Washington Irving, Daniel Webster, Ralph Waldo Emerson

Select American Classics

Washington Irving, Daniel Webster, Ralph Waldo Emerson

Select American Classics

ISBN/EAN: 9783741187636

Manufactured in Europe, USA, Canada, Australia, Japa

Cover: Foto ©Andreas Hilbeck / pixelio.de

Manufactured and distributed by brebook publishing software
(www.brebook.com)

Washington Irving, Daniel Webster, Ralph Waldo Emerson

Select American Classics

AMER[ICAN CL]ASSICS

IRVING'S SKETCH [... AND] EMERSON'S ESSAYS
AS PUB[...] CLASSICS.

NEW [...]
AMER[...]

TEN SELECTIONS

FROM

THE SKETCH-BOOK

BY

WASHINGTON IRVING

"Go, little booke, God send thee good passage,
And specially let this be thy prayere,
Unto them all that thee will read or hear,
Where thou art wrong, after their help to call,
Thee to correct in any part or all."
CHAUCER.

NEW YORK ·:· CINCINNATI ·:· CHICAGO
AMERICAN BOOK COMPANY

INTRODUCTION.

WASHINGTON IRVING, the eighth and youngest son of William and Sarah Irving, was born in a house on William Street, in New York City, April 3, 1783. His father was a descendant of an old Orkney family, and his mother was a native of Falmouth, England. Young Washington began his school days at the age of four. At the age of sixteen his school days were over, and he began the study of law. Though his education was of a rudimentary and incomplete character, consisting of a smattering of Latin, music, and the ordinary English branches, he gave early signs of a natural avidity for reading, and of a power of rapidly assimilating what he read. Sinbad, Robinson Crusoe, and Gulliver made a deep impression on his young mind. His early fondness for romance showed itself in many ways, and the theater in John Street possessed for him a seductive charm, to which he succumbed as often as he could steal away from home; for his father, of the stern ways and habits of the Scotch Covenanter, looked upon theaters with hearty disfavor. In 1802 he entered the law office of Josiah Ogden Hoffman, and, together with his " Blackstone," he read general literature voraciously. About this time his health began to fail, and he made frequent trips up the Hudson and the Mohawk, to Ogdensburg, Montreal, Albany, Schenectady, and Saratoga. While in Judge Hoffman's office, he offset the tedium of his studies by writing, over the name of "Jonathan Oldstyle," a series of papers for the "Morning Chronicle," a newspaper planned on the style of the "Spectator" and "Tatler." His health continuing poor, in May he went to Europe, spent six weeks in Bordeaux, studying the language, seeing life, and enlarging the scope of his powers of observation. Then he visited the Mediterranean, gathering more material, seeing new cities, studying the strong characters he met. Sicily, Genoa, Naples, Rome, came beneath his eye, and he saw Nelson's fleet spreading its sails for Trafalgar. At Rome a critical epoch in his life occurred. The atmosphere of music, of which he was passionately fond, of art, and especially painting, all tended to work powerfully on the artistic side of his nature, and appealed strongly to the poetic temperament, that, in spite of his keen sense of humor, was deep within him. At this time, and in this atmosphere, he met Washington Allston, the artist, and was almost persuaded by him to take up art; but Irving, convinced that his inclination was more the effect of his present surroundings than of a deep latent artistic power within himself, refrained, and continued his journey, seeking new faces and new scenes. Irving was essentially a traveler. He saw at a glance all those peculiarities and oddities of form and character that attract and amuse; and he had a happy way of putting up with inconveniences, getting the best out of everything that came before his notice, and entering thoroughly into the spirit of his surroundings. Switzerland, the Netherlands, Paris, London, were in turn visited. In London he saw John Kemble, Cooke, and Mrs. Siddons. In February, 1806, he returned to this country, and was admitted to the bar, but he never practiced law. He soon engaged, with his brother William and James K. Paulding, in the issue (1807) of a humorously satirical semi-monthly periodical called "Salmagundi, or the Whim-Whams and Opinions of Launcelot Langstaff, Esq., and Others." It was quite successful in its local hits, and in it Irving first awoke to a conception of his power. In 1809 appeared the droll "History of New York by Diedrich Knickerbocker. From the Beginning of the World to the End of the Dutch Dynasty." It won for its author instant fame. The book was cleverly advertised before it appeared, the newspapers containing descriptions of a gentleman named Diedrich Knickerbocker, who was said to have mysteriously disappeared without paying his board bill, but leaving behind him a curious manuscript which his creditor was about to publish. Just before the book was completed, Irving underwent the great anguish of his life. The second daughter of Judge Hoffman, Matilda, with whom he was in love, died in her eighteenth year. He remained true to her memory, and never married. The "Knickerbocker History" was highly praised by Scott, who recognized its merit; and detected in it strong resemblances to the style of Swift. The work was begun by Washington and his brother Peter as a travesty on Dr. Samuel Mitchell's "Handbook of New York;" but Peter sailed for Europe when five chapters only were completed, and left Washington to finish the work. The next year (1810) Washington became a silent partner, with a fifth interest, in the commercial house established in New York and Liverpool by his brothers, and (1813–14) was editorially connected with the "Analectic Magazine" of Philadelphia, and contributed a number of biographical sketches of American naval commanders. In 1814 he served four months as aide-de-camp and military secretary to Gov. Tompkins, and in 1815 sailed again for Europe. About this time financial troubles began to gather over the business house; and Washington, on arriving in England, found his brother Peter ill, and thus considerable work of a commercial nature devolved upon him.   Yet in the midst of business cares he found time for quiet rovings through Warwickshire and other parts of England, gathering material for "The Sketch-Book," and mingling in society with the literary men of the time.   But the business troubles of the house increased, and 1816 and 1817 were anxious years.   It was in the latter year that he met Scott in his home at Abbotsford, and felt the charm of his family circle.   In 1818 the house went into bankruptcy. Irving, declining a clerkship in the Navy Department, and deferring an editorship which Scott held out to him, preferred to follow his own literary pursuits, and brought out "The Sketch-Book" (1819) in America.   It was unqualifiedly successful; and Irving, who had heretofore been held as the ornamental feature of the family, became its financial stay, graciously returning the kind favors of earlier days.   Irving offered "The Sketch-Book" to Murray & Constable for republication; but they declined it, in spite of Scott's recommendation.   Irving then started to publish it himself, but, his publisher failing, its issue was stopped. Scott induced Murray to buy it for two hundred pounds, which was doubled on the success of the book.   In 1820 Irving was in Paris, and in 1821 wrote "Bracebridge Hall," bringing it out in 1822.   This year he was in Dresden.   He returned to Paris in 1823, and the next year brought out "Tales of a Traveller."   It was severely criticised.   The year 1826 found him in Madrid as *attaché* of the legation commissioned by A. H. Everett, United States minister to Spain, to translate various documents relating to Columbus, collected by Navarrete; and from this work Irving produced (1828) the "History of the Life and Voyages of Christopher Columbus." For it he got three thousand guineas, and the fifty-guinea medal offered by George IV. for historical composition. A pleasant sojourn in the south of Spain gave him further insight into Spanish lore, and in 1829 the "Chronicles of the Conquest of Granada" was given to the public. In the quiet seclusion of the Alhambra, the same year, he wove a portion of that graceful fabric which he gave the world in 1832. While in the Alhambra he received word of his appointment as secretary to the legation at London, and, reluctantly accepting it, returned there. In 1831 appeared his "Companions of Columbus," and the same year he received from Oxford the degree of LL.D. The next year he returned to New York, after a foreign sojourn of seventeen years, and was welcomed with tremendous enthusiasm. He bought Sunnyside, below Tarrytown on the Hudson, and prepared to settle quietly down to literary work; but the restless spirit of travel he had imbibed abroad induced him to take a flying trip through the West before doing so, and the summer of the same year found him with Commissioner Ellsworth, interested in the removal of the Indian tribes across the Mississippi. The literary outcome of this digression was the "Tour on the Prairies," which came out in 1835. With it came also "Abbotsford" and "Newstead Abbey," and the "Legends of the Conquest of Spain," making up the "Crayon Miscellany." In 1836 came "Astoria;" and from 1839 to 1841 he contributed articles for the "Knickerbocker Magazine," which were afterward gathered into "Wolfert's Roost" (1855). From 1842 to 1846 Irving was United States minister to Spain. Returning to his home, he spent the remaining years of his life at Sunnyside, engaged in literary work, chiefly the "Life of Mahomet" and the "Life of Washington." The final volume of this last was completed only three months before he died. He passed away at Sunnyside, Nov. 28, 1859.

Washington Irving was the first American who was admitted by Englishmen on equal terms into the great republic of letters. By him American literature was enriched in form and elegance, and its scope enlarged. He opened the treasure-house of Spanish history and romance, and gave an impulse to historical and biographical research. As an historian and biographer, his conclusions were carefully drawn, and just, and have stood the test of time.

Possessed of a broad and genial nature, a rich poetic temperament, a fancy that was as nimble as it was sprightly, a facile and ornate power of vivid and graphic description, and a pure and graceful style that rivals that of Addison, he was the very prince of story-tellers and the most fascinating of fireside companions. His delicacy of touch was equal to the task of adding beauty to the exquisite tracery of the Alhambra, and his refined imagination revivified the romantic legends of Granada, while his genial humor created a cherished ancestry for his native city. With such inimitable drollery did he place in succession upon his canvas the Dutch forefathers of New Amsterdam, that Diedrich Knickerbocker, fleeing through the dormer-windowed streets of New York, left behind him the legacy of a name as real and as enduring as that of Peter Stuyvesant.

Yet it is in "The Sketch-Book," perhaps, more than in any other of his works, that the qualities of style and mind which have so characterized Washington Irving, and endeared him to English-reading people, appear in their freshest, most varied form, covering a wider range of humanity. bubbling over with a humor that seems to have the inexhaustible spontaneity of a spring. Here drollery, grace, pathos, grandeur, in turn touch the heart and move the fancy. A broad, genial atmosphere pervades it, fresh and open as the blue sky, in which its characters live, move, and have their being, drawn with a portraiture as real as life, and with a gentle satire that has no trace of bitterness.

It is "The Sketch-Book" that affords such charming glimpses of the good old English Christmas, and such graceful reflections, under the shadow of the venerable Abbey; while with its tatterdemalion Rip Van Winkle, and its soft but timid-hearted pedagogue Ichabod Crane, it is "The Sketch-Book" which has given to our noble Hudson the weird witchery of legend, charming as the blue outline of the Catskills, and fascinating as the shades of Sleepy Hollow.

CONTENTS.

THE SKETCH-BOOK.

THE AUTHOR'S ACCOUNT OF HIMSELF.

" I am of this mind with Homer, that as the snaile that crept out of her shel was turned eftsoones [1] into a toad, and thereby was forced to make a stoole to sit on ; so the traveller that stragleth from his owne country is in a short time transformed into so monstrous a shape, that he is faine to alter his mansion with his manners, and to live where he can, not where he would."

LYLY's Euphues.[2]

I WAS always fond of visiting new scenes, and observing strange characters and manners. Even when a mere child I began my travels, and made many tours of discovery into foreign parts and unknown regions of my native city, to the frequent alarm of my parents, and the emolument of the town-crier. As I grew into boyhood, I extended the range of my observations. My holiday afternoons were spent in rambles about the surrounding country. I made myself familiar with all its places famous in history or fable. I knew every spot where a murder or robbery had been committed, or a ghost seen. I visited the neighboring villages, and added greatly to my stock of knowledge by noting their habits and customs, and conversing with their sages and great men. I even journeyed one long summer's day to the

[1] Speedily; at once.

[2] John Lyly, Lylie, Lyllie, or Lilly (1553–1609) was an English wit and writer of Shakespeare's time. He wrote several plays, but is best known from his novel Euphues, the style of which was intended to reform and purify that of the English language. This book immediately became the rage in the court circles, and for many years was the court standard.

summit of the most distant hill, from whence I stretched my eye over many a mile of *terra incognita*, and was astonished to find how vast a globe I inhabited.

This rambling propensity strengthened with my years. Books of voyages and travels became my passion; and, in devouring their contents, I neglected the regular exercises of the school. How wistfully would I wander about the pier-heads in fine weather, and watch the parting ships, bound to distant climes! With what longing eyes would I gaze after their lessening sails, and waft myself in imagination to the ends of the earth!

Further reading and thinking, though they brought this vague inclination into more reasonable bounds, only served to make it more decided. I visited various parts of my own country; and, had I been merely influenced by a love of fine scenery, I should have felt little desire to seek elsewhere its gratification, for on no country have the charms of Nature been more prodigally lavished. Her mighty lakes, like oceans of liquid silver; her mountains, with their bright aerial tints; her valleys, teeming with wild fertility; her tremendous cataracts, thundering in their solitudes; her boundless plains, waving with spontaneous verdure; her broad, deep rivers, rolling in solemn silence to the ocean; her trackless forests, where vegetation puts forth all its magnificence; her skies, kindling with the magic of summer clouds and glorious sunshine,—no, never need an American look beyond his own country for the sublime and beautiful of natural scenery.

But Europe held forth all the charms of storied and poetical association. There were to be seen the masterpieces of art, the refinements of highly cultivated society, the quaint peculiarities of ancient and local custom. My native country was full of youthful promise: Europe was rich in the accumulated treasures of age. Her very ruins told the history of times gone by, and every moldering stone was a chronicle. I longed to wander over the scenes of renowned achievement; to tread, as it were, in the footsteps of antiquity; to loiter about the ruined castle; to meditate on the falling tower; to escape, in short, from the commonplace realities of the present, and lose myself among the shadowy grandeurs of the past.

I had, beside all this, an earnest desire to see the great men of the earth. We have, it is true, our great men in America: not a city but has an ample share of them. I have mingled among them in my time, and been almost withered by the shade into which they cast me; for there is nothing so baleful to a small man as the shade of a great one, particularly the great man of a city. But I was anxious to see the great men of Europe; for I had read in the works of various philosophers, that all animals degenerated in America, and man among the number. A great man of Europe, thought I, must therefore be as superior to a great man of America as a peak of the Alps to a highland of the Hudson; and in this idea I was confirmed by observing the comparative importance and swelling magnitude of many English travelers among us, who, I was assured, were very little people in their own country. I will visit this land of wonders, thought I, and see the gigantic race from which I am degenerated.

It has been either my good or evil lot to have my roving passion gratified. I have wandered through different countries, and witnessed many of the shifting scenes of life. I cannot say that I have studied them with the eye of a philosopher, but rather with the sauntering gaze with which humble lovers of the picturesque stroll from the window of one print-shop to another; caught sometimes by the delineations of beauty, sometimes by the distortions of caricature, and sometimes by the loveliness of landscape. As it is the fashion for modern tourists to travel pencil in hand, and bring home their portfolios filled with sketches, I am disposed to get up a few for the entertainment of my friends. When, however, I look over the hints and memorandums I have taken down for the purpose, my heart almost fails me at finding how my idle humor has led me aside from the great objects studied by every regular traveler who would make a book. I fear I shall give equal disappointment with an unlucky landscape painter, who had traveled on the Continent, but, following the bent of his vagrant inclination, had sketched in nooks and corners and by-places. His sketch-book was accordingly crowded with cottages and landscapes and obscure ruins; but he had neglected to paint St. Peter's[1] or the Colosseum,[2] the cascade of Terni[3] or the Bay of Naples,[4] and had not a single glacier or volcano in his whole collection.

THE VOYAGE.

> "*Ships, ships, I will descrie you*
> *Amidst the main,*
> *I will come and try you,*
> *What you are protecting,*
> *And projecting,*
> *What's your end and aim.*
> *One goes abroad for merchandise and trading,*
> *Another stays to keep his country from invading,*
> *A third is coming home with rich and wealthy lading,*
> *Hallo! my fancie, whither wilt thou go?*"
>
> OLD POEM.

TO an American visiting Europe, the long voyage he has to make is an excellent preparative. The temporary absence of worldly scenes and employments produces a state of mind peculiarly fitted to receive new and vivid impressions. The vast space of waters that separates the hemispheres is like a blank

[1] The Church of St. Peter in Rome is built upon the site of the religious edifice erected in the time of Constantine (306), and consecrated as the "Basilica of St. Peter."

[2] A vast amphitheater in Rome, begun by the Emperor Vespasian, A.D. 72, and dedicated A.D. 80. For nearly five hundred years it was the popular resort of Rome. In the year 555 the whole of the city was overflowed by the Tiber, and the lower part of the Colosseum was then destroyed.

[3] A town of Italy in the province of Perugia, noted for the Falls of Velino, which, for volume and beauty, take a very high place among European waterfalls.

[4] No other place in the world combines within the same compass so much natural beauty with so many objects of interest to the antiquary, the historian, and the geologist, as the Bay of Naples.

page in existence. There is no gradual transition, by which, as in Europe, the features and population of one country blend almost imperceptibly with those of another. From the moment you lose sight of the land you have left, all is vacancy until you step on the opposite shore, and are launched at once into the bustle and novelties of another world.

In traveling by land there is a continuity of scene, and a connected succession of persons and incidents, that carry on the story of life, and lessen the effect of absence and separation. We drag, it is true, "a lengthening chain"[1] at each remove of our pilgrimage; but the chain is unbroken: we can trace it back link by link; and we feel that the last of them still grapples us to home. But a wide sea voyage severs us at once. It makes us conscious of being cast loose from the secure anchorage of settled life, and sent adrift upon a doubtful world. It interposes a gulf, not merely imaginary, but real, between us and our homes, — a gulf subject to tempest and fear and uncertainty, that makes distance palpable, and return precarious.

Such, at least, was the case with myself. As I saw the last blue line of my native land fade away like a cloud in the horizon, it seemed as if I had closed one volume of the world and its concerns, and had time for meditation before I opened another. That land, too, now vanishing from my view, which contained all that was most dear to me in life, — what vicissitudes might occur in it, what changes might take place in me, before I should visit it again! Who can tell, when he sets forth to wander, whither he may be driven by the uncertain currents of existence, or when he may return, or whether it may be ever his lot to revisit the scenes of his childhood?

I said that at sea all is vacancy. I should correct the expres-

---

1 Goldsmith's Traveller, line 10. Better explained in the first paragraph of his third letter in Citizen of the World; i.e., " The farther I travel I feel the pain of separation with stronger force: those ties that bind me to my native country and you, are still unbroken. By every move I only drag a greater length of chain."

2

sion. To one given to day-dreaming, and fond of losing himself in reveries, a sea voyage is full of subjects for meditation; but then they are the wonders of the deep and of the air, and rather tend to abstract the mind from worldly themes. I delighted to loll over the quarter railing, or climb to the maintop, of a calm day, and muse for hours together on the tranquil bosom of a summer's sea; to gaze upon the piles of golden clouds just peering above the horizon, fancy them some fairy realms, and people them with a creation of my own; to watch the gentle, undulating billows, rolling their silver volumes, as if to die away on those happy shores.

There was a delicious sensation of mingled security and awe with which I looked down, from my giddy height, on the monsters of the deep at their uncouth gambols, — shoals of porpoises, tumbling about the bow of the ship; the grampus, slowly heaving his huge form above the surface; or the ravenous shark, darting, like a specter, through the blue waters. My imagination would conjure up all that I had heard or read of the watery world beneath me, — of the finny herds that roam its fathomless valleys, of the shapeless monsters that lurk among the very foundations of the earth, and of those wild phantasms that swell the tales of fishermen and sailors.

Sometimes a distant sail, gliding along the edge of the ocean, would be another theme of idle speculation. How interesting this fragment of a world, hastening to rejoin the great mass of existence! What a glorious monument of human invention, that has thus triumphed over wind and wave; has brought the ends of the world into communion; has established an interchange of blessings, pouring into the sterile regions of the north all the luxuries of the south; has diffused the light of knowledge and the charities of cultivated life; and has thus bound together those scattered portions of the human race between which Nature seemed to have thrown an insurmountable barrier.

We one day descried some shapeless object drifting at a distance. At sea everything that breaks the monotony of the surrounding expanse attracts attention. It proved to be the mast of a ship that must have been completely wrecked; for there were the remains of handkerchiefs, by which some of the crew had fastened themselves to this spar, to prevent their being washed off by the waves. There was no trace by which the name of the ship could be ascertained. The wreck had evidently drifted about for many months. Clusters of shell-fish had fastened about it, and long seaweeds flaunted at its sides. But where, thought I, is the crew? Their struggle has long been over; they have gone down amidst the roar of the tempest; their bones lie whitening among the caverns of the deep. Silence, oblivion, like the waves, have closed over them, and no one can tell the story of their end. What sighs have been wafted after that ship! what prayers offered up at the deserted fireside of home! How often has the mistress, the wife, the mother, pored over the daily news to catch some casual intelligence of this rover of the deep! How has expectation darkened into anxiety, anxiety into dread, and dread into despair! Alas! not one memento shall ever return for love to cherish. All that shall ever be known, is that she sailed from her port, "and was never heard of more."

The sight of this wreck, as usual, gave rise to many dismal anecdotes. This was particularly the case in the evening, when the weather, which had hitherto been fair, began to look wild and threatening, and gave indications of one of those sudden storms that will sometimes break in upon the serenity of a summer voyage. As we sat round the dull light of a lamp in the cabin, that made the gloom more ghastly, every one had his tale of shipwreck and disaster. I was particularly struck with a short one related by the captain.

"As I was once sailing," said he, "in a fine stout ship across the Banks of Newfoundland,[1] one of those heavy fogs that prevail in those parts rendered it impossible for us to see far ahead

---

[1] The shoals to the southeast of the Island of Newfoundland, a great resort for fishermen.

even in the daytime; but at night the weather was so thick that
we could not distinguish any object at twice the length of the
ship. I kept lights at the mast-head, and a constant watch forward to look out for fishing-smacks, which are accustomed to lie
at anchor on the Banks. The wind was blowing a smacking
breeze, and we were going at a great rate through the water.
Suddenly the watch gave the alarm of 'A sail ahead!' It was
scarcely uttered before we were upon her. She was a small
schooner, at anchor, with her broadside toward us. The crew
were all asleep, and had neglected to hoist a light. We struck
her just amidships. The force, the size, and weight of our vessel
bore her down below the waves. We passed over her, and were
hurried on our course. As the crashing wreck was sinking beneath us, I had a glimpse of two or three half-naked wretches
rushing from her cabin. They just started from their beds, to be
swallowed, shrieking, by the waves. I heard their drowning cry
mingling with the wind. The blast that bore it to our ears swept
us out of all further hearing. I shall never forget that cry. It
was some time before we could put the ship about, she was under
such headway. We returned, as nearly as we could guess, to
the place where the smack had anchored. We cruised about for
several hours in the dense fog. We fired signal guns, and listened if we might hear the halloo of any survivors; but all was
silent. We never saw or heard anything of them more."

I confess these stories, for a time, put an end to all my fine
fancies. The storm increased with the night. The sea was
lashed into tremendous confusion. There was a fearful, sullen
sound of rushing waves and broken surges. Deep called unto
deep. At times the black volume of clouds overhead seemed
rent asunder by flashes of lightning that quivered along the
foaming billows, and made the succeeding darkness doubly terrible. The thunders bellowed over the wild waste of waters, and
were echoed and prolonged by the mountain waves. As I saw
the ship staggering and plunging among these roaring caverns, it
seemed miraculous that she regained her balance, or preserved

her buoyancy. Her yards would dip into the water. Her bow was almost buried beneath the waves. Sometimes an impending surge appeared ready to overwhelm her, and nothing but a dexterous movement of the helm preserved her from the shock.

When I retired to my cabin, the awful scene still followed me. The whistling of the wind through the rigging sounded like funereal wailings. The creaking of the masts, the straining and groaning of bulk-heads, as the ship labored in the weltering sea, were frightful. As I heard the waves rushing along the side of the ship, and roaring in my very ear, it seemed as if Death were raging round this floating prison, seeking for his prey. The mere starting of a nail, the yawning of a seam, might give him entrance.

A fine day, however, with a tranquil sea and favoring breeze, soon put all these dismal reflections to flight. It is impossible to resist the gladdening influence of fine weather and fair wind at sea. When the ship is decked out in all her canvas, every sail swelled, and careering gayly over the curling waves, how lofty, how gallant, she appears! How she seems to lord it over the deep! I might fill a volume with the reveries of a sea voyage, — for with me it is almost a continual reverie, — but it is time to get to shore.

It was a fine, sunny morning when the thrilling cry of "Land!" was given from the mast-head. None but those who have experienced it can form an idea of the delicious throng of sensations which rush into an American's bosom when he first comes in sight of Europe. There is a volume of associations with the very name. It is the land of promise, teeming with everything of which his childhood has heard, or on which his studious years have pondered.

From that time until the moment of arrival, it was all feverish excitement. The ships of war, that prowled like guardian giants along the coast; the headlands of Ireland, stretching out into the Channel; the Welsh mountains, towering into the clouds, — all were objects of intense interest. As we sailed up the Mersey,[1] I reconnoitered the shores with a telescope.　My eye dwelt with delight on neat cottages, with their trim shrubberies and green grass plots.　I saw the moldering ruin of an abbey overrun with ivy, and the taper spire of a village church rising from the brow of a neighboring hill.　All were characteristic of England.

The tide and wind were so favorable that the ship was enabled to come at once to the pier.　It was thronged with people, — some idle lookers-on, others eager expectants of friends or relatives.　I could distinguish the merchant to whom the ship was consigned.　I knew him by his calculating brow and restless air. His hands were thrust into his pockets.　He was whistling thoughtfully, and walking to and fro, a small space having been accorded him by the crowd, in deference to his temporary importance.　There were repeated cheerings and salutations interchanged between the shore and the ship as friends happened to recognize each other.　I particularly noticed one young woman of humble dress but interesting demeanor.　She was leaning forward from among the crowd.　Her eye hurried over the ship as it neared the shore, to catch some wished-for countenance.　She seemed disappointed and agitated, when I heard a faint voice call her name.　It was from a poor sailor who had been ill all the voyage, and had excited the sympathy of every one on board. When the weather was fine, his messmates had spread a mattress for him on deck in the shade; but of late his illness had so increased, that he had taken to his hammock, and only breathed a wish that he might see his wife before he died.　He had been helped on deck as we came up the river, and was now leaning against the shrouds, with a countenance so wasted, so pale, so ghastly, that it was no wonder even the eye of affection did not recognize him.　But at the sound of his voice, her eye darted on his features.　It read at once a whole volume of sorrow.　She clasped her hands, uttered a faint shriek, and stood wringing them in silent agony.

[1] A river in the county of Lancaster, England, which opens into a fine estuary before reaching the sea at Liverpool.

All now was hurry and bustle, — the meetings of acquaintances, the greetings of friends, the consultations of men of business. I alone was solitary and idle. I had no friend to meet, no cheering to receive. I stepped upon the land of my forefathers, but felt that I was a stranger in the land.

CHRISTMAS.[1]

" But is old, old, good old Christmas gone? Nothing but the hair of his good, gray, old head and beard left? Well, I will have that, seeing I cannot have more of him." — HUE AND CRY AFTER CHRISTMAS.

> *" A man might then behold*
>   *At Christmas, in each hall,*
> *Good fires to curb the cold,*
>   *And meat for great and small.*
> *The neighbors were friendly bidden,*
>   *And all had welcome true,*
> *The poor from the gates were not chidden,*
>   *When this old cap was new."*
>
> OLD SONG.[2]

THERE is nothing in England that exercises a more delightful spell over my imagination than the lingerings of the holiday customs and rural games of former times. They recall the pictures my fancy used to draw in the May morning of life, when as yet I only knew the world through books, and believed it to be all that poets had painted it; and they bring with them the flavor of those honest days of yore, in which, perhaps, with equal fallacy, I am apt to think the world was more homebred, social, and joyous than at present. I regret to say that they are daily growing more and more faint, being gradually worn away

[1] Christ and Mass (Anglo-Saxon *Maessa*, "a holy day or feast"), the Christian festival of the Nativity. The festival properly begins on the evening of Dec. 24, and lasts until Epiphany, Jan. 6, the whole being termed "Christmas-tide." Dec. 25, however, is the day more specifically observed.

[2] From Guild Hall Giants, by Thomas Hood, a famous English humorist and popular author (born in London, 1798; died, 1845).

by time, but still more obliterated by modern fashion. They resemble those picturesque morsels of Gothic architecture which
we see crumbling in various parts of the country, partly dilapidated by the waste of ages, and partly lost in the additions and
alterations of latter days. Poetry, however, clings with cherish-
ing fondness about the rural game and holiday revel, from which
it has derived so many of its themes,—as the ivy winds its rich
foliage about the Gothic arch and moldering tower, gratefully
repaying their support by clasping together their tottering remains, and, as it were, embalming them in verdure.

Of all the old festivals, however, that of Christmas awakens
the strongest and most heartfelt associations. There is a tone
of solemn and sacred feeling that blends with our conviviality,
and lifts the spirit to a state of hallowed and elevated enjoyment.
The services of the church about this season are extremely tender
and inspiring. They dwell on the beautiful story of the origin of
our faith, and the pastoral scenes that accompanied its announcement. They gradually increase in fervor and pathos during the
season of Advent,[1] until they break forth in full jubilee on the
morning that brought peace and good will to men.[2] I do not
know a grander effect of music on the moral feelings than to
hear the full choir and the pealing organ performing a Christmas
anthem in a cathedral, and filling every part of the vast pile with
triumphant harmony.

It is a beautiful arrangement, also, derived from days of yore,
that this festival, which commemorates the announcement of the
religion of peace and love, has been made the season for gathering together of family connections, and drawing closer again those

---

[1] The season of moral and religious preparation, between St. Andrew's
Day (Nov. 30) and Christmas. Its observance dates from the fourth century, and from the sixth century it has been recognized as the beginning of
the ecclesiastical year. At one time it was observed as strictly as Lent.
Advent fasting is now confined to the week in which Ember Day (Dec. 13)
occurs.

[2] No war was declared, and no capital executions were permitted to take
place, during this season of good will.

bands of kindred hearts which the cares and pleasures and sorrows of the world are continually operating to cast loose; of calling back the children of a family, who have launched forth in life, and wandered widely asunder, once more to assemble about the paternal hearth, that rallying-place of the affections, there to grow young and loving again among the endearing mementos of childhood.

There is something in the very season of the year that gives a charm to the festivity of Christmas. At other times we derive a great portion of our pleasures from the mere beauties of nature. Our feelings sally forth and dissipate themselves over the sunny landscape, and we "live abroad and everywhere." The song of the bird; the murmur of the stream; the breathing fragrance of spring; the soft voluptuousness of summer; the golden pomp of autumn; earth, with its mantle of refreshing green; and heaven, with its deep, delicious blue and its cloudy magnificence,—all fill us with mute but exquisite delight, and we revel in the luxury of mere sensation. But in the depth of winter, when Nature lies despoiled of every charm, and wrapped in her shroud of sheeted snow, we turn for our gratifications to moral sources. The dreariness and desolation of the landscape, the short, gloomy days and darksome nights, while they circumscribe our wanderings, shut in our feelings also from rambling abroad, and make us more keenly disposed for the pleasures of the social circle. Our thoughts are more concentrated, our friendly sympathies more aroused. We feel more sensibly the charm of each other's society, and are brought more closely together by dependence on each other for enjoyment. Heart calleth unto heart; and we draw our pleasures from the deep wells of living kindness, which lie in the quiet recesses of our bosoms, and which, when resorted to, furnish forth the pure element of domestic felicity.

The pitchy gloom without makes the heart dilate on entering the room filled with the glow and warmth of the evening fire. The ruddy blaze diffuses an artificial summer and sunshine through the room, and lights up each countenance into a kindlier welcome. Where does the honest face of hospitality expand into a broader and more cordial smile, where is the shy glance of love more sweetly eloquent, than by the winter fireside? and as the hollow blast of wintry wind rushes through the hall, claps the distant door, whistles about the casement, and rumbles down the chimney, what can be more grateful than that feeling of sober and sheltered security with which we look round upon the comfortable chamber and the scene of domestic hilarity?

The English, from the great prevalence of rural habits throughout every class of society, have always been fond of those festivals and holidays which agreeably interrupt the stillness of country life, and they were in former days particularly observant of the religious and social rites of Christmas.[1] It is inspiring to read even the dry details which some antiquaries have given of the quaint humors, the burlesque pageants, the complete abandonment to mirth and good-fellowship, with which this festival was celebrated. It seemed to throw open every door, and unlock every heart. It brought the peasant and the peer together, and blended all ranks in one warm generous flow of joy and kindness.[2] The old halls of castles and manor-houses resounded with the harp and the Christmas carol,[3] and their ample boards groaned under the weight of hospitality. Even the poorest cottage welcomed the festive season with green decorations of bay[4]

[1] Christmas Day, in the primitive Church, was always observed as the sabbath day, and, like that, preceded by an eve or vigil: hence our present Christmas Eve.

[2] In farmhouses in the north of England the servants used to lay a large knotty block for their Christmas fire, and during the time it lasted they were entitled by custom to ale at their meals.

[3] The well-known hymn, "Gloria in Excelsis," sung by the angels to the shepherds at our Lord's nativity, was the earliest Christmas carol. We next hear of one sung in the thirteenth century. It is in the British Museum, and written in Anglo-Norman.

[4] Since the days of the ancient Romans, this tree, a species of laurel, the aromatic leaves of which are often found packed with figs, has at all times been dedicated to all purposes of joyous commemoration; and its branches have been used as the emblems of peace, victory, and joy.

and holly.[1]   The cheerful fire glanced its rays through the lattice, inviting the passenger to raise the latch, and join the gossip knot huddled round the hearth, beguiling the long evening with legendary jokes and oft-told Christmas tales.

One of the least pleasing effects of modern refinement is the havoc it has made among the hearty old holiday customs.   It has completely taken off the sharp touchings and spirited reliefs of these embellishments of life, and has worn down society into a more smooth and polished, but certainly a less characteristic surface.   Many of the games and ceremonials of Christmas have entirely disappeared, and, like the sherris sack of old Falstaff,[2] are become matters of speculation and dispute among commentators. They flourished in times full of spirit and lustihood, when men enjoyed life roughly, but heartily and vigorously, — times wild and picturesque, which have furnished poetry with its richest materials, and the drama with its most attractive variety of characters and manners.   The world has become more worldly.   There is more of dissipation, and less of enjoyment.   Pleasure has expanded into a broader but a shallower stream, and has forsaken many of those deep and quiet channels where it flowed sweetly through the calm bosom of domestic life.   Society has acquired a more enlightened and elegant tone; but it has lost many of its strong local peculiarities, its home-bred feelings, its honest fireside delights.   The traditionary customs of golden-hearted antiquity, its feudal hospitalities, and lordly wassailings, have passed away with the baronial castles and stately manor-houses in which they were celebrated. They comported with the shadowy hall, the great oaken gallery, and the tapestried parlor, but are unfitted for the light, showy saloons and gay drawing-rooms of the modern villa.[3]

[1] A plant of the genus *Ilex*.   The common holly grows from twenty to thirty feet in height.   It is especially used about Christmas time to decorate the inside of houses and churches, — a relic, it is thought, of Druidism.

[2] Second Henry IV., act iv. sc. 3.

[3] In 1589 an order was issued to the gentlemen of Norfolk and Suffolk, commanding them " to depart from London before Christmas, and to repair to their country homes, there to keep hospitality amongst their neighbors."

Shorn, however, as it is, of its ancient and festive honors, Christmas is still a period of delightful excitement in England. It is gratifying to see that home feeling completely aroused which holds so powerful a place in every English bosom. The preparations making on every side for the social board that is again to unite friends and kindred; the presents[1] of good cheer passing and repassing, those tokens of regard, and quickeners of kind feelings; the evergreens distributed about houses and churches, emblems of peace and gladness,— all these have the most pleasing effect in producing fond associations, and kindling benevolent sympathies. Even the sound of the waits,[2] rude as may be their minstrelsy, breaks upon the mid-watches of a winter night with the effect of perfect harmony. As I have been awakened by them in that still and solemn hour "when deep sleep falleth upon man," I have listened with a hushed delight, and, connecting them with the sacred and joyous occasion, have almost fancied them into another celestial choir,[3] announcing peace and good will to mankind. How delightfully the imagination, when wrought upon by these moral influences, turns everything to melody and beauty! The very crowing of the cock, heard sometimes in the profound repose of the country, "telling the night watches to his feathery dames," was thought by the common people to announce the approach of this sacred festival.

> " Some say that ever 'gainst that season comes
> Wherein our Saviour's birth is celebrated,
> The bird of dawning singeth all night long:
> And then, they say, no spirit dare stir abroad;
> The nights are wholesome; then no planets strike,
> No fairy takes, no witch hath power to charm,
> So hallowed and so gracious is the time."[4]

---

[1] The practice of giving presents at Christmas was undoubtedly founded on the Pagan custom of New-Year's gifts, with which in these times it is blended.

[2] Or wayte, originally a kind of night-watchman who sounded the hours of his watch, and guarded the streets; later, a musician who sang out of doors at Christmas time, going from house to house.

[3] Luke ii. 13, 14.   [4] Hamlet, act i. sc. 1.

Amidst the general call to happiness, the bustle of the spirits, and stir of the affections, which prevail at this period, what bosom can remain insensible?   It is, indeed, the season of regenerated feeling,— the season for kindling, not merely the fire of hospitality in the hall, but the genial flame of charity in the heart. The scene of early love again rises green to memory beyond the sterile waste of years; and the idea of home, fraught with the fragrance of home-dwelling joys, reanimates the drooping spirit, as the Arabian breeze will sometimes waft the freshness of the distant fields to the weary pilgrim of the desert.

Stranger and sojourner as I am in the land,— though for me no social hearth may blaze, no hospitable roof throw open its doors, nor the warm grasp of friendship welcome me at the threshold, —yet I feel the influence of the season beaming into my soul from the happy looks of those around me.   Surely happiness is reflective, like the light of heaven; and every countenance, bright with smiles, and glowing with innocent enjoyment, is a mirror transmitting to others the rays of a supreme and ever-shining be-nevolence.   He who can turn churlishly away from contemplating the felicity of his fellow-beings, and can sit down darkling and repining in his loneliness when all around is joyful, may have his moments of strong excitement and selfish gratification, but he wants the genial and social sympathies which constitute the charm of a merry Christmas.

THE STAGECOACH.

*" Omne benè
Sine panâ
Tempus est ludendi
Venit hora
Absque morâ
Libros deponendi."* [1]
OLD HOLIDAY SCHOOL SONG.

IN the preceding paper I have made some general observations on the Christmas festivities of England, and am tempted to illustrate them by some anecdotes of a Christmas passed in the country; in perusing which I would most courteously invite my reader to lay aside the austerity of wisdom, and to put on that genuine holiday spirit which is tolerant of folly, and anxious only for amusement.

In the course of a December tour in Yorkshire,[2] I rode for a long distance in one of the public coaches on the day preceding Christmas. The coach was crowded, both inside and out, with passengers, who, by their talk, seemed principally bound to the mansions of relations or friends, to eat the Christmas dinner. It was loaded also with hampers of game, and baskets and boxes of delicacies; and hares hung dangling their long ears about the coachman's box, presents from distant friends for the impending feast. I had three fine rosy-cheeked schoolboys for my fellow-passengers inside, full of the buxom health and manly spirit which I have observed in the children of this country. They were returning home for the holidays in high glee, and promising themselves a world of enjoyment. It was delightful to hear the

---

[1] Free translation : —

" There's a time for hard playing,
With nothing to fear.
Drop books without delaying —
The hour is here."

[2] A northern county of England, famed for the beauty of its river scenery, in which respect it is scarcely surpassed by Scotland.

gigantic plans of pleasure of the little rogues, and the impractica-
ble feats they were to perform during their six-weeks' emancipation
from the abhorred thraldom of book, birch, and pedagogue. They
were full of the anticipations of the meeting with the family and
household, down to the very cat and dog, and of the joy they
were to give their little sisters by the presents with which their
pockets were crammed; but the meeting to which they seemed
to look forward with the greatest impatience was with Bantam,
which I found to be a pony, and, according to their talk, possessed of more virtues than any steed since the days of Buceph-
alus.[1] How he could trot! How he could run! And then such
leaps as he would take! There was not a hedge in the whole
country that he could not clear.

They were under the particular guardianship of the coachman,
to whom, whenever an opportunity presented, they addressed a
host of questions, and pronounced him one of the best fellows in
the whole world. Indeed, I could not but notice the more than
ordinary air of bustle and importance of the coachman, who wore
his hat a little on one side, and had a large bunch of Christmas
greens stuck in the buttonhole of his coat. He is always a personage full of mighty care and business, but he is particularly so
during this season, having so many commissions to execute in
consequence of the great interchange of presents. And here,
perhaps, it may not be unacceptable to my untraveled readers to
have a sketch that may serve as a general representation of this
very numerous and important class of functionaries, who have a
dress, a manner, a language, an air, peculiar to themselves, and
prevalent throughout the fraternity; so that, wherever an English
stagecoach-man may be seen, he cannot be mistaken for one of
any other craft or mystery.

He has commonly a broad, full face, curiously mottled with
red, as if the blood had been forced by hard feeding into every
vessel of the skin. He is swelled into jolly dimensions by frequent potations of malt liquors; and his bulk is still further in-

<hr>

[1] The horse of Alexander the Great.

creased by a multiplicity of coats, in which he is buried like a
cauliflower, the upper one reaching to his heels. He wears a
broad-brimmed, low-crowned hat; a huge roll of colored handkerchief about his neck, knowingly knotted, and tucked in at the
bosom; and has in summer time a large bouquet of flowers in
his buttonhole, — the present, most probably, of some enamored
country lass. His waistcoat is commonly of some bright color,
striped, and his small-clothes extend far below the knees, to meet
a pair of jockey boots which reach about halfway up his legs.

All this costume is maintained with much precision. He has
a pride in having his clothes of excellent materials; and, notwithstanding the seeming grossness of his appearance, there is still
discernible that neatness and propriety of person which is almost
inherent in an Englishman. He enjoys great consequence and
consideration along the road; has frequent conferences with the
village housewives, who look upon him as a man of great trust
and dependence; and he seems to have a good understanding
with every bright-eyed country lass. The moment he arrives
where the horses are to be changed, he throws down the reins
with something of an air, and abandons the cattle to the care of
the hostler, his duty being merely to drive them from one stage
to another. When off the box,[1] his hands are thrust in the pockets of his great-coat, and he rolls about the inn yard with an air
of the most absolute lordliness. Here he is generally surrounded
by an admiring throng of hostlers, stable-boys, shoeblacks, and
those nameless hangers-on that infest inns and taverns, and run
errands, and do all kind of odd jobs, for the privilege of batten-
ing on the drippings of the kitchen and the leakage of the tap-
room. These all look up to him as to an oracle; treasure up his
cant phrases; echo his opinions about horses and other topics of
jockey lore; and, above all, endeavor to imitate his air and carriage. Every ragamuffin that has a coat to his back, thrusts his
hands in the pockets, rolls in his gait, talks slang, and is an em-
bryo coachey.[2]

[1] The place beneath the driver's seat on a coach: hence the seat itself.
[2] Coachman; stage-driver.

Perhaps it might be owing to the pleasing serenity that reigned in my own mind, that I fancied I saw cheerfulness in every countenance throughout the journey. A stagecoach, however, carries animation always with it, and puts the world in motion as it whirls along. The horn, sounded at the entrance of a village, produces a general bustle. Some hasten forth to meet friends; some, with bundles and bandboxes, to secure places, and, in the hurry of the moment, can hardly take leave of the group that accompanies them. In the mean time the coachman has a world of small commissions to execute: sometimes he delivers a hare or pheasant; sometimes jerks a small parcel or newspaper to the door of a public house; and sometimes, with knowing leer and words of sly import, hands to some half-blushing, half-laughing housemaid an odd-shaped billet-doux [1] from some rustic admirer. As the coach rattles through the village, every one runs to the window, and you have glances on every side of fresh country faces and blooming giggling girls. At the corners are assembled juntos [2] of village idlers and wise men, who take their stations there for the important purpose of seeing company pass; but the sagest knot is generally at the blacksmith's, to whom the passing of the coach is an event fruitful of much speculation. The smith, with the horse's heel in his lap, pauses as the vehicle whirls by; the cyclops [3] round the anvil suspend their ringing hammers, and suffer the iron to grow cool; and the sooty specter, in brown paper cap, laboring at the bellows, leans on the handle for a moment, and permits the asthmatic engine to heave a long-drawn sigh, while he glares through the murky smoke and sulphureous gleams of the smithy.

[1] French, *billet* ("small letter") and *doux* ("sweet"): hence a love-letter.

[2] Originally private councils; here merely in the sense of gossiping groups.

[3] The cyclops, according to Greek mythology and story, were a race of stalwart giants with one eye in their foreheads: hence their name (Greek *kuklopes, kuklos*, "a circle;" and *ops*, "eye"), the round-eyed. They forged the thunderbolts of Zeus, the trident of Poseidon, and the helmet of Pluto. The allusion is to their size and strength as gigantic blacksmiths.

3

Perhaps the impending holiday might have given a more than usual animation to the country, for it seemed to me as if everybody was in good looks and good spirits. Game, poultry, and other luxuries of the table, were in brisk circulation in the villages. The grocers', butchers', and fruiterers' shops were thronged with customers. The housewives were stirring briskly about, putting their dwellings in order; and the glossy branches of holly, with their bright-red berries, began to appear at the windows. The scene brought to mind an old writer's account of Christmas preparations: "Now capons and hens, besides turkeys, geese, and ducks, with beef and mutton — must all die — for in twelve days a multitude of people will not be fed with a little. Now plums and spice, sugar and honey, square it among pies and broth. Now or never must music be in tune, for the youth must dance and sing to get them a heat, while the aged sit by the fire. The country maid leaves half her market, and must be sent again, if she forgets a pack of cards[1] on Christmas Eve. Great is the contention of holly and ivy, whether master or dame wears the breeches. Dice and cards benefit the butler; and if the cook do not lack wit, he will sweetly lick his fingers."[2]

I was roused from this fit of luxurious meditation by a shout from my little traveling companions. They had been looking out of the coach windows for the last few miles, recognizing every tree and cottage as they approached home, and now there was a general burst of joy. "There's John, and there's old Carlo, and there's Bantam!" cried the happy little rogues, clapping their hands.

At the end of a lane there was an old, sober-looking servant

---

[1] Cards furnished one of the great resources at this season of long evenings and indoor amusements, as they appear also to have formed an express feature of the Christmas entertainments of all ranks of people in old times. We are told that the squire in Queen Anne's time "never played cards but at Christmas, when the family pack was produced from the mantelpiece."

[2] Stevenson, in Twelve Months (1661).

in livery, waiting for them. He was accompanied by a superannuated pointer, and by the redoubtable Bantam,— a little old rat of a pony, with a shaggy mane, and long, rusty tail, who stood dozing quietly by the roadside, little dreaming of the bustling times that awaited him.

I was pleased to see the fondness with which the little fellows leaped about the steady old footman, and hugged the pointer, who wriggled his whole body for joy. But Bantam was the great object of interest. All wanted to mount at once; and it was with some difficulty that John arranged that they should ride by turns, and the eldest should ride first.

Off they set at last,— one on the pony, with the dog bounding and barking before him; and the others holding John's hands, both talking at once, and overpowering him with questions about home, and with school anecdotes. I looked after them with a feeling in which I do not know whether pleasure or melancholy predominated; for I was reminded of those days when, like them, I had neither known care nor sorrow, and a holiday was the summit of earthly felicity. We stopped a few moments afterwards to water the horses, and, on resuming our route, a turn of the road brought us in sight of a neat country seat. I could just distinguish the forms of a lady and two young girls in the portico; and I saw my little comrades, with Bantam, Carlo, and old John, trooping along the carriage road. I leaned out of the coach window, in hopes of witnessing the happy meeting, but a grove of trees shut it from my sight.

In the evening we reached a village where I had determined to pass the night. As we drove into the great gateway of the inn, I saw on one side the light of a rousing kitchen fire beaming through a window. I entered, and admired, for the hundredth time, that picture of convenience, neatness, and broad, honest enjoyment, the kitchen of an English inn. It was of spacious dimensions, hung round with copper and tin vessels highly polished, and decorated here and there with a Christmas green. Hams, tongues, and flitches of bacon were suspended from the ceiling; a smoke-jack[1] made its ceaseless clanking beside the fireplace; and a clock ticked in one corner. A well-scoured deal table extended along one side of the kitchen, with a cold round of beef and other hearty viands upon it, over which two foaming tankards of ale seemed mounting guard. Travelers of inferior order were preparing to attack this stout repast, while others sat smoking and gossiping over their ale on two high-backed oaken settles[2] beside the fire. Trim housemaids were hurrying backwards and forwards under the directions of a fresh bustling landlady, but still seizing an occasional moment to exchange a flippant word, and have a rallying laugh, with the group round the fire. The scene completely realized Poor Robin's[3] humble idea of the comforts of mid-winter:—

> " Now trees their leafy hats do bare
> To reverence Winter's silver hair,
> A handsome hostess, merry host,
> A pot of ale, and now a toast,
> Tobacco and a good coal fire,
> Are things this season doth require."

I had not been long at the inn when a post-chaise drove up to the door. A young gentleman stepped out, and by the light of the lamps I caught a glimpse of a countenance which I thought I knew. I moved forward to get a nearer view, when his eye caught mine. I was not mistaken: it was Frank Bracebridge, a sprightly, good-humored young fellow, with whom I had once traveled on the Continent. Our meeting was extremely cordial, for the countenance of an old fellow-traveler always brings up the recollection of a thousand pleasant scenes, odd adventures, and excellent jokes. To discuss all these in a transient interview

---

[1] A machine, consisting of fly-wheels used to rotate a roasting-spit, and operated by the current of rising air in a chimney.

[2] Benches.

[3] " Poor Robin " was the pseudonym of Robert Herrick, the poet, under which he issued a series of almanacs (begun in 1661). The quotation is from the almanac for 1684.

at an inn was impossible; and finding that I was not pressed for time, and was merely making a tour of observation, he insisted that I should give him a day or two at his father's country seat, to which he was going to pass the holidays, and which lay at a few miles' distance. "It is better than eating a solitary Christmas dinner at an inn," said he, "and I can assure you of a hearty welcome in something of the old-fashioned style." His reasoning was cogent, and I must confess the preparation I had seen for universal festivity and social enjoyment had made me feel a little impatient of my loneliness. I closed, therefore, at once, with his invitation: the chaise drove up to the door, and in a few moments I was on my way to the family mansion of the Bracebridges.

CHRISTMAS EVE.

> *" Saint Francis and Saint Benedight*
> *Blesse this house from wicked wight;*
> *From the night-mare and the goblin,*
> *That is hight good fellow Robin;*
> *Keep it from all evil spirits,*
> *Fairies, weazles, rats, and ferrets:*
> *From curfew-time*
> *To the next prime."*
>
> CARTWRIGHT.[1]

IT was a brilliant moonlight night, but extremely cold. Our chaise whirled rapidly over the frozen ground. The post-boy smacked his whip incessantly, and a part of the time his horses were on a gallop. "He knows where he is going," said my companion, laughing, "and is eager to arrive in time for some of the merriment and good cheer of the servants' hall.[2] My father, you

---

[1] William Cartwright (1611–43), an English poet and clergyman, was very popular in his time, especially about Oxford, where he was educated, and where he afterwards preached.

[2] The servants had enlarged privileges during this season, not only by custom, but by positive enactment; and certain games, which at other periods they were prohibited from engaging in, were allowed at Christmas time.

must know, is a bigoted devotee of the old school, and prides himself upon keeping up something of old English hospitality. He is a tolerable specimen of what you will rarely meet with nowadays in its purity, — the old English country gentleman; for our men of fortune spend so much of their time in town, and fashion is carried so much into the country, that the strong, rich peculiarities of ancient rural life are almost polished away. My father, however, from early years, took honest Peacham [1] for his text-book, instead of Chesterfield.[2] He determined in his own mind that there was no condition more truly honorable and enviable than that of a country gentleman on his paternal lands, and therefore passes the whole of his time on his estate. He is a strenuous advocate for the revival of the old rural games and holiday observances, and is deeply read in the writers, ancient and modern, who have treated on the subject. Indeed, his favorite range of reading is among the authors who flourished at least two centuries since, who, he insists, wrote and thought more like true Englishmen than any of their successors. He even regrets sometimes that he had not been born a few centuries earlier, when England was itself, and had its peculiar manners and customs. As he lives at some distance from the main road, in rather a lonely part of the country, without any rival gentry near him, he has that most enviable of all blessings to an Englishman, an opportunity of indulging the bent of his own humor without molestation. Being representative of the oldest family in the neighborhood, and a great part of the peasantry being his tenants, he is much looked up to, and, in general, is known simply by the appellation of 'The Squire,' — a title which has been accorded to the head of the family since time immemorial. I think it best to give you these hints about my worthy old father, to

---

[1] Henry Peacham (born in Hertfordshire, England, in the sixteenth century) was the author of The Complete Gentleman (1622).

[2] Chesterfield (Philip Dormer Stanhope) was an English courtier, orator, and wit, renowned as a model of politeness, and criterion of taste. He was born in London in 1694.

prepare you for any little eccentricities that might otherwise
appear absurd."

We had passed for some time along the wall of a park, and at
length the chaise stopped at the gate.   It was in a heavy, magnificent old style, of iron bars, fancifully wrought at top into
flourishes and flowers.   The huge, square columns that supported
the gate were surmounted by the family crest.   Close adjoining
was the porter's lodge, sheltered under dark fir-trees, and almost
buried in shrubbery.

The post-boy rang a large porter's bell, which resounded
through the still, frosty air, and was answered by the distant
barking of dogs, with which the mansion-house seemed garri-
soned.   An old woman immediately appeared at the gate.   As
the moonlight fell strongly upon her, I had a full view of a
little primitive dame, dressed very much in antique taste, with a
neat kerchief and stomacher,[1] and her silver hair peeping from
under a cap of snowy whiteness.   She came courtesying forth,
with many expressions of simple joy at seeing her young master.
Her husband, it seemed, was up at the house keeping Christmas
Eve in the servants' hall.   They could not do without him, as he
was the best hand at a song and story in the household.

My friend proposed that we should alight, and walk through
the park to the hall, which was at no great distance, while the
chaise should follow on.   Our road wound through a noble avenue of trees, among the naked branches of which the moon glittered, as she rolled through the deep vault of a cloudless sky.
The lawn beyond was sheeted with a slight covering of snow,
which here and there sparkled as the moonbeams caught a frosty
crystal; and at a distance might be seen a thin, transparent
vapor, stealing up from the low grounds, and threatening gradually to shroud the landscape.

My companion looked round him with transport.   "How
often," said he, "have I scampered up this avenue, on returning

1 The portion of a dress forming, generally, the lower part of the bodice,
extending down in front into the skirt, and usually overlapping it.

home on school vacations! How often have I played under these trees when a boy! I feel a degree of filial reverence for them, as we look up to those who have cherished us in childhood. My father was always scrupulous in exacting our holidays, and having us around him on family festivals. He used to direct and superintend our games with the strictness that some parents do the studies of their children. He was very particular that we should play the old English games according to their original form, and consulted old books for precedent and authority for every 'merrie disport;' yet I assure you there never was pedantry so delightful. It was the policy of the good old gentleman to make his children feel that home was the happiest place in the world; and I value this delicious home feeling as one of the choicest gifts a parent could bestow."

We were interrupted by the clamor of a troop of dogs of all sorts and sizes, — "mongrel, puppy, whelp, and hound, and curs of low degree," — that, disturbed by the ringing of the porter's bell and the rattling of the chaise, came bounding, open-mouthed, across the lawn.

> "The little dogs and all,
>   Tray, Blanch, and Sweet-heart, see, they bark at me." [1]

cried Bracebridge, laughing. At the sound of his voice, the bark was changed into a yelp of delight, and in a moment he was surrounded and almost overpowered by the caresses of the faithful animals.

We had now come in full view of the old family mansion, partly thrown in deep shadow, and partly lit up by the cold moonshine. It was an irregular building of some magnitude, and seemed to be of the architecture of different periods. One wing was evidently very ancient, with heavy stone-shafted bow-windows jutting out and overrun with ivy, from among the foliage of which the small, diamond-shaped panes of glass glittered with the moonbeams. The rest of the house was in the French

---

[1] King Lear, act iii. sc. 6.

taste of Charles II.'s [1] time, having been repaired and altered, as my friend told me, by one of his ancestors, who returned with that monarch at the Restoration.[2] The grounds about the house were laid out in the old formal manner of artificial flower-beds, clipped shrubberies, raised terraces, and heavy stone balustrades, ornamented with urns, a leaden statue or two, and a jet of water. The old gentleman, I was told, was extremely careful to preserve this obsolete finery in all its original state. He admired this fashion in gardening: it had an air of magnificence, was courtly and noble, and befitting good old family style. The boasted imitation of nature in modern gardening had sprung up with modern republican notions, but did not suit a monarchical government: it smacked of the leveling system. I could not help smiling at this introduction of politics into gardening, though I expressed some apprehension that I should find the old gentleman rather intolerant in his creed. Frank assured me, however, that it was almost the only instance in which he had ever heard his father meddle with politics; and he believed he had got this notion from a member of Parliament who once passed a few weeks with him. The Squire was glad of any argument to defend his clipped yew-trees and formal terraces, which had been occasionally attacked by modern landscape-gardeners.

As we approached the house, we heard the sound of music, and now and then a burst of laughter, from one end of the building. This, Bracebridge said, must proceed from the servants' hall, where a great deal of revelry was permitted, and even encouraged by the Squire, throughout the twelve days [3] of Christmas, provided every thing was done conformably to ancient

[1] Charles II. (born, 1630) was proclaimed king by the Scottish Parliament in 1649. He landed in Scotland in 1650, and was crowned the following year. He marched into England against Cromwell, but was defeated at Worcester in 1651.

[2] In English history, the reëstablishing of the monarchy with Charles II. in 1660, and the period of his reign.

[3] Referring to the period between Christmas and Epiphany, or from Dec. 25 to Jan. 6.

usage.   Here were kept up the old games of hoodman blind,
shoe the wild mare, hot cockles, steal the white loaf, bob-apple,
and snap-dragon.   The Yule clog[1] and Christmas candle were
regularly burnt; and the mistletoe, with its white berries, hung
up, to the imminent peril of all the pretty house-maids.[2]

So intent were the servants upon their sports, that we had to
ring repeatedly before we could make ourselves heard.   On our
arrival being announced, the Squire came out to receive us, accompanied by his two other sons, — one a young officer in the
army, home on leave of absence; the other an Oxonian, just
from the university.   The Squire was a fine, healthy-looking old
gentleman, with silver hair curling lightly round an open, florid
countenance, in which a physiognomist, with the advantage, like
myself, of a previous hint or two, might discover a singular mixture of whim and benevolence.

[1] IRVING'S NOTE. — The Yule clog is a great log of wood, sometimes the
root of a tree, brought into the house with great ceremony on Christmas Eve,
laid in the fireplace, and lighted with the brand of last year's clog.   While
it lasted, there was great drinking, singing, and telling of tales.   Sometimes
it was accompanied by Christmas candles, but in the cottages the only light
was from the ruddy blaze of the great wood fire.   The Yule clog was to burn
all night: if it went out, it was considered a sign of ill luck.   Herrick mentions it in one of his songs : —

> "Come, bring with a noise,
>   My merrie, merrie boyes,
> The Christmas log to the firing;
>   While my good dame, she
>   Bids ye all be free,
> And drink to your hearts desiring."

The Yule clog is still burnt in many farmhouses and kitchens in England,
particularly in the north, and there are several superstitions connected with
it among the peasantry.   If a squinting person come to the house while it is
burning, or a person barefooted, it is considered an ill omen.   The brand
remaining from the Yule clog is carefully put away to light the next year's
Christmas fire.

[2] IRVING'S NOTE. — The mistletoe is still hung up in farmhouses and
kitchens at Christmas, and the young men have the privilege of kissing the
girls under it, plucking each time a berry from the bush.   When the berries
are all plucked, the privilege ceases.

The family meeting was warm and affectionate. As the evening was far advanced, the Squire would not permit us to change our traveling dresses, but ushered us at once to the company, which was assembled in a large, old-fashioned hall. It was composed of different branches of a numerous family connection, where there were the usual proportions of old uncles and aunts, comfortable married dames, superannuated spinsters, blooming country cousins, half-fledged striplings, and bright-eyed boarding-school hoidens. They were variously occupied,— some at a round game of cards; others conversing around the fireplace; at one end of the hall was a group of the young folks, some nearly grown up, others of a more tender and budding age, fully engrossed by a merry game; and a profusion of wooden horses, penny trumpets, and tattered dolls about the floor, showed traces of a troop of little fairy beings, who, having frolicked through a happy day, had been carried off to slumber through a peaceful night.

While the mutual greetings were going on between young Bracebridge and his relatives, I had time to scan the apartment. I have called it a hall, for so it had certainly been in old times, and the Squire had evidently endeavored to restore it to something of its primitive state. Over the heavy projecting fireplace was suspended a picture of a warrior in armor, standing by a white horse; and on the opposite wall hung a helmet, buckler, and lance. At one end an enormous pair of antlers were inserted in the wall, the branches serving as hooks on which to suspend hats, whips, and spurs; and in the corners of the apartment were fowling-pieces, fishing-rods, and other sporting implements. The furniture was of the cumbrous workmanship of former days, though some articles of modern convenience had been added, and the oaken floor had been carpeted; so that the whole presented an odd mixture of parlor and hall.

The grate had been removed from the wide, overwhelming fireplace, to make way for a fire of wood, in the midst of which was an enormous log, glowing and blazing, and sending forth a vast volume of light and heat: this I understood was the Yule clog, which the Squire was particular in having brought in and illumined on a Christmas Eve, according to ancient custom.

It was really delightful to see the old Squire seated in his hereditary elbow chair, by the hospitable fireside of his ancestors, and looking around him like the sun of a system, beaming warmth and gladness to every heart. Even the very dog that lay stretched at his feet, as he lazily shifted his position and yawned, would look fondly up in his master's face, wag his tail against the floor, and stretch himself again to sleep, confident of kindness and protection. There is an emanation from the heart in genuine hospitality which cannot be described, but is immediately felt, and puts the stranger at once at his ease. I had not been seated many minutes by the comfortable hearth of the worthy old cavalier, before I found myself as much at home as if I had been one of the family.

Supper was announced shortly after our arrival. It was served up in a spacious oaken chamber, the panels of which shone with wax, and around which were several family portraits decorated with holly and ivy.[1] Beside the accustomed lights, two great wax tapers, called Christmas candles,[2] wreathed with greens, were placed on a highly polished beaufet among the family plate. The table was abundantly spread with substantial fare; but the Squire made his supper of frumenty,— a dish made of wheat cakes boiled in milk, with rich spices, being a standing dish in old times for Christmas Eve.

I was happy to find my old friend, minced pie,[3] in the retinue

[1] Ivy was used not only as a vintner's sign, but also among the evergreens at funerals.

[2] Christmas was called the " Feast of Lights " in the Western or Latin Church, because they used many lights or candles at the feast; or, rather, because Christ, the Light of all lights, that true Light, came into the world: hence the Christmas candle.

[3] By some it has been supposed, from the Oriental ingredients which enter into its composition, to have a reference to the offerings made by the Wise Men of the East; and it was anciently the custom to make these pies of an

of the feast; and finding him to be perfectly orthodox, and that I need not be ashamed of my predilection, I greeted him with all the warmth wherewith we usually greet an old and very genteel acquaintance.

The mirth of the company was greatly promoted by the humors of an eccentric personage whom Mr. Bracebridge always addressed with the quaint appellation of Master Simon. He was a tight, brisk little man, with the air of an arrant old bachelor. His nose was shaped like the bill of a parrot; his face, slightly pitted with the small-pox, with a dry, perpetual bloom on it, like a frost-bitten leaf in autumn. He had an eye of great quickness and vivacity, with a drollery and lurking waggery of expression that was irresistible. He was evidently the wit of the family, dealing very much in sly jokes and innuendoes with the ladies, and making infinite merriment by harpings upon old themes; which, unfortunately, my ignorance of the family chronicles did not permit me to enjoy. It seemed to be his great delight during supper to keep a young girl next him in a continual agony of stifled laughter, in spite of her awe of the reproving looks of her mother, who sat opposite. Indeed, he was the idol of the younger part of the company, who laughed at everything he said or did, and at every turn of his countenance. I could not wonder at it, for he must have been a miracle of accomplishments in their eyes. He could imitate Punch and Judy; make an old woman of his hand, with the assistance of a burnt cork and pocket-handkerchief; and cut an orange into such a ludicrous caricature that the young folks were ready to die with laughing.

I was let briefly into his history by Frank Bracebridge. He was an old bachelor, of a small, independent income, which, by careful management, was sufficient for all his wants. He revolved through the family system like a vagrant comet in its orbit; sometimes visiting one branch, and sometimes another quite remote, as is often the case with gentlemen of extensive

oblong form, thereby representing the manger in which, on that occasion, these sages found the infant Jesus.

connections and small fortunes in England. He had a chirping, buoyant disposition, always enjoying the present moment; and his frequent change of scene and company prevented his acquiring those rusty, unaccommodating habits, with which old bachelors are so uncharitably charged. He was a complete family chronicle, being versed in the genealogy, history, and intermarriages of the whole house of Bracebridge, which made him a great favorite with the old folks; he was a beau of all the elder ladies and superannuated spinsters, among whom he was habitually considered rather a young fellow, and he was master of the revels among the children; so that there was not a more popular being in the sphere in which he moved than Mr. Simon Bracebridge. Of late years he had resided almost entirely with the Squire, to whom he had become a factotum, and whom he particularly delighted by jumping with his humor in respect to old times, and by having a scrap of an old song to suit every occasion. We had presently a specimen of his last-mentioned talent, for no sooner was supper removed, and spiced wines and other beverages peculiar to the season introduced, than Master Simon was called on for a good old Christmas song. He bethought himself for a moment, and then, with a sparkle of the eye, and a voice that was by no means bad, excepting that it ran occasionally into a falsetto, like the notes of a split reed, he quavered forth a quaint old ditty: —

> "Now Christmas is come,
> Let us beat up the drum,
> And call all our neighbors together;
> And when they appear,
> Let us make such a cheer
> As will keep out the wind and the weather," etc.

The supper had disposed every one to gayety, and an old harper was summoned from the servants' hall, where he had been strumming all the evening, and to all appearance comforting himself with some of the Squire's home-brewed. He was a kind of hanger-on, I was told, of the establishment, and, though ostensibly a resident of the village, was oftener to be found in the Squire's kitchen than his own home, the old gentleman being fond of the sound of "harp in hall."

The dance, like most dances after supper, was a merry one. Some of the older folks joined in it, and the Squire himself figured down several couple with a partner with whom he affirmed he had danced at every Christmas for nearly half a century. Master Simon, who seemed to be a kind of connecting link between the old times and the new, and to be withal a little antiquated in the taste of his accomplishments, evidently piqued himself on his dancing, and was endeavoring to gain credit by the heel and toe, rigadoon, and other graces of the ancient school; but he had unluckily assorted himself with a little romping girl from boarding-school, who, by her wild vivacity, kept him continually on the stretch, and defeated all his sober attempts at elegance — such are the ill-assorted matches to which antique gentlemen are unfortunately prone!

The young Oxonian, on the contrary, had led out one of his maiden aunts, on whom the rogue played a thousand little knaveries with impunity. He was full of practical jokes, and his delight was to tease his aunts and cousins; yet, like all madcap youngsters, he was a universal favorite among the women. The most interesting couple in the dance was the young officer and a ward of the Squire's, a beautiful, blushing girl of seventeen. From several shy glances which I had noticed in the course of the evening, I suspected there was a little kindness growing up between them; and, indeed, the young soldier was just the hero to captivate a romantic girl. He was tall, slender, and handsome, and, like most young British officers of late years, had picked up various small accomplishments on the Continent, — he could talk French and Italian, draw landscapes, sing very tolerably, dance divinely, — but, above all, he had been wounded at Waterloo.[1] What girl of seventeen, well read in

[1] The French under Napoleon were defeated by the English, June 18, 1815, at Waterloo, a village in Belgium.

poetry and romance, could resist such a mirror of chivalry and perfection!

The moment the dance was over, he caught up a guitar, and, lolling against the old marble fireplace, in an attitude which I am half inclined to suspect was studied, began the little French air of the "Troubadour." The Squire, however, exclaimed against having anything on Christmas Eve but good old English; upon which the young minstrel, casting up his eye for a moment, as if in an effort of memory, struck into another strain, and, with a charming air of gallantry, gave Herrick's[1] "Night-Piece to Julia:"—

> "Her eyes the glow-worm lend thee.
> The shooting stars attend thee,
> 　　And the elves also,
> 　　Whose little eyes glow
> Like the sparks of fire, befriend thee.
>
> "No Will-o'-the-Wisp mislight thee;
> Nor snake or slow-worm bite thee;
> 　　But on, on thy way,
> 　　Not making a stay, ·
> Since ghost there is none to affright thee.
>
> "Then let not the dark thee cumber;
> What though the moon does slumber,
> 　　The stars of the night
> 　·　Will lend thee their light,
> Like tapers clear without number.
>
> "Then, Julia, let me woo thee,
> Thus, thus to come unto me;
> 　　And when I shall meet
> 　　Thy silvery feet,
> My soul I'll pour into thee."

The song might or might not have been intended in compliment to the fair Julia, for so I found his partner was called. She, however, was certainly unconscious of any such application,

---

[1] An English poet and clergyman (1591–1674). As a writer of pastoral lyrics, Herrick takes a high rank in English literature.

for she never looked at the singer, but kept her eyes cast upon the floor. Her face was suffused, it is true, with a beautiful blush, and there was a gentle heaving of the bosom ; but all that was doubtless caused by the exercise of the dance. Indeed, so great was her indifference, that she was amusing herself with plucking to pieces a choice bouquet of hothouse flowers, and by the time the song was concluded the nosegay lay in ruins on the floor.

The party now broke up for the night with the kind-hearted old custom of shaking hands. As I passed through the hall, on my way to my chamber, the dying embers of the Yule clog still sent forth a dusky glow; and, had it not been the season when "no spirit dare stir abroad,"[1] I should have been half tempted to steal from my room at midnight, and peep whether the fairies might not be at their revels about the hearth.

My chamber was in the old part of the mansion, the ponderous furniture of which might have been fabricated in the days of the giants. The room was paneled with cornices of heavy carved work, in which flowers and grotesque faces were strangely intermingled; and a row of black-looking portraits stared mournfully at me from the walls. The bed was of rich though faded damask, with a lofty tester,[2] and stood in a niche opposite a bow-window. I had scarcely got into bed, when a strain of music seemed to break forth in the air just below the window. I listened, and found it proceeded from a band, which I concluded to be the waits[3] from some neighboring village. They went round the house, playing under the windows. I drew aside the curtains to hear them more distinctly. The moonbeams fell through the upper part of the casement, partially lighting up the antiquated apartment. The sounds, as they receded, became more soft and

---

[1] It is an old superstition, that on the eve of Christmas "the bird of dawning singeth all night long" to scare away all evil things from infesting the hallowed hours.

[2] Old French, *testiere* ("a headpiece"); Latin, *testa* ("a shell"). The material stretched over a four-posted bed, forming a canopy over it.

[3] See Note 2, p. 28.

4

aerial, and seemed to accord with quiet and moonlight. I listened and listened. They became more and more tender and remote; and, as they gradually died away, my head sunk upon the pillow, and I fell asleep.

CHRISTMAS DAY.

> *" Dark and dull night flie hence away,*
> *And give the honor to this day*
> *That sees December turn'd to May.*
>
> .   .   .   .   .   .
>
> *Why does the chilling winter's morne*
> *Smile like a field beset with corn?*
> *Or smell like to a meade new-shorne,*
> *Thus on the sudden?—come and see*
> *The cause, why things thus fragrant be."*
>
> HERRICK.

WHEN I woke the next morning, it seemed as if all the events of the preceding evening had been a dream, and nothing but the identity of the ancient chamber convinced me of their reality. While I lay musing on my pillow, I heard the sound of little feet pattering outside of the door, and a whispering consultation. Presently a choir of small voices chanted forth an old Christmas carol, the burden of which was,—

> " Rejoice, our Saviour he was born
> On Christmas Day in the morning."

I rose softly, slipped on my clothes, opened the door suddenly, and beheld one of the most beautiful little fairy groups that a painter could imagine. It consisted of a boy and two girls, the eldest not more than six, and lovely as seraphs. They were going the rounds of the house, singing at every chamber door; but my sudden appearance frightened them into mute bashfulness. They remained for a moment playing on their lips with their fingers, and now and then stealing a shy glance from under their eyebrows; until, as if by one impulse, they scampered away, and, as they turned an angle of the gallery, I heard them laughing in triumph at their escape.

Everything conspired to produce kind and happy feelings in this stronghold of old-fashioned hospitality. The window of my chamber looked out upon what in summer would have been a beautiful landscape. There was a sloping lawn, a fine stream winding at the foot of it, and a tract of park beyond, with noble clumps of trees, and herds of deer. At a distance was a neat hamlet, with the smoke from the cottage chimneys hanging over it, and a church with its dark spire in strong relief against the clear, cold sky. The house was surrounded with evergreens, according to the English custom, which would have given almost an appearance of summer; but the morning was extremely frosty. The light vapor of the preceding evening had been precipitated by the cold, and covered all the trees and every blade of grass with its fine crystallizations. The rays of a bright morning sun had a dazzling effect among the glittering foliage. A robin, perched upon the top of a mountain ash that hung its clusters of red berries just before my window, was basking himself in the sunshine, and piping a few querulous notes; and a peacock was displaying all the glories of his train, and strutting with the pride and gravity of a Spanish grandee [1] on the terrace walk below.

I had scarcely dressed myself, when a servant appeared to invite me to family prayers. He showed me the way to a small chapel in the old wing of the house, where I found the principal part of the family already assembled in a kind of gallery, furnished with cushions, hassocks, and large prayer-books: the servants were seated on benches below. The old gentleman read prayers from a desk in front of the gallery, and Master Simon acted as clerk, and made the responses; and I must do him the justice to say that he acquitted himself with great gravity and decorum.

The service was followed by a Christmas carol, which Mr.

---

[1] A Spanish nobleman, especially one of the first rank (Spanish, *grande*).

Bracebridge himself had constructed from a poem of his favorite author, Herrick; and it had been adapted to a church melody by Master Simon. As there were several good voices among the household, the effect was extremely pleasing; but I was particularly gratified by the exaltation of heart, and sudden sally of grateful feeling, with which the worthy Squire delivered one stanza; his eye glistening, and his voice rambling out of all the bounds of time and tune, —

> " 'Tis thou that crown'st my glittering hearth
> With guiltless mirth,
> And giv'st me Wassaile bowles to drink
> Spic'd to the brink:
> Lord, 'tis thy plenty-dropping hand
> That soiles my land: [1]
> And giv'st me for my bushell sowne,
> Twice ten for one."

I afterwards understood that early morning service was read on every Sunday and saint's day throughout the year, either by Mr. Bracebridge or some member of the family. It was once almost universally the case at the seats of the nobility and gentry of England, and it is much to be regretted that the custom is falling into neglect; for the dullest observer must be sensible of the order and serenity prevalent in those households where the occasional exercise of a beautiful form of worship in the morning gives, as it were, the keynote to every temper for the day, and attunes every spirit to harmony.

Our breakfast consisted of what the Squire denominated true old English fare. He indulged in some bitter lamentations over modern breakfasts of tea and toast, which he censured as among the causes of modern effeminacy and weak nerves, and the decline of old English heartiness; and, though he admitted them to his table to suit the palates of his guests, yet there was a brave display of cold meats, wine, and ale on the sideboard.

After breakfast I walked about the grounds with Frank Brace-

---

[1] Enriches the soil, and sends a plentiful harvest.

bridge and Master Simon, or Mr. Simon, as he v.as called by everybody but the Squire. We were escorted by a number of gentlemanlike dogs, that seemed loungers about the establishment, from the frisking spaniel to the steady old stag-hound, the last of which was of a race that had been in the family time out of mind. They were all obedient to a dog-whistle which hung to Master Simon's buttonhole, and in the midst of their gambols would glance an eye occasionally upon a small switch he carried in his hand.

The old mansion had a still more venerable look in the yellow sunshine than by pale moonlight; and I could not but feel the force of the Squire's idea, that the formal terraces, heavily molded balustrades, and clipped yew-trees, carried with them an air of proud aristocracy.

There appeared to be an unusual number of peacocks about the place; and I was making some remarks upon what I termed a flock of them, that were basking under a sunny wall, when I was gently corrected in my phraseology by Master Simon, who told me, that, according to the most ancient and approved treatise on hunting, I must say a *muster* of peacocks. "In the same way," added he, with a slight air of pedantry, "we say a flight of doves or swallows; a bevy of quails; a herd of deer, of wrens, or cranes; a skulk of foxes; or a building of rooks." He went on to inform me, that, according to Sir Anthony Fitzherbert,[1] we ought to ascribe to this bird "both understanding and glory; for, being praised, he will presently set up his tail, chiefly against the sun, to the intent you may the better behold the beauty thereof. But at the fall of the leaf, when his tail falleth, he will mourn and hide himself in corners, till his tail come again as it was."[2]

---

[1] An eminent English lawyer, who wrote, in 1523, The Book of Husbandry, — the first published work on agriculture in the English language.

[2] The peacock is said to be the vainest of birds. It came originally from India. It was there that Alexander the Great saw it for the first time. He was so impressed with its magnificent plumage, that he forbade all persons, under pain of death, to kill any.

I could not help smiling at this display of small erudition on so whimsical a subject: but I found that the peacocks were birds of some consequence at the hall; for Frank Bracebridge informed me that they were great favorites with his father, who was extremely careful to keep up the breed, partly because they belonged to chivalry, and were in great request at the stately banquets of the olden time,[1] and partly because they had a pomp and magnificence about them highly becoming an old family mansion. Nothing, he was accustomed to say, had an air of greater state and dignity than a peacock perched upon an antique stone balustrade.

Master Simon had now to hurry off, having an appointment at the parish church with the village choristers, who were to perform some music of his selection. There was something extremely agreeable in the cheerful flow of animal spirits of the little man; and I confess I had been somewhat surprised at his apt quotations from authors who certainly were not in the range of every-day reading. I mentioned this last circumstance to Frank Bracebridge, who told me with a smile that Master Simon's whole stock of erudition was confined to some half a dozen old authors, which the Squire had put into his hands, and which he read over and over whenever he had a studious fit, as he sometimes had on a rainy day or a long winter evening. Sir Anthony Fitzherbert's "Book of Husbandry;" Markham's "Country Contentments;"[2] the "Tretyse of Hunting," by Sir Thomas Cockayne,[3] Knight; Izaak Walton's[4] "Angler;" and two or three more such ancient

---

[1] Quintus Hortensius, the orator, was the first to have peacocks served at a banquet. After this no banquet was complete without this dish.

[2] See Note 2, p. 55.

[3] Cokaine or Cokayn (written also Cockaine), an English Catholic (born in Derbyshire, 1608; died, 1684), was a Royalist in the civil war. He composed some worthless plays and doggerel poems, which are only worthy of notice on account of the anecdotes they furnish of contemporary authors or actors.

[4] A celebrated English writer (born at Stafford, 1593; died, 1683). His principal work, The Complete Angler or Contemplative Man's Recreation, was published in 1653.

worthies of the pen,— were his standard authorities; and, like all men who know but a few books, he looked up to them with a kind of idolatry, and quoted them on all occasions. As to his songs, they were chiefly picked out of old books in the Squire's library, and adapted to tunes that were popular among the choice spirits of the last century. His practical application of scraps of literature, however, had caused him to be looked upon as a prodigy of book knowledge by all the grooms, huntsmen, and small sportsmen of the neighborhood.

While we were talking, we heard the distant toll of the village bell, and I was told that the Squire was a little particular in having his household at church on a Christmas morning, considering it a day of pouring out of thanks and rejoicing; for, as old Tusser [1] observed,—

> " At Christmas be merry, *and thankful withal,*
> And feast thy poor neighbors, the great with the small."

"If you are disposed to go to church," said Frank Bracebridge, "I can promise you a specimen of my cousin Simon's musical achievements. As the church is destitute of an organ, he has formed a band from the village amateurs, and established a musical club for their improvement; he has also sorted a choir, as he sorted my father's pack of hounds, according to the directions of Jervaise Markham [2] in his ' Country Contentments.' For the bass he has sought out all the ' deep, solemn mouths,' and for the tenor the ' loud-ringing mouth,' among the country bumpkins; and for ' sweet mouths,' he has culled with curious taste among the prettiest lasses in the neighborhood, though these last, he affirms, are the most difficult to keep in tune, your pretty fe-

---

[1] Thomas Tusser (1527–80), poet, was born at Essex, England. His poems on husbandry have the charm of simplicity and directness, and during his life they went through a number of editions.

[2] Jervaise (or Gervase) Markham, an English soldier and miscellaneous writer, was born in Nottinghamshire about 1570. He served in the Royalist army in the civil war, and died in 1655.

male singer being exceedingly wayward and capricious, and very liable to accident."

As the morning, though frosty, was remarkably fine and clear, the most of the family walked to the church, which was a very old building of gray stone, and stood near a village, about half a mile from the park gate. Adjoining it was a low, snug parsonage, which seemed coeval with the church. The front of it was perfectly matted with a yew-tree that had been trained against its walls, through the dense foliage of which apertures had been formed to admit light into the small antique lattices. As we passed this sheltered nest, the parson issued forth, and preceded us.

I had expected to see a sleek, well-conditioned pastor, such as is often found in a snug living in the vicinity of a rich patron's table, but I was disappointed. The parson was a little, meager, black-looking man, with a grizzled wig that was too wide, and stood off from each ear, so that his head seemed to have shrunk away within it, like a dried filbert in its shell. He wore a rusty coat, with great skirts, and pockets that would have held the church Bible and Prayer Book; and his small legs seemed still smaller, from being planted in large shoes decorated with enormous buckles.

I was informed by Frank Bracebridge that the parson had been a chum of his father's at Oxford,[1] and had received this living shortly after the latter had come to his estate. He was a complete black-letter [2] hunter, and would scarcely read a work printed in the Roman character. The editions of Caxton and Wynkin de Worde were his delight; and he was indefatigable in his researches after such Old English writers as have fallen into oblivion from their worthlessness. In deference, perhaps, to the notions of Mr. Bracebridge, he had made diligent investigations

[1] The famous university situated in Oxford, the county town of Oxfordshire.

[2] A type which appeared in England about the year 1480. It was used especially for Bibles, law-books, royal proclamations, etc.

into the festive rites and holiday customs of former times, and
had been as zealous in the inquiry as if he had been a boon companion; but it was merely with that plodding spirit with which
men of adust temperament follow up any track of study, merely
because it is denominated learning; indifferent to its intrinsic
nature, whether it be the illustration of the wisdom or of the ribaldry and obscenity of antiquity. He had pored over these old volumes so intensely, that they seemed to have been reflected into
his countenance; which, if the face be indeed an index of the
mind, might be compared to a title-page of black-letter.

On reaching the church porch, we found the parson rebuking
the gray-headed sexton for having used mistletoe among the
greens with which the church was decorated. It was, he observed, an unholy plant, profaned by having been used by the
Druids in their mystic ceremonies; and though it might be inno-
cently employed in the festive ornamenting of halls and kitchens,
yet it had been deemed by the fathers of the Church as unhal-
lowed, and totally unfit for sacred purposes. So tenacious was
he on this point, that the poor sexton was obliged to strip down
a great part of the humble trophies of his taste, before the parson
would consent to enter upon the service of the day.

The interior of the church was venerable but simple. On the
walls were several mural monuments of the Bracebridges; and
just beside the altar was a tomb of ancient workmanship, on
which lay the effigy of a warrior in armor, with his legs crossed,
— a sign of his having been a crusader. I was told it was one
of the family who had signalized himself in the Holy Land, and
the same whose picture hung over the fireplace in the hall.

During service, Master Simon stood up in the pew, and repeated the responses very audibly, evincing that kind of ceremo-
nious devotion punctually observed by a gentleman of the old
school, and a man of old family connections. I observed, too,
that he turned over the leaves of a folio Prayer Book with something of a flourish; possibly to show off an enormous seal-ring
which enriched one of his fingers, and which had the look of a

family relic. But he was evidently most solicitous about the musical part of the service, keeping his eye fixed intently on the choir, and beating time with much gesticulation and emphasis.

The orchestra was in a small gallery, and presented a most whimsical grouping of heads, piled one above the other, among which I particularly noticed that of the village tailor, a pale fellow with a retreating forehead and chin, who played on the clarinet, and seemed to have blown his face to a point; and there was another, a short, pursy man, stooping and laboring at a bass viol, so as to show nothing but the top of a round, bald head, like the egg of an ostrich. There were two or three pretty faces among the female singers, to which the keen air of a frosty morning had given a bright, rosy tint; but the gentlemen choristers had evidently been chosen, like old Cremona [1] fiddles, more for tone than looks; and, as several had to sing from the same book, there were clusterings of odd physiognomies, not unlike those groups of cherubs we sometimes see on country tombstones.

The usual services of the choir were managed tolerably well, the vocal parts generally lagging a little behind the instrumental, and some loitering fiddler now and then making up for lost time by traveling over a passage with prodigious celerity, and clearing more bars than the keenest fox-hunter to be in at the death. But the great trial was an anthem that had been prepared and arranged by Master Simon, and on which he had founded great expectation. Unluckily, there was a blunder at the very outset. The musicians became flurried; Master Simon was in a fever; everything went on lamely and irregularly until they came to a chorus beginning, "Now let us sing with one accord," which seemed to be a signal for parting company. All became discord and confusion. Each shifted for himself, and got to the end as

---

[1] The capital of a province of Lombardy, also named Cremona, formerly celebrated for its violins and other musical instruments. Great prices were paid for violins made in Cremona. The manufacture of these has now declined.

well, or rather as soon, as he could, excepting one old chorister in a pair of horn spectacles, bestriding and pinching a long, sonorous nose, who, happening to stand a little apart, and being wrapped up in his own melody, kept on a quivering course, wriggling his head, ogling his book, and winding all up by a nasal solo of at least three bars' duration.

The parson gave us a most erudite sermon on the rites and ceremonies of Christmas, and the propriety of observing it not merely as a day of thanksgiving, but of rejoicing; supporting the correctness of his opinions by the earliest usages of the Church, and enforcing them by the authorities of Theophilus of Cæsarea,[1] St. Cyprian,[2] St. Chrysostom,[3] St. Augustine,[4] and a cloud more of saints and fathers, from whom he made copious quotations. I was a little at a loss to perceive the necessity of such a mighty array of forces to maintain a point which no one present seemed inclined to dispute, but I soon found that the good man had a legion of ideal adversaries to contend with, having, in the course of his researches on the subject of Christmas, got completely embroiled in the sectarian controversies of the Revolution, when the Puritans made such a fierce assault upon the ceremonies of the Church, and poor old Christmas was driven out of the land by proclamation of Parliament.[5] The worthy parson lived but with times past, and knew but little of the present.

[1] Instructor of Justinian, and abbot of St. Alexander at Prisrend in Macedonia, afterwards Bishop of Sardica in 517.

[2] Bishop of Carthage in the third century, one of the most illustrious men in the early history of the Church, and one of the most notable of its early martyrs. He was ordered to be beheaded Sept. 14, 258, by Emperor Valerian.

[3] The most famous of the Greek fathers (born at Antioch about 347). The festival of St. Chrysostom is observed both in the Greek and in the Latin Church, — by the former on Nov. 13, and by the latter on Jan. 27.

[4] The greatest of the four great fathers of the Latin Church (born in Numidia, Nov. 13, A.D. 354).

[5] "The House spent much time this day about the business of the Navy, for settling the affairs at sea, and before they rose, were presented with a ter-

Shut up among worm-eaten tomes in the retirement of his antiquated little study, the pages of old times were to him as the gazettes of the day, while the era of the Revolution was mere modern history. He forgot that nearly two centuries had elapsed since the fiery persecution of poor mince pie throughout the land, when plum porridge was denounced as "mere popery," and roastbeef as anti-Christian, and that Christmas had been brought in again triumphantly with the merry court of King Charles at the Restoration. He kindled into warmth with the ardor of his contest, and the host of imaginary foes with whom he had to combat. He had a stubborn conflict with old Prynne[1] and two or three other forgotten champions of the Roundheads,[2] on the subject of Christmas festivity, and concluded by urging his hearers, in the most solemn and affecting manner, to stand to the traditional customs of their fathers, and feast and make merry on this joyful anniversary of the Church.

I have seldom known a sermon attended apparently with more immediate effects; for, on leaving the church, the congregation seemed, one and all, possessed with the gayety of spirit so ear-

---

rible remonstrance against Christmas day, grounded upon divine Scriptures, 2 Cor. v. 16, 1 Cor. xv. 14, 17; and in honor of the Lord's Day, grounded upon these Scriptures, John xx. 1, Rev. i. 10, Psalms cxviii. 24, Lev. xxiii. 7, 11, Mark xv. 8, Psalms lxxxiv. 10; in which Christmas is called Antichrist's masse, and those Masse-mongers and Papists who observe it, etc. In consequence of which Parliament spent some time in consultation about the abolition of Christmas day, passed orders to that effect, and resolved to sit on the following day, which was commonly called Christmas day."— *Flying Eagle* (a small gazette published Dec. 24, 1652).

[1] William Prynne (1600–69) was a Puritan to the core. He published in 1633 a book (Histrio-Mastix) which was an attack upon stage plays. The Queen was very much interested in the drama at this time, and Prynne's offensive words were supposed to apply to her. Prynne was sentenced by the Star Chamber to fine, imprisonment, and to be set in the pillory, where he was to lose both his ears.

[2] Adherents of the Parliamentary or Puritan party, as opposed to the Royalists; called Roundheads in derisive allusion to their close-cut hair, the Royalists usually wearing theirs long.

nestly enjoined by their pastor. The elder folks gathered in knots in the churchyard, greeting and shaking hands; and the children ran about crying, "Ule! Ule!" and repeating some uncouth rhymes,[1] which the parson, who had joined us, informed me had been handed down from days of yore. The villagers doffed their hats to the Squire as he passed, giving him the good wishes of the season with every appearance of heartfelt sincerity, and were invited by him to the hall, to take something to keep out the cold of the weather; and I heard blessings uttered by several of the poor, which convinced me, that, in the midst of his enjoyments, the worthy old cavalier had not forgotten the true Christmas virtue of charity.

On our way homeward his heart seemed overflowing with generous and happy feelings. As we passed over a rising ground which commanded something of a prospect, the sounds of rustic merriment now and then reached our ears. The Squire paused for a few moments, and looked around with an air of inexpressible benignity. The beauty of the day was of itself sufficient to inspire philanthropy. Notwithstanding the frostiness of the morning, the sun, in his cloudless journey, had acquired sufficient power to melt away the thin covering of snow from every southern declivity, and to bring out the living green which adorns an English landscape even in mid-winter. Large tracts of smiling verdure contrasted with the dazzling whiteness of the shaded slopes and hollows. Every sheltered bank on which the broad rays rested yielded its silver rill of cold and limpid water, glittering through the dripping grass, and sent up slight exhalations to contribute to the thin haze that hung just above the surface of the earth. There was something truly cheering in this triumph of warmth and verdure over the frosty thraldom of winter: it was, as the Squire observed, an emblem of Christmas hospital-

---

[1] IRVING'S NOTE: —

> "Ule! Ule!
> Three puddings in a pule;
> Crack nuts and cry ule!"

ity, breaking through the chills of ceremony and selfishness, and thawing every heart into a flow. He pointed with pleasure to the indications of good cheer reeking from the chimneys of the comfortable farmhouses and low thatched cottages. "I love," said he, "to see this day well kept by rich and poor. It is a great thing to have one day in the year, at least, when you are sure of being welcome wherever you go, and of having, as it were, the world all thrown open to you; and I am almost disposed to join with Poor Robin, in his malediction on every churlish enemy to this honest festival: —

> " ' Those who at Christmas do repine,
> And would fain hence dispatch him,
> May they with old Duke Humphry dine,
> Or else may Squire Ketch[1] catch 'em.' "

The Squire went on to lament the deplorable decay of the games and amusements which were once prevalent at this season among the lower orders, and countenanced by the higher, when the old halls of castles and manor-houses were thrown open at daylight, when the tables were covered with brawn and beef and humming ale, when the harp and the carol resounded all day long, and when rich and poor were alike welcome to enter and make merry.[2] "Our old games and local customs," said he, "had a great effect in making the peasant fond of his home, and the promotion of them by the gentry made him fond of his lord.

---

[1] Alluding to Jack Ketch, the hangman (1678). Ketch executed Lord Russell and the Duke of Monmouth. The name has become proverbial for hangmen.

[2] " An English gentleman at the opening of the great day, i.e. on Christmas day in the morning, had all his tenants and neighbors enter his hall by daybreak. The strong beer was broached, and the black jacks went plentifully about with toast, sugar, and nutmeg, and good Cheshire cheese. The Hackin (the great sausage) must be boiled by daybreak, or else two young men must take the maiden (i.e. the cook) by the arms and run her round the market place till she is shamed of her laziness." — *Round about our Sea-Coal Fire.*

They made the times merrier and kinder and better, and I can truly say, with one of our old poets,—

> " 'I like them well—the curious preciseness
> And all-pretended gravity of those
> That seek to banish hence these harmless sports,
> Have thrust away much ancient honesty.'

" The nation," continued he, "is altered. We have almost lost our simple, true-hearted peasantry. They have broken asunder from the higher classes, and seem to think their interests are separate. They have become too knowing, and begin to read newspapers, listen to ale-house politicians, and talk of reform. I think one mode to keep them in good humor in these hard times would be for the nobility and gentry to pass more time on their estates, mingle more among the country people, and set the merry old English games going again."

Such was the good Squire's project for mitigating public discontent; and, indeed, he had once attempted to put his doctrine in practice, and a few years before had kept open house during the holidays in the old style. The country people, however, did not understand how to play their parts in the scene of hospitality. Many uncouth circumstances occurred. The manor was overrun by all the vagrants of the country, and more beggars drawn into the neighborhood in one week than the parish officers could get rid of in a year. Since then he had contented himself with inviting the decent part of the neighboring peasantry to call at the hall on Christmas Day, and with distributing beef and bread and ale among the poor, that they might make merry in their own dwellings.

We had not been long home, when the sound of music was heard from a distance. A band of country lads, without coats, their shirt-sleeves fancifully tied with ribbons, their hats decorated with greens, and clubs in their hands, were seen advancing up the avenue, followed by a large number of villagers and peasantry. They stopped before the hall door, where the music struck up a peculiar air, and the lads performed a curious and intricate dance, advancing, retreating, and striking their clubs together, keeping exact time to the music; while one, whimsically crowned with a fox's skin, the tail of which flaunted down his back, kept capering round the skirts of the dance, and rattling a Christmas box [1] with many antic gesticulations.

The Squire eyed this fanciful exhibition with great interest and delight, and gave me a full account of its origin, which he traced to the times when the Romans held possession of the island; plainly proving that this was a lineal descendant of the sword dance of the ancients. It was now, he said, nearly extinct, but he had accidentally met with traces of it in the neighborhood, and had encouraged its revival; though, to tell the truth, it was too apt to be followed up by rough cudgel play,[2] and broken heads in the evening.

After the dance was concluded, the whole party was entertained with brawn and beef, and stout home-brewed. The Squire himself mingled among the rustics, and was received with awkward demonstrations of deference and regard. It is true, I perceived two or three of the younger peasants, as they were raising their tankards to their mouths, when the Squire's back was turned, making something of a grimace, and giving each other the wink; but, the moment they caught my eye, they pulled grave faces,

---

[1] This title has been said to have been derived from the box which was kept on board of every vessel that sailed upon a distant voyage, for the reception of donations to the priest, who, in return, was expected to offer masses for the safety of the expedition, to the particular saint having charge of the ship, and, above all, of the box. The mass was at that time called "Christ mass," and the boxes kept to pay for it were of course called "Christ-mass boxes." The poor were in the habit of begging from the rich to contribute to the mass boxes, and hence the title which has descended to our day. A relic of these ancient boxes yet exists, in the earthen or wooden box, with a slit in it, which still bears the same name, and is carried by servants and children for the purpose of gathering money at Christmas, being broken only when the period of collection is supposed to be over.

[2] A bout with cudgels. Cudgels were thick short sticks, or staves.

and were exceedingly demure. With Master Simon, however, they all seemed more at their ease. His varied occupations and amusements had made him well known throughout the neighborhood. He was a visitor at every farmhouse and cottage; gossiped with the farmers and their wives; romped with their daughters; and, like that type of a vagrant bachelor the humble-bee, tolled the sweets from all the rosy lips of the country round.

The bashfulness of the guests soon gave way before good cheer and affability. There is something genuine and affectionate in the gayety of the lower orders, when it is excited by the bounty and familiarity of those above them. The warm glow of gratitude enters into their mirth; and a kind word or a small pleasantry, frankly uttered by a patron, gladdens the heart of the dependant more than oil and wine. When the Squire had retired, the merriment increased; and there was much joking and laughter, particularly between Master Simon and a hale, ruddy-faced, white-headed farmer, who appeared to be the wit of the village, for I observed all his companions to wait with open mouths for his retorts, and burst into a gratuitous laugh before they could well understand them.

The whole house, indeed, seemed abandoned to merriment. As I passed to my room to dress for dinner, I heard the sound of music in a small court, and, looking through a window that commanded it, I perceived a band of wandering musicians, with pandean[1] pipes and tambourine. A pretty, coquettish house-maid was dancing a jig with a smart country lad, while several of the other servants were looking on. In the midst of her sport, the girl caught a glimpse of my face at the window, and, coloring up, ran off with an air of roguish affected confusion.

---

[1] Pan, in Greek mythology, was the god of forests, pastures, and flocks, and was the attributed inventor of the shepherd's flute or pipe, the syrinx, — a series of graduated tubes set together (open at one end, and closed at the other), played by blowing across the open ends.

5

THE CHRISTMAS DINNER.

" Lo, now is come our joyful'st feast!
Let every man be jolly,
Each roome with yvie leaves is drest,
And every post with holly.
Now all our neighbours' chimneys smoke,
And Christmas blocks are burning;
Their ovens they with bak't meats choke,
And all their spits are turning.
Without the door let sorrow lie,
And if, for cold, it hap to die,
Wee'l bury 't in a Christmas pye,
And evermore be merry."

WITHERS,[1] *Juvenilia.*

I HAD finished my toilet, and was loitering with Frank Bracebridge in the library, when we heard a distant thwacking
sound, which he informed me was a signal for the serving-up of
the dinner. The Squire kept up old customs in kitchen as well
as hall; and the rolling-pin, struck upon the dresser by the cook,
summoned the servants to carry in the meats.

" Just in this nick the cook knock'd thrice,
And all the waiters in a trice,
His summons did obey;
Each serving man, with dish in hand,
Marched boldly up, like our train band,
Presented, and away." [2]

The dinner was served up in the great hall, where the Squire
always held his Christmas banquet. A blazing, crackling fire of
logs had been heaped on to warm the spacious apartment, and
the flame went sparkling and wreathing up the wide-mouthed
chimney. The great picture of the crusader and his white horse
had been profusely decorated with greens for the occasion; and

---

[1] Written also Wither and Wyther. An English poet, satirist, and political writer (1588–1667).

[2] From Sir John Suckling, an English poet (born in Middlesex about
1608, died about 1642), celebrated as a wit at the court of Charles I.

holly and ivy had likewise been wreathed round the helmet and weapons on the opposite wall, which I understood were the arms of the same warrior. I must own, by the by, I had strong doubts about the authenticity of the painting and armor as having belonged to the crusader, they certainly having the stamp of more recent days; but I was told that the painting had been so considered time out of mind, and that, as to the armor, it had been found in a lumber-room, and elevated to its present situation by the Squire, who at once determined it to be the armor of the family hero; and, as he was absolute authority on all such subjects in his own household, the matter had passed into current acceptation. A sideboard was set out just under this chivalric trophy, on which was a display of plate that might have vied (at least in variety) with Belshazzar's[1] parade of the vessels of the temple, — "flagons, cans, cups, beakers, goblets, basins, and ewers," the gorgeous utensils of good companionship that had gradually accumulated through many generations of jovial housekeepers. Before these stood the two Yule candles,[2] beaming like two stars of the first magnitude; other lights were distributed in branches; and the whole array glittered like a firmament of silver.

We were ushered into this banqueting scene with the sound of minstrelsy; the old harper being seated on a stool beside the fireplace, and twanging his instrument with a vast deal more power than melody. Never did Christmas board display a more goodly and gracious assemblage of countenances. Those who were not handsome were at least happy, and happiness is a rare improver of your hard-favored visage. I always consider an old English family as well worth studying as a collection of Holbein's[3] por-

---

[1] Son of Nabunahid, King of Babylon; conquered by the Persians and Cyrus, 556 B.C. (Compare Daniel v. 2.)

[2] These were large candles lighted and burned at Christmas Eve festivities. It was considered by many bad luck if the candle burned out before the close of the evening: and any portion left was kept to be burned at the corpse watch, or lich wake, of the owner.

[3] Hans Holbein (born at Grünstadt in 1497, died in 1543) was one of the

traits or Albert Dürer's [1] prints.   There is much antiquarian lore
to be acquired, much knowledge of the physiognomies of former
times.   Perhaps it may be from having continually before their
eyes those rows of old family portraits with which the mansions
of this country are stocked: certain it is, that the quaint features
of antiquity are often most faithfully perpetuated in these ancient
lines; and I have traced an old family nose through a whole
picture gallery, legitimately handed down from generation to
generation, almost from the time of the Conquest.   Something
of the kind was to be observed in the worthy company around
me.   Many of their faces had evidently originated in a Gothic
age, and been merely copied by succeeding generations; and
there was one little girl in particular, of staid demeanor, with a
high Roman nose and an antique vinegar aspect, who was a
great favorite of the Squire's, being, as he said, a Bracebridge
all over, and the very counterpart of one of his ancestors who
figured in the court of Henry VIII.[2]

The parson said grace, which was not a short familiar one,
such as is commonly addressed to the Deity in these unceremo-
nious days, but a long, courtly, well-worded one of the ancient
school.   There was now a pause, as if something was expected,
when suddenly the butler entered the hall with some degree of
bustle.   He was attended by a servant on each side with a large
wax-light, and bore a silver dish on which was an enormous pig's

most celebrated German painters.   Henry VIII. gave him abundant employment, and also bestowed upon him a large pension.   Holbein was also a
skillful architect and wood-engraver.   His greatest pictures were, " Dance of
Death," the " Adoration of the Shepherds and the Kings," and the " Last
Supper."

[1] Albrecht Dürer (born at Nuremberg in 1471; died there, April, 1528)
has a name, in the history of art, equal to that of the greatest Italians.   A
very choice collection of his drawings (a large volume), forming part of Lord
Arundel's collection, is in the British Museum.

[2] Henry VIII. (born at Greenwich, England, in 1491; died in 1547)
ascended the English throne in the year 1509.   He was the father of Queen
Elizabeth.

head decorated with rosemary,[1] with a lemon in its mouth, which was placed with great formality at the head of the table. The moment this pageant made its appearance, the harper struck up a flourish; at the conclusion of which the young Oxonian, on receiving a hint from the Squire, gave, with an air of the most comic gravity, an old carol, the first verse of which was as follows :—

> " Caput apri defero,[2]
> Reddens laudes Domino.[3]
> The boar's head in hand bring I,
> With garlands gay and rosemary.
> I pray you all synge merily
> Qui estis in convivio." [4]

Though prepared to witness many of these little eccentricities, from being apprised of the peculiar hobby of mine host, yet, I confess, the parade with which so odd a dish was introduced somewhat perplexed me, until I gathered from the conversation of the Squire and the parson that it was meant to represent the bringing-in of the boar's head,— a dish formerly served up with much ceremony, and the sound of minstrelsy and song, at great tables on Christmas Day. "I like the old custom," said the Squire, "not merely because it is stately and pleasing in itself, but because it was observed at the college at Oxford[5] at which I was educated. When I hear the old song chanted, it brings to mind the time when I was young and gamesome; and the noble old college hall; and my fellow-students loitering about in their black gowns, many of whom, poor lads, are now in their graves."

The parson, however, whose mind was not haunted by such

---

[1] Old English, *rosmarine ;* Latin, *rosmarinus* (*ros,* " dew ; " and *marinus,* " of the sea "). So called because it flourishes best in places near the sea. It is very fragrant, and symbolic of remembrance. Compare Hamlet (act iv. sc. 5): " There's rosemary, that's for remembrance."

[2] " I bring the boar's head."

[3] " Returning praises to the Lord."

[4] " As many as are at the banquet."

[5] The famous university situated in the county of Oxfordshire.

associations, and who was always more taken up with the text
than the sentiment, objected to the Oxonian's version of the
carol, which he affirmed was different from that sung at college.
He went on, with the dry perseverance of a commentator, to
give the college reading, accompanied by sundry annotations,
addressing himself at first to the company at large; but, finding
their attention gradually diverted to other talk and other objects,
he lowered his tone as his number of auditors diminished, until
he concluded his remarks in an under-voice to a fat-headed old
gentleman next him, who was silently engaged in the discussion
of a huge plateful of turkey.[1]

The table was literally loaded with good cheer, and presented
an epitome of country abundance, in this season of overflowing
larders.   A distinguished post was allotted to "ancient sirloin,"[2]

---

[1] IRVING'S NOTE. — The old ceremony of serving up the boar's head on
Christmas Day is still observed in the hall of Queen's College, Oxford.   I
was favored by the parson with a copy of the carol as now sung; and as it
may be acceptable to such of my readers as are curious in these grave and
learned matters, I give it entire: —

> " The boar's head in hand bear I,
> Bedeck'd with bays and rosemary;
> And I pray you, my masters, be merry,
>   Quot estis in convivio.
>   Caput apri defero,
>   Reddens laudes Domino.

> " The boar's head, as I understand,
> Is the rarest dish in all this land,
> Which thus bedeck'd with a gay garland
>   Let us servire cantico.
>   Caput apri defero,
>   Reddens laudes Domino.

> " Our steward hath provided this
> In honour of the King of Bliss,
> Which on this day to be served is
>   In Reginensi Atrio.
>   Caput apri defero,
>   Reddens laudes Domino."

[2] James I., on his return from a hunting excursion. so much enjoyed
his dinner, consisting of a loin of roast beef, that he laid his sword across

as mine host termed it; being, as he added, "the standard of old English hospitality, and a joint of goodly presence, and full of expectation." There were several dishes quaintly decorated, and which had evidently something traditional in their embellishments, but about which, as I did not like to appear over-curious, I asked no questions.

I could not, however, but notice a pie, magnificently decorated with peacocks' feathers, in imitation of the tail of that bird, which overshadowed a considerable tract of the table. This, the Squire confessed with some little hesitation, was a pheasant pie, though a peacock pie was certainly the most authentical; but there had been such a mortality among the peacocks this season, that he could not prevail upon himself to have one killed.[1]

It would be tedious, perhaps, to my wiser readers, who may not have that foolish fondness for odd and obsolete things to which I am a little given, were I to mention the other makeshifts of this worthy old humorist, by which he was endeavoring to follow up, though at humble distance, the quaint customs of antiquity. I was pleased, however, to see the respect shown to his whims by his children and relatives; who, indeed, entered readily

it, and dubbed it "Sir Loin." Etymologically, however, the word is from the French *surlonge*, "a sirloin:" *sur* (Latin, *super*), "over;" and *longe*, "loin."

[1] IRVING'S NOTE. — The peacock was anciently in great demand for stately entertainments. Sometimes it was made into a pie, at one end of which the head appeared above the crust in all its plumage, with the beak richly gilt: at the other end the tail was displayed. Such pies were served up at the solemn banquets of chivalry, when knights-errant pledged themselves to undertake any perilous enterprise, whence came the ancient oath, used by Justice Shallow, "by cock and pie." The peacock was also an important dish for the Christmas feast; and Massinger, in his City Madam, gives some idea of the extravagance with which this, as well as other dishes, was prepared for the gorgeous revels of the olden times : —

"Men may talk of Country Christmasses,
  Their thirty pound butter'd eggs, their pies of carps' tongues:
  Their pheasants drench'd with ambergris; *the carcases of three fat wethers
  bruised for gravy to make sauce for a single peacock!*"

into the full spirit of them, and seemed all well versed in their parts, having doubtless been present at many a rehearsal. I was amused, too, at the air of profound gravity with which the butler and other servants executed the duties assigned them, however eccentric. They had an old-fashioned look, — having, for the most part, been brought up in the household, and grown into keeping with the antiquated mansion, and the humors of its lord, — and most probably looked upon all his whimsical regulations as the established laws of honorable housekeeping.

When the cloth was removed, the butler brought in a huge silver vessel of rare and curious workmanship, which he placed before the Squire. Its appearance was hailed with acclamation, being the wassail bowl, so renowned in Christmas festivity. The contents had been prepared by the Squire himself; for it was a beverage in the skillful mixture of which he particularly prided himself, alleging that it was too abstruse and complex for the comprehension of an ordinary servant. It was a potation, indeed, that might well make the heart of a toper leap within him, being composed of the richest and raciest wines, highly spiced and sweetened, with roasted apples bobbing about the surface.[1]

The old gentleman's whole countenance beamed with a serene look of indwelling delight as he stirred this mighty bowl. Having raised it to his lips with a hearty wish of a merry Christmas to all present, he sent it brimming round the board, for every one to follow his example, according to the primitive style, pronoun-

---

[1] IRVING'S NOTE. — The wassail bowl was sometimes composed of ale instead of wine, with nutmeg, sugar, toast, ginger, and roasted crabs. In this way the nut-brown beverage is still prepared in some old families, and round the hearth of substantial farmers at Christmas. It is also called "lamb's wool," and it is celebrated by Herrick in his Twelfth Night:—

> "Next crowne the bowle full
> With gentle Lamb's Wool,
> Add sugar, nutmeg, and ginger,
> With store of ale too;
> And thus ye must doe
> To make the Wassaile a swinger."

cing it " the ancient fountain of good feeling, where all hearts met together."[1]

There was much laughing and rallying as the honest emblem of Christmas joviality circulated, and was kissed rather coyly by the ladies; but when it reached Master Simon, he raised it in both hands, and, with the air of a boon companion, struck up an old wassail chanson: [2] —

> " The brown bowle,
>   The merry brown bowle,
>   As it goes round about-a,
>   Fill
>   Still,
>   Let the world say what it will,
>   And drink your fill all out-a,

> " The deep canne,
>   The merry deep canne,
>   As thou dost freely quaff-a,
>   Sing
>   Fling,
>   Be as merry as a king,
>   And sound a lusty laugh-a." [3]

Much of the conversation during dinner turned upon family topics, to which I was a stranger. There was, however, a great deal of rallying of Master Simon about some gay widow, with whom he was accused of having a flirtation. This attack was commenced by the ladies; but it was continued throughout the dinner by the fat-headed old gentleman next the parson, with the persevering assiduity of a slowhound,[4] being one of those long-winded jokers, who, though rather dull at starting game, are un-rivaled for their talents in hunting it down. At every pause in the general conversation, he renewed his bantering in pretty

---

[1] " The custom of drinking out of the same cup gave place to each having his cup. When the steward came to the doore with the Wassel, he was to cry three times, *Wassel, Wassel, Wassel*, and then the chappell (chaplain) was to answer with a song."—*Archæologia.*

[2] Song.   [3] From Poor Robin's Almanack.   [4] Bloodhound.

much the same terms, winking hard at me with both eyes whenever he gave Master Simon what he considered a home thrust.
The latter, indeed, seemed fond of being teased on the subject,
as old bachelors are apt to be; and he took occasion to inform
me, in an undertone, that the lady in question was a prodigiously
fine woman, and drove her own curricle.

The dinner-time passed away in this flow of innocent hilarity,
and, though the old hall may have resounded in its time with
many a scene of broader rout and revel, yet I doubt whether it
ever witnessed more honest and genuine enjoyment. How easy
it· is for one benevolent being to diffuse pleasure around him;
and how truly is a kind heart a fountain of gladness, making
everything in its vicinity to freshen into smiles! The joyous disposition of the worthy Squire was perfectly contagious. He was
happy himself, and disposed to make all the world happy; and
the little eccentricities of his humor did but season, in a manner,
the sweetness of his philanthropy.

After the dinner-table was removed, the hall was given up to
the younger members of the family, who, prompted to all kind
of noisy mirth by the Oxonian and Master Simon, made its old
walls ring with their merriment, as they played at romping games.
I delight in witnessing the gambols of children, and particularly
at this happy holiday season, and could not help stealing out of
the drawing-room on hearing one of their peals of laughter. I
found them at the game of blind-man's-buff. Master Simon,
who was the leader of their revels, and seemed on all occasions
to fulfill the office of that ancient potentate, the Lord of Misrule,[1]
was blinded in the midst of the hall. The little beings were as
busy about him as the mock fairies about Falstaff,[2] pinching

---

[1] " At Christmasse there was in the Kinges house, wheresoever hee was
lodged, a lorde of misrule, or mayster of merie disportes, and the like had ye
in the house of every nobleman of honor, or good worshippe, were he spirit-
uall or temporall."— *Stow.*

[2] Sir John Falstaff, one of Shakespeare's characters in The Merry Wives
of Windsor and in the two parts of Henry IV.

him, plucking at the skirts of his coat, and tickling him with straws. One fine blue-eyed girl of about thirteen, with her flaxen hair all in beautiful confusion, her frolic face in a glow, her frock half torn off her shoulders, a complete picture of a romp, was the chief tormentor; and from the slyness with which Master Simon avoided the smaller game, and hemmed this wild little nymph in corners, and obliged her to jump, shrieking, over chairs, I suspected the rogue of being not a whit more blinded than was convenient.

When I returned to the drawing-room, I found the company seated round the fire, listening to the parson, who was deeply ensconced in a high-backed, oaken chair, the work of some cunning artificer of yore, which had been brought from the library for his particular accommodation. From this venerable piece of furniture, with which his shadowy figure and dark, weazen face so admirably accorded, he was dealing forth strange accounts of the popular superstitions and legends of the surrounding country, with which he had become acquainted in the course of his antiquarian researches. I am half inclined to think that the old gentleman was himself somewhat tinctured with superstition, as men are very apt to be who live a recluse and studious life in a sequestered part of the country, and pore over black-letter tracts, so often filled with the marvelous and supernatural. He gave us several anecdotes of the fancies of the neighboring peasantry concerning the effigy of the crusader, which lay on the tomb by the church altar. As it was the only monument of the kind in that part of the country, it had always been regarded with feelings of superstition by the good wives of the village. It was said to get up from the tomb and walk the rounds of the churchyard in stormy nights, particularly when it thundered; and one old woman, whose cottage bordered on the churchyard, had seen it through the windows of the church, when the moon shone, slowly pacing up and down the aisles. It was the belief that some wrong had been left unredressed by the deceased, or some treasure hidden, which kept the spirit in a state of trouble and restlessness. Some talked of gold and jewels buried in the tomb, over which the specter kept watch; and there was a story current of a sexton in old times, who endeavored to break his way to the coffin at night, but, just as he reached it, received a violent blow from the marble hand of the effigy, which stretched him senseless on the pavement. These tales were often laughed at by some of the sturdier among the rustics, yet, when night came on, there were many of the stoutest unbelievers that were shy of venturing alone in the footpath that led across the churchyard.

From these and other anecdotes that followed, the crusader appeared to be the favorite hero of ghost stories throughout the vicinity. His picture, which hung up in the hall, was thought by the servants to have something supernatural about it; for they remarked, that, in whatever part of the hall you went, the eyes of the warrior were still fixed on you. The old porter's wife, too, at the lodge, who had been born and brought up in the family, and was a great gossip among the maid-servants, affirmed that in her young days she had often heard say, that on midsummer eve, when it was well known all kinds of ghosts, goblins, and fairies become visible and walk abroad, the crusader used to mount his horse, come down from his picture, ride about the house, down the avenue, and so to the church to visit the tomb, on which occasion the church door most civilly swung open of itself; not that he needed it, for he rode through closed gates and even stone walls, and had been seen by one of the dairy-maids to pass between two bars of the great park gate, making himself as thin as a sheet of paper.

All these superstitions I found had been very much countenanced by the Squire, who, though not superstitious himself, was very fond of seeing others so. He listened to every goblin tale of the neighboring gossips with infinite gravity, and held the porter's wife in high favor on account of her talent for the marvelous. He was himself a great reader of old legends and romances, and often lamented that he could not believe in them; for a superstitious person, he thought, must live in a kind of fairyland.

Whilst we were all attention to the parson's stories, our ears were suddenly assailed by a burst of heterogeneous sounds from the hall, in which were mingled something like the clang of rude minstrelsy, with the uproar of many small voices and girlish laughter. The door suddenly flew open, and a train came trooping into the room, that might almost have been mistaken for the breaking-up of the court of Fairy. That indefatigable spirit Master Simon, in the faithful discharge of his duties as Lord of Misrule, had conceived the idea of a Christmas mummery or masking; and having called in to his assistance the Oxonian and the young officer, who were equally ripe for anything that should occasion romping and merriment, they had carried it into instant effect. The old housekeeper had been consulted; the antique clothes-presses and wardrobes rummaged, and made to yield up the relics of finery that had not seen the light for several generations. The younger part of the company had been privately convened from parlor and hall, and the whole had been bedizened out into a burlesque imitation of an antique mask.[1]

Master Simon led the van as Ancient Christmas, quaintly appareled in a ruff, a short cloak which had very much the aspect of one of the old housekeeper's petticoats, and a hat that might have served for a village steeple, and must indubitably have figured in the days of the Covenanters.[2] From under this, his nose curved boldly forth, flushed with a frost-bitten bloom that seemed the very trophy of a December blast. He was accompanied by the blue-eyed romp, dished up as Dame Mince Pie, in the venerable magnificence of faded brocade, long stomacher, peaked

[1] IRVING'S NOTE. — Maskings, or mummeries, were favorite sports at Christmas in old times; and the wardrobes at halls and manor-houses were often laid under contribution to furnish dresses and fantastic disguisings. I strongly suspect Master Simon to have taken the idea of his from Ben Jonson's Masque of Christmas.

[2] In Scottish history, the name applied to a party embracing the great majority of the people, who, during the seventeenth century, bound themselves to establish and maintain the Presbyterian doctrine as the sole religion of the country.

hat, and high-heeled shoes.   The young officer appeared as
Robin Hood,[1] in a sporting dress of Kendal green [2] and a for-
aging cap with a gold tassel.

The costume, to be sure, did not bear testimony to deep research, and there was an evident eye to the picturesque, natural
to a young gallant in presence of his mistress.   The fair Julia
hung on his arm in a pretty rustic dress, as Maid Marian.[3]   The
rest of the train had been metamorphosed in various ways, — the
girls trussed up in the finery of the ancient belles of the Bracebridge line;   and the striplings bewhiskered with burnt cork, and
gravely clad in broad skirts, hanging sleeves, and full-bottomed
wigs, to represent the characters of Roast Beef, Plum Pudding,
and other worthies celebrated in ancient maskings.   The whole
was under the control of the Oxonian, in the appropriate character of Misrule;   and I observed that he exercised rather a mischievous sway with his wand over the smaller personages of the
pageant.

The irruption of this motley crew, with beat of drum, according
to ancient custom, was the consummation of uproar and merriment.   Master Simon covered himself with glory by the state-
liness with which, as Ancient Christmas, he walked a minuet[4]
with the peerless though giggling Dame Mince Pie.   It was followed by a dance from all the characters, which, from its medley
of costumes, seemed as though the old family portraits had skipped
down from their frames to join in the sport.   Different centuries

---

[1] The famous legendary outlaw (born at Locksley, in Notts, in the reign
of Henry II., 1160).   His real name was Fitzooth, and it is commonly said
he was the Earl of Huntingdon.

[2] Woolen cloth of coarse texture, called Kendal from the town of that
name in Westmoreland, England, where it was first made.

[3] A name assumed by Matilda, daughter of Robert Lord Fitzwalter, while
Robin Hood (her lover) remained in a state of outlawry.

[4] A slow, very graceful dance, performed in $\frac{3}{4}$ or $\frac{3}{8}$ time; originated, it is
said, in Poitou, France, about the middle of the seventeenth century.   Its
name is from the French *menuet* (Latin, *minutus*, " small "), the steps taken
in the dance being small.

were figuring at cross hands and right and left: the dark ages were cutting pirouettes[1] and rigadoons;[2] and the days of Queen Bess jigging merrily down the middle, through a line of succeeding generations.

The worthy Squire contemplated these fantastic sports, and this resurrection of his old wardrobe, with the simple relish of childish delight. He stood chuckling, and rubbing his hands, and scarcely hearing a word the parson said, notwithstanding that the latter was discoursing most authentically on the ancient and stately dance of the pavon, or peacock, from which he conceived the minuet to be derived.[3] For my part, I was in a continual excitement from the varied scenes of whim and innocent gayety passing before me. It was inspiring to see wild-eyed Frolic and warm-hearted Hospitality breaking out from among the chills and glooms of winter, and Old Age throwing off his apathy, and catching once more the freshness of youthful enjoyment. I felt also an interest in the scene, from the consideration that these fleeting customs were posting fast into oblivion, and that this was perhaps the only family in England in which the whole of them were still punctiliously observed. There was a quaintness, too, mingled with all this revelry, that gave it a peculiar zest: it was suited to the time and place; and, as the old manor-house almost reeled with mirth and wassail, it seemed echoing back the joviality of long-departed years.

But enough of Christmas and its gambols: it is time for me to pause in this garrulity. Methinks I hear the question asked by my graver readers, "To what purpose is all this? How is the

---

[1] Whirling on the tip of one foot.

[2] French, *rigodon*. A dance said to have come from Provence, France. It is gay and brisk in character.

[3] Sir John Hawkins, speaking of the dance called pavon, from *pavo* ("a peacock"), says, "It is a grave and majestic dance; the method of dancing it anciently was by gentlemen dressed with caps and swords, by those of the long robe in their gowns, by the peers in their mantles, and by the ladies in gowns with long trains, the motion whereof, in dancing, resembled that of a peacock." — *History of Music.*

world to be made wiser by this talk?" Alas! is there not wisdom enough extant for the instruction of the world? and if not, are there not thousands of abler pens laboring for its improvement? It is so much pleasanter to please than to instruct, — to play the companion rather than the preceptor.

What, after all, is the mite of wisdom that I could throw into the mass of knowledge, or how am I sure that my sagest deductions may be safe guides for the opinions of others? But in writing to amuse, if I fail, the only evil is in my own disappointment. If, however, I can by any lucky chance, in these days of evil, rub out one wrinkle from the brow of care, or beguile the heavy heart of one moment of sorrow; if I can now and then penetrate through the gathering film of misanthropy, prompt a benevolent view of human nature, and make my reader more in good humor with his fellow-beings and himself, — surely, surely, I shall not then have written entirely in vain.

WESTMINSTER ABBEY.[1]

ON one of those sober and rather melancholy days in the latter part of autumn, when the shadows of morning and evening almost mingle together, and throw a gloom over the decline of the year, I passed several hours in rambling about Westminster Abbey. There was something congenial to the season in the mournful magnificence of the old pile; and, as I passed its threshold, it seemed like stepping back into the regions of antiquity, and losing myself among the shades of former ages.

---

[1] The coronation church of the sovereigns of England from the time of Harold (1066). It occupies the site of a chapel built by Siebert in honor of St. Peter, on a slightly elevated spot rising from the marshy ground bordering the Thames. The Abbey was fifteen years in building, and was the first cruciform church in England. It contains the tombs and monuments of many of the sovereigns of Great Britain, and the memorials of England's greatest men in all walks of life.

I entered from the inner court of Westminster School,[1] through a long, low, vaulted passage, that had an almost subterranean look, being dimly lighted in one part by circular perforations in the massive walls. Through this dark avenue I had a distant view of the cloisters,[2] with the figure of an old verger[3] in his black gown, moving along their shadowy vaults, and seeming like a specter from one of the neighboring tombs. The approach to the Abbey through these gloomy monastic remains prepares the mind for its solemn contemplation. The cloister still retains something of the quiet and seclusion of former days. The gray walls are discolored by damps, and crumbling with age; a coat of hoary moss has gathered over the inscriptions of the mural monuments, and obscured the death's heads and other funeral emblems; the sharp touches of the chisel are gone from the rich tracery of the arches; the roses which adorned the keystones have lost their leafy beauty; everything bears marks of the gradual dilapidations of time, which yet has something touching and pleasing in its very decay.

The sun was pouring down a yellow autumnal ray into the square of the cloisters, beaming upon a scanty plot of grass in the center, and lighting up an angle of the vaulted passage with a kind of dusty splendor. From between the arcades the eye glanced up to a bit of blue sky or a passing cloud, and beheld the sun-gilt pinnacles of the Abbey towering into the azure heaven.

As I paced the cloisters, sometimes contemplating this mingled picture of glory and decay, and sometimes endeavoring to deci-

---

[1] This school was in existence in 1540, established by charter of Henry VIII. Under the reign of Mary the whole school was swept away. It was restored by Elizabeth in 1560, who gave to the college the statutes which are more or less observed to this day.

[2] Old French, *cloistre;* Latin, *claustrum.* That which shuts off; in monastic buildings, an arched passage, usually running about an interior court, and used as a place of recreation for monks.

[3] Old French, *vergier;* Latin, *virga* ("a rod"). A church officer who bore the verge or staff of office for ecclesiastical dignitaries.

6

pher the inscriptions on the tombstones, which formed the pavement beneath my feet, my eye was attracted to three figures,
rudely carved in relief, but nearly worn away by the footsteps of
many generations.   They were the effigies of three of the early
abbots.   The epitaphs were entirely effaced.   The names alone
remained, having, no doubt, been renewed in later times, — Vitalis[1] (Abbas, 1082), and Gislebertus Crispinus[2] (Abbas, 1114), and
Laurentius[3] (Abbas, 1176).   I remained some little while, musing over these casual relics of antiquity, thus left like wrecks
upon this distant shore of time, telling no tale but that such
beings had been and had perished; teaching no moral but the
futility of that pride which hopes still to exact homage in its
ashes, and to live in an inscription.   A little longer, and even
these faint records will be obliterated, and the monument will
cease to be a memorial.   Whilst I was yet looking down upon
these gravestones, I was roused by the sound of the Abbey clock,
reverberating from buttress to buttress, and echoing among the
cloisters.   It is almost startling to hear this warning of departed
time sounding among the tombs, and telling the lapse of the hour,
which, like a billow, has rolled us onward towards the grave.

I pursued my walk to an arched door opening to the interior of the Abbey.   On entering here, the magnitude of the

---

[1] Vitalis was a Norman.   He was an abbot at Bernay in Normandy, and
was expressly sent for by the King (William the Conqueror) to govern at
Westminster.   He had the character of a wise and prudent man.   He died
June 19, 1082, and was interred in the south cloister.

[2] Gislebertus Crispinus (Gilbert Crispin) was a Norman of noble rank.
He was particularly famous as a sound theologist and a ready disputant.
After a long life of piety and good deeds, he died Dec. 6, 1114, and was
buried at the feet of Vitalis, his predecessor.

[3] Laurentius (or Lawrence) was educated, and resided for many years, at
St. Albans.   He was chosen for Westminster Abbey about the year 1159,
through the influence of Henry II., who thought highly of him.   He was a
man of talents.   He was appointed by the King, the Pope, and the Arch-
bishop of Canterbury, to decide several disputed causes.   He was buried in
the south walk of the cloister.

building breaks fully upon the mind, contrasted with the vaults of the cloisters. The eye gazes with wonder at clustered columns of gigantic dimensions, with arches springing from them to such an amazing height; and man wandering about their bases, shrunk into insignificance in comparison with his own handiwork. The spaciousness and gloom of this vast edifice produce a profound and mysterious awe. We step cautiously and softly about, as if fearful of disturbing the hallowed silence of the tomb; while every footfall whispers along the walls, and chatters among the sepulchers, making us more sensible of the quiet we have interrupted.

It seems as if the awful nature of the place presses down upon the soul, and hushes the beholder into noiseless reverence. We feel that we are surrounded by the congregated bones of the great men of past times, who have filled history with their deeds, and the earth with their renown. And yet it almost provokes a smile at the vanity of human ambition, to see how they are crowded together and jostled in the dust; what parsimony is observed in doling out a scanty nook, a gloomy corner, a little portion of earth, to those whom, when alive, kingdoms could not satisfy; and how many shapes and forms and artifices are devised to catch the casual notice of the passenger, and save from forgetfulness for a few short years a name which once aspired to occupy ages of the world's thought and admiration.

I passed some time in Poet's Corner,[1] which occupies an end of one of the transepts or cross aisles of the Abbey. The monuments are generally simple, for the lives of literary men afford no striking themes for the sculptor. Shakespeare[2] and Addison[3] have statues erected to their memories; but the greater part have

---

[1] The poet Chaucer, who died Oct. 25, 1400, was the first to be buried in Poet's Corner, through the royal favor of Henry IV.; but no monument was placed over him until during the reign of Edward VI., in 1551.

[2] The remains of Shakespeare (1564–1616) were never moved from Stratford, but a monument was erected in the Abbey in 1740.

[3] Addison (1672–1719) is buried in the chapel of Henry VII., in the vault

busts, medallions, and sometimes mere inscriptions. Notwithstanding the simplicity of these memorials, I have always observed that the visitors to the Abbey remain longest about them. A kinder and fonder feeling takes place of that cold curiosity or vague admiration with which they gaze on the splendid monuments of the great and the heroic. They linger about these as about the tombs of friends and companions; for, indeed, there is something of companionship between the author and the reader. Other men are known to posterity only through the medium of history, which is continually growing faint and obscure; but the intercourse between the author and his fellowmen is ever new, active, and immediate. He has lived for them more than for himself; he has sacrificed surrounding enjoyments, and shut himself up from the delights of social life, that he might the more intimately commune with distant minds and distant ages. Well may the world cherish his renown; for it has been purchased, not by deeds of violence and blood, but by the diligent dispensation of pleasure. Well may posterity be grateful to his memory; for he has left it an inheritance, not of empty names and sounding actions, but whole treasures of wisdom, bright gems of thought, and golden veins of language.

From Poet's Corner I continued my stroll towards that part of the Abbey which contains the sepulchers of the kings. I wandered among what once were chapels, but which are now occupied by the tombs and monuments of the great. At every turn I met with some illustrious name, or the cognizance of some powerful house renowned in history. As the eye darts into these dusky chambers of death, it catches glimpses of quaint effigies, — some kneeling in niches, as if in devotion; others stretched upon the tombs, with hands piously pressed together; warriors in armor, as if reposing after battle; prelates with crosiers and miters; and nobles in robes and coronets, lying, as it were, in state. In

of the House of Albemarle. A monument of him stands in the Poet's Corner, and was erected in 1808.

glancing over this scene, so strangely populous, yet where every form is so still and silent, it seems almost as if we were treading a mansion of that fabled city, where every being had been suddenly transmuted into stone.

I paused to contemplate a tomb on which lay the effigy of a knight in complete armor. A large buckler was on one arm; the hands were pressed together in supplication upon the breast; the face was almost covered by the morion; the legs were crossed, in token of the warrior's having been engaged in the holy war. It was the tomb of a crusader, — of one of those military enthusiasts who so strangely mingled religion and romance, and whose exploits form the connecting link between fact and fiction, between the history and the fairy tale. There is something extremely picturesque in the tombs of these adventurers, decorated as they are with rude armorial bearings and Gothic sculpture. They comport with the antiquated chapels in which they are generally found; and in considering them, the imagination is apt to kindle with the legendary associations, the romantic fictions, the chivalrous pomp and pageantry, which poetry has spread over the wars for the sepulcher of Christ. They are the relics of times utterly gone by, of beings passed from recollection, of customs and manners with which ours have no affinity. They are like objects from some strange and distant land, of which we have no certain knowledge, and about which all our conceptions are vague and visionary. There is something extremely solemn and awful in those effigies on Gothic tombs, extended as if in the sleep of death, or in the supplication of the dying hour. They have an effect infinitely more impressive on my feelings than the fanciful attitudes, the overwrought conceits, and allegorical groups, which abound on modern monuments. I have been struck, also, with the superiority of many of the old sepulchral inscriptions. There was a noble way, in former times, of saying things simply, and yet saying them proudly; and I do not know an epitaph that breathes a loftier consciousness of family worth and honorable lineage than one which affirms, of a noble house, that "all the brothers were brave, and all the sisters virtuous."[1]

In the opposite transept to Poet's Corner stands a monument which is among the most renowned achievements of modern art, but which to me appears horrible rather than sublime. It is the tomb of Mrs. Nightingale,[2] by Roubiliac.[3] The bottom of the monument is represented as throwing open its marble doors, and a sheeted skeleton is starting forth. The shroud is falling from his fleshless frame as he launches his dart at his victim. She is sinking into her affrighted husband's arms, who strives, with vain and frantic effort, to avert the blow. The whole is executed with terrible truth and spirit: we almost fancy we hear the gibbering yell of triumph bursting from the distended jaws of the specter. But why should we thus seek to clothe death with unnecessary terrors, and to spread horrors round the tomb of those we love? The grave should be surrounded by everything that might inspire tenderness and veneration for the dead, or that might win the living to virtue. It is the place, not of disgust and dismay, but of sorrow and meditation.

While wandering about these gloomy vaults and silent aisles, studying the records of the dead, the sound of busy existence from without occasionally reaches the ear, — the rumbling of the passing equipage, the murmur of the multitude, or perhaps the

---

[1] A portion of the inscription upon the tomb of " the loyal " Duke of Newcastle and the Duchess. This nobleman was one of the firmest supporters of Charles I.

[2] In memory of Joseph Gascoigne Nightingale, Esq., of Minehead, Devonshire, who died in 1752; and the Lady Elizabeth, his wife, who died soon after marriage. A tradition of the Abbey records that a robber, coming into the Abbey by moonlight, was so startled by the figure as to have fled in dismay, and left his crowbar on the pavement.

[3] Roubiliac (1695-1762) was an able French sculptor, born at Lyons. He settled in London in 1720, and soon became the most popular sculptor of the time in England. His chief works in the Abbey are the monuments of Handel, Admiral Warren, Marshal Wade, Mrs. Nightingale, and the Duke of Argyll.

light laugh of pleasure. The contrast is striking with the death-like repose around; and it has a strange effect upon the feelings, thus to hear the surges of active life hurrying along, and beating against the very walls of the sepulcher.

I continued in this way to move from tomb to tomb, and from chapel to chapel. The day was gradually wearing away; the distant tread of loiterers about the Abbey grew less and less frequent; the sweet-tongued bell was summoning to evening prayer; and I saw at a distance the choristers, in their white surplices, crossing the aisle and entering the choir. I stood before the entrance to Henry VII.'s Chapel.[1] A flight of steps leads up to it, through a deep and gloomy but magnificent arch. Great gates of brass, richly and delicately wrought, turn heavily upon their hinges, as if proudly reluctant to admit the feet of common mortals into this most gorgeous of sepulchers.

On entering, the eye is astonished by the pomp of architecture, and the elaborate beauty of sculptured detail. The very walls are wrought into universal ornament, incrusted with tracery, and scooped into niches crowded with the statues of saints and martyrs. Stone seems, by the cunning labor of the chisel, to have been robbed of its weight and density, suspended aloft as if by magic, and the fretted roof achieved with the wonderful minuteness and airy security of a cobweb.

Along the sides of the chapel are the lofty stalls of the Knights of the Bath[2] richly carved of oak, though with the grotesque dec-

---

[1] Designed by Henry VII. as a burying place for himself and his successors; and he expressly enjoined in his will that none but those of royal blood should be buried there. The first to be buried there was his wife, Elizabeth of York, who died in 1503. Six years later he died, and was buried by the side of his queen, not in the raised tomb, but in the vault beneath. His effigy was completed within twenty years after his death, by Torrigiano, a Florentine sculptor.

[2] This Order of the Knights of the Bath originated, it is said, in 1399, at Henry IV.'s coronation. In the earlier coronations it had been the practice of the sovereigns to create a number of knights before they started on their procession from the Tower. These knights, being made in time of peace,

orations of Gothic architecture. On the pinnacles of the stalls
are affixed the helmets and crests of the knights, with their scarfs
and swords; and above them are suspended their banners, em-
blazoned with armorial bearings, and contrasting the splendor of
gold and purple and crimson with the cold, gray fretwork of the
roof. In the midst of this grand mausoleum stands the sepulcher
of its founder,[1] — his effigy, with that of his queen, extended on
a sumptuous tomb, and the whole surrounded by a superbly
wrought brazen railing.

There is a sad dreariness in this magnificence; this strange
mixture of tombs and trophies, these emblems of living and aspiring ambition, close beside mementos which show the dust and
oblivion in which all must sooner or later terminate. Nothing
impresses the mind with a deeper feeling of loneliness, than to
tread the silent and deserted scene of former throng and pageant.
On looking round on the vacant stalls of the knights and their
esquires, and on the rows of dusty but gorgeous banners that were
once borne before them, my imagination conjured up the scene
when this hall was bright with the valor and beauty of the land,
glittering with the splendor of jeweled rank and military array,
alive with the tread of many feet and the hum of an admiring
multitude. All had passed away: the silence of death had settled again upon the place, interrupted only by the casual chirping of birds, which had found their way into the chapel, and built
their nests among its friezes and pendants, — sure signs of soli-
tariness and desertion.

were not enrolled in any existing order, and for a long period had no special
designation; but inasmuch as one of the most striking and characteristic parts
of their admission was the complete ablution of their persons on the eve of
their knighthood, as an emblem of the cleanliness and purity of their profession, they were called "Knights of the Bath." The King himself bathed on
this occasion with them. The ceremony took place at Westminster; the
bath, in the Painted or Prince's Chamber; and the vigils, either before the
Confessor's shrine or in Henry VII.'s Chapel.

[1] Edward the Confessor (1004–66). He acceded to the throne in 1043.
He rebuilt the ancient Abbey of Westminster.

When I read the names inscribed on the banners, they were those of men scattered far and wide about the world, some tossing upon distant seas, some under arms in distant lands, some mingling in the busy intrigues of courts and cabinets, all seeking to deserve one more distinction in this mansion of shadowy honors, — the melancholy reward of a monument.

Two small aisles on each side of this chapel present a touching instance of the equality of the grave, which brings down the oppressor to a level with the oppressed, and mingles the dust of the bitterest enemies together. In one is the sepulcher of the haughty Elizabeth:[1] in the other is that of her victim, the lovely and unfortunate Mary.[2] Not an hour in the day but some ejaculation of pity is uttered over the fate of the latter, mingled with indignation at her oppressor. The walls of Elizabeth's sepulcher continually echo with the sighs of sympathy heaved at the grave of her rival.

A peculiar melancholy reigns over the aisle where Mary lies buried. The light struggles dimly through windows darkened by dust. The greater part of the place is in deep shadow, and the walls are stained and tinted by time and weather. A marble figure of Mary is stretched upon the tomb, round which is an iron railing, much corroded, bearing her national emblem, — the thistle.[3] I was weary with wandering, and sat down to rest myself

---

[1] Elizabeth (born in 1533) reigned as Queen of England from 1558 to 1603, when she died. She was the last of the Tudors, and was called " the lion-hearted Elizabeth." James I. had the body of Queen Elizabeth taken from the Cathedral Church of Peterborough, and a monument erected over her in Westminster Abbey.

[2] Mary Queen of Scots, daughter of James V. of Scotland, was born in 1542. She was charged by Queen Elizabeth with having entered into a conspiracy against the life of the latter, and ordered to be executed. Queen Elizabeth signed the death warrant on the 1st of February, 1587; and on the morning of the 8th of February, Mary Queen of Scots, protesting her innocence, was beheaded.

[3] The thistle, which gives name to the Scottish order, is also an heraldic bearing in that country.

by the monument, revolving in my mind the checkered and disastrous story of poor Mary.

The sound of casual footsteps had ceased from the Abbey. I could only hear now and then the distant voice of the priest repeating the evening service, and the faint responses of the choir. These paused for a time, and all was hushed. The stillness, the desertion and obscurity, that were gradually prevailing around, gave a deeper and more solemn interest to the place:

> For in the silent grave no conversation,
> No joyful tread of friends, no voice of lovers,
> No careful father's counsel, — nothing's heard,
> For nothing is, but all oblivion,
> Dust and an endless darkness.

Suddenly the notes of the deep-laboring organ burst upon the ear, falling with doubled and redoubled intensity, and rolling, as it were, huge billows of sound. How well do their volume and grandeur accord with this mighty building! With what pomp do they swell through its vast vaults, and breathe their awful harmony through these caves of death, and make the silent sepulcher vocal! And now they rise in triumph and acclamation, heaving higher and higher their accordant notes, and piling sound on sound. And now they pause, and the soft voices of the choir break out into sweet gushes of melody: they soar aloft and warble along the roof, and seem to play about these lofty vaults like the pure airs of heaven. Again the pealing organ heaves its thrilling thunders, compressing air into music, and rolling it forth upon the soul. What long-drawn cadences! What solemn sweeping concords! It grows more and more dense and powerful; it fills the vast pile, and seems to jar the very walls; the ear is stunned; the senses are overwhelmed. And now it is winding up in full jubilee. It is rising from the earth to heaven. The very soul seems rapt away and floated upwards on this swelling tide of harmony.

I sat for some time lost in that kind of reverie which a strain of music is apt sometimes to inspire. The shadows of evening were gradually thickening around me, the monuments began to cast deeper and deeper gloom, and the distant clock again gave token of the slowly waning day.

I rose, and prepared to leave the Abbey. As I descended the flight of steps which lead into the body of the building, my eye was caught by the shrine[1] of Edward the Confessor; and I ascended the small staircase that conducts to it, to take from thence a general survey of this wilderness of tombs. The shrine is elevated upon a kind of platform, and close around it are the sepulchers of various kings and queens. From this eminence the eye looks down between pillars and funeral trophies to the chapels and chambers below, crowded with tombs, where warriors, prelates, courtiers, and statesmen lie moldering in their "beds of darkness." Close by me stood the great chair of coronation,[2] rudely carved of oak, in the barbarous taste of a remote and Gothic age. The scene seemed almost as if contrived, with theatrical artifice, to produce an effect upon the beholder. Here was a type of the beginning and the end of human pomp and power: here it was literally but a step from the throne to the sepulcher. Would not one think that these incongruous mementos had been gathered together as a lesson to living greatness? — to show it, even in the moment of its proudest exaltation, the neglect and dishonor to which it must soon arrive; how soon that crown which encircles its brow must pass away, and it must lie down in the dust and disgraces of the tomb, and be trampled

---

[1] Erected by Henry III. on the canonizing of Edward, King of England, by Pope Alexander III., who caused his name to be placed in the catalogue of saints. The shrine was the work of the Italian artist Cavallini. This shrine was a constant object of pilgrimages from all parts of England all through the middle ages.

[2] This chair must have been specially constructed for the reception of the famous stone which Edward I. brought from Scotland in 1296. It has been constantly used at coronations ever since. The coronation takes place while the sovereign is seated in the chair. The last time it was brought out from the chapel where it stands was at the Jubilee Thanksgiving service (1888), when the Queen sat in it during the ceremonial.

upon by the feet of the meanest of the multitude: for, strange to tell, even the grave is here no longer a sanctuary. There is a shocking levity in some natures, which leads them to sport with awful and hallowed things; and there are base minds, which delight to revenge on the illustrious dead the abject homage and groveling servility which they pay to the living. The coffin of Edward the Confessor has been broken open, and his remains despoiled of their funeral ornaments; the scepter has been stolen from the hand of the imperious Elizabeth; and the effigy of Henry V. lies headless.[1] Not a royal monument but bears some proof how false and fugitive is the homage of mankind. Some are plundered, some mutilated, some covered with ribaldry and insult, all more or less outraged and dishonored.

The last beams of day were now faintly streaming through the painted windows in the high vaults above me. The lower parts of the Abbey were already wrapped in the obscurity of twilight. The chapels and aisles grew darker and darker. The effigies of the kings faded into shadows; the marble figures of the monuments assumed strange shapes in the uncertain light; the evening breeze crept through the aisles like the cold breath of the grave; and even the distant footfall of a verger, traversing the Poet's Corner, had something strange and dreary in its sound. I slowly retraced my morning's walk; and as I passed out at the portal of the cloisters, the door, closing with a jarring noise behind me, filled the whole building with echoes.

I endeavored to form some arrangement in my mind of the objects I had been contemplating, but found they were already falling into indistinctness and confusion. Names, inscriptions, trophies, had all become confounded in my recollection, though I had scarcely taken my foot from off the threshold. What, thought I, is this vast assemblage of sepulchers, but a treasury of

---

[1] The effigy is said to have originally been plated with silver, and the *head* to have been of solid silver. Nothing is now left but the wooden form upon which the gilded plates were fastened. Henry V. was King of England from 1413 to 1422.

humiliation, — a huge pile of reiterated homilies on the emptiness of renown and the certainty of oblivion?   It is, indeed, the empire of Death; his great, shadowy palace, where he sits in state, mocking at the relics of human glory, and spreading dust and forgetfulness on the monuments of princes.   How idle a boast, after all, is the immortality of a name!   Time is ever silently turning over his pages.   We are too much engrossed by the story of the present to think of the characters and anecdotes that gave interest to the past; and each age is a volume thrown aside to be speedily forgotten.   The idol of to-day pushes the hero of yesterday out of our recollection, and will, in turn, be supplanted by his successor of to-morrow.   " Our fathers," says Sir Thomas Brown,[1] " find their graves in our short memories, and sadly tell us how we may be buried in our survivors."   History fades into fable, fact becomes clouded with doubt and controversy, the inscription molders from the tablet, the statue falls from the pedestal.   Columns, arches, pyramids — what are they but heaps of sand, and their epitaphs but characters written in the dust?   What is the security of the tomb, or the perpetuity of an embalmment?   The remains of Alexander the Great[2] have been scattered to the wind, and his empty sarcophagus is now the mere curiosity of a museum.   " The Egyptian mummies, which Cambyses[3] or

---

[1] A distinguished English writer, born in London in 1605.   He graduated at Oxford in 1626; studied medicine and practiced in Oxfordshire, and received the degree of M.D. at the University of Leyden.   He published a work, Religio Medici, which was a success, and he became celebrated as a man of letters.   In 1671 he was made a knight by Charles II.

[2] Alexander III. (commonly called " the Great ") was born at Pella, 356 B.C.   He was a great warrior, and successful in all his exploits, conquering all the world then known.   He died after a reign of less than thirteen years, and before he had reached the age of thirty-three.

[3] The elder son and successor of Cyrus, who reigned over the Persian Empire for seven years and five months (529–521 B.C.).   He made a conquest of Egypt in 525 B.C.   He assumed the responsibilities and titles proper to a king of Egypt, taking as his throne name that of " Kambath-Remesot, Lord of Upper and Lower Egypt."

time hath spared, avarice now consumeth. Mizraim[1] cures wounds, and Pharaoh[2] is sold for balsams."[3]

What, then, is to insure this pile which now towers above me from sharing the fate of mightier mausoleums? The time must come when its gilded vaults, which now spring so loftily, shall lie in rubbish beneath the feet; when, instead of the sound of melody and praise, the wind shall whistle through the broken arches, and the owl hoot from the shattered tower; when the garish sunbeam shall break into these gloomy mansions of death, and the ivy twine round the fallen column, and the fox-glove hang its blossoms about the nameless urn as if in mockery of the dead. Thus man passes away; his name perishes from record and recollection; his history is as a tale that is told; and his very monument becomes a ruin.

THE LEGEND OF SLEEPY HOLLOW.

[*Found among the Papers of the Late Diedrich Knickerbocker.*]

> "*A pleasing land of drowsy head it was,*
> *Of dreams that wave before the half-shut eye,*
> *And of gay castles in the clouds that pass,*
> *Forever flushing round a summer sky.*"
> CASTLE OF INDOLENCE.[4]

IN the bosom of one of those spacious coves which indent the eastern shore of the Hudson, at that broad expansion of the river denominated by the ancient Dutch navigators the Tappan

---

[1] Mizraim, or Mizri, is the Hebrew name for Egypt.

[2] The title of Pharaoh was applied to the kings of Egypt, from Menes to Solomon.

[3] From Sir T. Brown. In the sixteenth and part of the seventeenth centuries, mummy formed one of the ordinary drugs, and was found in the shops of all the apothecaries. Tombs were searched, and as many mummies as could be obtained were broken into pieces for the purpose of sale. Physicians of all nations commonly prescribed it in cases of bruises and wounds.

[4] James Thomson (1700–48) was the son of a Scotch minister, and author

Zee,[1] and where they always prudently shortened sail, and implored the protection of St. Nicholas[2] when they crossed, there lies a small market town or rural port, which by some is called Greensburgh, but which is more generally and properly known by the name of "Tarrytown."[3] This name was given it, we are told, in former days, by the good housewives of the adjacent country, from the inveterate propensity of their husbands to linger about the village tavern on market days. Be that as it may, I do not vouch for the fact, but merely advert to it for the sake of being precise and authentic. Not far from this village, perhaps about three miles, there is a little valley, or rather lap of land, among high hills, which is one of the quietest places in the whole world. A small brook glides through it, with just murmur enough to lull one to repose; and the occasional whistle of a quail, or tapping of a woodpecker, is almost the only sound that ever breaks in upon the uniform tranquillity.

I recollect, that, when a stripling, my first exploit in squirrel-shooting was in a grove of tall walnut-trees that shades one side of the valley. I had wandered into it at noontime, when all nature is peculiarly quiet, and was startled by the roar of my own gun, as it broke the sabbath stillness around, and was prolonged and reverberated by the angry echoes. If ever I should wish for a retreat, whither I might steal from the world and its distrac-

of The Seasons, which gave him a great reputation. The Castle of Indolence, from which the above verse is quoted, was his last work, and was published the year he died. Till the advent of Scott and Byron, Thomson was the most widely popular poet in our language.

[1] The expansion of the Hudson River between Haverstraw and Piermont, having a length of about twelve miles, and a breadth in the neighborhood of from four to five miles.

[2] Bishop of Myra in the fourth century. He was also the mariner's saint, and is the present patron of those who lead a seafaring life (as Neptune was of old).

[3] Tarrytown is twenty-seven miles from New York. It is famous both historically and from its connection with Washington Irving, whose cottage, "Sunnyside," is in the vicinity.

tions, and dream quietly away the remnant of a troubled life, I
know of none more promising than this little valley.

From the listless repose of the place, and the peculiar character of its inhabitants, who are descendants from the original
Dutch settlers, this sequestered glen has long been known by
the name of "Sleepy Hollow," and its rustic lads are called the
"Sleepy Hollow Boys" throughout all the neighboring country.
A drowsy, dreamy influence seems to hang over the land, and
to pervade the very atmosphere. Some say that the place was
bewitched by a high German doctor during the early days of the
settlement; others, that an old Indian chief, the prophet or wiz-
ard of his tribe, held his powwows there before the country was
discovered by Master Hendrick Hudson.[1] Certain it is, the
place still continues under the sway of some witching power, that
holds a spell over the minds of the good people, causing them to
walk in a continual reverie. They are given to all kinds of marvelous beliefs; are subject to trances and visions; and frequently
see strange sights, and hear music and voices in the air. The
whole neighborhood abounds with local tales, haunted spots,
and twilight superstitions; stars shoot and meteors glare oftener
across the valley than in any other part of the country; and the
nightmare, with her whole ninefold,[2] seems to make it the favorite scene of her gambols.

The dominant spirit, however, that haunts this enchanted region, and seems to be commander-in-chief of all the powers of
the air, is the apparition of a figure on horseback without a head.
It is said by some to be the ghost of a Hessian[3] trooper, whose

---

[1] A distinguished English navigator, who made four voyages, attempting
to find a shorter passage to China than by the way of the Cape of Good Hope.
On the third of these voyages he entered the bay now called New York Bay,
and (Sept. 11, 1609) sailed up what is now the Hudson River. During his
fourth voyage, two years later, he penetrated the straits and discovered the
great bay of Canada which now bears his name. Here his mutinous sailors
cast him adrift in a small boat, and left him to die.

[2] See King Lear, act iii. sc. 4.

[3] These Hessians came from a province of western Germany called Hesse-

head had been carried away by a cannon-ball in some nameless battle during the Revolutionary war, and who is ever and anon seen by the country folk hurrying along in the gloom of night, as if on the wings of the wind. His haunts are not confined to the valley, but extend at times to the adjacent roads, and especially to the vicinity of a church that is at no great distance. Indeed, certain of the most authentic historians of those parts, who have been careful in collecting and collating the floating facts concerning this specter, allege that, the body of the trooper having been buried in the churchyard, the ghost rides forth to the scene of battle in nightly quest of his head; and that the rushing speed with which he sometimes passes along the hollow, like a midnight blast, is owing to his being belated, and in a hurry to get back to the churchyard before daybreak.

Such is the general purport of this legendary superstition, which has furnished materials for many a wild story in that region of shadows; and the specter is known at all the country firesides by the name of "The Headless Horseman of Sleepy Hollow."

It is remarkable that the visionary propensity I have mentioned is not confined to the native inhabitants of the valley, but is unconsciously imbibed by every one who resides there for a time. However wide-awake they may have been before they entered that sleepy region, they are sure, in a little time, to inhale the witching influence of the air, and begin to grow imaginative, — to dream dreams, and see apparitions.

I mention this peaceful spot with all possible laud: for it is in such little retired Dutch valleys, found here and there embosomed in the great State of New York, that population, manners, and customs remain fixed; while the great torrent of migration and improvement, which is making such incessant changes in other parts of this restless country, sweeps by them

Cassel. They were brought to America by the British in 1776, having been hired by them to fight against the American troops.

7

unobserved. They are like those little nooks of still water which border a rapid stream, where we may see the straw and bubble riding quietly at anchor, or slowly revolving in their mimic harbor, undisturbed by the rush of the passing current. Though many years have elapsed since I trod the drowsy shades of Sleepy Hollow, yet I question whether I should not still find the same trees and the same families vegetating in its sheltered bosom.

In this by-place of Nature there abode, in a remote period of American history,—that is to say, some thirty years since,—a worthy wight of the name of Ichabod Crane, who sojourned, or, as he expressed it, "tarried," in Sleepy Hollow, for the purpose of instructing the children of the vicinity. He was a native of Connecticut,—a State which supplies the Union with pioneers for the mind as well as for the forest, and sends forth yearly its legions of frontier woodmen and country schoolmasters. The cognomen of Crane was not inapplicable to his person. He was tall, but exceedingly lank, with narrow shoulders, long arms and legs, hands that dangled a mile out of his sleeves, feet that might have served for shovels, and his whole frame most loosely hung together. His head was small, and flat at top, with huge ears, large green glassy eyes, and a long snipe nose, so that it looked like a weathercock perched upon his spindle neck to tell which way the wind blew. To see him striding along the profile of a hill on a windy day, with his clothes bagging and fluttering about him, one might have mistaken him for the genius of famine descending upon the earth, or some scarecrow eloped from a cornfield.

His schoolhouse was a low building of one large room, rudely constructed of logs; the windows partly glazed, and partly patched with leaves of old copy-books. It was most ingeniously secured at vacant hours by a withe twisted in the handle of the door, and stakes set against the window-shutters; so that, though a thief might get in with perfect ease, he would find some embarrassment in getting out,—an idea most probably borrowed by the architect, Yost Van Houten, from the mystery of an eel-pot.[1] The schoolhouse stood in a rather lonely but pleasant situation, just at the foot of a woody hill, with a brook running close by, and a formidable birch-tree growing at one end of it. From hence the low murmur of his pupils' voices, conning over their lessons, might be heard of a drowsy summer's day, like the hum of a beehive; interrupted now and then by the authoritative voice of the master in the tone of menace or command, or, per-adventure, by the appalling sound of the birch as he urged some tardy loiterer along the flowery path of knowledge. Truth to say, he was a conscientious man, that ever bore in mind the golden maxim, "Spare the rod and spoil the child."[2] Ichabod Crane's scholars certainly were not spoiled.

I would not have it imagined, however, that he was one of those cruel potentates of the school who joy in the smart of their subjects: on the contrary, he administered justice with discrimi-nation rather than severity; taking the burthen off the backs of the weak, and laying it on those of the strong. Your mere puny stripling, that winced at the least flourish of the rod, was passed by with indulgence; but the claims of justice were satisfied by inflicting a double portion on some little, tough, wrong-headed, broad-skirted Dutch urchin, who sulked and swelled and grew dogged and sullen beneath the birch. All this he called " doing his duty by their parents;" and he never inflicted a chastisement without following it by the assurance, so consolatory to the smart-ing urchin, that "he would remember it and thank him for it the longest day he had to live."

When school hours were over, he was even the companion and playmate of the larger boys, and on holiday afternoons would convoy some of the smaller ones home, who happened to have pretty sisters, or good housewives for mothers, noted for the

[1] A box or basket for catching eels. The only opening is at the bottom of a funnel-shaped entrance, and is so small and so located, that, having entered it, the eels cannot easily find it again in order to get out.

[2] King Solomon's.

comforts of the cupboard. Indeed, it behooved him to keep on good terms with his pupils. The revenue arising from his school was small, and would have been scarcely sufficient to furnish him with daily bread, for he was a huge feeder, and, though lank, had the dilating powers of an anaconda;[1] but to help out his maintenance, he was, according to country custom in those parts, boarded and lodged at the houses of the farmers whose children he instructed. With these he lived successively a week at a time; thus going the rounds of the neighborhood, with all his worldly effects tied up in a cotton handkerchief.

That all this might not be too onerous on the purses of his rustic patrons, who are apt to consider the costs of schooling a grievous burthen, and schoolmasters as mere drones, he had various ways of rendering himself both useful and agreeable. He assisted the farmers occasionally in the lighter labors of their farms, helped to make hay, mended the fences, took the horses to water, drove the cows from pasture, and cut wood for the winter fire. He laid aside, too, all the dominant dignity and absolute sway with which he lorded it in his little empire the school, and became wonderfully gentle and ingratiating. He found favor in the eyes of the mothers by petting the children, particularly the youngest; and like "the lion bold," which whilom so magnanimously "the lamb did hold,"[2] he would sit with a child on one knee, and rock a cradle with his foot for whole hours together.

In addition to his other vocations, he was the singing-master of the neighborhood, and picked up many bright shillings by instructing the young folks in psalmody. It was a matter of no little vanity to him on Sundays, to take his station in front of the

---

[1] A reptile possessing extraordinary powers of dilation. It kills by constriction.

[2] The New England Primer, published in Walpole, N.H., in 1814, contains an illustrated alphabet. The letter *L* is illustrated by a lion with one of its paws resting upon a lamb which is lying down, and the following lines : —

> "The Lion bold
> The Lamb doth hold."

church gallery with a band of chosen singers, where, in his own mind, he completely carried away the palm from the parson.[1] Certain it is, his voice resounded far above all the rest of the congregation ; and there are peculiar quavers still to be heard in that church, and which may even be heard half a mile off, quite to the opposite side of the mill-pond, on a still Sunday morning, which are said to be legitimately descended from the nose of Ichabod Crane. Thus, by divers little makeshifts in that ingenious way which is commonly denominated "by hook and by crook,"[2] the worthy pedagogue got on tolerably enough, and was thought, by all who understood nothing of the labor of headwork, to have a wonderfully easy life of it.

The schoolmaster is generally a man of some importance in the female circle of a rural neighborhood, being considered a kind of idle, gentlemanlike personage, of vastly superior taste and accomplishments to the rough country swains, and, indeed, inferior in learning only to the parson. His appearance, therefore, is apt to occasion some little stir at the tea-table of a farmhouse, and the addition of a supernumerary dish of cakes or sweet-meats, or, peradventure, the parade of a silver teapot. Our man of letters, therefore, was peculiarly happy in the smiles of all the country damsels. How he would figure among them in the churchyard, between services on Sundays! gathering grapes for them from the wild vines that overrun the surrounding trees ; reciting for their amusement all the epitaphs on the tombstones ; or sauntering with a whole bevy of them along the banks of the adjacent mill-pond ; while the more bashful country bumpkins hung sheepishly back, envying his superior elegance and address.

From his half itinerant life, also, he was a kind of traveling

---

[1] Surpassed the parson in point of excellence.

[2] Formerly the poor of a manor were allowed to go into the forests with a hook and crook to get wood. What they could not reach, they might pull down with their crook. This sort of living was very precarious, but eagerly sought. Boundary stones, beyond which " the hook and crook folk " might not pass, exist still.

gazette, carrying the whole budget of local gossip from house to house; so that his appearance was always greeted with satisfaction. He was, moreover, esteemed by the women as a man of great erudition, for he had read several books quite through, and was a perfect master of Cotton Mather's[1] "History of New England Witchcraft;" in which, by the way, he most firmly and potently believed.

He was, in fact, an odd mixture of small shrewdness and simple credulity. His appetite for the marvelous, and his powers of digesting it, were equally extraordinary; and both had been increased by his residence in this spell-bound region. No tale was too gross or monstrous for his capacious swallow. It was often his delight, after his school was dismissed in the afternoon, to stretch himself on the rich bed of clover bordering the little brook that whimpered by his schoolhouse, and there con over old Mather's direful tales, until the gathering dusk of evening made the printed page a mere mist before his eyes. Then, as he wended his way, by swamp and stream and awful woodland, to the farmhouse where he happened to be quartered, every sound of Nature, at that witching hour, fluttered his excited imagination, — the moan of the whip-poor-will[2] from the hillside; the boding cry of the tree-toad, that harbinger of storm; the dreary hooting of the screech-owl; or the sudden rustling in the thicket of birds frightened from their roost. The fire-flies, too, which sparkled most vividly in the darkest places, now and then startled him, as one of uncommon brightness would stream across his path; and if by chance a huge blockhead of a beetle came winging his

---

[1] A celebrated theologian and writer, born in Boston in 1663. He was ordained as a minister in 1684, and preached in Boston. From the first he was eager to bring to trial and punishment those supposed to be guilty of witchcraft; and, when others began clearly to see the folly and injustice of these cruel persecutions, he earnestly, though vainly, strove to stem the reaction in the popular mind.

[2] A whip-poor-will is a bird which is only heard at night. It receives its name from its note, which is thought to resemble those words.

blundering flight against him, the poor varlet was ready to give up the ghost, with the idea that he was struck with a witch's token. His only resource on such occasions, either to drown thought or drive away evil spirits, was to sing psalm tunes; and the good people of Sleepy Hollow, as they sat by their doors of an evening, were often filled with awe at hearing his nasal melody, "in linked sweetness long drawn out,"[1] floating from the distant hill or along the dusky road.

Another of his sources of fearful pleasure was to pass long winter evenings with the old Dutch wives, as they sat spinning by the fire, with a row of apples roasting and sputtering along the hearth, and listen to their marvelous tales of ghosts and goblins, and haunted fields, and haunted brooks, and haunted bridges, and haunted houses, and particularly of the headless horseman, or "Galloping Hessian of the Hollow," as they sometimes called him. He would delight them equally by his anecdotes of witchcraft, and of the direful omens and portentous sights and sounds in the air, which prevailed in the earlier times of Connecticut,[2] and would frighten them wofully with speculations upon comets and shooting stars, and with the alarming fact that the world did absolutely turn round, and that they were half the time topsy-turvy.

But if there was a pleasure in all this, while snugly cuddling in the chimney corner of a chamber that was all of a ruddy glow from the crackling wood fire, and where, of course, no specter dared to show its face, it was dearly purchased by the terrors of his subsequent walk homewards. What fearful shapes and shadows beset his path amidst the dim and ghastly glare of a snowy night! With what wistful look did he eye every trembling ray of light streaming across the waste fields from some dis-

---

[1] From Milton's L'Allegro.

[2] In New England, in 1692, many people believed in witches. Such firm believers were they in witchcraft, that it was very easy to create a suspicion against a person as a witch. Many were thrown into prison, and some were hung, in consequence.

tant window!   How often was he appalled by some shrub covered with snow, which, like a sheeted specter, beset his very
path!   How often did he shrink with curdling awe at the sound
of his own steps on the frosty crust beneath his feet, and dread
to look over his shoulder, lest he should behold some uncouth
being tramping close behind him! and how often was he thrown
into complete dismay by some rushing blast, howling among the
trees, in the idea that it was the Galloping Hessian on one of his
nightly scourings!

All these, however, were mere terrors of the night, phantoms
of the mind that walk in darkness; and though he had seen
many specters in his time, and been more than once beset by
Satan in divers shapes in his lonely perambulations, yet daylight
put an end to all these evils; and he would have passed a pleasant life of it, in despite of the Devil and all his works, if his path
had not been crossed by a being that causes more perplexity to
mortal man than ghosts, goblins, and the whole race of witches
put together, and that was — a woman.

Among the musical disciples who assembled one evening in
each week to receive his instructions in psalmody, was Katrina
Van Tassel, the daughter and only child of a substantial Dutch
farmer.   She was a blooming lass of fresh eighteen; plump as a
partridge; ripe and melting and rosy-cheeked as one of her
father's peaches; and universally famed, not merely for her
beauty, but her vast expectations. She was, withal, a little of a
coquette, as might be perceived even in her dress, which was a
mixture of ancient and modern fashions, as most suited to set off
her charms.   She wore the ornaments of pure yellow gold which
her great-great-grandmother had brought over from Saardam;[1]
the tempting stomacher of the olden time; and, withal, a pro-
vokingly short petticoat, to display the prettiest foot and ankle
in the country round.

---

[1] Zaandam, Zaanredam, or Saardam, is a village of Holland in the province of North Holland, five miles by rail from Amsterdam.   Peter the Great
of Russia wrought at Saardam as a ship carpenter in 1697.

Ichabod Crane had a soft and foolish heart towards the sex; and it is not to be wondered at that so tempting a morsel soon found favor in his eyes, more especially after he had visited her in her paternal mansion. ' Old Baltus Van Tassel was a perfect picture of a thriving, contented, liberal-hearted farmer. He seldom, it is true, sent either his eyes or his thoughts beyond the boundaries of his own farm; but within these everything was snug, happy, and well-conditioned. He was satisfied with his wealth, but not proud of it, and piqued himself upon the hearty abundance rather than the style in which he lived. His stronghold was situated on the banks of the Hudson, in one of those green, sheltered, fertile nooks in which the Dutch farmers are so fond of nestling. A great elm-tree spread its broad branches over it, at the foot of which bubbled up a spring of the softest and sweetest water in a little well formed of a barrel, and then stole sparkling away through the grass to a neighboring brook that babbled along among alders and dwarf willows. Hard by the farmhouse was a vast barn that might have served for a church, every window and crevice of which seemed bursting forth with the treasures of the farm. The flail was busily resounding within it from morning to night; swallows and martins skimmed twittering about the eaves; and rows of pigeons — some with one eye turned up, as if watching the weather; some with their heads under their wings or buried in their bosoms; and others swelling, and cooing, and bowing about their dames — were enjoying the sunshine on the roof. Sleek, unwieldy porkers were grunting in the repose and abundance of their pens; from whence sallied forth, now and then, troops of sucking pigs, as if to snuff the air. A stately squadron of snowy geese were riding in an adjoining pond, convoying whole fleets of ducks. Regiments of turkeys were gobbling through the farmyard, and guinea-fowls fretting about it like ill-tempered housewives, with their peevish, discontented cry. Before the barn door strutted the gallant cock, that pattern of a husband, a warrior, and a fine gentleman, clapping his burnished wings and crowing in the pride and gladness of his heart, sometimes tearing up the earth with his feet, and then generously calling his ever-hungry family of wives and children to enjoy the rich morsel which he had discovered.

The pedagogue's mouth watered as he looked upon this sumptuous promise of luxurious winter fare.   In his devouring mind's eye he pictured to himself every roasting pig running about " with a pudding in its belly "[1] and an apple in its mouth; the pigeons were snugly put to bed in a comfortable pie, and tucked in with a coverlet of crust; the geese were swimming in their own gravy; and the ducks pairing cosily in dishes, like snug married couples, with a decent competency of onion sauce.   In the porkers he saw carved out the future sleek side of bacon, and juicy, relishing ham; not a turkey but he beheld daintily trussed up, with its gizzard under its wing, and, peradventure, a necklace of savory sausages; and even bright chanticleer[2] himself lay sprawling on his back, in a side-dish, with uplifted claws, as if craving that quarter which his chivalrous spirit disdained to ask while living.

As the enraptured Ichabod fancied all this, and as he rolled his great green eyes over the fat meadow-lands, the rich fields of wheat, of rye, of buckwheat and Indian corn, and the orchards burthened with ruddy fruit, which surrounded the warm tenement of Van Tassel, his heart yearned after the damsel who was to inherit these domains; and his imagination expanded with the idea, how they might be readily turned into cash, and the money invested in immense tracts of wild land, and shingle palaces in the wilderness.   Nay, his busy fancy already realized his hopes, and presented to him the blooming Katrina, with a whole family of children, mounted on the top of a wagon loaded with household

---

[1] From Shakespeare, Henry IV., Part I. act ii. sc. 4.

[2] A cock.   Old French, *chantecler* (from *chanter*, " to sing;" and *cler*, " clear"), the name of the cock in the poem Reynard the Fox.   The Middle English forms of the word were *chauntecleer, chaunteclere, chanteclere.* Compare Chaucer, Nun's Priest's Tale, l. 501: " This chauntecleer his wynges gan to bete."

trumpery, with pots and kettles dangling beneath; and he beheld himself bestriding a pacing mare, with a colt at her heels, setting out for Kentucky, Tennessee, or the Lord knows where.

When he entered the house, the conquest of his heart was complete. It was one of those spacious farmhouses, with high-ridged but lowly-sloping roofs, built in the style handed down from the first Dutch settlers; the low, projecting eaves forming a piazza along the front, capable of being closed up in bad weather. Under this were hung flails, harness, various utensils of husbandry, and nets for fishing in the neighboring river. Benches were built along the sides for summer use; and a great spinning-wheel at one end, and a churn at the other, showed the various uses to which this important porch might be devoted. From this piazza the wonderful Ichabod entered the hall, which formed the center of the mansion, and the place of usual residence. Here rows of resplendent pewter, ranged on a long dresser, dazzled his eyes. In one corner stood a huge bag of wool ready to be spun; in another, a quantity of linsey-woolsey[1] just from the loom. Ears of Indian corn, and strings of dried apples and peaches, hung in gay festoons along the walls, mingled with the gaud of red peppers: and a door left ajar gave him a peep into the best parlor, where the claw-footed chairs and dark mahogany tables shone like mirrors; and irons, with their accompanying shovel and tongs, glistened from their covert of asparagus tops; mock-oranges and conch-shells decorated the mantelpiece; strings of various colored bird's eggs were suspended above it; a great ostrich egg was hung from the center of the room; and a corner cupboard, knowingly left open, displayed immense treasures of old silver and well-mended china.

From the moment Ichabod laid his eyes upon these regions of delight, the peace of his mind was at an end, and his only study was how to gain the affections of the peerless daughter of Van Tassel. In this enterprise, however, he had more real difficulties

1 Coarse cloth, having a linen warp and a woolen woof.

than generally fell to the lot of a knight-errant[1] of yore, who seldom had anything but giants, enchanters, fiery dragons, and suchlike easily conquered adversaries to contend with; and had to make his way merely through gates of iron and brass, and walls of adamant, to the castle keep, where the lady of his heart was confined, — all which he achieved as easily as a man would carve his way to the center of a Christmas pie, and then the lady gave him her hand as a matter of course. Ichabod, on the contrary, had to win his way to the heart of a country coquette, beset with a labyrinth of whims and caprices, which were forever presenting new difficulties and impediments; and he had to encounter a host of fearful adversaries of real flesh and blood, the numerous rustic admirers, who beset every portal to her heart, keeping a watchful and angry eye upon each other, but ready to fly out in the common cause against any new competitor.

Among these the most formidable was a burly, roaring, roystering blade, of the name of Abraham, or, according to the Dutch abbreviation, Brom Van Brunt, the hero of the country round, which rang with his feats of strength and hardihood. He was broad-shouldered and double-jointed, with short, curly black hair, and a bluff but not unpleasant countenance, having a mingled air of fun and arrogance. From his Herculean frame and great powers of limb, he had received the nickname of " Brom Bones," by which he was universally known. He was famed for great knowledge and skill in horsemanship, being as dexterous on horseback as a Tartar.[2] He was foremost at all races and cock-fights, and, with the ascendency which bodily strength always acquires in rustic life, was the umpire in all disputes, setting his hat on one side, and giving his decisions with an air and tone that admitted of no gainsay or appeal. He was always ready for either a fight or a frolic; had more mischief than ill will in his composition; and, with all his overbearing roughness, there was a strong dash

---

[1] A knight who wandered in search of adventure.

[2] The Tartars were a nomadic tribe of Central Asia, noted for their fine horsemanship.

of waggish good-humor at bottom. He had three or four boon companions of his own stamp, who regarded him as their model, and at the head of whom he scoured the country, attending every scene of feud or merriment for miles around. In cold weather he was distinguished by a fur cap, surmounted with a flaunting fox's tail; and when the folks at a country gathering descried this well-known crest at a distance, whisking about among a squad of hard riders, they always stood by for a squall. Sometimes his crew would be heard dashing along past the farmhouses at midnight, with whoop and halloo, like a troop of Don Cossacks;[1] and the old dames, startled out of their sleep, would listen for a moment till the hurry-scurry had clattered by, and then exclaim, "Ay, there goes Brom Bones and his gang!" The neighbors looked upon him with a mixture of awe, admiration, and good will, and, when any madcap prank or rustic brawl occurred in the vicinity, always shook their heads, and warranted Brom Bones was at the bottom of it.

This rantipole[2] hero had for some time singled out the blooming Katrina for the object of his uncouth gallantries, and though his amorous toyings were something like the gentle caresses and endearments of a bear, yet it was whispered that she did not altogether discourage his hopes. Certain it is, his advances were signals for rival candidates to retire, who felt no inclination to cross a lion in his amours; insomuch, that when his horse was seen tied to Van Tassel's paling on a Sunday night, — a sure sign that his master was courting, or, as it is termed, "sparking," within, — all other suitors passed by in despair, and carried the war into other quarters.

Such was the formidable rival with whom Ichabod Crane had to contend; and, considering all things, a stouter man than he would have shrunk from the competition, and a wiser man would

---

1 The Russian tribes who settled on the River Don. They are a restless and warlike race. They form a first-rate irregular cavalry, and render excellent service as scouts and skirmishers.

2 Wild.

have despaired. He had, however, a happy mixture of pliability and perseverance in his nature. He was in form and spirit like a supple-jack,—yielding, but tough; though he bent, he never broke; and though he bowed beneath the slightest pressure, yet, the moment it was away—jerk! he was as erect, and carried his head as high, as ever.

To have taken the field openly against his rival would have been madness; for he was not a man to be thwarted in his amours, any more than that stormy lover Achilles.[1] Ichabod, therefore, made his advances in a quiet and gently insinuating manner. Under cover of his character of singing-master, he made frequent visits at the farmhouse; not that he had anything to apprehend from the meddlesome interference of parents, which is so often a stumbling-block in the path of lovers. Balt Van Tassel was an easy, indulgent soul. He loved his daughter better even than his pipe, and, like a reasonable man and an excellent father, let her have her way in everything. His notable little wife, too, had enough to do to attend to her housekeeping and manage the poultry; for, as she sagely observed, ducks and geese are foolish things, and must be looked after, but girls can take care of themselves. Thus, while the busy dame bustled about the house, or plied her spinning-wheel at one end of the piazza, honest Balt would sit smoking his evening pipe at the other, watching the achievements of a little wooden warrior, who, armed with a sword in each hand, was most valiantly fighting the wind on the pinnacle of the barn. In the mean time Ichabod would carry on his suit with the daughter by the side of the spring under the great elm, or sauntering along in the twilight, that hour so favorable to the lover's eloquence.

---

[1] A famous Greek warrior of Homer's Iliad. Achilles, in a dispute about his lady-love Briseis, becomes angered against Agamemnon, commander-in-chief of the allied Greeks besieging Troy or Ilion (hence the name " Iliad "), and refuses to fight. The Trojans prevail for a time. Patroclus, Achilles' friend, falls; and Achilles in wrath flies to battle, kills Hector (chief of the Trojans), and turns the tide of battle against them.

I profess not to know how women's hearts are wooed and won. To me they have always been matters of riddle and admiration. Some seem to have but one vulnerable point, or door of access; while others have a thousand avenues, and may be captured in a thousand different ways. It is a great triumph of skill to gain the former, but a still greater proof of generalship to maintain possession of the latter, for a man must battle for his fortress at every door and window. He who wins a thousand common hearts is therefore entitled to some renown; but he who keeps undisputed sway over the heart of a coquette is indeed a hero. Certain it is, this was not the case with the redoubtable Brom Bones; and, from the moment Ichabod Crane made his advances, the interests of the former evidently declined. His horse was no longer seen tied at the palings on Sunday nights, and a deadly feud gradually arose between him and the preceptor of Sleepy Hollow.

Brom, who had a degree of rough chivalry in his nature, would fain have carried matters to open warfare, and settled their pretensions to the lady according to the mode of those most concise and simple reasoners, the knights-errant of yore, by single combat; but Ichabod was too conscious of the superior might of his adversary to enter the lists against him. He had overheard the boast of Bones, that he would "double the schoolmaster up and put him on a shelf;" and he was too wary to give him an opportunity. There was something extremely provoking in this obstinately pacific system: it left Brom no alternative but to draw upon the funds of rustic waggery in his disposition, and to play off boorish practical jokes upon his rival. Ichabod became the object of whimsical persecution to Bones and his gang of rough riders. They harried his hitherto peaceful domains; smoked out his singing-school by stopping up the chimney; broke into the schoolhouse at night, in spite of its formidable fastenings of withe and window stakes, and turned everything topsy-turvy: so that the poor schoolmaster began to think all the witches in the country held their meetings there. But, what was still more annoying,

Brom took all opportunities of turning him into ridicule in presence of his mistress, and had a scoundrel dog whom he taught to whine in the most ludicrous manner, and introduced as a rival of Ichabod's to instruct her in psalmody.

In this way matters went on for some time, without producing any material effect on the relative situations of the contending powers. On a fine autumnal afternoon, Ichabod, in pensive mood, sat enthroned on the lofty stool from whence he usually watched all the concerns of his little literary realm. In his hand he swayed a ferule, that scepter of despotic power; the birch of justice reposed on three nails behind the throne, a constant terror to evil doers; while on the desk before him might be seen sundry contraband articles and prohibited weapons, detected upon the persons of idle urchins, such as half-munched apples, pop-guns, whirligigs, fly-cages, and whole legions of rampant little paper game-cocks. Apparently there had been some appalling act of justice recently inflicted; for his scholars were all busily intent upon their books, or slyly whispering behind them with one eye kept upon the master, and a kind of buzzing stillness reigned throughout the schoolroom. It was suddenly interrupted by the appearance of a negro, in tow-cloth jacket and trousers, a round-crowned fragment of a hat, like the cap of Mercury,[1] and mounted on the back of a ragged, wild, half-broken colt, which he managed with a rope by way of halter. He came clattering up to the school door with an invitation to Ichabod to attend a merry-making, or "quilting frolic," to be held that evening at Mynheer Van Tassel's; and having delivered his message with that air of importance, and effort at fine language, which a negro is apt to display on petty embassies of the kind, he dashed over the brook, and was seen scampering away up the hollow, full of the importance and hurry of his mission.

All was now bustle and hubbub in the late quiet schoolroom. The scholars were hurried through their lessons without stopping

---

[1] The Roman god who presided over barter, trade, and all commercial dealings.

at trifles. Those who were nimble skipped over half with impunity; and those who were tardy had a smart application now
and then in the rear, to quicken their speed, or help them over a
tall word. Books were flung aside without being put away on
the shelves; inkstands were overturned, benches thrown down;
and the whole school was turned loose an hour before the usual
time, bursting forth like a legion of young imps, yelping and
racketing about the green, in joy at their early emancipation.

The gallant Ichabod now spent at least an extra half hour at
his toilet, brushing and furbishing up his best and indeed only suit
of rusty black, and arranging his looks by a bit of broken look-
ing-glass that hung up in the schoolhouse. That he might make
his appearance before his mistress in the true style of a cavalier,
he borrowed a horse from the farmer with whom he was domi-
ciliated, a choleric old Dutchman of the name of Hans Van Ripper, and, thus gallantly mounted, issued forth, like a knight-errant
in quest of adventures. But it is meet I should, in the true spirit
of romantic story, give some account of the looks and equipments
of my hero and his steed. The animal he bestrode was a broken-
down plow-horse, that had outlived almost everything but his
viciousness. He was gaunt and shagged, with a ewe neck, and
a head like a hammer. His rusty mane and tail were tangled
and knotted with burrs. One eye had lost its pupil, and was
glaring and spectral, but the other had the gleam of a genuine
devil in it. Still he must have had fire and mettle in his day, if
we may judge from his name, which was Gunpowder. He had,
in fact, been a favorite steed of his master's, the choleric Van
Ripper, who was a furious rider, and had infused, very probably,
some of his own spirit into the animal; for, old and broken-down
as he looked, there was more of the lurking devil in him than in
any young filly in the country.

Ichabod was a suitable figure for such a steed. He rode with
short stirrups, which brought his knees nearly up to the pommel
of the saddle; his sharp elbows stuck out like grasshoppers'; he
carried his whip perpendicularly in his hand, like a scepter; and,

8

as the horse jogged on, the motion of his arms was not unlike the flapping of a pair of wings. A small wool hat rested on the top of his nose, for so his scanty strip of forehead might be called; and the skirts of his black coat fluttered out almost to the horse's tail. Such was the appearance of Ichabod and his steed, as they shambled out of the gate of Hans Van Ripper; and it was altogether such an apparition as is seldom to be met with in broad daylight.

It was, as I have said, a fine autumnal day. The sky was clear and serene, and nature wore that rich and golden livery which we always associate with the idea of abundance. The forests had put on their sober brown and yellow, while some trees of the tenderer kind had been nipped by the frost into brilliant dyes of orange, purple, and scarlet. Streaming files of wild ducks began to make their appearance high in the air. The bark of the squirrel might be heard from the groves of beech and hickory nuts, and the pensive whistle of the quail at intervals from the neighboring stubble-field.

The small birds were taking their farewell banquets. In the fullness of their revelry, they fluttered, chirping and frolicking, from bush to bush, and tree to tree, capricious from the very profusion and variety around them. There was the honest cock-robin, the favorite game of stripling sportsmen, with its loud, querulous note; and the twittering blackbirds flying in sable clouds; and the golden-winged woodpecker, with his crimson crest, his broad, black gorget, and splendid plumage; and the cedar bird, with its red-tipped wings and yellow-tipped tail, and its little monteiro cap[1] of feathers; and the blue jay, that noisy coxcomb, in his gay, light-blue coat and white underclothes, screaming and chattering, nodding and bobbing and bowing, and pretending to be on good terms with every songster of the grove.

---

[1] Montero cap (Spanish, *montera*), a kind of cap, originally a hunting-cap; from *montero* ("a huntsman"). It has a spherical crown, and a flap round it that may be drawn down over the ears.

As Ichabod jogged slowly on his way, his eye, ever open to every symptom of culinary abundance, ranged with delight over the treasures of jolly autumn. On all sides he beheld vast store of apples, — some hanging in oppressive opulence on the trees, some gathered into baskets and barrels for the market, others heaped up in rich piles for the cider-press. Farther on he beheld great fields of Indian corn, with its golden ears peeping from their leafy coverts, and holding out the promise of cakes and hasty pudding; and the yellow pumpkins lying beneath them, turning up their fair, round bellies to the sun, and giving ample prospects of the most luxurious of pies; and anon he passed the fragrant buckwheat fields, breathing the odor of the beehive; and as he beheld them, soft anticipations stole over his mind of dainty slapjacks, well buttered, and garnished with honey or treacle, by the delicate little dimpled hand of Katrina Van Tassel.

Thus feeding his mind with many sweet thoughts and "sugared suppositions," he journeyed along the sides of a range of hills which look out upon some of the goodliest scenes of the mighty Hudson. The sun gradually wheeled his broad disk down into the west. The wide bosom of the Tappan Zee lay motionless and glassy, excepting that here and there a gentle undulation waved, and prolonged the blue shadow of the distant mountain. A few amber clouds floated in the sky, without a breath of air to move them. The horizon was of a fine, golden tint, changing gradually into a pure apple-green, and from that into the deep-blue of the mid-heaven. A slanting ray lingered on the woody crests of the precipices that overhung some parts of the river, giving greater depth to the dark gray and purple of their rocky sides. A sloop was loitering in the distance, dropping slowly down with the tide, her sail hanging uselessly against the mast; and, as the reflection of the sky gleamed along the still water, it seemed as if the vessel was suspended in the air.

It was toward evening that Ichabod arrived at the castle of the Herr Van Tassel, which he found thronged with the pride

and flower of the adjacent country, — old farmers, a spare, leath-
ern-faced race, in homespun coats and breeches, blue stockings,
huge shoes, and magnificent pewter buckles; their brisk, withered
little dames, in close crimped caps, long-waisted gowns, homespun petticoats, with scissors and pincushions, and gay calico
pockets hanging on the outside; buxom lasses, almost as antiquated as their mothers, excepting where a straw hat, a fine
ribbon, or perhaps a white frock, gave symptoms of city inno-
vations; the sons, in short, square-skirted coats with rows of
stupendous brass buttons, and their hair generally queued in the
fashion of the times, especially if they could procure an eel-skin
for the purpose, it being esteemed throughout the country as a
potent nourisher and strengthener of the hair.

Brom Bones, however, was the hero of the scene, having come
to the gathering on his favorite steed Daredevil, — a creature,
like himself, full of mettle and mischief, and which no one but
himself could manage. He was, in fact, noted for preferring
vicious animals, given to all kinds of tricks, which kept the rider
in constant risk of his neck; for he held a tractable, well-broken
horse as unworthy of a lad of spirit.

Fain would I pause to dwell upon the world of charms that
burst upon the enraptured gaze of my hero, as he entered the
state parlor of Van Tassel's mansion; not those of the bevy of
buxom lasses, with their luxurious display of red and white, but
the ample charms of a genuine Dutch country tea-table, in the
sumptuous time of autumn. Such heaped-up platters of cakes
of various and almost indescribable kinds, known only to experienced Dutch housewives! There was the doughty doughnut,
the tender oly-koek,[1] and the crisp and crumbling cruller;
sweet cakes and short cakes, ginger cakes and honey cakes, and
the whole family of cakes; and then there were apple pies and
peach pies and pumpkin pies; besides slices of ham and smoked
beef; and, moreover, delectable dishes of preserved plums, and

---

[1] A kind of Dutch cake, made of dough sweetened, and fried in lard.

peaches, and pears, and quinces; not to mention broiled shad and roasted chickens; together with bowls of milk and cream; all mingled higgledy-piggledy, pretty much as I have enumerated them, with the motherly teapot sending up its clouds of vapor from the midst — Heaven bless the mark! I want breath and time to discuss this banquet as it deserves, and am too eager to get on with my story. Happily, Ichabod Crane was not in so great a hurry as his historian, but did ample justice to every dainty.

He was a kind and thankful creature, whose heart dilated in proportion as his skin was filled with good cheer, and whose spirits rose with eating as some men's do with drink. He could not help, too, rolling his large eyes round him as he ate, and chuckling with the possibility that he might one day be lord of all this scene of almost unimaginable luxury and splendor. Then, he thought, how soon he'd turn his back upon the old school-house; snap his fingers in the face of Hans Van Ripper, and every other niggardly patron; and kick any itinerant pedagogue out of doors that should dare to call him comrade!

Old Baltus Van Tassel moved about among his guests with a face dilated with content and good humor, round and jolly as the harvest moon. His hospitable attentions were brief but expressive, being confined to a shake of the hand, a slap on the shoulder, a loud laugh, and a pressing invitation to "fall to, and help themselves."

And now the sound of the music from the common room, or hall, summoned to the dance. The musician was an old gray-headed negro, who had been the itinerant orchestra of the neighborhood for more than half a century. His instrument was as old and battered as himself. The greater part of the time he scraped away on two or three strings, accompanying every movement of the bow with a motion of the head, bowing almost to the ground, and stamping with his foot whenever a fresh couple were to start.

Ichabod prided himself upon his dancing as much as upon his

vocal powers. Not a limb, not a fiber about him, was idle; and to have seen his loosely hung frame in full motion, and clattering about the room, you would have thought St. Vitus[1] himself, that blessed patron of the dance, was figuring before you in person. He was the admiration of all the negroes, who, having gathered, of all ages and sizes, from the farm and the neighborhood, stood forming a pyramid of shining black faces at every door and window, gazing with delight at the scene, rolling their white eyeballs, and showing grinning rows of ivory from ear to ear. How could the flogger of urchins be otherwise than animated and joyous? The lady of his heart was his partner in the dance, and smiling graciously in reply to all his amorous oglings; while Brom Bones, sorely smitten with love and jealousy, sat brooding by himself in one corner.

When the dance was at an end, Ichabod was attracted to a knot of the sager folks, who, with old Van Tassel, sat smoking at one end of the piazza, gossiping over former times, and drawling out long stories about the war.

This neighborhood, at the time of which I am speaking, was one of those highly favored places which abound with chronicle and great men. The British and American line had run near it during the war: it had therefore been the scene of marauding, and infested with refugees, cowboys, and all kinds of border chivalry. Just sufficient time had elapsed to enable each story-teller to dress up his tale with a little becoming fiction, and, in the indistinctness of his recollection, to make himself the hero of every exploit.

There was the story of Doffue Martling, a large, blue-bearded Dutchman, who had nearly taken a British frigate with an old iron nine-pounder from a mud breastwork, only that his gun burst at the sixth discharge. And there was an old gentleman who

---

[1] The patron saint of dancers and actors, and invoked against the disease known as "St. Vitus's dance." He is the patron of Saxony, Bohemia, and Sicily, and throughout Germany ranks as one of the fourteen "Nothelfer" of the Church.

shall be nameless, being too rich a mynheer[1] to be lightly mentioned, who in the battle of Whiteplains,[2] being an excellent master of defense, parried a musket-ball with a small sword, insomuch that he absolutely felt it whiz round the blade, and glance off at the hilt, in proof of which he was ready at any time to show the sword, with the hilt a little bent. There were several more that had been equally great in the field, not one of whom but was persuaded that he had a considerable hand in bringing the war to a happy termination.

But all these were nothing to the tales of ghosts and apparitions that succeeded. The neighborhood is rich in legendary treasures of the kind. Local tales and superstitions thrive best in these sheltered, long-settled retreats, but are trampled under foot by the shifting throng that forms the population of most of our country places. Besides, there is no encouragement for ghosts in most of our villages, for they have scarcely had time to finish their first nap, and turn themselves in their graves, before their surviving friends have traveled away from the neighborhood ; so that, when they turn out at night to walk their rounds, they have no acquaintance left to call upon. This is, perhaps, the reason why we so seldom hear of ghosts, except in our long-established Dutch communities.

The immediate cause, however, of the prevalence of supernatural stories in these parts, was doubtless owing to the vicinity of Sleepy Hollow. There was a contagion in the very air that blew from that haunted region: it breathed forth an atmosphere of dreams and fancies infecting all the land. Several of the Sleepy Hollow people were present at Van Tassel's, and, as usual, were doling out their wild and wonderful legends. Many dismal tales

---

[1] From the Dutch *mijn heer*, equivalent to the German *mein Herr* ("my master," "my lord"), our "sir" or "Mr.," a term of respectful address employed by the Dutch; hence also a Dutchman.

[2] At Whiteplains, twenty-five miles northeast of New York, the Americans were driven back by the British under Gen. Howe, and compelled to withdraw to New Jersey, October, 1776.

were told about funeral trains, and mourning cries and wailings, heard and seen about the great tree where the unfortunate Major André[1] was taken, and which stood in the neighborhood. Some mention was made also of the woman in white that haunted the dark glen at Raven Rock, and was often heard to shriek on winter nights before a storm, having perished there in the snow. The chief part of the stories, however, turned upon the favorite specter of Sleepy Hollow, the headless horseman, who had been heard several times of late, patrolling the country, and, it was said, tethered his horse nightly among the graves in the churchyard.

The sequestered situation of this church seems always to have made it a favorite haunt of troubled spirits. It stands on a knoll, surrounded by locust-trees and lofty elms, from among which its decent, whitewashed walls shine modestly forth, like Christian purity beaming through the shades of retirement. A gentle slope descends from it to a silver sheet of water, bordered by high trees, between which peeps may be caught at the blue hills of the Hudson. To look upon its grass-grown yard, where the sunbeams seem to sleep so quietly, one would think that there, at least, the dead might rest in peace. On one side of the church extends a wide, woody dell, along which raves a large brook among broken rocks and trunks of fallen trees. Over a deep black part of the stream, not far from the church, was formerly thrown a wooden bridge. The road that led to it, and the bridge itself, were thickly shaded by overhanging trees, which cast a gloom about it, even in the daytime, but occasioned a fearful

---

[1] John André was born in London in 1751. He became an adjutant-general in the British army of the American Revolution. Benedict Arnold, who commanded the American fortress of West Point, made arrangements to betray that place into the hands of the British general Sir Henry Clinton. André was associated with Arnold in this plot, which was frustrated and defeated by the capture of André, who had been sent by Arnold with letters. André was tried by a court-martial, and condemned to be hung as a spy. He was executed at Tappantown, Oct. 2, 1780. In 1821 his remains were transferred to England, and interred in Westminster Abbey.

darkness at night. Such was one of the favorite haunts of the headless horseman, and the place where he was most frequently encountered. The tale was told of old Brouwer, a most heretical disbeliever in ghosts, — how he met the horseman returning from his foray into Sleepy Hollow, and was obliged to get up behind him; how they galloped over bush and brake, over hill and swamp, until they reached the bridge, when the horseman suddenly turned into a skeleton, threw old Brouwer into the brook, and sprang away over the tree-tops with a clap of thunder.

This story was immediately matched by a thrice marvelous adventure of Brom Bones, who made light of the Galloping Hessian as an arrant jockey. He affirmed, that, on returning one night from the neighboring village of Sing Sing, he had been overtaken by this midnight trooper; that he had offered to race with him for a bowl of punch, and should have won it, too (for Daredevil beat the goblin horse all hollow), but, just as they came to the church bridge, the Hessian bolted, and vanished in a flash of fire.

All these tales told in that drowsy undertone with which men talk in the dark, the countenances of the listeners only now and then receiving a casual gleam from the glare of a pipe, sank deep in the mind of Ichabod. He repaid them in kind with large extracts from his invaluable author Cotton Mather, and added many marvelous events that had taken place in his native State of Connecticut, and fearful sights which he had seen in his nightly walks about Sleepy Hollow.

The revel now gradually broke up. The old farmers gathered together their families in their wagons, and were heard for some time rattling along the hollow roads, and over the distant hills. Some of the damsels mounted on pillions[1] behind their favorite swains; and their light-hearted laughter, mingling with the clatter of hoofs, echoed along the silent woodlands, sounding fainter and fainter until they gradually died away, and the late scene of

[1] A cushion adjusted to a saddle at the back, serving as a kind of seat for another person riding behind.

noise and frolic was all silent and deserted. Ichabod only lingered behind, according to the custom of country lovers, to have
a *tête-à-tête* with the heiress, fully convinced that he was now on
the high road to success. What passed at this interview I will
not pretend to say, for in fact I do not know. Something, however, I fear me, must have gone wrong; for he certainly sallied
forth, after no very great interval, with an air quite desolate and
chopfallen. Oh these women, these women! Could that girl
have been playing off any of her coquettish tricks? Was her
encouragement of the poor pedagogue all a mere sham to secure
her conquest of his rival? Heaven only knows, not I! Let it
suffice to say, Ichabod stole forth with the air of one who had
been sacking a hen-roost rather than a fair lady's heart. Without looking to the right or left to notice the scene of rural wealth
on which he had so often gloated, he went straight to the stable,
and, with several hearty cuffs and kicks, roused his steed most
uncourteously from the comfortable quarters in which he was
soundly sleeping, dreaming of mountains of corn and oats, and
whole valleys of timothy and clover.

It was the very witching time of night, that Ichabod, heavy
hearted and crestfallen, pursued his travel homewards along the
sides of the lofty hills which rise above Tarrytown, and which
he had traversed so cheerily in the afternoon. The hour was as
dismal as himself. Far below him the Tappan Zee spread its
dusky and indistinct waste of waters, with here and there the tall
mast of a sloop riding quietly at anchor under the land. In the
dead hush of midnight he could even hear the barking of the
watch-dog from the opposite shore of the Hudson, but it was so
vague and faint as only to give an idea of his distance from this
faithful companion of man. Now and then, too, the long-drawn
crowing of a cock, accidentally awakened, would sound far, far
off, from some farmhouse away among the hills; but it was like
a dreaming sound in his ear. No signs of life occurred near
him, but occasionally the melancholy chirp of a cricket, or
perhaps the guttural twang of a bull-frog from a neighboring

marsh, as if sleeping uncomfortably, and turning suddenly in his bed.

All the stories of ghosts and goblins that he had heard in the afternoon, now came crowding upon his recollection. The night grew darker and darker. The stars seemed to sink deeper in the sky, and driving clouds occasionally hid them from his sight. He had never felt so lonely and dismal. He was, moreover, approaching the very place where many of the scenes of the ghost stories had been laid. In the center of the road stood an enormous tulip-tree, which towered like a giant above all the other trees of the neighborhood, and formed a kind of landmark. Its limbs were gnarled and fantastic, large enough to form trunks for ordinary trees, twisting down almost to the earth, and rising again into the air. It was connected with the tragical story of the unfortunate André who had been taken prisoner hard by, and was universally known by the name of Major André's tree. The common people regarded it with a mixture of respect and superstition, partly out of sympathy for the fate of its ill-starred namesake, and partly from the tales of strange sights and doleful lamentations told concerning it.

As Ichabod approached this fearful tree, he began to whistle. He thought his whistle was answered: it was but a blast sweeping sharply through the dry branches. As he approached a little nearer, he thought he saw something white hanging in the midst of the tree. He paused, and ceased whistling, but, on looking more narrowly, perceived that it was a place where the tree had been scathed by lightning, and the white wood laid bare. Suddenly he heard a groan. His teeth chattered, and his knees smote against the saddle. It was but the rubbing of one huge bough upon another, as they were swayed about by the breeze. He passed the tree in safety, but new perils lay before him.

About two hundred yards from the tree a small brook crossed the road, and ran into a marshy and thickly wooded glen, known by the name of Wiley's Swamp. A few rough logs laid side by side served for a bridge over this stream. On that side of the road where the brook entered the wood, a group of oaks and chestnuts, matted thick with wild grape-vines, threw a cavernous gloom over it. To pass this bridge was the severest trial. It was at this identical spot that the unfortunate André was captured, and under the covert of those chestnuts and vines were the sturdy yeomen concealed who surprised him. This has ever since been considered a haunted stream, and fearful are the feelings of the schoolboy who has to pass it alone after dark.

As he approached the stream his heart began to thump. He summoned up, however, all his resolution, gave his horse half a score of kicks in the ribs, and attempted to dash briskly across the bridge; but, instead of starting forward, the perverse old animal made a lateral movement, and ran broadside against the fence. Ichabod, whose fears increased with the delay, jerked the reins on the other side, and kicked lustily with the contrary foot. It was all in vain. His steed started, it is true, but it was only to plunge to the opposite side of the road into a thicket of brambles and alder bushes. The schoolmaster now bestowed both whip and heel upon the starveling ribs of old Gunpowder, who dashed forward, snuffling and snorting, but came to a stand just by the bridge with a suddenness that had nearly sent his rider sprawling over his head. Just at this moment a plashy tramp by the side of the bridge caught the sensitive ear of Ichabod. In the dark shadow of the grove, on the margin of the brook, he beheld something huge, misshapen, black, and towering. It stirred not, but seemed gathered up in the gloom, like some gigantic monster ready to spring upon the traveler.

The hair of the affrighted pedagogue rose upon his head with terror. What was to be done? To turn and fly was now too late; and, besides, what chance was there of escaping ghost or goblin, if such it was, which could ride upon the wings of the wind? Summoning up, therefore, a show of courage, he demanded in stammering accents, "Who are you?" He received no reply. He repeated his demand in a still more agitated voice. Still there was no answer. Once more he cudgeled the sides of the inflexible Gunpowder, and, shutting his eyes, broke forth with involuntary fervor into a psalm tune. Just then the shadowy object of alarm put itself in motion, and, with a scramble and a bound, stood at once in the middle of the road. Though the night was dark and dismal, yet the form of the unknown might now in some degree be ascertained. He appeared to be a horseman of large dimensions, and mounted on a black horse of powerful frame. He made no offer of molestation or sociability, but kept aloof on one side of the road, jogging along on the blind side of old Gunpowder, who had now got over his fright and waywardness.

Ichabod, who had no relish for this strange midnight companion, and bethought himself of the adventure of Brom Bones with the Galloping Hessian, now quickened his steed, in hopes of leaving him behind. The stranger, however, quickened his horse to an equal pace. Ichabod pulled up, and fell into a walk, thinking to lag behind: the other did the same. His heart began to sink within him. He endeavored to resume his psalm tune; but his parched tongue clove to the roof of his mouth, and he could not utter a stave. There was something in the moody and dogged silence of this pertinacious companion that was mysterious and appalling. It was soon fearfully accounted for. On mounting a rising ground, which brought the figure of his fellow-traveler in relief against the sky, gigantic in height, and muffled in a cloak, Ichabod was horror-struck on perceiving that he was headless; but his horror was still more increased on observing that the head, which should have rested on his shoulders, was carried before him on the pommel of his saddle. His terror rose to desperation. He reined a shower of kicks and blows upon Gunpowder, hoping, by a sudden movement, to give his companion the slip; but the specter started full jump with him. Away then they dashed, through thick and thin; stones flying, and sparks flashing, at every bound. Ichabod's flimsy garments fluttered in the air, as he stretched his long, lank body away over his horse's head, in the eagerness of his flight.

They had now reached the road which turns off to Sleepy Hollow; but Gunpowder, who seemed possessed with a demon, instead of keeping up it, made an opposite turn, and plunged headlong downhill to the left. This road leads through a sandy hollow, shaded by trees for about a quarter of a mile, where it crosses the bridge famous in goblin story; and just beyond swells the green knoll on which stands the whitewashed church.

As yet the panic of the steed had given his unskillful rider an apparent advantage in the chase; but, just as he had got halfway through the hollow, the girths of the saddle gave way, and he felt it slipping from under him. He seized it by the pommel, and endeavored to hold it firm, but in vain; and had just time to save himself by clasping old Gunpowder round the neck, when the saddle fell to the earth, and he heard it trampled under foot by his pursuer. For a moment the terror of Hans Van Ripper's wrath passed across his mind, for it was his Sunday saddle; but this was no time for petty fears. The goblin was hard on his haunches; and (unskillful rider that he was) he had much ado to maintain his seat, sometimes slipping on one side, sometimes on another, and sometimes jolted on the high ridge of his horse's backbone with a violence that he verily feared would cleave him asunder.

An opening in the trees now cheered him with the hopes that the church bridge was at hand. The wavering reflection of a silver star in the bosom of the brook told him that he was not mistaken. He saw the walls of the church dimly glaring under the trees beyond. He recollected the place where Brom Bones's ghostly competitor had disappeared. "If I can but reach that bridge," thought Ichabod, "I am safe." Just then he heard the black steed panting and blowing close behind him. He even fancied that he felt his hot breath. Another convulsive kick in the ribs, and old Gunpowder sprang upon the bridge; he thundered over the resounding planks; he gained the opposite side; and now Ichabod cast a look behind to see if his pursuer should vanish, according to rule, in a flash of fire and brimstone. Just then he saw the goblin rising in his stirrups, and in the very act of hurling his head at him. Ichabod endeavored to dodge the horrible missile, but too late. It encountered his cranium with a tremendous crash. He was tumbled headlong into the dust; and Gunpowder, the black steed, and the goblin rider, passed by like a whirlwind.

The next morning the old horse was found without his saddle, and with the bridle under his feet, soberly cropping the grass at his master's gate. Ichabod did not make his appearance at breakfast. Dinner-hour came, but no Ichabod. The boys assembled at the schoolhouse, and strolled idly about the banks of the brook; but no schoolmaster. Hans Van Ripper now began to feel some uneasiness about the fate of poor Ichabod and his saddle. An inquiry was set on foot, and after diligent investigation they came upon his traces. In one part of the road leading to the church was found the saddle trampled in the dirt. The tracks of horses' hoofs deeply dented in the road, and evidently at furious speed, were traced to the bridge, beyond which, on the bank of a broad part of the brook, where the water ran deep and black, was found the hat of the unfortunate Ichabod, and close beside it a shattered pumpkin.

The brook was searched, but the body of the schoolmaster was not to be discovered. Hans Van Ripper, as executor of his estate, examined the bundle which contained all his worldly effects. They consisted of two shirts and a half; two stocks for the neck; a pair or two of worsted stockings; an old pair of corduroy small-clothes; a rusty razor; a book of psalm tunes, full of dogs' ears; and a broken pitchpipe. As to the books and furniture of the schoolhouse, they belonged to the community, excepting Cotton Mather's " History of Witchcraft," a " New England Almanac," and a book of dreams and fortune-telling; in which last was a sheet of foolscap much scribbled and blotted by several fruitless attempts to make a copy of verses in honor of the heiress of Van Tassel. These magic books and the poetic scrawl were forthwith consigned to the flames by Hans Van Ripper, who from that time forward determined to send his children no more to school, observing that he never knew any good come of this same reading and writing. Whatever money the schoolmaster possessed, and he had received his quarter's pay but a day or two before, he must have had about his person at the time of his disappearance.

The mysterious event caused much speculation at the church on the following Sunday. Knots of gazers and gossips were collected in the churchyard, at the bridge, and at the spot where the hat and pumpkin had been found. The stories of Brouwer, of Bones, and a whole budget of others, were called to mind; and when they had diligently considered them all, and compared them with the symptoms of the present case, they shook their heads, and came to the conclusion that Ichabod had been carried off by the Galloping Hessian. As he was a bachelor, and in nobody's debt, nobody troubled his head any more about him. The school was removed to a different quarter of the hollow, and another pedagogue reigned in his stead.

It is true, an old farmer, who had been down to New York on a visit several years after, and from whom this account of the ghostly adventure was received, brought home the intelligence that Ichabod Crane was still alive; that he had left the neighborhood, partly through fear of the goblin and Hans Van Ripper, and partly in mortification at having been suddenly dismissed by the heiress; that he had changed his quarters to a distant part of the country, had kept school and studied law at the same time, had been admitted to the bar, turned politician, electioneered, written for the newspapers, and finally had been made a justice of the Ten Pound Court. Brom Bones, too, who shortly after his rival's disappearance conducted the blooming Katrina in triumph to the altar, was observed to look exceedingly knowing whenever the story of Ichabod was related, and always burst into a hearty laugh at the mention of the pumpkin, which led some to suspect that he knew more about the matter than he chose to tell.

The old country wives, however, who are the best judges of these matters, maintain to this day that Ichabod was spirited away by supernatural means; and it is a favorite story often told about the neighborhood round the winter evening fire. The bridge became more than ever an object of superstitious awe; and that may be the reason why the road has been altered of late years, so as to approach the church by the border of the mill-pond. The schoolhouse, being deserted, soon fell to decay, and was reported to be haunted by the ghost of the unfortunate pedagogue; and the plow-boy, loitering homeward of a still summer evening, has often fancied his voice at a distance, chanting a melancholy psalm tune among the tranquil solitudes of Sleepy Hollow.

POSTSCRIPT.

[Found in the handwriting of Mr. Knickerbocker.]

THE preceding tale is given almost in the precise words in which I heard it related at a corporation meeting of the ancient city of the Manhattoes,[1] at which were present many of its sagest and most illustrious burghers. The narrator was a pleasant, shabby, gentlemanly old fellow, in pepper-and-salt clothes, with a sadly humorous face; and one whom I strongly suspected of being poor, he made such efforts to be entertaining. When his story was concluded, there was much laughter and approbation, particularly from two or three deputy aldermen, who had been asleep the greater part of the time. There was, however, one tall, dry-looking old gentleman, with beetling eye-brows, who maintained a grave and rather severe face throughout; now and then folding his arms, inclining his head, and looking down upon the floor, as if turning a doubt over in his mind. He was one of your wary men, who never laugh but upon good grounds, when they have reason and the law on their side. When the mirth of the rest of the company had subsided and silence was restored, he leaned one arm on the elbow of his chair, and, sticking the other akimbo, demanded, with a slight but exceedingly sage motion of the head and contraction of the brow, what was the moral of the story, and what it went to prove.

The story-teller, who was just putting a glass of wine to his lips, as a refreshment after his toils, paused for a moment, looked at his inquirer with an

---

[1] Manhattan, i.e., New York.

9

air of infinite deference, and, lowering the glass slowly to the table, observed
that the story was intended most logically to prove, —

"That there is no situation in life but has its advantages and pleasures,
provided we will but take a joke as we find it.

"That therefore he that runs races with goblin troopers is likely to have
rough riding of it.

"Ergo, for a country schoolmaster to be refused the hand of a Dutch heiress, is a certain step to high preferment in the State."

The cautious old gentleman knit his brows tenfold closer after this explanation, being sorely puzzled by the ratiocination of the syllogism; while,
methought, the one in pepper-and-salt eyed him with something of a
triumphant leer.   At length he observed that all this was very well, but still
he thought the story a little on the extravagant: there were one or two points
on which he had his doubts.

"Faith, sir," replied the story-teller, "as to that matter, I don't believe
one half of it myself."

D. K.

RIP VAN WINKLE.

[A Posthumous Writing of Diedrich Knickerbocker.]

'By Woden, God of Saxons,
From whence comes Wensday, that is Wodensday,
Truth is a thing that ever I will keep
Unto thylke day in which I creep into
My supulchre."

CARTWRIGHT.

WHOEVER has made a voyage up the Hudson must remember the Catskill Mountains. They are a dismembered
branch of the great Appalachian family, and are seen away to
the west of the river, swelling up to a noble height, and lording
it over the surrounding country.   Every change of season, every
change of weather, indeed every hour of the day, produces some
change in the magical hues and shapes of these mountains; and
they are regarded by all the good wives, far and near, as perfect
barometers.   When the weather is fair and settled, they are
clothed in blue and purple, and print their bold outlines on the

clear evening sky; but sometimes, when the rest of the landscape is cloudless, they will gather a hood of gray vapors about their summits, which, in the last rays of the setting sun, will glow and light up like a crown of glory.

At the foot of these fairy mountains the voyager may have descried the light smoke curling up from a village, whose shingle-roofs gleam among the trees, just where the blue tints of the upland melt away into the fresh green of the nearer landscape. It is a little village, of great antiquity, having been founded by some of the Dutch colonists in the early times of the province, just about the beginning of the government of the good Peter Stuyvesant;[1] (may he rest in peace!) and there were some of the houses of the original settlers standing within a few years, built of small, yellow bricks brought from Holland, having latticed windows and gable fronts, surmounted with weathercocks.

In that same village, and in one of these very houses (which, to tell the precise truth, was sadly time-worn and weather-beaten), there lived many years since, while the country was yet a province of Great Britain, a simple, good-natured fellow of the name of Rip Van Winkle. He was a descendant of the Van Winkles who figured so gallantly in the chivalrous days of Peter Stuyvesant, and accompanied him to the siege of Fort Christina.[2] He inherited, however, but little of the martial character of his ancestors. I have observed that he was a simple, good-natured man; he was, moreover, a kind neighbor, and an obedient, henpecked husband. Indeed, to the latter circumstance might be owing that meekness of spirit which gained him such universal popularity; for those men are most apt to be obsequious and conciliating abroad, who are under the discipline of shrews at home. Their tempers, doubtless, are rendered pliant and malleable in the fiery furnace of domestic tribulation; and a curtain

---

[1] Governor of Manhattan Island in 1647.

[2] Fort Christina, or Christiana, was a Swedish fort, situated five miles north of Fort Cassimir (now Newcastle, Del.), attacked and captured by the Dutch of New Netherlands in 1655.

lecture is worth all the sermons in the world for teaching the virtues of patience and long-suffering. A termagant wife may therefore, in some respects, be considered a tolerable blessing; and, if so, Rip Van Winkle was thrice blessed.

Certain it is, that he was a great favorite among all the good wives of the village, who, as usual with the amiable sex, took his part in all family squabbles, and never failed, whenever they talked those matters over in their evening gossipings, to lay all the blame on Dame Van Winkle. The children of the village, too, would shout with joy whenever he approached. He assisted at their sports, made their playthings, taught them to fly kites and shoot marbles, and told them long stories of ghosts, witches, and Indians. Whenever he went dodging about the village, he was surrounded by a troop of them, hanging on his skirts, clambering on his back, and playing a thousand tricks on him with impunity; and not a dog would bark at him throughout the neighborhood.

The great error in Rip's composition was an insuperable aversion to all kinds of profitable labor. It could not be from the want of assiduity or perseverance; for he would sit on a wet rock, with a rod as long and heavy as a Tartar's[1] lance, and fish all day without a murmur, even though he should not be encouraged by a single nibble. He would carry a fowling-piece on his shoulder for hours together, trudging through woods and swamps, and up hill and down dale, to shoot a few squirrels or wild pigeons. He would never refuse to assist a neighbor even in the roughest toil, and was a foremost man at all country frolics for husking Indian corn or building stone fences. The women of the village, too, used to employ him to run their errands, and to do such little odd jobs as their less obliging husbands would not do for them. In a word, Rip was ready to attend to anybody's business but his own; but as to doing family duty, and keeping his farm in order, he found it impossible.

In fact, he declared it was of no use to work on his farm. It

---

[1] See note, p. 108.

was the most pestilent little piece of ground in the whole country. Everything about it went wrong, and would go wrong, in spite of him. His fences were continually falling to pieces; his cow would either go astray, or get among the cabbages; weeds were sure to grow quicker in his fields than anywhere else; the rain always made a point of setting in just as he had some outdoor work to do: so that, though his patrimonial estate had dwindled away under his management acre by acre, until there was little more left than a mere patch of Indian corn and potatoes, yet it was the worst-conditioned farm in the neighborhood.

His children, too, were as ragged and wild as if they belonged to nobody. His son Rip, an urchin begotten in his own likeness, promised to inherit the habits with the old clothes of his father. He was generally seen trooping like a colt at his mother's heels, equipped in a pair of his father's cast-off galligaskins,[1] which he had much ado to hold up with one hand, as a fine lady does her train in bad weather.

Rip Van Winkle, however, was one of those happy mortals, of foolish, well-oiled dispositions, who take the world easy, eat white bread or brown, whichever can be got with least thought or trouble, and would rather starve on a penny than work for a pound. If left to himself, he would have whistled life away in perfect contentment; but his wife kept continually dinning in his ears about his idleness, his carelessness, and the ruin he was bringing on his family.

Morning, noon, and night, her tongue was incessantly going, and everything he said or did was sure to produce a torrent of household eloquence. Rip had but one way of replying to all lectures of the kind, and that, by frequent use, had grown into a habit. He shrugged his shoulders, shook his head, cast up his eyes, but said nothing. This, however, always provoked a fresh volley from his wife; so that he was fain to draw off his forces, and take to the outside of the house,— the only side which, in truth, belongs to a hen-pecked husband.

<hr>

[1] A kind of wide breeches.

Rip's sole domestic adherent was his dog Wolf, who was as much hen-pecked as his master; for Dame Van Winkle regarded them as companions in idleness, and even looked upon Wolf with an evil eye, as the cause of his master's going so often astray. True it is, in all points of spirit befitting an honorable dog, he was as courageous an animal as ever scoured the woods; but what courage can withstand the ever-during and all-besetting terrors of a woman's tongue? The moment Wolf entered the house, his crest fell; his tail drooped to the ground or curled between his legs; he sneaked about with a gallows air, casting many a sidelong glance at Dame Van Winkle; and, at the least flourish of a broomstick or ladle, he would fly to the door with yelping precipitation.

Times grew worse and worse with Rip Van Winkle as years of matrimony rolled on. A tart temper never mellows with age, and a sharp tongue is the only edged tool that grows keener with constant use. For a long while he used to console himself, when driven from home, by frequenting a kind of perpetual club of the sages, philosophers, and other idle personages of the village, which held its sessions on a bench before a small inn, designated by a rubicund portrait of his Majesty George III.[1] Here they used to sit in the shade of a long, lazy, summer's day, talking listlessly over village gossip, or telling endless sleepy stories about nothing. But it would have been worth any statesman's money to have heard the profound discussions which sometimes took place, when by chance an old newspaper fell into their hands from some passing traveler. How solemnly they would listen to the contents, as drawled out by Derrick Van Bummel, the schoolmaster, — a dapper, learned little man, who was not to be daunted by the most gigantic word in the dictionary! and how sagely they would deliberate upon public events some months after they had taken place!

The opinions of this junto were completely controlled by

---

[1] George III. (1738–1820) ascended the English throne in 1760, and reigned sixty years.

Nicholas Vedder, a patriarch of the village, and landlord of the inn, at the door of which he took his seat from morning till night, just moving sufficiently to avoid the sun, and keep in the shade of a large tree; so that the neighbors could tell the hour by his movements as accurately as by a sun-dial. It is true, he was rarely heard to speak, but smoked his pipe incessantly. His adherents, however (for every great man has his adherents), perfectly understood him, and knew how to gather his opinions. When anything that was read or related displeased him, he was observed to smoke his pipe vehemently, and to send forth short, frequent, and angry puffs; but, when pleased, he would inhale the smoke slowly and tranquilly, and emit it in light and placid clouds, and sometimes, taking the pipe from his mouth, and letting the fragrant vapor curl about his nose, would gravely nod his head in token of perfect approbation.

From even this stronghold the unlucky Rip was at length routed by his termagant wife, who would suddenly break in upon the tranquillity of the assemblage, and call the members all to naught; nor was that august personage, Nicholas Vedder himself, sacred from the daring tongue of this terrible virago, who charged him outright with encouraging her husband in habits of idleness.

Poor Rip was at last reduced almost to despair; and his only alternative, to escape from the labor of the farm and the clamor of his wife, was to take gun in hand and stroll away into the woods. Here he would sometimes seat himself at the foot of a tree, and share the contents of his wallet with Wolf, with whom he sympathized as a fellow-sufferer in persecution. "Poor Wolf," he would say, "thy mistress leads thee a dog's life of it; but never mind, my lad, whilst I live thou shalt never want a friend to stand by thee!" Wolf would wag his tail, look wistfully in his master's face, and, if dogs can feel pity, I verily believe he reciprocated the sentiment with all his heart.

In a long ramble of the kind on a fine autumnal day, Rip had unconsciously scrambled to one of the highest parts of the Catskill Mountains. He was after his favorite sport of squirrel shooting, and the still solitudes had echoed and reëchoed with the reports of his gun. Panting and fatigued, he threw himself, late in the afternoon, on a green knoll, covered with mountain herbage, that crowned the brow of a precipice. From an opening between the trees he could overlook all the lower country for many a mile of rich woodland. He saw at a distance the lordly Hudson, far, far below him, moving on its silent but majestic course, with the reflection of a purple cloud, or the sail of a lagging bark, here and there sleeping on its glassy bosom, and at last losing itself in the blue highlands.

On the other side he looked down into a deep mountain glen, wild, lonely, and shagged, the bottom filled with fragments from the impending cliffs, and scarcely lighted by the reflected rays of the setting sun. For some time Rip lay musing on this scene. Evening was gradually advancing; the mountains began to throw their long, blue shadows over the valleys; he saw that it would be dark long before he could reach the village, and he heaved a heavy sigh when he thought of encountering the terrors of Dame Van Winkle.

As he was about to descend, he heard a voice from a distance, hallooing, "Rip Van Winkle! Rip Van Winkle!" He looked around, but could see nothing but a crow winging its solitary flight across the mountain. He thought his fancy must have deceived him, and turned again to descend, when he heard the same cry ring through the still evening air, "Rip Van Winkle! Rip Van Winkle!" At the same time Wolf bristled up his back, and, giving a low growl, skulked to his master's side, looking fearfully down into the glen. Rip now felt a vague apprehension stealing over him. He looked anxiously in the same direction, and perceived a strange figure slowly toiling up the rocks, and bending under the weight of something he carried on his back. He was surprised to see any human being in this lonely and unfrequented place, but, supposing it to be some one of the neighborhood in need of his assistance, he hastened down to yield it.

On nearer approach he was still more surprised at the singularity of the stranger's appearance. He was a short, square-built old fellow, with thick, bushy hair, and a grizzled beard. His dress was of the antique Dutch fashion,— a cloth jerkin[1] strapped round the waist; several pair of breeches, the outer one of ample volume, decorated with rows of buttons down the sides, and bunches at the knees. He bore on his shoulders a stout keg, that seemed full of liquor, and made signs for Rip to approach and assist him with the load. Though rather shy and distrustful of this new acquaintance, Rip complied with his usual alacrity; and, mutually relieving each other, they clambered up a narrow gully, apparently the dry bed of a mountain torrent. As they ascended, Rip every now and then heard long, rolling peals, like distant thunder, that seemed to issue out of a deep ravine, or rather cleft, between lofty rocks, toward which their rugged path conducted. He paused for an instant, but, supposing it to be the muttering of one of those transient thunder-showers which often take place in mountain heights, he proceeded. Passing through the ravine, they came to a hollow, like a small amphitheater, surrounded by perpendicular precipices, over the brinks of which impending trees shot their branches, so that you only caught glimpses of the azure sky and the bright evening cloud. During the whole time, Rip and his companion had labored on in silence; for, though the former marveled greatly what could be the object of carrying a keg of liquor up this wild mountain, yet there was something strange and incomprehensible about the unknown, that inspired awe and checked familiarity.

On entering the amphitheater, new objects of wonder presented themselves. On a level spot in the center was a company of odd-looking personages playing at ninepins. They were dressed in a quaint, outlandish fashion. Some wore short doublets;[2] others, jerkins, with long knives in their belts; and most of them

---

[1] A close jacket much worn in the sixteenth and seventeenth centuries.

[2] A close-fitting outer garment, covering the body from the neck to below the waist.

had enormous breeches, of similar style with that of the guide's.
Their visages, too, were peculiar.   One had a large head, broad
face, and small, piggish eyes.   The face of another seemed to
consist entirely of nose, and was surmounted by a white sugar-
loaf hat, set off with a little red cock's tail. They all had beards,
of various shapes and colors.   There was one who seemed to be
the commander.   He was a stout old gentleman, with a weather-
beaten countenance.   He wore a laced doublet, broad belt and
hanger,[1] high-crowned hat and feather, red stockings, and high-
heeled shoes with roses in them.   The whole group reminded Rip
of the figures in an old Flemish painting in the parlor of Domi-
nie Van Schaick, the village parson, and which had been brought
over from Holland at the time of the settlement.

What seemed particularly odd to Rip was, that, though these
folks were evidently amusing themselves, yet they maintained the
gravest faces, the most mysterious silence, and were, withal, the
most melancholy party of pleasure he had ever witnessed.   Nothing interrupted the stillness of the scene but the noise of the balls,
which, whenever they were rolled, echoed along the mountains
like rumbling peals of thunder.

As Rip and his companion approached them, they suddenly
desisted from their play, and stared at him with such fixed,
statue-like gaze, and such strange, uncouth, lack-luster countenances, that his heart turned within him, and his knees smote together.   His companion now emptied the contents of the keg
into large flagons, and made signs to him to wait upon the company.   He obeyed with fear and trembling.   They quaffed the
liquor in profound silence, and then returned to their game.

By degrees Rip's awe and apprehension subsided.   He even
ventured, when no eye was fixed upon him, to taste the beverage, which he found had much of the flavor of excellent Hol-
lands.[2]   He was naturally a thirsty soul, and was soon tempted

---

[1] A short broadsword worn from the girdle, and slightly curved at the
point.

[2] Holland gin.

to repeat the draught. One taste provoked another; and he re-iterated his visits to the flagon so often, that at length his senses were overpowered, his eyes swam in his head, his head gradually declined, and he fell into a deep sleep.

On waking, he found himself on the green knoll whence he had first seen the old man of the glen. He rubbed his eyes. It was a bright, sunny morning. The birds were hopping and twitter-ing among the bushes; and the eagle was wheeling aloft, and breasting the pure mountain breeze. "Surely," thought Rip, "I have not slept here all night." He recalled the occurrences before he fell asleep,—the strange man with a keg of liquor, the mountain ravine, the wild retreat among the rocks, the woe-begone party at ninepins, the flagon. "Oh, that wicked flagon!" thought Rip: "what excuse shall I make to Dame Van Winkle!"

He looked round for his gun, but in place of the clean, well-oiled fowling-piece, he found an old firelock lying by him, the barrel incrusted with rust, the lock falling off, and the stock worm-eaten. He now suspected that the grave roysters of the mountain had put a trick upon him, and, having dosed him with liquor, had robbed him of his gun. Wolf, too, had disappeared; but he might have strayed away after a squirrel or partridge. He whistled after him, and shouted his name, but all in vain: the echoes repeated his whistle and shout, but no dog was to be seen.

He determined to revisit the scene of the last evening's gam-bol, and, if he met with any of the party, to demand his dog and gun. As he rose to walk, he found himself stiff in the joints, and wanting in his usual activity. "These mountain beds do not agree with me," thought Rip; "and, if this frolic should lay me up with a fit of the rheumatism, I shall have a blessed time with Dame Van Winkle." With some difficulty he got down into the glen. He found the gully up which he and his companion had ascended the preceding evening; but, to his astonishment, a mountain stream was now foaming down it, leaping from rock to rock, and filling the glen with babbling murmurs. He, however, made shift to scramble up its sides, working his toilsome way through thickets of birch, sassafras, and witch-hazel, and sometimes tripped up or entangled by the wild grape-vines that twisted their coils and tendrils from tree to tree, and spread a kind of network in his path.

At length he reached to where the ravine had opened through the cliffs to the amphitheater; but no traces of such opening remained. The rocks presented a high, impenetrable wall, over which the torrent came tumbling in a sheet of feathery foam, and fell into a broad, deep basin, black from the shadows of the surrounding forest. Here, then, poor Rip was brought to a stand. He again called and whistled after his dog. He was only answered by the cawing of a flock of idle crows, sporting high in air about a dry tree that overhung a sunny precipice, and who, secure in their elevation, seemed to look down and scoff at the poor man's perplexities. What was to be done? The morning was passing away, and Rip felt famished for want of his breakfast. He grieved to give up his dog and gun, he dreaded to meet his wife; but it would not do to starve among the mountains. He shook his head, shouldered the rusty firelock, and, with a heart full of trouble and anxiety, turned his steps homeward.

As he approached the village, he met a number of people, but none whom he knew; which somewhat surprised him, for he had thought himself acquainted with every one in the country round. Their dress, too, was of a different fashion from that to which he was accustomed. They all stared at him with equal marks of surprise, and, whenever they cast their eyes upon him, invariably stroked their chins. The constant recurrence of this gesture induced Rip involuntarily to do the same, when, to his astonishment, he found his beard had grown a foot long.

He had now entered the skirts of the village. A troop of strange children ran at his heels, hooting after him, and pointing at his gray beard. The dogs, too, not one of which he recognized for an old acquaintance, barked at him as he passed. The very village was altered: it was larger and more populous. There were rows of houses which he had never seen before, and those which had been his familiar haunts had disappeared. Strange names were over the doors, strange faces at the windows: everything was strange. His mind now misgave him. He began to doubt whether both he and the world around him were not bewitched. Surely this was his native village, which he had left but the day before. There stood the Catskill Mountains; there ran the silver Hudson at a distance; there was every hill and dale precisely as it had always been. Rip was sorely perplexed. "That flagon last night," thought he, "has addled my poor head sadly."

It was with some difficulty that he found the way to his own house, which he approached with silent awe, expecting every moment to hear the shrill voice of Dame Van Winkle. He found the house gone to decay,—the roof fallen in, the windows shattered, and the doors off the hinges. A half-starved dog that looked like Wolf was skulking about it. Rip called him by name; but the cur snarled, showed his teeth, and passed on. This was an unkind cut, indeed. "My very dog," sighed poor Rip, "has forgotten me!"

He entered the house, which, to tell the truth, Dame Van Winkle had always kept in neat order. It was empty, forlorn, and apparently abandoned. This desolateness overcame all his connubial fears. He called loudly for his wife and children: the lonely chambers rang for a moment with his voice, and then all again was silence.

He now hurried forth, and hastened to his old resort, the village inn; but it, too, was gone. A large, rickety, wooden building stood in its place, with great, gaping windows, some of them broken and mended with old hats and petticoats; and over the door was painted, "The Union Hotel, by Jonathan Doolittle." Instead of the great tree that used to shelter the quiet little Dutch inn of yore, there now was reared a tall, naked pole, with some-

thing on the top that looked like a red night-cap;[1] and from
it was fluttering a flag, on which was a singular assemblage of
stars and stripes.   All this was strange and incomprehensible.
He recognized on the sign, however, the ruby face of King
George, under which he had smoked so many a peaceful pipe;
but even this was singularly metamorphosed.   The red coat was
changed for one of blue and buff, a sword was held in the hand
instead of a scepter, the head was decorated with a cocked hat,
and underneath was painted in large characters, "General Washington."

There was, as usual, a crowd of folk about the door, but none
that Rip recollected.   The very character of the people seemed
changed.   There was a busy, bustling, disputatious tone about it,
instead of the accustomed phlegm and drowsy tranquillity.   He
looked in vain for the sage Nicholas Vedder, with his broad face,
double chin, and fair long pipe, uttering clouds of tobacco-smoke
instead of idle speeches; or Van Bummel, the schoolmaster, doling forth the contents of an ancient newspaper.   In place of
these, a lean, bilious-looking fellow, with his pockets full of
handbills, was haranguing vehemently about the rights of citizens,
election, members of Congress, liberty, Bunker's Hill,[2] heroes of
seventy-six, and other words, that were a perfect Babylonish
jargon to the bewildered Van Winkle.

The appearance of Rip, with his long, grizzled beard, his rusty
fowling-piece, his uncouth dress, and the army of women and
children that had gathered at his heels, soon attracted the attention of the tavern politicians.   They crowded round him, eying

---

[1] Cap of liberty worn in the Roman states by manumitted slaves.   It was
made thus according to a coin of Brutus after the death of Cæsar, and worn
by Brutus and his rebels, as a token of their *republican* sentiment.   Its shape
was copied from the Phrygian cap, which had become a symbol or emblem
of personal and political freedom.

[2] A celebrated height in Charlestown, Mass. (now a part of Boston), famous as the place where a battle was fought between the British and American
forces June 17, 1775.

him from head to foot with great curiosity. The orator bustled up to him, and, drawing him partly aside, inquired on which side he voted. Rip stared in vacant stupidity. Another short but busy little fellow pulled him by the arm, and, rising on tiptoe, inquired in his ear whether he was a Federal or a Democrat. Rip was equally at a loss to comprehend the question, when a knowing, self-important old gentleman in a sharp cocked hat made his way through the crowd, putting them to the right and left with his elbows as he passed, and, planting himself before Van Winkle,— with one arm akimbo, the other resting on his cane; his keen eyes and sharp hat penetrating, as it were, into his very soul,— demanded in an austere tone what brought him to the election with a gun on his shoulder and a mob at his heels, and whether he meant to breed a riot in the village. "Alas! gentlemen," cried Rip, somewhat dismayed, "I am a poor, quiet man, a native of the place, and a loyal subject to the King, God bless him!"

Here a general shout burst from the bystanders: "A Tory, a Tory! A spy! A refugee! Hustle him! Away with him!" It was with great difficulty that the self-important man in the cocked hat restored order, and, having assumed a tenfold austerity of brow, demanded again of the unknown culprit what he came there for, and whom he was seeking. The poor man humbly assured him that he meant no harm, but merely came there in search of some of his neighbors, who used to keep about the tavern.

"Well, who are they? Name them."

Rip bethought himself a moment, and inquired, "Where's Nicholas Vedder?"

There was a silence for a little while, when an old man replied in a thin, piping voice, "Nicholas Vedder! Why, he is dead and gone these eighteen years! There was a wooden tombstone in the churchyard that used to tell all about him, but that's rotten and gone, too."

"Where's Brom Dutcher?"

"Oh, he went off to the army in the beginning of the war.

Some say he was killed at the storming of Stony Point;[1] others say he was drowned in the squall at the foot of Anthony's Nose.[2] I don't know: he never came back again."

"Where's Van Bummel, the schoolmaster?"

"He went off to the wars, too, was a great militia general, and is now in Congress."

Rip's heart died away at hearing of these sad changes in his home and friends, and finding himself thus alone in the world. Every answer puzzled him, too, by treating of such enormous lapses of time, and of matters which he could not understand,—war, Congress, Stony Point. He had no courage to ask after any more friends, but cried out in despair, "Does nobody here know Rip Van Winkle?"

"Oh, Rip Van Winkle!" exclaimed two or three. "Oh, to be sure! that's Rip Van Winkle yonder, leaning against the tree."

Rip looked, and beheld a precise counterpart of himself, as he went up the mountain, apparently as lazy, and certainly as ragged. The poor fellow was now completely confounded. He doubted his own identity, and whether he was himself or another man. In the midst of his bewilderment, the man in the cocked hat demanded who he was, and what was his name.

"God knows!" exclaimed he, at his wits' end. "I'm not myself: I'm somebody else. That's me yonder. No, that's somebody else got into my shoes. I was myself last night: but I fell asleep on the mountain; and they've changed my gun; and everything's changed; and I'm changed; and I can't tell what's my name, or who I am!"

The bystanders began now to look at each other, nod, wink

---

[1] The well-known promontory on the Hudson River, forty-two miles north of New York, where, July 16, 1779, Gen. "Mad Anthony" Wayne took by storm the fort upon its rocky heights.

[2] Anthony's or St. Anthony's Nose is a headland fifty-seven miles from New York, on the east side of the Hudson, in Putnam County. It juts from the south side of Breakneck Hill at the north entrance of the Highlands.

significantly, and tap their fingers against their foreheads. There was a whisper, also, about securing the gun, and keeping the old fellow from doing mischief, at the very suggestion of which the self-important man in the cocked hat retired with some precipitation. At this critical moment a fresh, comely woman pressed through the throng to get a peep at the gray-bearded man. She had a chubby child in her arms, which, frightened at his looks, began to cry. "Hush, Rip!" cried she. "Hush, you little fool! The old man won't hurt you."

The name of the child, the air of the mother, the tone of her voice, all awakened a train of recollections in his mind. "What is your name, my good woman?" asked he.

"Judith Gardenier."

"And your father's name?"

"Ah, poor man, his name was Rip Van Winkle. It's twenty years since he went away from home with his gun, and never has been heard of since. His dog came home without him; but whether he shot himself, or was carried away by the Indians, nobody can tell. I was then but a little girl."

Rip had but one question more to ask, but he put it with a faltering voice : —

"Where's your mother?"

Oh, she too had died but a short time since. She broke a blood-vessel in a fit of passion at a New England peddler.

There was a drop of comfort, at least, in this intelligence. The honest man could contain himself no longer. He caught his daughter and her child in his arms. "I am your father!" cried he, — "young Rip Van Winkle once, old Rip Van Winkle now! Does nobody know poor Rip Van Winkle?"

All stood amazed, until an old woman, tottering out from among the crowd, put her hand to her brow, and, peering under it in his face for a moment, exclaimed, "Sure enough! It is Rip Van Winkle! It is himself! Welcome home again, old neighbor! Why, where have you been these twenty long years?"

Rip's story was soon told, for the whole twenty years had been to him but as one night.   The neighbors stared when they heard it.   Some were seen to wink at each other, and put their tongues in their cheeks; and the self-important man in the cocked hat, who, when the alarm was over, had returned to the field, screwed down the corners of his mouth, and shook his head, upon which there was a general shaking of the head throughout the assemblage.

It was determined, however, to take the opinion of old Peter Vanderdonk, who was seen slowly advancing up the road.   He was a descendant of the historian of that name, who wrote one of the earliest accounts of the province.   Peter was the most ancient inhabitant of the village, and well versed in all the wonderful events and traditions of the neighborhood.   He recollected Rip at once, and corroborated his story in the most satisfactory manner.   He assured the company that it was a fact, handed down from his ancestor the historian, that the Catskill Mountains had always been haunted by strange beings; that it was affirmed that the great Hendrick Hudson,[1] the first discoverer of the river and country, kept a kind of vigil there every twenty years, with his crew of the Half-moon,[2] being permitted in this way to revisit the scenes of his enterprise, and keep a guardian eye upon the river, and the great city called by his name; that his father had once seen them in their old Dutch dresses, playing at ninepins in the hollow of the mountain; and that he himself had heard, one summer afternoon, the sound of their balls, like distant peals of thunder.

To make a long story short, the company broke up, and returned to the more important concerns of the election.   Rip's daughter took him home to live with her.   She had a snug, well-furnished house, and a stout, cheery farmer for a husband, whom Rip recollected for one of the urchins that used to climb upon his back.   As to Rip's son and heir, who was the ditto of himself, seen leaning against the tree, he was employed to work on the farm, but evinced an hereditary disposition to attend to anything else but his business.

---

[1] See Note 1, p. 96.   [2] Hendrick Hudson's ship.

Rip now resumed his old walks and habits. He soon found many of his former cronies, though all rather the worse for the wear and tear of time, and preferred making friends among the rising generation, with whom he soon grew into great favor.

Having nothing to do at home, and being arrived at that happy age when a man can do nothing with impunity, he took his place once more on the bench at the inn door, and was reverenced as one of the patriarchs of the village, and a chronicle of the old times "before the war." It was some time before he could get into the regular track of gossip, or could be made to comprehend the strange events that had taken place during his torpor,— how that there had been a revolutionary war; that the country had thrown off the yoke of old England, and that, instead of being a subject of his Majesty George III., he was now a free citizen of the United States. Rip, in fact, was no politician,— the changes of states and empires made but little impression on him,— but there was one species of despotism under which he had long groaned, and that was, petticoat government. Happily, that was at an end. He had got his neck out of the yoke of matrimony, and could go in and out whenever he pleased, without dreading the tyranny of Dame Van Winkle. Whenever her name was mentioned, however, he shook his head, shrugged his shoulders, and cast up his eyes; which might pass either for an expression of resignation to his fate, or joy at his deliverance.

He used to tell his story to every stranger that arrived at Mr. Doolittle's hotel. He was observed at first to vary on some points every time he told it, which was doubtless owing to his having so recently awaked. It at last settled down precisely to the tale I have related; and not a man, woman, or child in the neighborhood but knew it by heart. Some always pretended to doubt the reality of it, and insisted that Rip had been out of his head, and that this was one point on which he always remained flighty. The old Dutch inhabitants, however, almost universally gave it full credit. Even to this day they never hear a thunderstorm of a summer afternoon about the Catskill, but they say Hendrick Hudson and his crew are at their game of ninepins; and it is a common wish of all hen-pecked husbands in the neighborhood, when life hangs heavy on their hands, that they might have a quieting draught out of Rip Van Winkle's flagon.

NOTE.

THE foregoing tale, one would suspect, had been suggested to Mr. Knickerbocker by a little German superstition about the Emperor Frederick *der Rothbart* and the Kyphäuser Mountain; the subjoined note, however, which he had appended to the tale, shows that it is an absolute fact, narrated with his usual fidelity.

"The story of Rip Van Winkle may seem incredible to many; but nevertheless I give it my full belief, for I know the vicinity of our old Dutch settlements to have been very subject to marvelous events and appearances. Indeed, I have heard many stranger stories than this, in the villages along the Hudson, all of which were too well authenticated to admit of a doubt. I have even talked with Rip Van Winkle myself, who, when last I saw him, was a very venerable old man, and so perfectly rational and consistent on every other point, that I think no conscientious person could refuse to take this into the bargain; nay, I have seen a certificate on the subject taken before a country justice and signed with a cross, in the justice's own handwriting. The story, therefore, is beyond the possibility of doubt."

POSTSCRIPT.

The following are traveling notes from a memorandum-book of Mr. Knickerbocker: —

"The Kaatsberg, or Catskill Mountains, have always been a region full of fable. The Indians considered them the abode of spirits, who influenced the weather, spreading sunshine or clouds over the landscape, and sending good or bad hunting seasons. They were ruled by an old squaw spirit, said to be their mother. She dwelt on the highest peak of the Catskills, and had charge of the doors of day and night to open and shut them at the proper hour. She hung up the new moons in the skies, and cut up the old ones into stars. In times of drought, if properly propitiated, she would spin light summer clouds out of cobwebs and morning dew, and send them off from the crest of the mountain, flake after flake, like flakes of carded cotton, to float in the air; until, dissolved by the heat of the sun, they would fall in gentle showers, causing the grass to spring, the fruits to ripen, and the corn to grow an inch an hour. If displeased, however, she would brew up clouds black as ink, sitting in the midst of them like a bottle-bellied spider in the midst of its web; and when these clouds broke, woe betide the valleys!

"In old times, say the Indian traditions, there was a kind of Monitou, or Spirit, who kept about the wildest recesses of the Catskill Mountains, and took a mischievous pleasure in wreaking all kinds of evils and vexations upon the redmen. Sometimes he would assume the form of a bear, a panther, or a deer, lead the bewildered hunter a weary chase through tangled forests and among ragged rocks, and then spring off with a loud ' ho, ho!' leaving him aghast on the brink of a beetling precipice or raging torrent."

Danl. Webster

THE ORATIONS ON

BUNKER HILL MONUMENT
THE CHARACTER OF WASHINGTON
AND THE LANDING AT PLYMOUTH

BY

DANIEL WEBSTER

NEW YORK ·:· CINCINNATI ·:· CHICAGO
AMERICAN BOOK COMPANY

INTRODUCTION.

IT is a fact worthy of notice that, among all the masters of eloquence known to history, only four have produced works which have been generally recognized as contributions to the permanent literature of the world. These were Demosthenes in ancient Athens, Cicero in old Rome, Edmund Burke in Great Britain, and Daniel Webster in America. A comparison of the public discourses of these four great orators reveals, of course, many differences resulting from the diversity of race, time, circumstance, and the character of the audiences to whom they were addressed. A closer examination, however, will disclose numerous similarities in their fundamental construction, going far to show that the principles of true eloquence are always and everywhere the same, and that the art which swayed the minds of multitudes of men twenty centuries ago remains in essential points as unchanged as human thought itself. Between the orations of Demosthenes, so distinctively ancient and Grecian, and those of Webster, so distinctively modern and American, one may detect a striking resemblance. Both are characterized by the same sustained appeal to the understanding and by the same clear-cut, vigorous, and perfectly intelligible course of reasoning. In their unadorned simplicity each is the work of a sculptor rather than painter. "To test Webster's oratory, which has ever been very attractive to me," said the late Dr. Francis Lieber, "I read a portion of my favorite speeches of Demosthenes, and then read, always aloud, parts of Webster; then returned to the Athenian: and Webster stood the test." This resemblance was not the result of any study of ancient models on Mr. Webster's part, nor of any conscious or unconscious effort to imitate the masterpieces of Athenian eloquence. It was due rather to a similarity of intellectual powers wholly independent of time, or race, or other environment.

The quality of Webster's imagination, which was of an historical rather than poetic cast, had much to do with the power and peculiar charm of his oratory. But it was his simplicity of diction, and his perfect mastery of pure, idiomatic English, which gave to his discourses their distinctive classic elegance, and made them worthy of a permanent place in our literature. As specimens, therefore, of a correct, clear, and vigorous style of composition, full of warmth and vitality, these orations are worthy of the most careful attention of every one who would perfect himself in the use of the English tongue; as notable examples of persuasive discourse, logical, forcible, and convincing, they especially commend themselves to those who aspire to distinction as public speakers; as containing lessons of the purest and most disinterested patriotism, they appeal to Americans everywhere, and should be read and studied by every American youth.

Daniel Webster was born in Salisbury (now Franklin), N.H., Jan. 18, 1782. His father, who was a farmer, had served as a soldier in both the French and Indian and the Revolutionary Wars, and later became a member of the State Legislature, and judge of the county court. Being brought up in poverty, in a region at that time the very outskirts of civilization, the boy had none of the opportunities which are now supposed to be indispensable to the making of a great man. His mother taught him to read, and as the schools which he attended during his childhood were extremely inefficient, it is probable that the best part of his early education was acquired at home. Being a delicate child, he was generally exempt from the hard tasks required of other boys in his condition of life, and, while much of his time was devoted to play, he developed a passionate eagerness for books. " I read what I could get to read," he says, "went to school when I could, and when not at school was a farmer's youngest boy, not good for much, for want of health and strength, but expected to do something. In those boyish days there were two things which I did dearly love,—reading and playing, passions which did not cease to struggle when boyhood was over, (have they yet altogether ?) and in regard to which neither *cita mors* nor the *victoria laeta* could be said of either."

When fourteen years of age, he was sent to the Phillips Exeter Academy. There he made his first acquaintance with the world, suffering much from the ridicule of his schoolmates, to whom his rustic clothes and uncouth manners were a source of great merriment. Although he made rapid progress in his studies, his lack of self-confidence was such, that he found it impossible to stand up and "speak a piece" before the school. At the end of nine months it was thought best that he should return home; and his father made arrangements whereby he should continue his studies under the tuition of a clergyman, the Rev. Samuel Wood, at Boscawen. This change was made in order that the lad might the more quickly complete his preparation for college; for, notwithstanding the poverty of the family, his father had decided to give him as thorough an education as was then available. He remained with Dr. Wood only six months, and in August, 1797, contrived to enter Dartmouth College, from which he was duly graduated in 1801. The college was at that time scarcely equal in efficiency to any well-equipped high school of the present day; and Webster's scholarship was neither extensive nor profound. He read everything that came to hand, and whatever was worthy of remembrance he never forgot. He acquired a fair knowledge of Latin literature, and gained a smattering of Greek and mathematics. He was not only considered the best general scholar in the college, but he was looked upon by both the faculty and the students as a remarkable man with an extraordinary career before him. He soon overcame the boyish timidity which had been so much in his way at Exeter, and developed an especial inclination for public speaking. Indeed, the fame of his eloquence extended beyond the college walls; and in 1800 he was invited by the towns-people of Hanover to deliver the Fourth-of-July oration in their village. He had not then completed his eighteenth year; yet in that youthful speech, his first public utterance on questions of national import, there was a distinct foreshadowing of the enduring work which he was afterwards to perform for his countrymen and the world. It was, of course, crude and imitative, as would be expected of a boy; its language was florid in the extreme, and its general style was that of the " spread eagle," full of bombast and figures of rhetoric; but in its thought and leading purpose there breathed the same manly, patriotic spirit that runs through all his maturer utterances, and distinguishes them from the commonplace oratory of political demagogues.

Immediately after leaving college, Mr. Webster began the study of law in the office of Thomas W. Thompson of Salisbury; but, wishing to earn money to help his elder brother

Ezekiel to go through college, he soon afterwards went to Frye-
burg, Me., and took charge of a small academy there. In the
following year he returned to Salisbury, and remained with Mr.
Thompson until 1804; then, desiring better opportunities for
extending his legal knowledge, he went to Boston, where he entered the office of Christopher Gore, and where, in 1805, he was
admitted to the bar. He began practicing in Boscawen; and in
1807, having built up a fairly good business there, he turned it
over to his brother Ezekiel, and removed to Portsmouth, then
the capital of the State. Being now fairly established in his profession, he was married in 1808 to Grace Fletcher of Hopkin-
ton. He soon distinguished himself as the foremost lawyer in
the State, and attracted much attention by his eloquent utterances in opposing the declaration of war against Great Britain.
In 1812 he was elected to Congress by the Federalists, and on
taking his seat was placed on the Committee on Foreign Affairs.
The first public act which brought him into prominence as a
member of Congress was his introduction of a series of resolutions calling for an inquiry concerning the announcement to the
United States of the revocation of Napoleon's decrees against
American shipping. This was followed a few months later by
his first great speech in the House,—a speech in opposition
to a bill for the encouragement of enlistments. In 1814 he
was reëlected to Congress; and in 1816, at the expiration of his
second term, he removed to Boston, where for seven years he
devoted himself exclusively to the practice of his profession. In
1818, by his management of the celebrated Dartmouth College
case, he achieved a success which not only placed him at the
head of the American bar, but gave him great prominence as an
able exponent and uncompromising defender of the Federal Con-

stitution. The Legislature of New Hampshire had passed an act virtually abrogating the original charter of the college, and providing for the appointment of a new board of trustees. The old board contested the legality of this act; and a suit against the new board, in action of trover for the college seal, was carried to the Superior Court of the State, where it was decided in favor of the defendants. Thereupon the case was carried to the Supreme Court of the United States, where, through Mr. Webster's management, the judgment of the State court was reversed, and the act of the State Legislature was declared to be a violation of that clause of the Federal Constitution which prohibits the States from passing laws in impairment of contracts. The decision was of national importance, since it "went further, perhaps, than any other in our history towards limiting State sovereignty, and extending the jurisdiction of the Federal Supreme Court."

On Dec. 22, 1820, the two hundredth anniversary of the landing of the Pilgrims, Mr. Webster delivered his famous discourse on the " First Settlement of New England,"—the first of those great efforts which placed him among the foremost orators of the world. In 1822 he was again elected a representative to Congress, this time from Boston; and in 1824 and 1826 he was reëlected. In 1827 he resigned his membership in the House to accept a seat in the Senate, where he remained, by successive reëlections, until 1841. His oration on the laying of the corner stone of Bunker Hill Monument, in 1825, and that on Adams and Jefferson (1826), are among the noblest historical addresses ever delivered. "The spirit of these orations is that of the broadest patriotism enlightened by a clear perception of the fundamental importance of the Federal union between the States, and an ever-present consciousness of the mighty future of our

country, and its moral significance in the history of the world."
In the Bunker Hill oration he appeared at his best. His style
had been perfected, and he "touched his highest point in the
difficult task of commemorative oratory." Eighteen years later,
upon the completion of the monument, he was called upon to
deliver a second address at the same place and upon the same
theme. This later effort, although it failed to attain to the massive dignity and grandeur of the first, must always be regarded as
one of the finest examples of patriotic oratory to which Americans
have ever listened.

From the beginning of his career in the United States Senate,
Mr. Webster was naturally recognized as one of the most influ-
ential men in the nation, and, had he been more distinctively a
partisan, it is not improbable that he would eventually have
occupied the President's chair. But his patriotism was superior
to personal ambition ; and his powers as a statesman and orator,
instead of being directed to the aggrandizement of the party with
which he was affiliated, were devoted to the defense of the Constitution and the preservation of the Union. In 1830 he delivered his celebrated second speech on Foote's resolution, generally known as the " Reply to Hayne," in which he reached the
culmination of his career as an orator. It was delivered in refutation of a speech by Mr. Hayne accusing the New-England
States of attempting to aggrandize themselves at the expense of
all the rest of the Union, and defending South Carolina in her
proposed policy of nullification. Although Mr. Webster's fame
extended in the years which followed, and he made many other
speeches, he never again attained to so high a point as in that
remarkable and memorable discourse. It was a speech for
which, as he himself said, his whole life had been in a certain

sense a preparation.   Of all the speeches ever made in Congress there has probably never been another that has been so widely read, or has had so great influence in the shaping of men's thoughts.   In 1841 Mr. Webster was appointed Secretary of State by President Harrison, and upon the death of the latter he was continued in office by President Tyler until after the completion of the famous Ashburton Treaty with Great Britain, in 1842.   He then returned to the practice of law in Boston; but in 1844 he was again appointed to the Senate, where he distinguished himself by opposing the admission of Texas as a slave State, and strenuously combating the prosecution of the Mexican War.   In 1848 and again in 1852 he was a candidate before the national convention of Whigs for the nomination to the Presidency, but was defeated in the first case by General Taylor and in the second by General Scott.   In 1850, led by a zealous desire to promote peace between the opposing political factions, he was induced to give his adhesion to Clay's "compromise measures," and on the 7th of March delivered his last great speech,—a speech in which he favored the enforcement of the Fugitive Slave Law, and opposed the Wilmot Proviso for the exclusion of slavery from the new Territories thereafter acquired by the United States.   This speech was a great disappointment to his friends, and lost him the support and confidence of the Whig party.   In the latter part of the same year, however, he was appointed Secretary of State by President Fillmore.   This position he held until May, 1852, when he resigned on account of ill health, and retired to his home at Marshfield, Mass., where he died on the 24th of October in the same year.

In the great influence which Mr. Webster, as a public speaker, wielded over the minds of his hearers, he was aided by his remarkable physical attributes. He possessed in a wonderful degree an indefinable personal magnetism which impressed every one with a sense of his greatness. His face, his eyes, his voice, were such that whoever looked upon him and heard him speak, felt intuitively that he was a man of most extraordinary powers. Sydney Smith, when he saw him, exclaimed, " Good heavens! he is a small cathedral by himself; " and Carlyle, writing of him, said, " He is a magnificent specimen. As a logic fencer or parliamentary Hercules, one would incline to back him at first sight against all the extant world. The tanned complexion; the amorphous crag-like face; the dull black eyes under the precipice of brows, like dull anthracite furnaces needing only to be blown; the mastiff mouth accurately closed,—I have not traced so much of *silent Berserker rage* that I remember of in any man."

Of the quality of Webster's oratory, the Hon. Rufus Choate says, " His multiform eloquence became at once so much accession to permanent literature, in the strictest sense solid, attractive, and rich. Recall what pervaded all these forms of display, and every effort in every form: that union of naked intellect, in its largest measure, which penetrates to the exact truth of the matter in hand by intuition or by inference, and discerns everything which may make it intelligible, probable, and credible to another, with an emotional and moral nature profound, passionate, and ready to kindle, and with imagination enough to supply a hundredfold more of illustration and aggrandizement than his taste suffered him to accept; that union of greatness of soul with depth of heart which made his speaking almost more an exhibition of character than of mere genius; the style not merely pure, clear Saxon, but so constructed, so numerous as far as becomes prose, so forcible, so abounding in unlabored felicities, the words so choice, the epithet so pictured, the matter absolute truth, or the most exact and spacious resemblance the human wit can devise; the treatment of the subject, if you have regard to the kind of truth he had to handle,—political, ethical, legal,—as deep as Paley's, or Locke's, or Butler's, . . . yet that depth and that completeness of sense made transparent as crystal waters, raised on winged language, vivified, fused, and poured along in a tide of emotion fervid, and incapable to be withstood."

The history of Bunker Hill Monument and of the circumstances attending the delivery of Webster's famous orations—the one at the laying of its corner stone, the other at its completion—may be briefly narrated.

Gen. Joseph Warren, the hero of the battle of Bunker Hill, and the first prominent martyr of the Revolutionary War, was buried upon the hill on the day following the action, June 18, 1775. Early in the following year the Massachusetts Lodge of Masons, of which he had been the presiding officer, applied to the Provisional Government of the Colony for permission to take up his remains, and inter them with the usual ceremonies and solemnities of the order. The request was granted, on condition that nothing should be done that would prevent the government from erecting at some future time a monument to his memory. This may be regarded as the first movement made towards commemorating in any way the historic struggle on Bunker Hill; and yet, although a funeral procession was formed, and a fitting eulogy on Gen. Warren was delivered, no measures were taken towards the building of a monument.

On the 8th of April, 1777, however, a resolution was adopted by the Continental Congress, directing that monuments should be erected to Gen. Warren in Boston and to Gen. Mercer at Fredericksburg; but no steps were ever taken towards the carrying out of this resolution.

In 1794 the lodge of Masons at Charlestown decided to erect a monument to Gen. Warren at their own expense. Land for that purpose was donated to the lodge by the Hon. James Russell of Charlestown, and the monument was dedicated with appropriate ceremonies on the 2d of December of the same year. This monument was a wooden pillar, eighteen feet in height, raised on a pedestal eight feet square, at an elevation or ten feet from the ground. On the summit of the pillar was a gilt urn, and on the south side of the pedestal an appropriate inscription was engraved.

It was not until still thirty years later that any decisive steps were taken towards the building of a monument which should commemorate in a general way the battle of Bunker Hill, and should stand as the nation's expression of honor and gratitude to those who fell there in the defense of American liberty. In 1824 an association was formed, under the leadership of William Tudor, Esq., to whose enthusiasm and perseverance the final success of the undertaking was largely due. After various private conferences among those who were most deeply interested in the project, it was decided to lay the corner stone of the monument on the 17th of June, 1825, the fiftieth anniversary of the battle; and, in order to excite enthusiasm in favor of the work, Gen. Lafayette, at that time the nation's guest, was invited to be present, and participate in the ceremonies. Free transportation was offered to all surviving soldiers of the Revolution, and every effort was made to enlist a national interest in the patriotic occasion.

"The celebration," says Mr. Frothingham, "was unequaled in magnificence by anything of the kind that had been seen in

New England. The morning proved propitious. The air was cool, the sky was clear, and timely showers the previous day had brightened the vesture of Nature into its loveliest hue. Delighted thousands flocked into Boston to bear a part in the proceedings, or to witness the spectacle. At about ten o'clock a procession moved from the State House towards Bunker Hill. The military, in their fine uniforms, formed the van. About two hundred veterans of the Revolution, of whom forty were survivors of the battle, rode in barouches next to the escort. These venerable men, the relics of a past generation, with emaciated frames, tottering limbs, and trembling voices, constituted a touching spectacle. Some wore, as honorable decorations, their old fighting equipments; and some bore the scars of still more honorable wounds. Glistening eyes constituted their answer to the enthusiastic cheers of the grateful multitudes who lined their pathway, and cheered their progress. To this patriot band succeeded the Bunker Hill Monument Association; then the Masonic fraternity, in their splendid regalia, thousands in number; then Lafayette, continually welcomed by tokens of love and gratitude, and the invited guests; then a long array of societies, with their various badges and banners. It was a splendid procession, and of such length that the front nearly reached Charlestown Bridge ere the rear had left Boston Common. It proceeded to Breed's Hill, where the Grand Master of the Freemasons, the President of the Monument Association, and Gen. Lafayette performed the ceremony of laying the corner stone in the presence of a vast concourse of people." The procession then moved to the northern declivity of the hill, where Mr. Webster delivered his oration to a large and appreciative audience.

When the corner stone of the Bunker Hill Monument was thus

laid in 1825, no definite plan for its construction had been decided upon. Among other designs for the proposed monument, one submitted by Solomon Willard, an architect of Boston, was finally adopted; and in 1827 the foundation was laid and the work of construction begun. The funds on hand, amounting to about $55,000, were soon exhausted, however, and in the following year the work was temporarily abandoned. In 1834 a renewed effort was made, a considerable amount of money was raised by subscription, and the building of the great stone shaft was renewed. But the committee having the affair in charge soon found itself without further available means, and progress was again suspended. In 1840 the ladies of Boston and the vicinity took hold of the enterprise. A fair was held in Faneuil Hall, to which every woman in the United States had been invited to contribute, and every effort was made to increase the list of subscriptions. The result was, that a contract was soon afterwards entered into with Mr. Savage of Boston, to finish the monument for $43,000. The work was pushed forward with all reasonable dispatch, and the last stone was raised to the apex at six o'clock in the morning of July 23, 1842.

The monument, which is in the form of an obelisk, is built of Quincy granite, is thirty feet in diameter at the base, and about fifteen feet at the top of the truncated part. It consists of ninety courses of stone, six of them below the ground, and eighty-four above. It was intended that it should be two hundred and twenty feet high; but the precise height is two hundred and twenty-one feet. The observatory at the top is seventeen feet high, and eleven feet in diameter. The cap stone, or apex, is a single stone four feet square at the base, and three feet six inches in height, weighing two tons and a half.

It was arranged by the directors that the completion of the work should be celebrated on the 17th of the following June, the sixty-eighth anniversary of the battle; and Mr. Webster was invited to deliver the oration. "Many circumstances," says Edward Everett, "conspired to increase the interest of the occasion. . . . The President of the United States and his Cabinet had accepted invitations to be present; delegations of the descendants of New England were present from the remotest parts of the Union; one hundred and eight surviving veterans of the Revolution, among whom were some who were in the battle of Bunker Hill, imparted a touching interest to the scene. . . . Mr. Webster was stationed upon an elevated platform in front of the audience and of the monument towering in the background. According to Mr. Frothingham's estimate, a hundred thousand persons were gathered about the spot, and nearly half that number are supposed to have been within the reach of the orator's voice. The ground rises slightly between the platform and the Monument Square, so that the whole of this immense concourse —compactly crowded together, breathless with attention, swayed by one sentiment of admiration and delight—was within the full view of the speaker. The position and the occasion were the height of the moral sublime."

THE BUNKER HILL MONUMENT.

AN ADDRESS DELIVERED AT THE LAYING OF THE CORNER
STONE OF THE BUNKER HILL MONUMENT AT
CHARLESTOWN, MASS., ON THE 17TH
OF JUNE, 1825.

THIS uncounted multitude before me and around me proves the feeling which the occasion has excited. These thousands of human faces, glowing with sympathy and joy, and from the impulses of a common gratitude turned reverently to heaven in this spacious temple of the firmament, proclaim that the day, the place, and the purpose of our assembling, have made a deep impression on our hearts.

If, indeed, there be anything in local association fit to affect the mind of man, we need not strive to repress the emotions which agitate us. here. We are among the sepulchers of our fathers. We are on ground distinguished by their valor, their constancy, and the shedding of their blood. We are here, not to fix an uncertain date in our annals, nor to draw into notice an obscure and unknown spot. If our humble purpose had never been conceived, if we ourselves had never been born, the 17th of June, 1775, would have been a day on which all subsequent history would have poured its light, and the eminence where we stand, a point of attraction to the eyes of successive generations. But we are Americans. We live in what may be called the "early age" of this great continent; and we know that our posterity, through all time, are here to enjoy and suffer the allotments of humanity. We see before us a probable train of great events; we know that our own fortunes have been happily cast; and it is natural, therefore, that we should be moved by the contemplation of occurrences which have guided our destiny before many of us were born, and settled the condition in which we should pass that portion of our existence which God allows to men on earth.

We do not read even of the discovery of this continent without feeling something of a personal interest in the event, without being reminded how much it has affected our own fortunes and our own existence. It would be still more unnatural for us, therefore, than for others, to contemplate with unaffected minds that interesting, I may say that most touching and pathetic scene, when the great discoverer of America stood on the deck of his shattered bark, the shades of night falling on the sea, yet no man sleeping; tossed on the billows of an unknown ocean, yet the stronger billows of alternate hope and despair tossing his own troubled thoughts; extending forward his harassed frame, straining westward his anxious and eager eyes, till Heaven at last granted him a moment of rapture and ecstasy, in blessing his vision with the sight of the unknown world.

Nearer to our times, more closely connected with our fates, and therefore still more interesting to our feelings and affections, is the settlement of our own country by colonists from England. We cherish every memorial of these worthy ancestors; we celebrate their patience and fortitude; we admire their daring enterprise; we teach our children to venerate their piety; and we are justly proud of being descended from men who have set the world an example of founding civil institutions on the great and united principles of human freedom and human knowledge. To us their children, the story of their labors and sufferings can never be without its interest. We shall not stand unmoved on the shores of Plymouth while the sea continues to wash it; nor will our brethren in another early and ancient Colony forget the place of its first establishment till their river shall cease to flow

by it.[1] No vigor of youth, no maturity of manhood, will lead
the nation to forget the spots where its infancy was cradled and
defended.

But the great event in the history of the continent, which we
are now met here to commemorate, that prodigy of modern
times, at once the wonder and the blessing of the world, is the
American Revolution. In a day of extraordinary prosperity and
happiness, of high national honor, distinction, and power, we are
brought together in this place by our love of country, by our
admiration of exalted character, by our gratitude for signal services and patriotic devotion.

The Society whose organ I am [2] was formed for the purpose
of rearing some honorable and durable monument to the memory
of the early friends of American independence. They have
thought that for this object no time could be more propitious
than the present prosperous and peaceful period, that no place
could claim preference over this memorable spot, and that no
day could be more auspicious to the undertaking than the anniversary of the battle which was here fought. The foundation of
that monument we have now laid. With solemnities [3] suited to
the occasion, with prayers to Almighty God for his blessing, and
in the midst of this cloud of witnesses, we have begun the work.

[1] As nearly every one of the Colonies was founded on the bank of a river,
it is not clear which is alluded to here. Edward Everett, whose edition of
the orations appeared while Webster was still living, mentions the settlement
of the Maryland Colony on the St. Mary's River. "The ‘Ark’ and the
‘Dove,’" he says, "are remembered with scarcely less interest by the descendants of the sister Colony than is the ‘Mayflower’ in New England,
which thirteen years earlier, at the same season of the year, bore thither the
Pilgrim Fathers."

[2] Mr. Webster was at that time president of the Bunker Hill Monument
Association, having been appointed to that position as the successor of Gov.
John Brooks, the first president.

[3] Besides the laying of the corner stone with Masonic ceremonies, there
was prayer by the Rev. Joseph Thaxter, and an ode was read by the Rev.
John Pierpont of Boston.

We trust it will be prosecuted, and that, springing from a broad foundation, rising high in massive solidity and unadorned grandeur, it may remain as long as Heaven permits the works of man to last, a fit emblem, both of the events in memory of which it is raised, and of the gratitude of those who have reared it.

We know, indeed, that the record of illustrious actions is most safely deposited in the universal remembrance of mankind. We know that if we could cause this structure to ascend, not only till it reached the skies, but till it pierced them, its broad surfaces could still contain but part of that which, in an age of knowledge, hath already been spread over the earth, and which history charges itself with making known to all future times. We know that no inscription on entablatures less broad than the earth itself can carry information of the events we commemorate where it has not already gone; and that no structure which shall not outlive the duration of letters and knowledge among men can prolong the memorial. But our object is, by this edifice, to show our own deep sense of the value and importance of the achievements of our ancestors, and, by presenting this work of gratitude to the eye, to keep alive similar sentiments, and to foster a constant regard for the principles of the Revolution. Human beings are composed not of reason only, but of imagination also, and sentiment; and that is neither wasted nor misapplied which is appropriated to the purpose of giving right direction to sentiments, and opening proper springs of feeling in the heart. Let it not be supposed that our object is to perpetuate national hostility, or even to cherish a mere military spirit. It is higher, purer, nobler. We consecrate our work to the spirit of national independence, and we wish that the light of peace may rest upon it forever. We rear a memorial of our conviction of that unmeasured benefit which has been conferred on our own land, and of the happy influences which have been produced, by the same events, on the general interests of mankind. We come, as Americans, to mark a spot which must forever be dear to us and our posterity. We wish that whosoever, in all coming time, shall turn his eye hither may behold that the place is not undistinguished where the first great battle of the Revolution was fought. We wish that this structure may proclaim the magnitude and importance of that event to every class and every age. We wish that infancy may learn the purpose of its erection from maternal lips, and that weary and withered age may behold it, and be solaced by the recollections which it suggests. We wish that labor may look up here, and be proud in the midst of its toil. We wish that in those days of disaster, which, as they come upon all nations, must be expected to come upon us also, desponding patriotism may turn its eyes hitherward, and be assured that the foundations of our national power are still strong. We wish that this column, rising towards heaven among the pointed spires of so many temples dedicated to God, may contribute also to produce in all minds a pious feeling of dependence and gratitude. We wish, finally, that the last object to the sight of him who leaves his native shore, and the first to gladden his who revisits it, may be something which shall remind him of the liberty and the glory of his country. Let it rise! let it rise till it meet the sun in his coming; let the earliest light of the morning gild it, and parting day linger and play on its summit.

We live in a most extraordinary age. Events so various and so important that they might crowd and distinguish centuries, are in our times compressed within the compass of a single life. When has it happened that history has had so much to record, in the same term of years, as since the 17th of June, 1775? Our own Revolution, which, under other circumstances, might itself have been expected to occasion a war of half a century, has been achieved, twenty-four sovereign and independent States erected, and a general government established over them, so safe, so wise, so free, so practical, that we might well wonder its establishment should have been accomplished so soon, were it not far the greater wonder that it should have been established at all. Two or three millions of people have been augmented to twelve, the great forests of the West prostrated beneath the arm of successful industry, and the dwellers on the banks of the Ohio and the Mississippi become the fellow citizens and neighbors of those who cultivate the hills of New England.[1] We have a commerce that leaves no sea unexplored, navies which take no law from superior force, revenues adequate to all the exigencies of government, almost without taxation, and peace with all nations, founded on equal rights and mutual respect.

Europe, within the same period, has been agitated by a mighty revolution [2] which, while it has been felt in the individual condition and happiness of almost every man, has shaken to the center her political fabric, and dashed against one another thrones which had stood tranquil for ages. On this our continent, our own example has been followed, and colonies have sprung up to be nations. Unaccustomed sounds of liberty and free government have reached us from beyond the track of the sun; [3] and at this moment the dominion of European power in this continent,[4] from the place where we stand to the south pole, is annihilated forever.

In the mean time, both in Europe and America, such has been the general progress of knowledge, such the improvement in legislation, in commerce, in the arts, in letters, and, above all, in liberal ideas and the general spirit of the age, that the whole world seems changed.

---

[1] This has been more than realized by the introduction of railroads, making the people even of the Pacific coast neighbors of the people of New England. Edward Everett mentions as an interesting circumstance, the fact that the first railroad on the Western continent was built for the purpose of aiding in the erection of this monument. It was a horse railroad from Quincy to Boston, and was used for transporting the blocks of granite from the quarries.

[2] The French Revolution and the wars resulting from it.

[3] The allusion is to the then recent establishment of republican governments in South America.

[4] The Monroe Doctrine, enunciated by President Monroe in his message to Congress in 1823, was virtually a declaration that no European power should be permitted to secure further dominion on the American continent.

Yet, notwithstanding that this is but a faint abstract of the things which have happened since the day of the battle of Bunker Hill, we are but fifty years removed from it; and we now stand here to enjoy all the blessings of our own condition, and to look abroad on the brightened prospects of the world, while we still have among us some of those who were active agents in the scenes of 1775, and who are now here, from every quarter of New England,[1] to visit once more, and under circumstances so affecting, — I had almost said so overwhelming, — this renowned theater of their courage and patriotism.

VENERABLE MEN, you have come down to us from a former generation. Heaven has bounteously lengthened out your lives, that you might behold this joyous day. You are now where you stood fifty years ago this very hour, with your brothers and your neighbors, shoulder to shoulder, in the strife for your country. Behold, how altered! The same heavens are indeed over your heads; the same ocean rolls at your feet: but all else how changed! You hear now no roar of hostile cannon, you see no mixed volumes of smoke and flame rising from burning Charlestown. The ground strewed with the dead and the dying; the impetuous charge; the steady and successful repulse; the loud call to repeated assault; the summoning of all that is manly to repeated resistance; a thousand bosoms freely and fearlessly bared in an instant to whatever of terror there may be in war and death, —all these you have witnessed, but you witness them no more. All is peace. The heights of yonder metropolis,[2] its towers and roofs, —which you then saw filled with wives and children and countrymen in distress and terror, and looking with unutterable emotions for the issue of the combat,—have presented you to-day with the sight of its whole happy population come out to welcome and greet you with a universal jubilee. Yonder proud ships, by a

[1] There were nearly two hundred of them, forty of whom had been in the battle of Bunker Hill.
[2] Boston.

felicity of position appropriately lying at the foot of this mount,[1]
and seeming fondly to cling around it, are not means of annoy-
ance to you, but your country's own means of distinction and
defense. All is peace; and God has granted you this sight of
your country's happiness ere you slumber in the grave. He has
allowed you to behold and to partake the reward of your patriotic toils; and he has allowed us, your sons and countrymen,
to meet you here, and in the name of the present generation, in
the name of your country, in the name of liberty, to thank you.

But, alas! you are not all here. Time and the sword have
thinned your ranks. Prescott, Putnam, Stark, Brooks, Read,
Pomeroy, Bridge, — our eyes seek for you in vain amid this broken
band. You are gathered to your fathers, and live only to your
country in her grateful remembrance and your own bright example. But let us not too much grieve that you have met the
common fate of men. You lived at least long enough to know
that your work had been nobly and successfully accomplished.
You lived to see your country's independence established, and
to sheathe your swords from war. On the light of Liberty you
saw arise the light of Peace, like

> "Another morn,
> Risen on mid noon;"[2]

and the sky on which you closed your eyes was cloudless.

But ah! him, the first great martyr[3] in this great cause;
him, the premature victim of his own self-devoting heart;
him, the head of our civil councils and the destined leader of
our military bands, whom nothing brought hither but the un-
quenchable fire of his own spirit; him, cut off by Providence

---

[1] The United States Navy Yard at Charlestown is situated at the base of
Bunker Hill.

[2] Paradise Lost, v. 310.

[3] Gen. Joseph Warren, born in 1741, was a man of fine culture and
unusual promise. He had been elected president of the Provincial Congress,
and was one of the most ardent patriots of the time.

in the hour of overwhelming anxiety and thick gloom, falling ere he saw the star of his country rise, pouring out his generous blood like water before he knew whether it would fertilize a land of freedom or of bondage, — how shall I struggle with the emotions that stifle the utterance of thy name! Our poor work may perish; but thine shall endure. This monument may molder away; the solid ground it rests upon may sink down to a level with the sea: but thy memory shall not fail. Wheresoever among men a heart shall be found that beats to the transports of patriotism and liberty, its aspirations shall be to claim kindred with thy spirit.

But the scene amidst which we stand does not permit us to confine our thoughts or our sympathies to those fearless spirits who hazarded or lost their lives on this consecrated spot. We have the happiness to rejoice here in the presence of a most worthy representation of the survivors of the whole Revolutionary army.

VETERANS, you are the remnant of many a well-fought field. You bring with you marks of honor from Trenton and Monmouth, from Yorktown, Camden, Bennington, and Saratoga. VETERANS OF HALF A CENTURY, when in your youthful days you put everything at hazard in your country's cause, — good as that cause was, and sanguine as youth is, — still your fondest hopes did not stretch onward to an hour like this. At a period to which you could not reasonably have expected to arrive, at a moment of national prosperity such as you could never have foreseen, you are now met here to enjoy the fellowship of old soldiers, and to receive the overflowings of a universal gratitude.

But your agitated countenances and your heaving breasts inform me that even this is not an unmixed joy. I perceive that a tumult of contending feelings rushes upon you. The images of the dead, as well as the persons of the living, present themselves before you. The scene overwhelms you, and I turn from it. May the Father of all mercies smile upon your declining years, and bless them! And when you shall here have ex-

changed your embraces, when you shall once more have pressed
the hands which have been so often extended to give succor in
adversity, or grasped in the exultation of victory, then look abroad
upon this lovely land which your young valor defended, and
mark the happiness with which it is filled ; yea, look abroad upon
the whole earth, and see what a name you have contributed to
give to your country, and what a praise you have added to freedom, and then rejoice in the sympathy and gratitude which beam
upon your last days from the improved condition of mankind !

The occasion does not require of me any particular account of
the battle of the 17th of June, 1775, nor any detailed narrative
of the events which immediately preceded it. These are famil-
iarly known to all. In the progress of the great and interesting
controversy, Massachusetts and the town of Boston had become
early and marked objects of the displeasure of the British Parliament. This had been manifested in the act for altering the government of the Province, and in that for shutting up the port of
Boston.[1] Nothing sheds more honor on our early history, and
nothing better shows how little the feelings and sentiments of the
Colonies were known or regarded in England, than the impression which these measures everywhere produced in America. It
had been anticipated that, while the Colonies in general would
be terrified by the severity of the punishment inflicted on Massachusetts, the other seaports would be governed by a mere spirit
of gain ; and that, as Boston was now cut off from all commerce,
the unexpected advantage which this blow on her was calculated
to confer on other towns would be greedily enjoyed. How mis-
erably such reasoners deceived themselves ! How little they
knew of the depth and the strength and the intenseness of that
feeling of resistance to illegal acts of power which possessed the
whole American people ! Everywhere the unworthy boon was

[1] The Boston Port Bill, passed by the British Parliament in 1774, declared
that port to be closed, and transferred the seat of colonial government to
Salem.

rejected with scorn. The fortunate occasion was seized everywhere, to show to the whole world that the Colonies were swayed
by no local interest, no partial interest, no selfish interest. The
temptation to profit by the punishment of Boston was strongest
to our neighbors of Salem. Yet Salem was precisely the place
where this miserable proffer was spurned in a tone of the most
lofty self-respect and the most indignant patriotism. "We are
deeply affected," said its inhabitants, "with the sense of our public calamities; but the miseries that are now rapidly hastening
on our brethren in the capital of the Province greatly excite our
commiseration. By shutting up the port of Boston, some imagine
that the course of trade might be turned hither and to our benefit; but we must be dead to every idea of justice, lost to all feelings of humanity, could we indulge a thought to seize on wealth,
and raise our fortunes, on the ruin of our suffering neighbors."
These noble sentiments were not confined to our immediate vicinity. In that day of general affection and brotherhood, the
blow given to Boston smote on every patriotic heart from one
end of the country to the other. Virginia and the Carolinas, as
well as Connecticut and New Hampshire, felt and proclaimed
the cause to be their own. The Continental Congress, then
holding its first session in Philadelphia, expressed its sympathy
for the suffering inhabitants of Boston; and addresses were
received from all quarters assuring them that the cause was a
common one, and should be met by common efforts and common sacrifices. The Congress of Massachusetts responded to
these assurances; and in an address to the Congress at Philadelphia, bearing the official signature (perhaps among the last) of
the immortal Warren, notwithstanding the severity of its suffering and the magnitude of the dangers which threatened it, it was
declared that this Colony "is ready at all times to spend and to
be spent in the cause of America."

But the hour drew nigh which was to put professions to the
proof, and to determine whether the authors of these mutual
pledges were ready to seal them in blood. The tidings of Lex-

ington and Concord had no sooner spread than it was universally felt that the time was at last come for action. A spirit pervaded all ranks, not transient, not boisterous, but deep, solemn, determined,

> "Totamque infusa per artus
> Mens agitat molem, et magno se corpore miscet." [1]

War on their own soil and at their own doors was, indeed, a strange work to the yeomanry of New England; but their consciences were convinced of its necessity, their country called them to it, and they did not withhold themselves from the perilous trial. The ordinary occupations of life were abandoned; the plow was stayed in the unfinished furrow; wives gave up their husbands, and mothers gave up their sons, to the battles of a civil war. Death might come, in honor, on the field; it might come, in disgrace, on the scaffold: for either and for both they were prepared. The sentiment of Quincy [2] was full in their hearts. "Blandishments," said that distinguished son of genius and patriotism, "will not fascinate us, nor will threats of a halter intimidate; for, under God, we are determined that wheresoever, whensoever, or howsoever we shall be called to make our exit, we will die free men."

The 17th of June saw the four New-England Colonies [3] standing here side by side to triumph or to fall together; and there was with them, from that moment to the end of the war, what I hope will remain with them forever, one cause, one country, one heart.

The battle of Bunker Hill was attended with the most impor-

---

[1] Æneid, Lib. VI. 725, William Morris's translation: —

> "One soul is shed through all,
> That quickeneth all the mass, and with the mighty thing is blent."

[2] Josiah Quincy, Jr. (born in 1744; died at sea, 1775), was one of the most energetic opponents of British usurpation, and with Warren and James Otis exerted an early and very great influence in favor of the freedom of the American Colonies.

[3] Massachusetts, New Hampshire, Rhode Island, Connecticut.

tant effects beyond its immediate results as a military engagement. It created at once a state of open, public war. There could now be no longer a question of proceeding against individuals as guilty of treason or rebellion. That fearful crisis was past. The appeal lay to the sword; and the only question was, whether the spirit and the resources of the people would hold out till the object should be accomplished. Nor were its general consequences confined to our own country. The previous proceedings of the Colonies, their appeals, resolutions, and addresses, had made their cause known to Europe. Without boasting, we may say that in no age or country has the public cause been maintained with more force of argument, more power of illustration, or more of that persuasion which excited feeling and elevated principle can alone bestow, than the Revolutionary state papers exhibit. These papers will forever deserve to be studied, not only for the spirit which they breathe, but for the ability with which they were written.

To this able vindication of their cause, the Colonies had now added a practical and severe proof of their own true devotion to it, and given evidence also of the power which they could bring to its support. All now saw that, if America fell, she would not fall without a struggle. Men felt sympathy and regard, as well as surprise, when they beheld these infant states, remote, unknown, unaided, encounter the power of England, and, in the first considerable battle, leave more of their enemies dead on the field, in proportion to the number of combatants,[1] than had been recently known to fall in the wars of Europe.

Information of these events, circulating throughout the world, at length reached the ears of one who now hears me.[2] He has

---

1 There were engaged in the battle about 1,500 Americans and 2,500 British. The losses of the Americans were 115 killed, 305 wounded, 30 captured: total 450. The British lost 206 killed, 828 wounded: total 1,054.

2 " Among the earliest of the arrangements for the celebration of the 17th of June, 1825, was the invitation to Gen. Lafayette to be present; and he had so timed his progress through the other States as to return to Massachusetts in season for the great occasion."—EVERETT.

not forgotten the emotion which the fame of Bunker Hill and the name of Warren excited in his youthful breast.

SIR, we are assembled to commemorate the establishment of great public principles of liberty, and to do honor to the distinguished dead. The occasion is too severe for eulogy of the living. But, sir, your interesting relation to this country, the peculiar circumstances which surround you and surround us, call on me to express the happiness which we derive from your presence and aid in this solemn commemoration.

Fortunate, fortunate man!—with what measure of devotion will you not thank God for the circumstances of your extraordinary life! You are connected with both hemispheres and with two generations. Heaven saw fit to ordain that the electric spark of liberty should be conducted, through you, from the New World to the Old; and we who are now here to perform this duty of patriotism have all of us long ago received it in charge from our fathers to cherish your name and your virtues. You will account it an instance of your good fortune, sir, that you crossed the seas to visit us at a time which enables you to be present at this solemnity.[1] You now behold the field the renown of which reached you in the heart of France, and caused a thrill in your ardent bosom. You see the lines of the little redoubt thrown up by the incredible diligence of Prescott, defended to the last extremity by his lion-hearted valor, and within which the corner stone of our monument has now taken its position. You see where Warren fell, and where Parker, Gardner, McCleary, Moore, and other early patriots fell with him. Those who survived that day, and whose lives have been prolonged to the present hour, are now around you. Some of them you have known in the trying scenes of the war. Behold! they now

1 Gen. Lafayette made a tour of the United States as the "nation's guest" in 1824–25. His name stood at the head of the subscriptions for the Bunker Hill Monument; and he wrote, "In all my travels through the country, I have made Bunker Hill my polestar."

stretch forth their feeble arms to embrace you. Behold! they raise their trembling voices to invoke the blessing of God on you and yours forever.

Sir, you have assisted us in laying the foundation of this structure. You have heard us rehearse, with our feeble commendation, the names of departed patriots. Monuments and eulogy belong to the dead.[1] We give them this day to Warren and his associates. On other occasions they have been given to your more immediate companions in arms, to Washington, to Greene, to Gates, to Sullivan, and to Lincoln. We have become reluctant to grant these, our highest and last honors, further. We would gladly hold them yet back from the little remnant of that immortal band. *Serus in cœlum redeas.*[2] Illustrious as are your merits, yet far, oh, very far distant be the day[3] when any inscription shall bear your name, or any tongue pronounce its eulogy!

The leading reflection to which this occasion seems to invite us respects the great changes which have happened in the fifty years since the battle of Bunker Hill was fought. And it peculiarly marks the character of the present age, that, in looking at these changes and in estimating their effect on our condition, we are obliged to consider, not what has been done in our own country only, but in others also: In these interesting times, while nations are making separate and individual advances in improvement, they make, too, a common progress, like vessels on a common tide, propelled by the gales at different rates, according to their several structure and management, but all moved forward by one mighty current, strong enough to bear onward whatever does not sink beneath it.

---

1 " The thrilling eloquence of the address to the old soldiers of Bunker Hill, and of the apostrophe to Warren, and the superb reservation of eulogy with which he spoke of and to Gen. Lafayette, were perhaps unequaled, surely never surpassed, by Webster on any other occasion."—TICKNOR: *Life of Webster,* ii. p. 252.

2 " Late into heaven may you return."—HORACE, I. ii. 45.

3 Lafayette died May 20, 1834.

3

A chief distinction of the present day is a community of opinions and knowledge amongst men in different nations, existing in a degree heretofore unknown. Knowledge has in our time triumphed, and is triumphing, over distance, over difference of languages, over diversity of habits, over prejudice, and over bigotry. The civilized and Christian world is fast learning the great lesson, that difference of nation does not imply necessary hostility, and that all contact need not be war. The whole world is becoming a common field for intellect to act in. Energy of mind, genius, power, wheresoever it exists, may speak out in any tongue, and the *world* will hear it. A great chord of sentiment and feeling runs through two continents, and vibrates over both. Every breeze wafts intelligence from country to country; every wave rolls it; all give it forth, and all in turn receive it. There is a vast commerce of ideas; there are marts and exchanges for intellectual discoveries, and a wonderful fellowship of those individual intelligences which make up the mind and opinion of the age. Mind is the great lever of all things; human thought is the process by which human ends are ultimately answered; and the diffusion of knowledge, so astonishing in the last half century, has rendered innumerable minds, variously gifted by nature, competent to be competitors or fellow workers on the theater of intellectual operation.

From these causes, important improvements have taken place in the personal condition of individuals. Generally speaking, mankind are not only better fed and better clothed, but they are able also to enjoy more leisure; they possess more refinement and more self-respect. A superior tone of education, manners, and habits, prevails. This remark, most true in its application to our own country, is also partly true when applied elsewhere. It is proved by the vastly augmented consumption of those articles of manufacture and of commerce which contribute to the comforts and the decencies of life,—an augmentation which has far outrun the progress of population. And while the unexampled and almost incredible use of machinery would seem to supply the place of labor, labor still finds its occupation and its reward, so wisely has Providence adjusted men's wants and desires to their condition and their capacity.

Any adequate survey, however, of the progress made during the last half century in the polite and the mechanic arts, in machinery and manufactures, in commerce and agriculture, in letters and in science, would require volumes. I must abstain wholly from these subjects, and turn for a moment to the contemplation of what has been done on the great question of politics and government. This is the master topic of the age, and during the whole fifty years it has intensely occupied the thoughts of men. The nature of civil government, its ends and uses, have been canvassed and investigated, ancient opinions attacked and defended, new ideas recommended and resisted, by whatever power the mind of man could bring to the controversy. From the closet and the public halls, the debate has been transferred to the field; and the world has been shaken by wars of unexampled magnitude and the greatest variety of fortune. A day of peace has at length succeeded; and, now that the strife has subsided and the smoke cleared away, we may begin to see what has actually been done permanently changing the state and condition of human society. And, without dwelling on particular circumstances, it is most apparent, that, from the before-mentioned causes of augmented knowledge and improved individual condition, a real, substantial, and important change has taken place, and is taking place, highly favorable, on the whole, to human liberty and human happiness.

The great wheel of political revolution began to move in America. Here its rotation was guarded, regular, and safe. Transferred to the other continent, from unfortunate but natural causes, it received an irregular and violent impulse; it whirled along with a fearful celerity, till at length, like the chariot wheels in the races of antiquity, it took fire from the rapidity of its own motion, and blazed onward, spreading conflagration and terror around.[1]

[1] Alluding to the French Revolution (1793) and the Reign of Terror.

We learn from the result of this experiment how fortunate was our own condition, and how admirably the character of our people was calculated for setting the great example of popular governments. The possession of power did not turn the heads of the American people, for they had long been in the habit of exercising a great degree of self-control. Although the paramount authority of the parent state existed over them, yet a large field of legislation had always been open to our colonial assemblies. They were accustomed to representative bodies and the forms of free government; they understood the doctrine of the division of power among different branches, and the necessity of checks on each. The character of our countrymen, moreover, was sober, moral, and religious, and there was little in the change to shock their feelings of justice and humanity, or even to disturb an honest prejudice. We had no domestic throne to overturn, no privileged orders to cast down, no violent changes of property to encounter. In the American Revolution, no man sought or wished for more than to defend and enjoy his own. None hoped for plunder or for spoil. Rapacity was unknown to it; the ax was not among the instruments of its accomplishment; and we all know that it could not have lived a single day under any well-founded imputation of possessing a tendency adverse to the Christian religion.

It need not surprise us, that, under circumstances less auspicious, political revolutions elsewhere, even when well intended, have terminated differently. It is, indeed, a great achievement, it is the master work of the world, to establish governments entirely popular on lasting foundations; nor is it easy, indeed, to introduce the popular principle at all into governments to which it has been altogether a stranger. It cannot be doubted, however, that Europe has come out of the contest, in which she has been so long engaged, with greatly superior knowledge, and, in many respects, in a highly improved condition. Whatever benefit has been acquired is likely to be retained, for it consists mainly in the acquisition of more enlightened ideas. And although kingdoms and provinces may be wrested from the hands that hold them, in the same manner they were obtained; although ordinary and vulgar power may, in human affairs, be lost as it has been won; yet it is the glorious prerogative of the empire of knowledge, that what it gains it never loses. On the contrary, it increases by the multiple of its own power; all its ends become means; all its attainments, helps to new conquests. Its whole abundant harvest is but so much seed wheat, and nothing has limited, and nothing can limit, the amount of ultimate product.

Under the influence of this rapidly increasing knowledge, the people have begun, in all forms of government, to think and to reason on affairs of state. Regarding government as an institution for the public good, they demand a knowledge of its operations and a participation in its exercise. A call for the representative system wherever it is not enjoyed, and where there is already intelligence enough to estimate its value, is perseveringly made. Where men may speak out, they demand it; where the bayonet is at their throats, they pray for it.

When Louis XIV.[1] said, "I am the state," he expressed the essence of the doctrine of unlimited power. By the rules of that system, the people are disconnected from the state: they are its subjects; it is their lord. These ideas, founded in the love of power, and long supported by the excess and the abuse of it, are yielding, in our age, to other opinions; and the civilized world seems at last to be proceeding to the conviction of that fundamental and manifest truth, that the powers of government are but a trust, and that they cannot be lawfully exercised but for the good of the community. As knowledge is more and more extended, this conviction becomes more and more general. Knowledge, in truth, is the great sun in the firmament. Life and power are scattered with all its beams. The prayer of the Grecian champion when enveloped in unnatural clouds and darkness is the appropriate political supplication for the people of every country not yet blessed with free institutions:

[1] Louis XIV., King of France, 1643-1715.

> "Dispel this cloud, the light of heaven restore,
> Give me TO SEE,— and Ajax asks no more." [1]

We may hope that the growing influence of enlightened sentiment will promote the permanent peace of the world. Wars to maintain family alliances, to uphold or to cast down dynasties, and to regulate successions to thrones, which have occupied so much room in the history of modern times, if not less likely to happen at all, will be less likely to become general and involve many nations, as the great principle shall be more and more established, that the interest of the world is peace, and its first great statute, that every nation possesses the power of establishing a government for itself. But public opinion has attained, also, an influence over governments which do not admit the popular principle into their organization. A necessary respect for the judgment of the world operates, in some measure, as a control over the most unlimited forms of authority. It is owing, perhaps, to this truth, that the interesting struggle of the Greeks [2] has been suffered to go on so long without a direct interference, either to wrest that country from its present masters, or to execute the system of pacification by force, and with united strength lay the neck of Christian and civilized Greek at the foot of the barbarian Turk. Let us thank God that we live in an age when something has influence besides the bayonet, and when the sternest authority does not venture to encounter the scorching power of public reproach. Any attempt of the kind I have mentioned should be met by one universal burst of indignation ; the air of the civilized world ought to be made too warm to be comfortably breathed by any one who would hazard it.

It is, indeed, a touching reflection, that while, in the fullness of our country's happiness, we rear this monument to her honor, we

---

[1] Iliad, XVII. 729, Pope's translation.

[2] The Greek Revolution, against Turkish oppression and for the freedom of Greece, was then in progress. It had begun in 1820, and was terminated, with the success of the patriots, in 1829.

look for instruction in our undertaking to a country which is now in fearful contest, not for works of art or memorials of glory, but for her own existence. Let her be assured that she is not forgotten in the world, that her efforts are applauded, and that constant prayers ascend for her success. And let us cherish a confident hope for her final triumph. If the true spark of religious and civil liberty be kindled, it will burn. Human agency cannot extinguish it. Like the earth's central fire, it may be smothered for a time; the ocean may overwhelm it; mountains may press it down; but its inherent and unconquerable force will heave both the ocean and the land, and at some time or other, in some place or other, the volcano will break out, and flame up to heaven.

Among the great events of the half century we must reckon, certainly, the revolution of South America;[1] and we are not likely to overrate the importance of that revolution, either to the people of the country itself or to the rest of the world. The late Spanish colonies, now independent states, under circumstances less favorable, doubtless, than attended our own Revolution, have yet successfully commenced their national existence. They have accomplished the great object of establishing their independence; they are known and acknowledged in the world: and although in regard to their systems of government, their sentiments on religious toleration, and their provisions for public instruction, they may have yet much to learn, it must be admitted that they have risen to the condition of settled and established states more rapidly than could have been reasonably anticipated. They already furnish an exhilarating example of the difference between free governments and despotic misrule. Their commerce, at this moment, creates a new activity in all the great marts of the world. They show themselves able, by an exchange of commodities, to bear a useful part in the intercourse of nations.

1 The revolution of the South American colonies was at that time an event of but recent occurrence. It began in 1810, and ended in 1824, when Bolivia, the last of the Spanish colonies, was acknowledged independent.

A new spirit of enterprise and industry begins to prevail; all the great interests of society receive a salutary impulse; and the progress of information not only testifies to an improved condition, but itself constitutes the highest and most essential improvement.

When the battle of Bunker Hill was fought, the existence of South America was scarcely felt in the civilized world. The thirteen little Colonies of North America habitually called themselves the "Continent." Borne down by colonial subjugation, monopoly, and bigotry, these vast regions of the South were hardly visible above the horizon. But in our day there has been, as it were, a new creation. The southern hemisphere emerges from the sea. Its lofty mountains begin to lift themselves into the light of heaven; its broad and fertile plains stretch out in beauty to the eye of civilized man; and at the mighty bidding of the voice of political liberty the waters of darkness retire.

And now let us indulge an honest exultation in the conviction of the benefit which the example of our country has produced, and is likely to produce, on human freedom and human happiness. Let us endeavor to comprehend in all its magnitude, and to feel in all its importance, the part assigned to us in the great drama of human affairs. We are placed at the head of the system of representative and popular governments. Thus far our example shows that such governments are compatible, not only with respectability and power, but with repose, with peace, with security of personal rights, with good laws, and a just administration.

We are not propagandists. Wherever other systems are preferred, either as being thought better in themselves, or as better suited to existing condition, we leave the preference to be enjoyed. Our history hitherto proves, however, that the popular form is practicable, and that with wisdom and knowledge men may govern themselves; and the duty incumbent on us is to preserve the consistency of this cheering example, and take care that nothing may weaken its authority with the world. If, in our case, the representative system ultimately fail, popular governments must be pronounced impossible. No combination of circumstances more favorable to the experiment can ever be expected to occur. The last hopes of mankind, therefore, rest with us; and if it should be proclaimed that our example had become an argument against the experiment, the knell of popular liberty would be sounded throughout the earth.

These are excitements to duty, but they are not suggestions of doubt. Our history and our condition, all that is gone before us, and all that surrounds us, authorize the belief that popular governments, though subject to occasional variations, in form perhaps not always for the better, may yet, in their general character, be as durable and permanent as other systems. We know, indeed, that in our country any other is impossible. The *principle* of free governments adheres to the American soil. It is bedded in it, immovable as its mountains.

And let the sacred obligations which have devolved on this generation and on us sink deep into our hearts. Those who established our liberty and our government are daily dropping from among us. The great trust now descends to new hands. Let us apply ourselves to that which is presented to us as our appropriate object. We can win no laurels in a war for independence. Earlier and worthier hands have gathered them all. Nor are there places for us by the side of Solon [1] and Alfred [2] and other founders of states. Our fathers have filled them. But there remains to us a great duty of defense and preservation; and there is opened to us, also, a noble pursuit to which the spirit of the times strongly invites us. Our proper business

1 Solon, the most famous of the lawgivers of ancient Greece (born about 638 B.C.), established a new code of laws for Athens.

2 King Alfred the Great, of England (849–901), reduced the Anglo-Saxon laws to a system, and made great improvements in the administration of justice. He is sometimes regarded as the founder of the English monarchy.

is improvement.   Let our age be the age of improvement.   In
a day of peace, let us advance the arts of peace and the works
of peace.   Let us develop the resources of our land, call forth its
powers, build up its institutions, promote all its great interests,
and see whether we also, in our day and generation, may not perform something worthy to be remembered.   Let us cultivate a
true spirit of union and harmony.   In pursuing the great objects
which our condition points out to us, let us act under a settled
conviction and an habitual feeling, that these twenty-four States
are one country.   Let our conceptions be enlarged to the circle
of our duties.   Let us extend our ideas over the whole of the
vast field in which we are called to act.   Let our object be, OUR
COUNTRY, OUR WHOLE COUNTRY, AND NOTHING BUT OUR COUN-
TRY.   And, by the blessing of God, may that country itself
become a vast and splendid monument, not of oppression and
terror, but of Wisdom, of Peace, and of Liberty, upon which
the world may gaze with admiration forever !

THE COMPLETION OF THE BUNKER HILL MONUMENT.

AN ADDRESS DELIVERED ON BUNKER HILL, ON THE 17TH OF
JUNE, 1843, ON THE OCCASION OF THE COMPLETION
OF THE MONUMENT.

A DUTY has been performed. A work of gratitude and patriotism is completed. This structure, having its foundations in soil which drank deep of early Revolutionary blood, has at length reached its destined height, and now lifts its summit to the skies.

We have assembled to celebrate the accomplishment of this undertaking, and to indulge afresh in the recollection of the great event which it is designed to commemorate. Eighteen years, more than half the ordinary duration of a generation of mankind, have elapsed since the corner stone of this monument was laid. The hopes of its projectors rested on voluntary contributions, private munificence, and the general favor of the public. These hopes have not been disappointed. Donations have been made by individuals, in some cases of large amount; and smaller sums have been contributed by thousands. All who regard the object itself as important, and its accomplishment, therefore, as a good attained, will entertain sincere respect and gratitude for the unwearied efforts of the successive presidents, boards of directors, and committees of the Association which has had the general control of the work. The architect, equally entitled to our thanks and commendation, will find other reward, also, for his labor and skill, in the beauty and elegance of the obelisk itself, and the distinction which, as a work of art, it confers upon him.

At a period when the prospects of further progress in the undertaking were gloomy and discouraging, the Mechanic Association, by a most praiseworthy and vigorous effort, raised new funds for carrying it forward, and saw them applied with fidelity, economy, and skill. It is a grateful duty to make public acknowledgments of such timely and efficient aid.

The last effort and the last contribution were from a different source. Garlands of grace and elegance were destined to crown a work which had its commencement in manly patriotism. The winning power of the sex addressed itself to the public, and all that was needed to carry the monument to its proposed height, and to give to it its finish, was promptly supplied. The mothers and the daughters of the land contributed thus, most successfully, to whatever there is of beauty in the monument itself, or whatever of utility and public benefit and gratification there is in its completion.

Of those with whom the plan originated, of erecting on this spot a monument worthy of the event to be commemorated, many are now present; but others, alas! have themselves become subjects of monumental inscription. William Tudor—an accomplished scholar, a distinguished writer, a most amiable man, allied both by birth and sentiment to the patriots of the Revolution—died while on public service abroad, and now lies buried in a foreign land.[1] William Sullivan—a name fragrant of Revolutionary merit and of public service and public virtue, who himself partook in a high degree of the respect and confidence of the community, and yet was always most loved where best known—has also been gathered to his fathers. And last, George Blake—a lawyer of learning and eloquence, a man of wit and of

----

[1] William Tudor died at Rio de Janeiro, while *Chargé d'Affaires* of the United States, in 1830. See Introduction.

talent, of social qualities the most agreeable and fascinating, and of gifts which enabled him to exercise large sway over public assemblies — has closed his human career.[1] I know that in the crowds before me there are those from whose eyes tears will flow at the mention of these names. But such mention is due to their general character, their public and private virtues, and especially, on this occasion, to the spirit and zeal with which they entered into the undertaking which is now completed.

I have spoken only of those who are no longer numbered with the living. But a long life, now drawing towards its close, always distinguished by acts of public spirit, humanity, and charity, forming a character which has already become historical, and sanctified by public regard and the affection of friends, may confer even on the living the proper immunity of the dead, and be the fit subject of honorable mention and warm commendation. Of the early projectors of the design of this monument, one of the most prominent, the most zealous, and the most efficient, is Thomas H. Perkins.[2] It was beneath his ever hospitable roof that those whom I have mentioned, and others yet living and now present, having assembled for the purpose, adopted the first step towards erecting a monument on Bunker Hill. Long may he remain, with unimpaired faculties, in the wide field of his usefulness ! His charities have distilled like the dews of heaven ; he has fed the hungry, and clothed the naked ; he has given sight to the blind : and for such virtues there is a reward on high of which all human memorials, all language of brass and stone, are but humble types and attempted imitations.

Time and nature have had their course in diminishing the number of those whom we met here on the 17th of June, 1825. Most of the Revolutionary characters then present have since

---

1 William Sullivan died in Boston in 1839, George Blake, in 1841 ; both gentlemen of great political and legal eminence.

2 Thomas Handasyd Perkins, a distinguished merchant and philanthropist of Boston, founder of the Perkins Institution and Massachusetts School for the Blind. He died Jan. 11, 1854.

deceased; and Lafayette sleeps in his native land.   Yet the name and blood of Warren are with us; the kindred of Putnam are also here; and near me, universally beloved for his character and his virtues, and now venerable for his years, sits the son of the noble-hearted and daring Prescott.[1] Gideon Foster of Danvers, Enos Reynolds of Boxford, Phineas Johnson, Robert Andrews, Elijah Dresser, Josiah Cleaveland, Jesse Smith, Philip Bagley, Needham Maynard, Roger Plaisted, Joseph Stephens, Nehemiah Porter, and James Harvey, who bore arms for their country, either at Concord and Lexington on the 19th of April, or on Bunker Hill, all now far advanced in age, have come here to-day to look once more on the field where their valor was proved, and to receive a hearty outpouring of our respect.

They have long outlived the troubles and dangers of the Revolution; they have outlived the evils arising from the want of a united and efficient government; they have outlived the menace of imminent dangers to the public liberty; they have outlived nearly all their contemporaries: but they have not outlived, they cannot outlive, the affectionate gratitude of their country.   Heaven has not allotted to this generation an opportunity of rendering high services, and manifesting strong personal devotion, such as they rendered and manifested, and in such a cause as that which roused the patriotic fires of their youthful breasts, and nerved the strength of their arms.   But we may praise what we cannot equal, and celebrate actions which we were not born to perform.   *Pulchrum est benefacere reipublicæ, etiam benedicere haud absurdum est.*

The Bunker Hill Monument is finished.   Here it stands.   Fortunate in the high natural eminence on which it is placed, higher, infinitely higher, in its objects and purpose, it rises over the land and over the sea; and, visible at their homes to three hundred thousand of the people of Massachusetts, it stands a memorial of the last, and a monitor to the present, and to all succeeding

---

1 " William Prescott (since deceased, in 1844), son of Col. William Prescott, who commanded on the 17th of June, 1775, and father of William H. Prescott, the historian." — EVERETT.

generations. I have spoken of the loftiness of its purpose. If it had been without any other design than the creation of a work of art, the granite of which it is composed would have slept in its native bed. It has a purpose, and that purpose gives it its character. That purpose enrobes it with dignity and moral grandeur. That well-known purpose it is which causes us to look up to it with a feeling of awe. It is itself the orator of this occasion. It is not from my lips, it could not be from any human lips, that that strain of eloquence is this day to flow most competent to move and excite the vast multitudes around me. The powerful speaker stands motionless before us.[1] It is a plain shaft. It bears no inscriptions, fronting to the rising sun, from which the future antiquary shall wipe the dust. Nor does the rising sun cause tones of music to issue from its summit. But at the rising of the sun and at the setting of the sun, in the blaze of noonday, and beneath the milder effulgence of lunar light, it looks, it speaks, it acts, to the full comprehension of every American mind, and the awakening of glowing enthusiasm in every American heart. Its silent but awful utterance; its deep pathos as it brings to our contemplation the 17th of June, 1775, and the consequences which have resulted to us, to our country, and to the world, from the events of that day, and which we know must continue to rain influence on the destinies of mankind to the end of time ; the elevation with which it raises us high above the ordinary feelings of life,—surpass all that the study of the closet, or even the inspiration of genius, can produce. To-day it speaks to us: its future auditories will be the successive generations of men as they rise up before it and gather around it. Its speech will be of patriotism and courage, of civil and religious liberty, of free government, of the moral improvement and elevation of mankind, and of the immortal memory of those who, with heroic devotion, have sacrificed their lives for their country.

[1] It is related that at this point in his speech the orator was interrupted by a spontaneous burst of applause from his hearers, and that such was their enthusiasm, that it was several moments before he could proceed.

In the older world, numerous fabrics still exist, reared by human hands, but whose object has been lost in the darkness of ages.   They are now monuments of nothing but the labor and skill which constructed them.

The mighty Pyramid itself, half buried in the sands of Africa, has nothing to bring down and report to us but the power of kings and the servitude of the people.   If it had any purpose beyond that of a mausoleum, such purpose has perished from history and from tradition.   If asked for its moral object, its admonition, its sentiment, its instruction to mankind, or any high end in its erection, it is silent, — silent as the millions which lie in the dust at its base, and in the catacombs which surround it.   Without a just moral object, therefore, made known to man, though raised against the skies, it excites only conviction of power mixed with strange wonder.   But if the civilization of the present race of men — founded as it is in solid science, the true knowledge of nature, and vast discoveries in art, and which is elevated and purified by moral sentiment and by the truths of Christianity — be not destined to destruction before the final termination of human existence on earth, the object and purpose of this edifice will be known till that hour shall come.   And even if civilization should be subverted, and the truths of the Christian religion obscured by a new deluge of barbarism, the memory of Bunker Hill and the American Revolution will still be elements and parts of the knowledge which shall be possessed by the last man to whom the light of civilization and Christianity shall be extended.

This celebration is honored by the presence of the chief executive magistrate of the Union.   An occasion so national in its object and character, and so much connected with that Revolution from which the government sprang at the head of which he is placed, may well receive from him this mark of attention and respect.   Well acquainted with Yorktown,[1] the scene of the last

---

[1] President Tyler was a native of Virginia, and his birthplace was within less than forty miles of Yorktown.   The surrender of the British army under Cornwallis, at Yorktown, occurred Oct. 19, 1781.

great military struggle of the Revolution, his eye now surveys the field of Bunker Hill, the theater of the first of those important conflicts. He sees where Warren fell, where Putnam and Prescott and Stark and Knowlton and Brooks fought. He beholds the spot where a thousand trained soldiers of England were smitten to the earth, in the first effort of revolutionary war, by the arm of a bold and determined yeomanry contending for liberty and their country. And while all assembled here entertain towards him sincere personal good wishes and the high respect due to his elevated office and station, it is not to be doubted that he enters with true American feeling into the patriotic enthusiasm kindled by the occasion which animates the multitudes that surround him.

His Excellency the Governor of the Commonwealth, the Governor of Rhode Island, and the other distinguished public men whom we have the honor to receive as visitors and guests to-day, will cordially unite in a celebration connected with the great event of the Revolutionary War.

No name in the history of 1775 and 1776 is more distinguished than that borne by an ex-president of the United States,[1] whom we expected to see here, but whose ill health prevents his attendance. Whenever popular rights were to be asserted, an Adams was present; and when the time came for the formal Declaration of Independence, it was the voice of an Adams that shook the halls of Congress. We wish we could have welcomed to us this day the inheritor of Revolutionary blood, and the just and worthy representative of high Revolutionary names, merit, and services.

Banners and badges, processions and flags, announce to us that amidst this uncounted throng are thousands of natives of New England now residents in other States. Welcome, ye kindred names, with kindred blood ! From the broad savannas[2] of the South, from the newer regions of the West, from amidst

---

[1] John Quincy Adams (1767–1848), the sixth President of the United States (1825–29).

[2] Plains, or meadows.

4

the hundreds of thousands of men of Eastern origin who cultivate the rich valley of the Genesee, or live along the chain of
the Lakes, from the mountains of Pennsylvania, and from the
thronged cities of the coast, welcome, welcome !   Wherever else
you may be strangers, here you are all at home.   You assemble
at this shrine of liberty, near the family altars at which your earliest devotions were paid to Heaven, near to the temples of
worship first entered by you, and near to the schools and colleges
in which your education was received.   You come hither with a
glorious ancestry of liberty.   You bring names which are on the
rolls of Lexington, Concord, and Bunker Hill.   You come, some
of you, once more to be embraced by an aged Revolutionary
father, or to receive another, perhaps a last, blessing, bestowed in
love and tears, by a mother, yet surviving to witness and to
enjoy your prosperity and happiness.

But if family associations and the recollections of the past
bring you hither with greater alacrity, and mingle with your
greeting much of local attachment and private affection, greeting
also be given, free and hearty greeting, to every American citizen
who treads this sacred soil with patriotic feeling, and respires with
pleasure in an atmosphere perfumed with the recollections of
1775 !   This occasion is respectable,[1] nay, it is grand, it is sublime, by the nationality of its sentiment.   Among the seventeen
millions of happy people who form the American community,
there is not one who has not an interest in this monument, as
there is not one that has not a deep and abiding interest in that
which it commemorates.

Woe betide the man who brings to this day's worship feeling
less than wholly American !   Woe betide the man who can stand
here with the fires of local resentments burning, or the purpose
of fomenting local jealousies and the strifes of local interests fes-
tering and rankling in his heart !   Union, established in justice,
in patriotism, and the most plain and obvious common interest ;

---

[1] This is a favorite word with Webster, and he often gives to it an unusual
significance.

union, founded on the same love of liberty, cemented by blood shed in the same common cause,—union has been the source of all our glory and greatness thus far, and is the ground of all our highest hopes. This column stands on union. I know not that it might not keep its position if the American Union, in the mad conflict of human passions, and in the strife of parties and factions, should be broken up and destroyed. I know not that it would totter and fall to the earth, and mingle its fragments with the fragments of Liberty and the Constitution, when State should be separated from State, and faction and dismemberment obliterate forever all the hopes of the founders of our Republic and the great inheritance of their children. It might stand. But who, from beneath the weight of mortification and shame that would oppress him, could look up to behold it ? Whose eyeballs would not be seared by such a spectacle ? For my part, should I live to such a time, I shall avert my eyes from it forever.

It is not as a mere military encounter of hostile armies that the battle of Bunker Hill presents its principal claim to attention. Yet, even as a mere battle, there were circumstances attending it extraordinary in character, and entitling it to peculiar distinction. It was fought on this eminence, in the neighborhood of yonder city, in the presence of many more spectators than there were combatants in the conflict. Men, women, and children, from every commanding position, were gazing at the battle, and looking for its results with all the eagerness natural to those who knew that the issue was fraught with the deepest consequences to themselves personally, as well as to their country. Yet on the 16th of June, 1775, there was nothing around this hill but verdure and culture. There was, indeed, the note of awful preparation in Boston. There was the Provincial army at Cambridge, with its right flank resting on Dorchester, and its left on Chelsea. But here all was peace. Tranquillity reigned around. On the 17th, everything was changed. On this eminence had arisen, in the night, a redoubt, built by Prescott, and in which he held command. Perceived by the enemy at dawn, it was immediately cannonaded from the floating batteries in the river, and from the opposite shore. And then ensued the hurried movement in Boston, and soon the troops of Britain embarked in the attempt to dislodge the colonists. In an hour everything indicated an immediate and bloody conflict. Love of liberty on one side, proud defiance of rebellion on the other, hopes and fears, and courage and daring, on both sides, animated the hearts of the combatants as they hung on the edge of battle.

I suppose it would be difficult, in a military point of view, to ascribe to the leaders on either side any just motive for the engagement which followed. On the one hand, it could not have been very important to the Americans to attempt to hem the British within the town, by advancing one single post a quarter of a mile; while, on the other hand, if the British found it essential to dislodge the American troops, they had it in their power at no expense of life. By moving up their ships and batteries, they could have completely cut off all communication with the mainland over the Neck, and the forces in the redoubt would have been reduced to a state of famine in forty-eight hours.

But that was not the day for any such consideration on either side. Both parties were anxious to try the strength of their arms. The pride of England would not permit the "rebels," as she termed them, to defy her to the teeth; and, without for a moment calculating the cost, the British general determined to destroy the fort immediately. On the other side, Prescott and his gallant followers longed and thirsted for a decisive trial of strength and of courage. They wished a battle, and wished it at once. And this is the true secret of the movements on this hill.

I will not attempt to describe that battle. The cannonading, the landing of the British, their advance, the coolness with which the charge was met, the repulse, the second attack, the second repulse, the burning of Charlestown, and finally the closing assault and the slow retreat of the Americans,—the history of all these is familiar.

But the consequences of the battle of Bunker Hill were greater than those of any ordinary conflict, although between armies of far greater force, and terminating with more immediate advantage on the one side or the other. It was the first great battle of the Revolution, and not only the first blow, but the blow which determined the contest. It did not, indeed, put an end to the war; but, in the then existing hostile state of feeling, the difficulties could only be referred to the arbitration of the sword. And one thing is certain,—that, after the New-England troops had shown themselves able to face and repulse the regulars, it was decided that peace never could be established but upon the basis of the independence of the Colonies. When the sun of that day went down, the event of independence was no longer doubtful. In a few days Washington heard of the battle, and he inquired if the militia had stood the fire of the regulars. When told that they had not only stood that fire, but reserved their own till the enemy was within eight rods, and then poured it in with tremendous effect, "Then," exclaimed he, "the liberties of the country are safe!"

The consequences of this battle were just of the same importance as the Revolution itself.

If there was nothing of value in the principles of the American Revolution, then there is nothing valuable in the battle of Bunker Hill and its consequences. But if the Revolution was an era in the history of man favorable to human happiness, if it was an event which marked the progress of man all over the world from despotism to liberty, then this monument is not raised without cause. Then the battle of Bunker Hill is not an event undeserving celebrations, commemorations, and rejoicings, now and in all coming times.

What, then, is the true and peculiar principle of the American Revolution, and of the systems of government which it has confirmed and established? The truth is, that the American Revolution was not caused by the instantaneous discovery of principles of government before unheard of, or the practical adoption of political ideas such as had never before entered into the minds of men. It was but the full development of principles of government, forms of society, and political sentiments, the origin of all which lay back two centuries in English and American history.

The discovery of America, its colonization by the nations of Europe, the history and progress of the Colonies, from their establishment to the time when the principal of them threw off their allegiance to the respective states by which they had been planted, and founded governments of their own, constitute one of the most interesting portions of the annals of man. These events occupied three hundred years, during which period civilization and knowledge made steady progress in the Old World; so that Europe, at the commencement of the nineteenth century, had become greatly changed from that Europe which began the colonization of America at the close of the fifteenth or the commencement of the sixteenth. And what is most material to my present purpose is, that in the progress of the first of these centuries, that is to say, from the discovery of America to the settlements of Virginia and Massachusetts, political and religious events took place which most materially affected the state of society and the sentiments of mankind, especially in England and in parts of Continental Europe. After a few feeble and unsuccessful efforts by England, under Henry VII.,[1] to plant colonies in America, no designs of that kind were prosecuted for a long period, either by the English Government or any of its subjects. Without inquiring into the causes of this delay, its consequences are sufficiently clear and striking. England, in this lapse of a century, unknown to herself, but under the providence of God and the influence of events, was fitting herself for the work of colonizing North America, on such principles, and by such men, as should spread the English name and English blood, in time, over a great portion of the Western hemisphere.

[1] It was during the reign of Henry VII. that John Cabot, under a royal commission, discovered the coast of North America, — a discovery upon which the subsequent claims of the English to jurisdiction on this continent were based.

The commercial spirit was greatly fostered by several laws passed in the reign of Henry VII.; and in the same reign encouragement was given to arts and manufactures in the eastern counties, and some not unimportant modifications of the feudal system took place by allowing the breaking of entails.[1] These and other measures, and other occurrences, were making way for a new class of society to emerge and show itself in a military and feudal age; a middle class, between the barons or great landholders and the retainers of the Crown on the one side, and the tenants of the Crown and barons, and agricultural and other laborers, on the other side. With the rise and growth of this new class of society, not only did commerce and the arts increase, but better education, a greater degree of knowledge, juster notions of the true ends of government, and sentiments favorable to civil liberty, began to spread abroad, and become more and more common. But the plants springing from these seeds were of slow growth. The character of English society had indeed begun to undergo a change; but changes of national character are ordinarily the work of time. Operative causes were, however, evidently in existence, and sure to produce, ultimately, their proper effect. From the accession of Henry VII. to the breaking out of the civil wars,[2] England enjoyed much greater exemption from war, foreign and domestic, than for a long period before, and during the controversy between the houses of York and Lancaster.[3] These years of peace were favorable to commerce and the arts. Commerce and the arts augmented general and individual knowledge; and knowledge is the only fountain, both of the love and the principles of human liberty.

[1] Laws forbidding the owner of an estate to transfer it to any person except the legal heir.

[2] That is, from 1485 to about 1640.

[3] This conflict between the two great families of England, each claiming the right to the royal succession, is known in history as the War of the Roses. It began in 1455, and continued until the death of Richard III. in 1485.

Other powerful causes soon came into active play. The Reformation of Luther[1] broke out, kindling up the minds of men afresh, leading to new habits of thought, and awakening in individuals energies before unknown even to themselves. The religious controversies of this period changed society as well as religion: indeed, it would be easy to prove, if this occasion were proper for it, that they changed society to a considerable extent, where they did not change the religion of the state. They changed man himself, in his modes of thought, his consciousness of his own powers, and his desire of intellectual attainment. The spirit of commercial and foreign adventure, therefore, on the one hand, which had gained so much strength and influence since the time of the discovery of America; and, on the other, the assertion and maintenance of religious liberty, having their source indeed in the Reformation, but continued, diversified, and constantly strengthened by the subsequent divisions of sentiment and opinion among the Reformers themselves; and this love of religious liberty, drawing after it, or bringing along with it, as it always does, an ardent devotion to the principle of civil liberty also,— were the powerful influences under which character was formed, and men trained, for the great work of introducing English civilization, English law, and, what is more than all, Anglo-Saxon blood, into the wilderness of North America. Raleigh[2] and his companions may be considered as the creatures, principally, of the first of these causes. High-spirited, full of the love of personal adventure, excited, too, in some degree, by the hopes of sudden riches from the discovery of mines of the precious metals, and not unwilling to diversify the labors of settling a colony with occasional cruising against the Spaniards in the West Indian seas,

---

[1] This great religious and political movement, which engaged the attention of a large portion of Europe during the sixteenth century, is so called from Martin Luther, its most distinguished promoter. The Reformation was begun in Switzerland by Zwingli in 1516; in Germany, by Luther in 1517; and in England, by Henry VIII. in 1534.

[2] Sir Walter Raleigh (1552–1618).

they crossed and recrossed the ocean with a frequency which surprises us when we consider the state of navigation, and which evinces a most daring spirit.

The other cause peopled New England. The "Mayflower" sought our shores under no high-wrought spirit of commercial adventure, no love of gold, no mixture of purpose warlike or hostile to any human being. Like the dove from the ark, she had put forth only to find rest. Solemn supplications on the shore of the sea in Holland had invoked for her, at her departure, the blessings of Providence. The stars which guided her were the unobscured constellations of civil and religious liberty. Her deck was the altar of the living God. Fervent prayers on bended knees mingled, morning and evening, with the voices of ocean and the sighing of the wind in her shrouds. Every prosperous breeze which, gently swelling her sails, helped the Pilgrims onward in their course, awoke new anthems of praise; and when the elements were wrought into fury, neither the tempest, tossing their fragile bark like a feather, nor the darkness and howling of the midnight storm, ever disturbed in man or woman the firm and settled purpose of their souls, to undergo all and to do all that the meekest patience, the boldest resolution, and the highest trust in God, could enable human beings to suffer or to perform.

Some differences may, doubtless, be traced at this day between the descendants of the early colonists of Virginia and those of New England, owing to the different influences and different circumstances under which the respective settlements were made, but only enough to create a pleasing variety in the midst of a general family resemblance.

> "Facies non omnibus una,
> Nec diversa tamen; qualis decet sororum."[1]

But the habits, sentiments, and objects of both soon became modified by local causes, growing out of their condition in the

---

[1] "The features are not the same in all, nor yet very different: they are such as those of sisters ought to be." — OVID.

New World; and as this condition was essentially alike in both,
and as both at once adopted the same general rules and principles of English jurisprudence, and became accustomed to the
authority of representative bodies, these differences gradually
diminished.   They disappeared by the progress of time and the
influence of intercourse.   The necessity of some degree of union
and coöperation to defend themselves against the savage tribes,
tended to excite in them mutual respect and regard.   They
fought together in the wars against France.[1] The great and
common cause of the Revolution bound them to one another by
new links of brotherhood; and at length the present constitution
of government united them, happily and gloriously, to form the
great republic of the world, and bound up their interests and fortunes, till the whole earth sees that there is now for them, in present possession as well as in future hope, but " One Country, One
Constitution, and One Destiny."

The colonization of the tropical region, and the whole of the
southern parts of the continent, by Spain and Portugal, was conducted on other principles, under the influence of other motives,
and followed by far different consequences.   From the time of
its discovery, the Spanish Government pushed forward its settlements in America, not only with vigor, but with eagerness; so
that, long before the first permanent English settlement had been
accomplished in what is now the United States, Spain had conquered Mexico, Peru, and Chile, and stretched her power over
nearly all the territory she ever acquired on this continent.   The
rapidity of these conquests is to be ascribed, in a great degree, to
the eagerness, not to say the rapacity, of those numerous bands
of adventurers who were stimulated by individual interests and
private hopes to subdue immense regions, and take possession of
them in the name of the Crown of Spain.   The mines of gold
and silver were the incitements to these efforts; and accordingly

---

[1] Known in American history as King William's War (1689–97), Queen
Anne's War (1702–13), King George's War (1744–48), and the French and
Indian War (1754–63).

settlements were generally made, and Spanish authority established, immediately on the subjugation of territory, that the native population might be set to work by their new Spanish masters in the mines. From these facts, the love of gold—gold not produced by industry, nor accumulated by commerce, but gold dug from its native bed in the bowels of the earth, and that earth ravished from its rightful possessors by every possible degree of enormity, cruelty, and crime—was long the governing passion in Spanish wars and Spanish settlements in America. Even Columbus himself did not wholly escape the influence of this base motive. In his early voyages we find him passing from island to island, inquiring everywhere for gold, as if God had opened the New World to the knowledge of the Old, only to gratify a passion equally senseless and sordid, and to offer up millions of an unoffending race of men to the destruction of the sword, sharpened both by cruelty and rapacity. And yet Columbus was far above his age and country; enthusiastic, indeed, but sober, religious, and magnanimous; born to great things, and capable of high sentiments, as his noble discourse before Ferdinand and Isabella, as well as the whole history of his life, shows. Probably he sacrificed much to the known sentiments of others, and addressed to his followers motives likely to influence them. At the same time, it is evident that he himself looked upon the world which he discovered as a world of wealth all ready to be seized and enjoyed.

The conquerors and the European settlers of Spanish America were mainly military commanders and common soldiers. The monarchy of Spain was not transferred to this hemisphere; but it acted in it, as it acted at home, through its ordinary means and its true representative, military force. The robbery and destruction of the native race was the achievement of standing armies, in the right of the King and by his authority; fighting in his name, for the aggrandizement of his power and the extension of his prerogatives, with military ideas under arbitrary maxims,—a portion of that dreadful instrumentality by which a perfect despotism governs a people. As there was no liberty in Spain, how could liberty be transmitted to Spanish colonies ?

The colonists of English America were of the people, and a people already free. They were of the middle, industrious, and already prosperous class, the inhabitants of commercial and manufacturing cities, among whom liberty first revived and re-spired after a sleep of a thousand years in the bosom of the Dark Ages. Spain descended on the New World in the armed and terrible image of her monarchy and her soldiery; England ap-proached it in the winning and popular garb of personal rights, public protection, and civil freedom. England transplanted lib-erty to America; Spain transplanted power. England, through the agency of private companies and the efforts of individuals, colonized this part of North America by industrious individuals, making their own way in the wilderness, defending themselves against the savages, recognizing their right to the soil, and with a general honest purpose of introducing knowledge as well as Christianity among them. Spain stooped on South America like a vulture on its prey. Everything was force. Territories were acquired by fire and sword. Cities were destroyed by fire and sword. Hundreds of thousands of human beings fell by fire and sword. Even conversion to Christianity was attempted by fire and sword.

Behold, then, fellow citizens, the difference resulting from the operation of the two principles ! Here, to-day, on the summit of Bunker Hill, and at the foot of this monument, behold the difference ! I would that the fifty thousand voices present could proclaim it with a shout which should be heard over the globe. Our inheritance was of liberty, secured and regulated by law, and enlightened by religion and knowledge ; that of South America was of power,—stern, unrelenting, tyrannical, military power. And now look to the consequences of the two principles on the general and aggregate happiness of the human race. Behold the results in all the regions conquered by Cortes and Pizarro, and the con-trasted results here. I suppose the territory of the United States may amount to one eighth, or one tenth, of that colonized by Spain on this continent; and yet in all that vast region there are but between one and two millions of people of European color and European blood, while in the United States there are fourteen millions who rejoice in their descent from the people of the more northern part of Europe.

But we may follow the difference in the original principle of colonization, and in its character and objects, still further. We must look to moral and intellectual results; we must consider consequences, not only as they show themselves in hastening or retarding the increase of population and the supply of physical wants, but in their civilization, improvement, and happiness. We must inquire what progress has been made in the true science of liberty, in the knowledge of the great principles of self-government, and in the progress of man as a social, moral, and religious being.

I would not willingly say anything on this occasion discourteous to the new governments founded on the demolition of the power of the Spanish monarchy. They are yet on their trial, and I hope for a favorable result. But truth, sacred truth, and fidelity to the cause of civil liberty, compel me to say, that hitherto they have discovered quite too much of the spirit of that monarchy from which they separated themselves. Quite too frequent resort is made to military force; and quite too much of the substance of the people is consumed in maintaining armies, not for defense against foreign aggression, but for enforcing obedience to domestic authority. Standing armies are the oppressive instruments for governing the people in the hands of hereditary and arbitrary monarchs. A military republic, a government founded on mock elections and supported only by the sword, is a movement indeed, but a retrograde and disastrous movement, from the regular and old-fashioned monarchical systems. If men would enjoy the blessings of republican government, they must govern themselves by reason, by mutual counsel and consultation, by a sense and feeling of general interest, and by the acquiescence of the minority in the will of the majority, properly expressed; and, above all, the military must be kept, according to the language of our Bill of Rights, in strict subordination to the civil authority. Wherever this lesson is not both learned and practiced, there can be no political freedom. Absurd, preposterous is it, a scoff and a satire on free forms of constitutional liberty, for frames of government to be prescribed by military leaders, and the right of suffrage to be exercised at the point of the sword.

Making all allowance for situation and climate, it cannot be doubted by intelligent minds that the difference now existing between North and South America is justly attributable, in a great degree, to political institutions in the Old World and in the New. And how broad that difference is ! Suppose an assembly, in one of the valleys or on the side of one of the mountains of the southern half of the hemisphere, to be held this day in the neighborhood of a large city — what would be the scene presented ? Yonder is a volcano, flaming and smoking, but shedding no light, moral or intellectual. At its foot is the mine, sometimes yielding, perhaps, large gains to capital, but in which labor is destined to eternal and unrequited toil, and followed only by penury and beggary. The city is filled with armed men; not a free people, armed and coming forth voluntarily to rejoice in a public festivity, but hireling troops, supported by forced loans, excessive impositions on commerce, or taxes wrung from a half-fed and a half-clothed population. For the great there are palaces covered with gold; for the poor there are hovels of the meanest sort. There is an ecclesiastical hierarchy, enjoying the wealth of princes; but there are no means of education for the people. Do public improvements favor intercourse between place and place? So far from this, the traveler cannot pass from town to town without danger, every mile, of robbery and assassination. I would not overcharge or exaggerate this picture; but its principal features are all too truly sketched.

And how does it contrast with the scene now actually before

us ? Look round upon these fields; they are verdant and beautiful, well cultivated, and at this moment loaded with the riches of the early harvest. The hands which till them are those of the free owners of the soil, enjoying equal rights, and protected by law from oppression and tyranny. Look to the thousand vessels in our sight, filling the harbor, or covering the neighboring sea. They are the vehicles of a profitable commerce, carried on by men who know that the profits of their hardy enterprise, when they make them, are their own ; and this commerce is encouraged and regulated by wise laws, and defended, when need be, by the valor and patriotism of the country. Look to that fair city, the abode of so much diffused wealth, so much general happiness and comfort, so much personal independence, and so much general knowledge, and not undistinguished, I may be permitted to add, for hospitality and social refinement. She fears no forced contributions, no siege or sacking from military leaders of rival factions. The hundred temples in which her citizens worship God are in no danger of sacrilege. The regular administration of the laws encounters no obstacle. The long processions of children and youth which you see this day issuing by thousands from her free schools, prove the care and anxiety with which a popular government provides for the education and morals of the people. Everywhere there is order; everywhere there is security. Everywhere the law reaches to the highest, and reaches to the lowest, to protect all in their rights, and to restrain all from wrong ; and over all hovers Liberty, — that Liberty for which our fathers fought and fell on this very spot, — with her eye ever watchful and her eagle wing ever wide outspread.

The colonies of Spain, from their origin to their end, were subject to the sovereign authority of the mother country. Their government, as well as their commerce, was a strict home monopoly. If we add to this the established usage of filling important posts in the administration of the colonies exclusively by natives of Old Spain, thus cutting off forever all hopes of honorable preferment from every man born in the Western hemisphere, causes enough rise up before us at once to account fully for the subsequent history and character of these provinces. The viceroys and provincial governors of Spain were never at home in their governments in America. They did not feel that they were of the people whom they governed. Their official character and employment have a good deal of resemblance to those of the proconsuls of Rome in Asia, Sicily, and Gaul, but obviously no resemblance to those of Carver and Winthrop, and very little to those of the governors of Virginia after that Colony had established a popular House of Burgesses.

The English colonists in America, generally speaking, were men who were seeking new homes in a new world. They brought with them their families and all that was most dear to them. This was especially the case with the colonists of Plymouth and Massachusetts. Many of them were educated men, and all possessed their full share, according to their social condition, of the knowl-edge and attainments of that age. The distinctive characteristic of their settlement is the introduction of the civilization of Europe into a wilderness, without bringing with it the political institutions of Europe. The arts, sciences, and literature of England came over with the settlers. That great portion of the common law which regulates the social and personal relations and conduct of men came also. The jury came; the *habeas corpus* came; the testamentary power came; and the law of inheritance and descent came also, except that part of it which recognizes the rights of primogeniture,[1] which either did not come at all, or soon gave way to the rule of equal partition of estates among children. But the monarchy did not come, nor the aristocracy, nor the church, as an estate of the realm. Political institutions were to be framed anew, such as should be adapted to the state of things. But it could not be doubtful what should be the nature and character of these institutions. A general social equality prevailed among the settlers, and an equality of political rights seemed the

---

[1] "Rights of primogeniture," i.e., the law providing that the eldest son should inherit the entire estate of his father.

natural, if not the necessary consequence. After forty years of revolution, violence, and war, the people of France have placed at the head of the fundamental instrument of their government, as the great boon obtained by all their sufferings and sacrifices, the declaration that all Frenchmen are equal before the law. What France has reached only by the expenditure of so much blood and treasure, and the perpetration of so much crime, the English colonists obtained by simply changing their place, carrying with them the intellectual and moral culture of Europe, and the personal and social relations to which they were accustomed, but leaving behind their political institutions. It has been said with much vivacity, that the felicity of the American colonists consisted in their escape from the past. This is true so far as respects political establishments, but no farther. They brought with them a full portion of all the riches of the past, in science, in art, in morals, religion, and literature. The Bible came with them. And it is not to be doubted, that to the free and universal reading of the Bible, in that age, men were much indebted for right views of civil liberty. The Bible is a book of faith, and a book of doctrine, and a book of morals, and a book of religion, of especial revelation from God; but it is also a book which teaches man his own individual responsibility, his own dignity, and his equality with his fellow man.

Bacon and Locke, and Shakespeare and Milton, also came with the colonists. It was the object of the first settlers to form new political systems; but all that belonged to cultivated man, to family, to neighborhood, to social relations, accompanied them. In the Doric [1] phrase of one of our own historians, " They came to settle on bare creation ; " but their settlement in the wilderness, nevertheless, was not a lodgment of nomadic tribes, a mere resting place of roaming savages. It was the beginning of a permanent community, the fixed residence of cultivated men. Not only was English literature read, but English, good English, was spoken and written, before the ax had made way to let in the

---

[1] Plain, unadorned.

sun upon the habitations and fields of Plymouth and Massachusetts. And, whatever may be said to the contrary, a correct use of the English language is, at this day, more general throughout the United States than it is throughout England herself.

But another grand characteristic is, that in the English Colonies political affairs were left to be managed by the colonists themselves. This is another fact wholly distinguishing them in character, as it has distinguished them in fortune, from the colonists of Spain. Here lies the foundation of that experience in self-government which has preserved order and security and regularity amidst the play of popular institutions. Home government was the secret of the prosperity of the North-American settlements. The more distinguished of the New-England colonists, with a most remarkable sagacity and a long-sighted reach into futurity, refused to come to America unless they could bring with them charters providing for the administration of their affairs in this country. They saw from the first the evils of being governed in the New World by a power fixed in the Old. Acknowledging the general superiority of the Crown, they still insisted on the right of passing local laws, and of local administration. And history teaches us the justice and the value of this determination in the example of Virginia. The early attempts to settle that Colony failed, sometimes with the most melancholy and fatal consequences, from want of knowledge, care, and attention on the part of those who had the charge of their affairs in England; and it was only after the issuing of the third charter that its prosperity fairly commenced. The cause was, that by that third charter the people of Virginia, for by this time they deserved to be so called, were allowed to constitute and establish the first popular representative assembly which ever convened on this continent,—the Virginia House of Burgesses.[1]

The great elements, then, of the American system of government, originally introduced by the colonists, and which were early

[1] The first House of Burgesses in Virginia was convened by Gov. Yeardley in 1619, thirteen years after the landing at Jamestown.

in operation, and ready to be developed more and more as the progress of events should justify or demand, were: —

Escape from the existing political systems of Europe, including its religious hierarchies,[1] but the continued possession and enjoyment of its science and arts, its literature and its manners;

Home government, or the power of making in the Colony the municipal laws which were to govern it;

Equality of rights;

Representative assemblies, or forms of government founded on popular elections.

Few topics are more inviting, or more fit for philosophical discussion, than the effect on the happiness of mankind of institutions founded upon these principles; or, in other words, the influence of the New World upon the Old.

Her obligations to Europe for science and art, laws, literature, and manners, America acknowledges as she ought, with respect and gratitude. The people of the United States, descendants of the English stock, grateful for the treasures of knowledge derived from their English ancestors, admit also, with thanks and filial regard, that among those ancestors, under the culture of Hampden and Sidney [2] and other assiduous friends, that seed of popular liberty first germinated, which on our soil has shot up to its full height, until its branches overshadow all the land.

But America has not failed to make returns. If she has not wholly canceled the obligation, or equaled it by others of like weight, she has at least made respectable advances towards repaying the debt. And she admits that, standing in the midst of civilized nations and in a civilized age, a nation among nations, there is a high part which she is expected to act for the general advancement of human interests and human welfare.

---

[1] Governments by the priesthood.

[2] John Hampden (1594–1643) and Algernon Sidney (1622–83), English patriots distinguished for their fearless advocacy of the rights of the people in opposition to kingly tyranny.

American mines have filled the mints of Europe with the precious metals. The productions of the American soil and climate have poured out their abundance of luxuries for the tables of the rich and of necessaries for the sustenance of the poor. Birds and animals of beauty and value have been added to the European stocks; and transplantations from the unequaled riches of our forests have mingled themselves profusely with the elms and ashes and druidical oaks of England.

America has made contributions to Europe far more important. Who can estimate the amount, or the value, of the augmentation of the commerce of the world that has resulted from America? Who can imagine to himself what would now be the shock to the Eastern Continent, if the Atlantic were no longer traversable, or if there were no longer American productions or American markets?

But America exercises influences, or holds out examples, for the consideration of the Old World, of a much higher, because they are of a moral and political character.

America has furnished to Europe proof of the fact that popular institutions, founded on equality and the principle of representation, are capable of maintaining governments able to secure the rights of person, property, and reputation.

America has proved that it is practicable to elevate the mass of mankind, — that portion which in Europe is called the laboring, or lower class, — to raise them to self-respect, to make them competent to act a part in the great right and great duty of self-government; and she has proved that this may be done by education and the diffusion of knowledge. She holds out an example, a thousand times more encouraging than ever was presented before, to those nine tenths of the human race who are born without hereditary fortune or hereditary rank.

America has furnished to the world the character of Washington. And, if our American institutions had done nothing else, that alone would have entitled them to the respect of mankind.

Washington! " First in war, first in peace, and first in the hearts of his countrymen!"[1] Washington is all our own! The enthusiastic veneration and regard in which the people of the United States hold him prove them to be worthy of such a countryman; while his reputation abroad reflects the highest honor on his country. I would cheerfully put the question to-day to the intelligence of Europe and the world, What character of the century, upon the whole, stands out in the relief of history, most pure, most respectable, most sublime? and I doubt not, that, by a suffrage approaching to unanimity, the answer would be, Washington!

The structure now standing before us, by its uprightness, its solidity, its durability, is no unfit emblem of his character. His public virtues and public principles were as firm as the earth on which it stands; his personal motives, as pure as the serene heaven in which its summit is lost. But, indeed, though a fit, it is an inadequate emblem. Towering high above the column which our hands have builded, beheld, not by the inhabitants of a single city or a single State, but by all the families of man, ascends the colossal grandeur of the character and life of Washington. In all the constituents of the one, in all the acts of the other, in all its titles to immortal love, admiration, and renown, it is an American production. It is the embodiment and vindication of our Transatlantic liberty. Born upon our soil, of parents also born upon it; never for a moment having had sight of the Old World; instructed, according to the modes of his time, only in the spare, plain, but wholesome elementary knowledge which our institutions provide for the children of the people; growing up beneath and penetrated by the genuine influences of American society; living, from infancy to manhood and age, amidst our expanding but not luxurious civilization; partaking in our great destiny of labor, our long contest with unreclaimed nature and uncivilized man, our agony of glory, the war of Independence, our great victory of peace, the formation of the Union

[1] These words were first used by Henry Lee in his oration on the death of Washington.

and the establishment of the Constitution,—he is all, all our own !   Washington is ours.   That crowded and glorious life,—

> " Where multitudes of virtues passed along,
>   Each pressing foremost, in the mighty throng
>   Ambitious to be seen, then making room
>   For greater multitudes that were to come," —

that life was the life of an American citizen.

I claim him for America.   In all the perils, in every darkened moment of the state, in the midst of the reproaches of enemies and the misgivings of friends, I turn to that transcendent name for courage and for consolation.   To him who denies or doubts whether our fervid liberty can be combined with law, with order, with the security of property, with the pursuits and advancement of happiness ; to him who denies that our forms of government are capable of producing exaltation of soul and the passion of true glory ; to him who denies that we have contributed anything to the stock of great lessons and great examples,—to all these I reply by pointing to Washington.

And now, friends and fellow citizens, it is time to bring this discourse to a close.

We have indulged in gratifying recollections of the past, in the prosperity and pleasures of the present, and in high hopes for the future.   But let us remember that we have duties and obligations to perform corresponding to the blessings which we enjoy.   Let us remember the trust, the sacred trust, attaching to the rich inheritance which we have received from our fathers.   Let us feel our personal responsibility, to the full extent of our power and influence, for the preservation of the principles of civil and religious liberty.   And let us remember that it is only religion and morals and knowledge, that can make men respectable[1] and happy under any form of government.   Let us hold fast the great truth, that communities are responsible, as well as individ-

---

[1] See note, p. 50.

uals; that no government is respectable [1] which is not just; that without unspotted purity of public faith, without sacred public principle, fidelity, and honor, no mere forms of government, no machinery of laws, can give dignity to political society. In our day and generation let us seek to raise and improve the moral sentiment, so that we may look, not for a degraded, but for an elevated and improved future. And when both we and our children shall have been consigned to the house appointed for all living, may love of country and pride of country glow with equal fervor among those to whom our names and our blood shall have descended ! And then, when honored and decrepit age shall lean against the base of this monument, and troops of ingenuous youth shall be gathered round it, and when the one shall speak to the other of its objects, the purposes of its construction, and the great and glorious events with which it is connected, there shall rise from every youthful breast the ejaculation, "Thank God, I — I also — AM AN AMERICAN !"

[1] See note, p. 50.

THE CHARACTER OF WASHINGTON.

A SPEECH DELIVERED AT A PUBLIC DINNER IN THE CITY OF
WASHINGTON, ON THE 22D OF FEBRUARY, 1832, THE
CENTENNIAL ANNIVERSARY OF WASHINGTON'S
BIRTHDAY.

I RISE, gentlemen, to propose to you the name of that great
man in commemoration of whose birth, and in honor of
whose character and services, we are here assembled.

I am sure that I express a sentiment common to every one
present, when I say that there is something more than ordinarily
solemn and affecting in this occasion.

We are met to testify our regard for him whose name is intimately blended with whatever belongs most essentially to the
prosperity, the liberty, the free institutions, and the renown of our
country.   That name was of power to rally a nation in the hour
of thick-thronging public disasters and calamities; that name
shone, amid the storm of war, a beacon light, to cheer and guide
the country's friends; it flamed, too, like a meteor, to repel her
foes.   That name, in the days of peace, was a loadstone, attract-
ing to itself a whole people's confidence, a whole people's love,
and the whole world's respect.   That name, descending with all
time, spreading over the whole earth, and uttered in all the languages belonging to the tribes and races of men, will forever be
pronounced with affectionate gratitude by every one in whose
breast there shall arise an aspiration for human rights and human
liberty.

We perform this grateful duty, gentlemen, at the expiration of a hundred years from his birth, near the place, so cherished and beloved by him, where his dust now reposes, and in the capital which bears his own immortal name.

All experience evinces that human sentiments are strongly influenced by associations. The recurrence of anniversaries, or of longer periods of time, naturally freshens the recollection, and deepens the impression, of events with which they are historically connected. Renowned places, also, have a power to awaken feeling, which all acknowledge. No American can pass by the fields of Bunker Hill, Monmouth, and Camden, as if they were ordinary spots on the earth's surface. Whoever visits them feels the sentiment of love of country kindling anew, as if the spirit that belonged to the transactions which have rendered these places distinguished, still hovered round, with power to move and excite all who in future time may approach them.

But neither of these sources of emotion equals the power with which great moral examples affect the mind. When sublime virtues cease to be abstractions, when they become embodied in human character, and exemplified in human conduct, we should be false to our own nature if we did not indulge in the spontaneous effusions of our gratitude and our admiration. A true lover of the virtue of patriotism delights to contemplate its purest models; and that love of country may be well suspected which affects to soar so high into the regions of sentiment as to be lost and absorbed in the abstract feeling, and becomes too elevated or too refined to glow with fervor in the commendation or the love of individual benefactors. All this is unnatural. It is as if one should be so enthusiastic a lover of poetry as to care nothing for Homer or Milton; so passionately attached to eloquence as to be indifferent to Tully[1] and Chatham;[2] or such a devotee to the arts, in such an ecstasy with the elements of beauty, proportion, and expression, as to regard the masterpieces of Raphael[3]

---

[1] Marcus Tullius Cicero, the most famous Roman orator (106–43 B.C.).
[2] William Pitt, Earl of Chatham, the " Great Commoner " (1708–78).
[3] Raphael, or Raffaelle Santi d'Urbino, Italian painter (1483–1520).

and Michael Angelo [1] with coldness or contempt. We may be assured, gentlemen, that he who really loves the thing itself, loves its finest exhibitions. A true friend of his country loves her friends and benefactors, and thinks it no degradation to commend and commemorate them. The voluntary outpouring of the public feeling made to-day, from the North to the South, and from the East to the West, proves this sentiment to be both just and natural. In the cities and in the villages, in the public temples and in the family circles, among all ages and sexes, gladdened voices to-day bespeak grateful hearts and a freshened recollection of the virtues of the Father of his Country. And it will be so in all time to come, so long as public virtue is itself an object of regard. The ingenuous youth of America will hold up to themselves the bright model of Washington's example, and study to be what they behold; they will contemplate his character till all its virtues spread out and display themselves to their delighted vision, as the earliest astronomers, the shepherds on the plains of Babylon, gazed at the stars till they saw them form into clusters and constellations, overpowering at length the eyes of the beholders with the united blaze of a thousand lights.

Gentlemen, we are at a point of a century from the birth of Washington; and what a century it has been! During its course, the human mind has seemed to proceed with a sort of geometric velocity, accomplishing for human intelligence and human freedom more than had been done in fives or tens of centuries preceding. Washington stands at the commencement of a new era, as well as at the head of the New World. A century from the birth of Washington has changed the world. The country of Washington has been the theater on which a great part of that change has been wrought, and Washington himself a principal agent by which it has been accomplished. His age and his country are equally full of wonders; and of both he is the chief.

If the poetical prediction uttered a few years before his birth be true; if indeed it be designed by Providence that the grandest

[1] Michael Angelo Buonarroti, Italian painter and sculptor (1485-1564).

exhibition of human character and human affairs shall be made on this theater of the Western world; if it be true that

> " The four first acts already past,
> A fifth shall close the drama with the day:
> Time's noblest offspring is the last," [1] —

how could this imposing, swelling, final scene be appropriately opened, how could its intense interest be adequately sustained, but by the introduction of just such a character as our Washington ?

Washington had attained his manhood when that spark of liberty was struck out in his own country which has since kindled into a flame, and shot its beams over the earth. In the flow of a century from his birth, the world has changed in science, in arts, in the extent of commerce, in the improvement of navigation, and in all that relates to the civilization of man. But it is the spirit of human freedom, the new elevation of individual man, in his moral, social, and political character, leading the whole long train of other improvements, which has most remarkably distinguished the era. Society, in this century, has not made its progress, like Chinese skill, by a greater acuteness of ingenuity in trifles; it has not merely lashed itself to an increased speed round the old circles of thought and action; but it has assumed a new character; it has raised itself from *beneath* governments to a participation *in* governments; it has mixed moral and political objects with the daily pursuits of individual men; and, with a freedom and strength before altogether unknown, it has applied to these objects the whole power of the human understanding. It has been the era, in short, when the social principle has triumphed over the feudal principle; when society has maintained its rights against military power, and established, on foundations never hereafter to be shaken, its competency to govern itself.

[1] From a poem entitled On the Prospect of Planting Arts and Learning in America, written by Bishop Berkeley in 1724. The first line of the stanza is,
> " Westward the course of empire takes its way."

It was the extraordinary fortune of Washington, that having been intrusted in Revolutionary times with the supreme military command, and having fulfilled that trust with equal renown for wisdom and for valor, he should be placed at the head of the first government in which an attempt was to be made on a large scale to rear the fabric of social order on the basis of a written constitution and of a pure representative principle. A government was to be established, without a throne, without an aristocracy, without castes, orders, or privileges; and this government, instead of being a democracy, existing and acting within the walls of a single city, was to be extended over a vast country, of different climates, interests, and habits, and of various communions of our common Christian faith. The experiment certainly was entirely new. A popular government of this extent, it was evident, could be framed only by carrying into full effect the principle of representation or of delegated power; and the world was to see whether society could, by the strength of this principle, maintain its own peace and good government, carry forward its own great interests, and conduct itself to political renown and glory. By the benignity of Providence, this experiment, so full of interest to us and to our posterity forever, so full of interest, indeed, to the world in its present generation and in all its generations to come, was suffered to commence under the guidance of Washington. Destined for this high career, he was fitted for it by wisdom, by virtue, by patriotism, by discretion, by whatever can inspire confidence in man towards man. In entering on the untried scenes, early disappointment and the premature extinction of all hope of success would have been certain, had it not been that there did exist throughout the country, in a most extraordinary degree, an unwavering trust in him who stood at the helm.

I remarked, gentlemen, that the whole world was and is interested in the result of this experiment. And is it not so ? Do we deceive ourselves, or is it true that at this moment the career which this government is running is among the most attractive objects to the civilized world? Do we deceive ourselves, or is it true that at this moment that love of liberty, and that understanding of its true principles, which are flying over the whole earth as on the wings of all the winds, are really and truly of American origin?

At the period of the birth of Washington, there existed in Europe no political liberty in large communities, except in the provinces of Holland, and except that England herself had set a great example, so far as it went, by her glorious Revolution of 1688. Everywhere else despotic power was predominant, and the feudal or military principle held the mass of mankind in hopeless bondage. One half of Europe was crushed beneath the Bourbon scepter; and no conception of political liberty, no hope even of religious toleration, existed among that nation which was America's first ally. The king was the state,[1] the king was the country, the king was all. There was one king, with power not derived from his people, and too high to be questioned; and the rest were all subjects, with no political right but obedience. All above was intangible power; all below, quiet subjection. A recent occurrence in the French Chambers shows us how public opinion on these subjects is changed. A minister had spoken of the "king's subjects." "There are no subjects," exclaimed hundreds of voices at once, "in a country where the people make the king!"

Gentlemen, the spirit of human liberty and of free government, nurtured and grown into strength and beauty in America, has stretched its course into the midst of the nations. Like an emanation from Heaven, it has gone forth, and it will not return void. It must change, it is fast changing, the face of the earth. Our great, our high duty is to show, in our own example, that this spirit is a spirit of health as well as a spirit of power; that its benignity is as great as its strength; that its efficiency to secure individual rights, social relations, and moral order, is equal

---

[1] An allusion to the famous dictum of Louis XIV., "*L'état c'est moi*" ("I am the state"). See p. 37.

to the irresistible force with which it prostrates principalities and powers. The world at this moment is regarding us with a willing, but something of a fearful admiration. Its deep and awful anxiety is to learn whether free states may be stable, as well as free; whether popular power may be trusted, as well as feared: in short, whether wise, regular, and virtuous self-government is a vision for the contemplation of theorists, or a truth established, illustrated, and brought into practice in the country of Washington.

Gentlemen, for the earth which we inhabit and the whole circle of the sun, for all the unborn races of mankind, we seem to hold in our hands, for their weal or woe, the fate of this experiment. If we fail, who shall venture the repetition? If our example shall prove to be one, not of encouragement, but of terror, not fit to be imitated, but fit only to be shunned, where else shall the world look for free models? If this great *Western Sun* be struck out of the firmament, at what other fountain shall the lamp of liberty hereafter be lighted? What other orb shall emit a ray to glimmer even, on the darkness of the world?

There is no danger of our overrating or overstating the important part which we are now acting in human affairs. It should not flatter our personal self-respect; but it should reanimate our patriotic virtues, and inspire us with a deeper and more solemn sense, both of our privileges and of our duties. We cannot wish better for our country nor for the world than that the same spirit which influenced Washington may influence all who succeed him; and that the same blessing from above, which attended his efforts, may also attend theirs.

The principles of Washington's administration are not left doubtful. They are to be found in the Constitution itself, in the great measures recommended and approved by him, in his speeches to Congress, and in that most interesting paper, his "Farewell Address to the People of the United States." The success of the government under his administration is the highest proof of the soundness of these principles. And, after an experience of thirty-five years, what is there which an enemy could condemn ?   What is there which either his friends, or the friends of the country, could wish to have been otherwise ?   I speak, of course, of great measures and leading principles.

In the first place, all his measures were right in their intent. He stated the whole basis of his own great character, when he told the country, in the homely phrase of the proverb, that honesty is the best policy.   One of the most striking things ever said of him is, that "*he changed mankind's ideas of political greatness.*" [1] To commanding talents and to success, the common elements of such greatness, he added a disregard of self, a spotlessness of motive, a steady submission to every public and private duty, which threw far into the shade the whole crowd of vulgar great. The object of his regard was the whole country.   No part of it was enough to fill his enlarged patriotism.   His love of glory, so far as that may be supposed to have influenced him at all, spurned everything short of general approbation.   It would have been nothing to him, that his partisans or his favorites outnumbered, or outvoted, or outmanaged, or outclamored, those of other leaders.   He had no favorites; he rejected all partisanship; and, acting honestly for the universal good, he deserved what he has so richly enjoyed, — the universal love.

His principle it was, to act right, and to trust the people for support; his principle it was, not to follow the lead of sinister and selfish ends, nor to rely on the little arts of party delusion to obtain public sanction for such a course.   Born for his country and for the world, he did not give up to party what was meant for mankind.   The consequence is, that his fame is as durable as his principles, as lasting as truth and virtue themselves.   While the hundreds whom party excitement, and temporary circumstances, and casual combinations, have raised into transient notoriety, sink again, like thin bubbles, bursting and dissolving into the great ocean, Washington's fame is like the rock which bounds that ocean, and at whose feet its billows are destined to break harmlessly forever.

[1] Works of Fisher Ames.

The maxims upon which Washington conducted our foreign relations were few and simple. The first was an entire and indisputable impartiality towards foreign states. He adhered to this rule of public conduct against very strong inducements to depart from it, and when the popularity of the moment seemed to favor such a departure. In the next place, he maintained true dignity and unsullied honor in all communications with foreign states. It was among the high duties devolved upon him to introduce our new government into the circle of civilized states and powerful nations. Not arrogant or assuming, with no unbecoming or supercilious bearing, he yet exacted for it from all others entire and punctilious respect. He demanded, and he obtained at once, a standing of perfect equality for his country in the society of nations; nor was there a prince or potentate of his day whose personal character carried with it, into the intercourse of other states, a greater degree of respect and veneration.

He regarded other nations only as they stood in political relations to us. With their internal affairs, their political parties and dissensions, he scrupulously abstained from all interference; and, on the other hand, he repelled with spirit all such interference by others with us or our concerns. His sternest rebuke, the most indignant measure of his whole administration, was aimed against such an attempted interference. He felt it as an attempt to wound the national honor, and resented it accordingly.

The reiterated admonitions in his " Farewell Address " show his deep fears that foreign influence would insinuate itself into our counsels through the channels of domestic dissension, and obtain a sympathy with our own temporary parties. Against all such dangers, he most earnestly entreats the country to guard itself. He appeals to its patriotism, to its self-respect, to its own honor, to every consideration connected with its welfare and happiness, to resist, at the very beginning, all tendencies towards such connection of foreign interests with our own affairs. With a tone of earnestness nowhere else found, even in his last affectionate farewell advice to his countrymen, he says, " Against the insidious wiles of foreign influence (I conjure you to believe me, fellow citizens), the jealousy of a free people ought to be *constantly* awake, since history and experience prove that foreign influence is one of the most baneful foes of republican government."

Lastly, on the subject of foreign relations, Washington never forgot that we had interests peculiar to ourselves. The primary political concerns of Europe, he saw, did not affect us. We had nothing to do with her balance of power, her family compacts, or her successions to thrones. We were placed in a condition favorable to neutrality during European wars, and to the enjoyment of all the great advantages of that relation. "Why, then," he asks us, "why forego the advantages of so peculiar a situation? Why quit our own to stand upon foreign ground? Why, by interweaving our destiny with that of any part of Europe, entangle our peace and prosperity in the toils of European ambition, rivalship, interest, humor, or caprice?"

Indeed, gentlemen, Washington's "Farewell Address" is full of truths important at all times, and particularly deserving consideration at the present. With a sagacity which brought the future before him, and made it like the present, he saw and pointed out the dangers that even at this moment most imminently threaten us. I hardly know how a greater service of that kind could now be done to the community than by a renewed and wide diffusion of that admirable paper, and an earnest invitation to every man in the country to reperuse and consider it. Its political maxims are invaluable; its exhortations to love of country and to brotherly affection among citizens, touching; and the solemnity with which it urges the observance of moral duties, and impresses the power of religious obligation, gives to it the highest character of truly disinterested, sincere, parental advice.

The domestic policy of Washington found its polestar in the avowed objects of the Constitution itself. He sought so to administer that Constitution as to form a more perfect union, establish justice, insure domestic tranquillity, provide for the common defense, promote the general welfare, and secure the

6

blessings of liberty. These were objects interesting in the highest degree to the whole country; and his policy embraced the
whole country.

Among his earliest and most important duties was the organization of the government itself, the choice of his confidential
advisers, and the various appointments to office. This duty, so
important and delicate, when a whole government was to be
organized, and all its offices for the first time filled, was yet not
difficult to him; for he had no sinister ends to accomplish, no
clamorous partisans to gratify, no pledges to redeem, no object
to be regarded, but simply the public good. It was a plain,
straightforward matter, a mere honest choice of good men for
the public service.

His own singleness of purpose, his disinterested patriotism,
were evinced by the selection of his first Cabinet, and by the
manner in which he filled the seats of justice and other places
of high trust. He sought for men fit for offices, not for offices
which might suit men. Above personal considerations, above
local considerations, above party considerations, he felt that he
could only discharge the sacred trust which the country had
placed in his hands, by a diligent inquiry after real merit, and a
conscientious preference of virtue and talent. The whole country was the field of his selection. He explored that whole field,
looking only for whatever it contained most worthy and distinguished. He was, indeed, most successful; and he deserved success for the purity of his motives, the liberality of his sentiments,
and his enlarged and manly policy.

Washington's administration established the national credit,
made provision for the public debt and for that patriotic army
whose interests and welfare were always so dear to him, and,
by laws wisely framed and of admirable effect, raised the commerce and navigation of the country, almost at once, from de-
pression and ruin to a state of prosperity. Nor were his eyes
open to these interests alone. He viewed with equal concern its
agriculture and manufactures, and, so far as they came within the

regular exercise of the powers of this government, they experienced regard and favor.

It should not be omitted, even in this slight reference to the general measures and general principles of the first President, that he saw and felt the full value and importance of the judicial department of the government. An upright and able administration of the laws, he held to be alike indispensable to private happiness and public liberty. The temple of justice, in his opinion, was a sacred place, and he would profane and pollute it who should call any to minister in it not spotless in character, not incorruptible in integrity, not competent by talent and learning, not a fit object of unhesitating trust.

Among other admonitions, Washington has left us, in his last communication to his country, an exhortation against the excesses of party spirit. A fire not to be quenched, he yet conjures us not to fan and feed the flame. Undoubtedly, gentlemen, it is the greatest danger of our system and of our time. Undoubtedly, if that system should be overthrown, it will be the work of excessive party spirit, acting on the government, which is dangerous enough, or acting *in* the government, which is a thousand times more dangerous; for government then becomes nothing but organized party, and, in the strange vicissitudes of human affairs, it may come at last, perhaps, to exhibit the singular paradox of government itself being in opposition to its own powers, at war with the very elements of its own existence. Such cases are hopeless. As men may be protected against murder, but cannot be guarded against suicide, so government may be shielded from the assaults of external foes; but nothing can save it when it chooses to lay violent hands on itself.

Finally, gentlemen, there was in the breast of Washington one sentiment so deeply felt, so constantly uppermost, that no proper occasion escaped without its utterance. From the letter which he signed in behalf of the Convention when the Constitution was sent out to the people, to the moment when he put his hand to that last paper in which he addressed his countrymen, the Union

—the Union was the great object of his thoughts. In that first letter he tells them that, to him and his brethren of the Convention, union appears to be the greatest interest of every true American; and in that last paper he conjures them to regard that unity of government which constitutes them one people, as the very palladium [1] of their prosperity and safety, and the security of liberty itself. He regarded the union of these States less as one of our blessings than as the great treasure-house which contained them all. Here, in his judgment, was the great magazine of all our means of prosperity; here, as he thought, and as every true American still thinks, are deposited all our animating prospects, all our solid hopes for future greatness. He has taught us to maintain this union, not by seeking to enlarge the powers of the government, on the one hand, nor by surrendering them, on the other, but by an administration of them at once firm and moderate, pursuing objects truly national, and carried on in a spirit of justice and equity.

The extreme solicitude for the preservation of the Union, at all times manifested by him, shows not only the opinion he entertained of its importance, but his clear perception of those causes which were likely to spring up to endanger it, and which, if once they should overthrow the present system, would leave little hope of any future beneficial union. Of all the presumptions indulged by presumptuous man, that is one of the rashest which looks for repeated and favorable opportunities for the deliberate establishment of a united government over distinct and widely extended communities. Such a thing has happened once in human affairs, and but once: the event stands out as a prominent exception to all ordinary history; and, unless we suppose ourselves running into an age of miracles, we may not expect its repetition.

Washington, therefore, could regard, and did regard, nothing

---

[1] Preserver. This was the name applied to the statue of Pallas Athene, the presence of which within the walls of Troy was believed to assure the preservation of the city from the attacks of the Greeks.

as of paramount political interest but the integrity of the Union itself. With a united government well administered, he saw that we had nothing to fear; and without it, nothing to hope. The sentiment is just, and its momentous truth should solemnly impress the whole country. If we might regard our country as personated in the spirit of Washington; if we might consider him as representing her in her past renown, her present prosperity, and her future career, and as, in that character, demanding of us all to account for our conduct as political men or as private citizens, — how should he answer him who has ventured to talk of disunion and dismemberment? Or how should he answer him who dwells perpetually on local interests, and fans every kindling flame of local prejudice? How should he answer him who would array State against State, interest against interest, and party against party, careless of the continuance of that *unity of government which constitutes us one people?*

The political prosperity which this country has attained, and which it now enjoys, has been acquired mainly through the instrumentality of the present government. While this agent continues, the capacity of attaining to still higher degrees of prosperity exists also. We have, while this lasts, a political life capable of beneficial exertion, with power to resist or overcome misfortunes, to sustain us against the ordinary accidents of human affairs, and to promote, by active efforts, every public interest. But dismemberment strikes at the very being which preserves these faculties. It would lay its rude and ruthless hand on this great agent itself. It would sweep away, not only what we possess, but all power of regaining lost, or acquiring new possessions. It would leave the country not only bereft of its prosperity and happiness, but without limbs, or organs, or faculties by which to exert itself hereafter in the pursuit of that prosperity and happiness.

Other misfortunes may be borne, or their effects overcome. If disastrous war should sweep our commerce from the ocean, another generation may renew it; if it exhaust our treasury, future industry may replenish it; if it desolate and lay waste our fields, still, under a new cultivation, they will grow green again, and ripen to future harvests. It were but a trifle, even if the walls of yonder Capitol were to crumble, if its lofty pillars should fall, and its gorgeous decorations be all covered by the dust of the valley. All these might be rebuilt. But who shall reconstruct the fabric of demolished government? Who shall rear again the well-proportioned columns of constitutional liberty? Who shall frame together the skillful architecture which unites national sovereignty with State rights, individual security, and public prosperity? No, if these columns fall, they will be raised not again. Like the Coliseum [1] and the Parthenon,[2] they will be destined to a mournful, a melancholy immortality. Bitterer tears, however, will flow over them than were ever shed over the monuments of Roman or Grecian art; for they will be the remnants of a more glorious edifice than Greece or Rome ever saw,—the edifice of constitutional American liberty.

But let us hope for better things. Let us trust in that gracious Being who has hitherto held our country as in the hollow of his hand. Let us trust to the virtue and the intelligence of the people, and to the efficacy of religious obligation. Let us trust to the influence of Washington's example. Let us hope that that fear of Heaven which expels all other fear, and that regard to duty which transcends all other regard, may influence public men and private citizens, and lead our country still onward in her happy career. Full of these gratifying anticipations and hopes, let us look forward to the end of that century which is now commenced. A hundred years hence, other disciples of Washington will celebrate his birth, with no less of sincere admiration than we now commemorate it. When they shall meet, as we now meet, to do themselves and him that honor, so surely as they shall see the blue summits of his native mountains rise in the horizon, so surely as they shall behold the river on whose banks he lived, and on whose banks he rests, still flowing on to-

---

[1] The famous amphitheater at Rome, built by the Emperor Vespasian.

[2] The marble temple of Athene, on the Acropolis at Athens.

wards the sea, so surely may they see, as we now see, the flag of the Union floating on the top of the Capitol; and then, as now, may the sun in his course visit no land more free, more happy, more lovely, than this our own country !

Gentlemen, I propose

"THE MEMORY OF GEORGE WASHINGTON."

THE LANDING AT PLYMOUTH.

A SPEECH DELIVERED ON THE 22D OF DECEMBER, 1843, AT
THE PUBLIC DINNER OF THE NEW-ENGLAND SOCIETY
OF NEW YORK, IN COMMEMORATION OF THE
LANDING OF THE PILGRIMS.

MR. PRESIDENT, I have a grateful duty to perform
in acknowledging the kindness of the sentiment thus expressed towards me.[1]   And yet I must say, gentlemen, that I rise
upon this occasion under a consciousness that I may probably
disappoint highly raised, too highly raised expectations.   In the
scenes of this evening, and in the scene of this day, my part is a
humble one.   I can enter into no competition with the fresher
geniuses of those more eloquent gentlemen, learned and rever-

----

[1] On the 22d of December, 1843, the anniversary of the landing at Plymouth was celebrated with great success by the New-England Society of New
York.   The exercises were opened with a commemorative oration by the
Hon. Rufus Choate; and later in the day the Society and a number of invited
guests met at a public dinner at the Astor House.   After several appropriate
toasts had been given and responded to, George Griswold rose, and offered a
few complimentary remarks concerning Daniel Webster.   After referring to
that gentleman's public services, to his refutation of the doctrine of nullification, and to the wisdom of his course in connection with the treaty of Washington, Mr. Griswold gave the following toast : —

"DANIEL WEBSTER, — the gift of New England to his country, his whole
country, and nothing but his country."

When Mr. Webster rose to respond to this toast, he was greeted with nine
hearty and prolonged cheers ; and when quiet had been restored, he proceeded
to deliver this address.

end, who have addressed this Society. I may perform, however,
the humbler, but sometimes useful, duty of contrast, by adding
the dark ground of the picture, which shall serve to bring out
the more brilliant colors.

I must receive, gentlemen, the sentiment proposed by the
worthy and distinguished citizen of New York before me, as intended to convey the idea, that as a citizen of New England, as
a son, a child, a *creation*, of New England, I may be yet supposed
to entertain, in some degree, that enlarged view of my duty as a
citizen of the United States and as a public man, which may, in
some small measure, commend me to the regard of the whole
country. While I am free to confess, gentlemen, that there is
no compliment of which I am more desirous to be thought
worthy, I will add, that a compliment of that kind could have
proceeded from no source more agreeable to my own feelings
than from the gentleman who has proposed it,—an eminent
merchant, the member of a body of eminent merchants, known
throughout the world for their intelligence and enterprise. I the
more especially feel this, gentlemen, because, whether I view the
present state of things, or recur to the history of the past, I can
in neither case be ignorant how much that profession and its
distinguished members, from an early day of our history, have
contributed to make the country what it is, and the government
what it is.

Gentlemen, the free nature of our institutions, and the popular
form of those governments which have come down to us from
the Rock of Plymouth, give scope to intelligence, to talent, enterprise, and public spirit, from all classes making up the great
body of the community. And the country has received benefit,
in all its history and in all its exigencies, of the most eminent and
striking character, from persons of the class to which my friend
before me belongs. Who will ever forget that the first name
signed to our ever-memorable and ever-glorious Declaration of
Independence is the name of John Hancock, a merchant of
Boston ? Who will ever forget, that in the most disastrous days

of the Revolution, when the treasury of the country was bank-
rupt, with unpaid navies and starving armies, it was a merchant,
— Robert Morris of Philadelphia, — who by a noble sacrifice of
his own fortune, as well as by the exercise of his great financial
abilities, sustained and supported the wise men of the country in
council, and the brave men of the country in the field of battle ?
Nor are there wanting more recent instances. I have the pleasure to see near me, and near my friend who proposed this sentiment, the son of an eminent merchant of New England [Mr.
Goodhue], an early member of the Senate of the United States,
always consulted, always respected, in whatever belonged to the
duty and the means of putting in operation the financial and
commercial system of the country; and this mention of the
father of my friend brings to my mind the memory of his great
colleague, the early associate of Hamilton and of Ames, trusted
and beloved by Washington, consulted on all occasions connected
with the administration of the finances, the establishment of the
treasury department, the imposition of the first rates of duty, and
with everything that belonged to the commercial system of the
United States, — George Cabot of Massachusetts.

I will take this occasion to say, gentlemen, that there is no
truth better developed and established in the history of the United
States, from the formation of the Constitution to the present time,
than this, — that the mercantile classes, the great commercial
masses of the country, whose affairs connect them strongly with
every State in the Union and with all the nations of the earth,
whose business and profession give a sort of nationality to their
character, — that no class of men among us, from the beginning,
have shown a stronger and firmer devotion to whatsoever has
been designed, or to whatever has tended, to preserve the union
of these States and the stability of the free government under
which we live. The Constitution of the United States, in regard
to the various municipal regulations and local interests, has left
the States individual, disconnected, isolated. It has left them
their own codes of criminal law; it has left them their own sys-

tem of municipal regulations.   But there was one great interest, one great concern, which, from the very nature of the case, was no longer to be left under the regulations of the then thirteen, afterwards twenty, and now twenty-six States, but was committed, necessarily committed, to the care, the protection, and the regulation of one government; and this was that great unit, as it has been called, the commerce of the United States.   There is no commerce of New York, no commerce of Massachusetts, none of Georgia, none of Alabama or Louisiana.   All and singular, in the aggregate and in all its parts, is the commerce of the United States, regulated at home by a uniform system of laws under the authority of the general government, and protected abroad under the flag of our government, the glorious *E Pluribus Unum*,[1] and guarded, if need be, by the power of the general government all over the world.   There is, therefore, gentlemen, nothing more cementing, nothing that makes us more cohesive, nothing that more repels all tendencies to separation and dismemberment, than this great, this common, I may say this overwhelming interest of one commerce, one general system of trade and navigation, one everywhere and with every nation of the globe.   There is no flag of any particular American State seen in the Pacific seas, or in the Baltic; or in the Indian Ocean.   Who knows, or who hears, there of your proud State, or of my proud State ?   Who knows, or who hears, of anything, at the extremest north or south, or at the antipodes; in the remotest regions of the Eastern or Western sea,—who ever hears, or knows, of anything but an American ship, or of any American enterprise of a commercial character that does not bear the impression of the American Union with it ?

It would be a presumption of which I cannot be guilty, gentlemen, for me to imagine for a moment, that, among the gifts which New England has made to our common country, I am anything more than one of the most inconsiderable.   I readily bring to mind the great men, not only with whom I have met,

<hr>

[1] One out of many,—the motto of the United States.

but those of the generation before me, who now sleep with their fathers, distinguished in the Revolution, distinguished in the formation of the Constitution and in the early administration of the government, always and everywhere distinguished; and I shrink in just and conscious humiliation before their established character and established renown; and all that I venture to say, and all that I venture to hope may be thought true in the sentiment proposed, is, that so far as mind and purpose, so far as intention and will, are concerned, I may be found among those who are capable of embracing the whole country, of which they are members, in a proper, comprehensive, and patriotic regard. We all know that the objects which are nearest are the objects which are dearest. Family affections, neighborhood affections, social relations; these, in truth, are nearest and dearest to us all: but whosoever shall be able rightly to adjust the graduation of his affections, and to love his friends and his neighbors and his country as he ought to love them, merits the commendation pronounced by the philosophic poet upon him

"Qui didicit patriæ quid debeat, et quid amicis."[1]

Gentlemen, it has been my fortune, in the little part which I have acted in public life, for good or for evil to the community, to be connected entirely with that government, which, within the limits of constitutional power, exercises jurisdiction over all the States and all the people. My friend at the end of the table, on my left, has spoken pleasantly to us to-night of the reputed miracles of tutelar saints. In a sober sense, in a sense of deep conviction, I say that the emergence of this country from British domination, and its union, under its present form of government, beneath the general Constitution of the country, if not a miracle, is, I do not say the most, but one of the most, fortunate, the most admirable, the most auspicious, occurrences which have ever fallen to the lot of man. Circumstances have wrought out for

[1] "Who has learned what he owes to his country, and what to his friends." — HORACE.

us a state of things, which, in other times and other regions, philosophy has dreamed of, and theory has proposed, and speculation has suggested, but which man has never been able to accomplish. I mean the government of a great nation, over a vastly extended portion of the surface of the earth, *by means of local institutions for local purposes, and general institutions for general purposes.* I know of nothing in the history of the world, notwithstanding the great league of Grecian states, notwithstanding the success of the Roman system (and certainly there is no exception to the remark in modern history), — I know of nothing so suitable, on the whole, for the great interests of a great people spread over a large portion of the globe, as the provision of local legislation for local and municipal purposes, with, not a confederacy, nor a loose binding together of separate parts, but a limited, positive general government, for positive general purposes, over the whole. We may derive eminent proofs of this truth from the past and the present. What see we to-day in the agitations on the other side of the Atlantic ? I speak of them, of course, without expressing any opinion on questions of politics in a foreign country; but I speak of them as an occurrence which shows the great expediency, the utility, I may say the necessity, of local legislation. If, in a country on the other side of the water [Ireland], there be some who desire a severance of one part of the empire from another, under a proposition of repeal, there are others who propose a continuance of the existing relation under a federative system : and what is this ? No more and no less than an approximation to that system under which we live, which for local municipal purposes shall have a local legislature, and for general purposes a general legislature.

This becomes the more important when we consider that the United States stretch over so many degrees of latitude, that they embrace such a variety of climate, that various conditions and relations of society naturally call for different laws and regulations. Let me ask whether the Legislature of New York could wisely pass laws for the government of Louisiana, or whether the Legislature of Louisiana could wisely pass laws for Pennsylvania or New York. Everybody will say, " No." And yet the interests of New York and Pennsylvania and Louisiana, in whatever concerns their relations between themselves and their general relations with all the states of the world, are found to be perfectly well provided for, and adjusted with perfect congruity, by committing these general interests to one common government, the result of popular general elections among them all.

I confess, gentlemen, that having been, as I have said, in my humble career in public life, employed in that portion of the public service which is connected with the general government, I have contemplated, as the great object of every proceeding, not only the particular benefit of the moment, or the exigency of the occasion, but the preservation of this system; for I do consider it so much the result of circumstances, and that so much of it is due to fortunate concurrence as well as to the sagacity of the great men acting upon those occasions, that it is an experiment of such remarkable and renowned success, that he is a fool or a madman who would wish to try that experiment a second time. I see to-day, and we all see, that the descendants of the Puritans, who landed upon the Rock of Plymouth; the followers of Raleigh, who settled Virginia and North Carolina; he who lives where the truncheon of empire, so to speak, was borne by Smith; the inhabitants of Georgia; he who settled, under the auspices of France, at the mouth of the Mississippi; the Swede on the Delaware; the Quaker of Pennsylvania,—all find at this day their common interest, their common protection, their common *glory*, under the united government, which leaves them all, nevertheless, in the administration of their own municipal and local affairs, to be Frenchmen, or Swedes, or Quakers, or whatever they choose. And when one considers that this system of government, I will not say has produced, because God and nature and circumstances have had an agency in it,—but when it is considered that this system has not prevented, but has rather encouraged, the growth of the people of this country from three millions on

the glorious 4th of July, 1776, to seventeen millions now, who
is there that will say, upon this hemisphere, nay, who is there that
will stand up in any hemisphere, who is there in any part of the
world, that will say that the great experiment of a united republic has *failed* in America ?   And yet I know, gentlemen, I feel,
that this united system is held together by strong tendencies to
union, at the same time that it is kept from too much leaning towards consolidation by a strong tendency in the several States
to support each its own power and consideration.   In the physical world it is said, that

" All nature's difference keeps all nature's peace,"

and there is in the political world this same harmonious difference,
this regular play of the positive and negative powers (if I may so
say), which, at least for one glorious half century, has kept us as
we have been kept, and made us what we are.

But, gentlemen, I must not allow myself to pursue this topic.
It is a sentiment so commonly repeated by me upon all public
occasions, and upon all private occasions, and everywhere, that
I forbear to dwell upon it now.   It is the union of these States,
it is the system of government under which we live, beneath the
Constitution of the United States, happily framed, wisely adopted,
successfully administered for fifty years, — it is mainly this, I say,
that gives us power at home and credit abroad.   And, for one,
I never stop to consider the power, or wealth, or greatness of a
State.   I tell you, Mr. Chairman, I care nothing for your Empire
State as such.   Delaware and Rhode Island are as high in my
regard as New York.   In population, in power, in the government over us, you have a greater share.   You would have the
same share, if you were divided into forty States.   It is not,
therefore, as a State sovereignty, it is only because New York
is a vast portion of the whole American people, that I regard
this State, as I always shall regard her, as respectable [1] and honor
able.   But among State sovereignties there is no preference;

[1] See note, p. 50.

there is nothing high and nothing low ; every State is independent, and every State is equal.   If we depart from this great principle, then are we no longer one people, but we are thrown back again upon the Confederation, and upon that state of things in which the inequality of the States produced all the evils which befell us in times past, and a thousand ill-adjusted and jarring interests.

Mr. President, I wish, then, without pursuing these thoughts, without especially attempting to produce any fervid impression by dwelling upon them, to take this occasion to answer my friend who has proposed the sentiment, and to respond to it by saying, that whoever would serve his country in this our day, with whatever degree of talent, great or small, it may have pleased the Almighty Power to give him, he cannot serve it, he will not serve it, unless he be able, at least, to extend his political designs, purposes, and objects, till they shall comprehend the whole country of which he is a servant.

Sir, I must say a word in connection with that event which we have assembled to commemorate.   It has seemed fit to the dwellers in New York, New Englanders by birth or descent, to form this society.   They have formed it for the relief of the poor and distressed, and for the purpose of commemorating annually the great event of the settlement of the country from which they spring.   It would be great presumption in me to go back to the scene of that settlement, or to attempt to exhibit it in any colors, after the exhibition made to-day ; yet it is an event that in all time since, and in all time to come, and more in times to come than in times past, must stand out in great and striking characteristics to the admiration of the world.   The sun's return to his winter's solstice, in 1620, is the epoch from which he dates his first acquaintance with the small people, now one of the happiest, and destined to be one of the greatest, that his rays fall upon ; and his annual visitation, from that day to this, to our frozen region, has enabled him to see that progress, *progress*, was the characteristic of that small people.   He has seen them, from a handful that one of his beams coming through a keyhole might illuminate, spread over a hemisphere which he cannot enlighten under the slightest eclipse. Nor, though this globe should revolve round him for tens of hundreds of thousands of years, will he see such another incipient colonization upon any part of this attendant upon his mighty orb. What else he may see in those other planets which revolve around him, we cannot tell, at least until we have tried the fifty-foot telescope which Lord Rosse is preparing for that purpose.

There is not, gentlemen, and we may as well admit it, in any history of the past, another epoch from which so many great events have taken a turn,—events which, while important to us, are equally important to the country from whence we came. The settlement of Plymouth—concurring, I always wish to be understood, with that of Virginia—was the settlement of New England by colonies of Old England. Now, gentlemen, take these two ideas, and run out the thoughts suggested by both. What has been, and what is to be, Old England? What has been, what is, and what may be, in the providence of God, *New* England, with her neighbors and associates? I would not dwell, gentlemen, with any particular emphasis upon the sentiment, which I nevertheless entertain, with respect to the great diversity in the races of men. I do not know how far, in that respect, I might not encroach on those mysteries of Providence, which, while I adore, I may not comprehend; but it does seem to me to be very remarkable that we may go back to the time when New England, or those who founded it, were *subtracted* from Old England, and both Old England and New England went on, nevertheless, in their mighty career of progress and power.

Let me begin with New England for a moment. What has resulted, embracing, as I say, the nearly contemporaneous settlement of Virginia,—what has resulted from the planting upon this continent of two or three slender colonies from the mother country? Gentlemen, the great epitaph commemorative of the character and the worth, the discoveries and glory, of Columbus, was,

7

that he had *given a new world to the crowns of Castile and Aragon*. Gentlemen, this is a great mistake. It does not come up at all to the great merits of Columbus. He gave the territory of the southern hemisphere to the crowns of Castile and Aragon; but as a place for the plantation of colonies, as a place for the habitation of men, as a place to which laws and religion and manners and science were to be transferred, as a place in which the creatures of God should multiply and fill the earth, under friendly skies and with religious hearts, he gave it to the whole world, he gave it to universal man! From this seminal principle, and from a handful, — a hundred saints, blessed of God and ever honored of men, landed on the shores of Plymouth, and elsewhere along the coast, united, as I have said already more than once, in the process of time, with the settlement at Jamestown, — has sprung this great people of which we are a portion.

I do not reckon myself among quite the oldest of the land; and yet it so happens that very recently I recurred to an exulting speech or oration of my own,[1] in which I spoke of my country as consisting of nine millions of people. I could hardly persuade myself, that, within the short time which had elapsed since that epoch, our population had doubled; and that at the present moment there does exist most unquestionably as great a probability of its continued progress in the same ratio as has ever existed in any previous time. I do not know whose imagination is fertile enough, I do not know whose conjectures, I may almost say, are *wild* enough, to tell what may be the progress of wealth and population in the United States in half a century to come. All we know is, here is a people of from seventeen to twenty millions, intelligent, educated, freeholders, freemen, republicans, possessed of all the means of modern improvement, modern science, arts, literature, with the world before them! There is nothing to check them till they touch the shores of the Pacific,[2] and then,

[1] Oration on the First Settlement of New England, Dec. 22, 1820.

[2] Five years later, gold was discovered in California, and the first great movement of settlers towards the Pacific coast was begun.

they are so much accustomed to water, that *that's* a facility and no obstruction !

So much, gentlemen, for this branch of the English race. But what has happened, meanwhile, to England herself, since the period of the departure of the Puritans from the coast of Lincolnshire, from the English Boston ? Gentlemen, in speaking of the progress of English power, of English dominion and authority, from that period to the present, I shall be understood, of course, as neither entering into any defense, or any accusation, of the policy which has conducted her to her present state. As to the justice of her wars, the necessity of her conquests, the propriety of those acts by which she has taken possession of so great a portion of the globe, it is not the business of the present occasion to inquire. *Neque teneo, neque refello.*[1] But I speak of them, or intend to speak of them, as facts of the most extraordinary character, unequaled in the history of any nation on the globe, and the consequences of which may and must reach through a thousand generations. The Puritans left England in the reign of James I. England herself had then become somewhat settled and established in the Protestant faith, and in the quiet enjoyment of property, by the previous energetic, long, and prosperous reign of Elizabeth. Her successor was James VI. of Scotland, now become James I. of England; and here was a union of the crowns, but not of the kingdoms,—a very important distinction. Ireland was held by a military power; and one cannot but see that at that day, whatever may be true or untrue in more recent periods of her history, Ireland was held by England by the two great potencies,—the power of the sword and the power of confiscation. In other respects, England was nothing like the England which we now behold. Her foreign possessions were quite inconsiderable. She had some hold on the West India Islands ; she had Acadia, or Nova Scotia, which King James granted, by wholesale, for the endowment of the knights whom he created by hundreds. And what has been

[1] I neither support nor confute.

her progress? Did she then possess Gibraltar, the key to the Mediterranean? Did she possess a port in the Mediterranean? Was Malta hers? Were the Ionian Islands hers? Was the southern extremity of Africa, was the Cape of Good Hope hers? Were the whole of her vast possessions in India hers? Was her great Australian empire hers? While that branch of her population which followed the western star, and under its guidance committed itself to the duty of settling, fertilizing, and peopling an unknown wilderness in the West, were pursuing their destinies, other causes, providential doubtless, were leading English power eastward and southward, in consequence and by means of her naval prowess and the extent of her commerce, until in our day we have seen that within the Mediterranean, on the western coast and at the southern extremity of Africa, in Arabia, in hither India and farther India, she has a population *ten times* as great as that of the British Isles two centuries ago. And recently, as we have witnessed, — I will not say with how much truth and justice, policy or impolicy; I do not speak at all to the morality of the action, I only speak to the *fact*, — she has found admission into China, and has carried the Christian religion and the Protestant faith to the doors of three hundred millions of people.[1]

It has been said that whosoever would see the Eastern world before it turns into a Western world, must make his visit soon, because steamboats and omnibuses, commerce, and all the arts of Europe, are extending themselves from Egypt to Suez, from Suez to the Indian seas, and from the Indian seas all over the explored regions of the still farther East.

Now, gentlemen, I do not know what practical views, or what practical results, may take place from this great expansion of the power of the two branches of Old England. It is not for me to say. I only can see, that on this continent *all* is to be *Anglo-American*, from Plymouth Rock to the Pacific seas, from the

---

[1] The war between China and Great Britain, known as the " opium war," which began in 1834, was ended by the treaty of Aug. 26, 1842. By the conditions of this treaty, Hong-Kong was ceded to the British.

north pole to California.[1] That is certain; and in the Eastern world I only see that you can hardly place a finger on a map of the world, and be an *inch* from an English settlement.

Gentlemen, if there be anything in the supremacy of races, the experiment now in progress will develop it. If there be any truth in the idea that those who issued from the great Caucasian fountain, and spread over Europe, are to react on India and on Asia, and to act on the whole Western world, it may not be for us, nor our children, nor our grandchildren, to see it, but it will be for our descendants of some generation to see the extent of that progress and dominion of the favored races.

For myself, I believe there is no limit fit to be assigned to it by the human mind, because I find at work everywhere, on both sides of the Atlantic, under various forms and degrees of restriction on the one hand, and under various degrees of motive and stimulus on the other hand, in these branches of a common race, the great principle *of the freedom of human thought and the respectability of individual character*. I find everywhere an elevation of the character of man as man, an elevation of the individual as a component part of society. I find everywhere a rebuke of the idea that the many are made for the few, or that government is anything but an *agency* for mankind. And I care not beneath what zone, frozen, temperate, or torrid; I care not of what complexion, white or brown; I care not under what circumstances of climate or cultivation,—if I can find a race of men on an inhabitable spot of earth whose general sentiment it is, and whose general feeling it is, that government is made for man,—man as a religious, moral, and social being,—and not man for government, there I know that I shall find prosperity and happiness.

<hr>

[1] It is well to remember, that, when these words were spoken, California was a province of Mexico, inhabited only by Indians and a few people of Spanish descent.

ECLECTIC ENGLISH CLASSICS

THE AMERICAN SCHOLAR
SELF-RELIANCE
COMPENSATION

BY

RALPH WALDO EMERSON

NEW YORK · : · CINCINNATI · : · CHICAGO

AMERICAN BOOK COMPANY

INTRODUCTION.

Ralph Waldo Emerson, poet, essayist, and philosopher, was born in Boston, May 25, 1803. He was the second of five sons of the Rev. William Emerson, minister of the First (Congregational) Church in Boston. His mother was Ruth Haskins, a woman of strong character and superior mental abilities. He had a minister for an ancestor for eight generations back, either on the paternal or the maternal side. Thus he inherited his spiritual and intellectual tendencies from a long line of distinguished progenitors. His aunt, Mary Moody Emerson, a woman of rare intellectual attainments, was one of his early companions and exerted a remarkable influence over his development.

Emerson began his studies at the public grammar school at the age of eight, and four years later he attended the Latin School. In 1817 he entered Harvard. He was not distinguished for proficiency in the studies of the curriculum, but he was superior to most of his classmates in his knowledge of general literature. He was especially interested in the study of Greek and history, and much of his time was spent in the library. He graduated in 1821.

For five years after leaving college Emerson taught school. In 1823 he began to study for the ministry under Dr. Channing. He was "approbated to preach" in 1826 by the Middlesex

Association of Ministers, but owing to ill health he did not enter immediately upon his public duties, but spent the following winter in Florida. On his return from the South he preached in New Bedford, Northampton, Concord, and Boston. On March 11, 1829, he was ordained as a colleague of the Rev. Henry Ware, minister of the Second (Congregational Unitarian) Church in Boston. Eighteen months later, Dr. Ware resigned and the pastoral duties fell upon Emerson.

In September, 1829, he was married to Miss Ellen Louisa Tucker. Their married life was brief, as Mrs. Emerson died of consumption in February, 1832.

Emerson soon became troubled with doubts regarding his duties as a minister, and as sincerity was always his guiding star, he felt it his duty to proclaim these doubts to his congregation. Accordingly in September, 1832, he delivered a sermon on the Lord's Supper, in which he stated his scruples against administering that rite. As he and his congregation differed radically in these views, he resigned his pastorate and retired from public preaching.

In 1833 he visited Europe for the first time. There he met Coleridge, Wordsworth, and Carlyle, and formed with the last-named a lifelong friendship which resulted in their famous correspondence.

In the winter of 1833–34 he returned to the United States and began his career as a lecturer. At this period of his life he lived with Dr. Ripley in the "Old Manse," afterwards made famous by Hawthorne. The first lectures he delivered were "Water" and "The Relation of Man to the Globe." These were followed by three lectures on his European tour.

In 1834 he began his series of biographical lectures on Michael

Angelo, Milton, Luther, George Fox, and Edmund Burke. Those on Michael Angelo and George Fox were published later in the " North American Review."

In September, 1835, he was married to Miss Lydia Jackson of Plymouth, Mass. They went to live in "the plain, square, wooden house," in Concord, which was Emerson's home for the rest of his life.

During the next three winters Emerson delivered three courses of lectures in Boston: ten on English literature, in 1835; twelve on the philosophy of history, in 1836; and ten on human culture, in 1837.

In 1836 he wrote the "Concord Hymn" for the dedication ceremonies at the monument raised in honor of the Concord fight. It is one of the most beautiful poems he has written.

In 1836 his first volume, " Nature,"— a philosophic essay full of poetic thoughts,— was published anonymously. It was quite different from anything Emerson had written before, and it did not meet with a favorable reception. It was too vague for popular comprehension, and the time was not ripe for its full appreciation. It took five years to sell five hundred copies of it in the United States.

In 1836 the Symposium, or Transcendental Club, was organized, and Emerson became an active member. Among its other members were James Freeman Clarke, Theodore Parker, Bronson Alcott, Elizabeth P. Peabody, and Margaret Fuller. They discussed, besides a variety of other topics, religious justice, truth, mysticism, and the development of American genius.

From the last-named subject Emerson probably received the impulse which prompted him in 1837 to deliver his oration entitled "The American Scholar" before the Phi Beta Kappa

Society at Cambridge. The address was received by the audience with the utmost enthusiasm and approval.

On July 24, 1838, Emerson delivered an oration on literary ethics before the literary societies at Dartmouth College.

In the winter of 1838–39 he gave a course of ten lectures, — "The Doctrine of the Soul," "Home," "The School," "Love," "Genius," "The Protest," "Tragedy," "Comedy," "Duty," "Demonology."

His next address was "The Method of Nature," delivered before the Society of the Adelphi in Waterville, Me., Aug. 11, 1841. Other addresses delivered about this time were "Man, the Reformer," "Lecture on the Times," "The Transcendentalist," and "The Conservative."

In July, 1840, a transcendental magazine called "The Dial" began its career under the editorship of Margaret Fuller. Emerson soon succeeded her as editor, and he contributed numerous articles to the paper. It was not a financial success, and was abandoned in 1844.

In 1841 Emerson's first volume of collected essays was published. This volume now includes the following essays: "History," "Self-Reliance," "Compensation," "Spiritual Laws," "Love," "Friendship," "Prudence," "Heroism," "The Over-Soul," "Circles," "Intellect," "Art," "The Young American." The last named was not published till 1844, but it now forms part of the "First Series of Essays."

In February, 1842, Emerson wrote the pathetic "Threnody," on the death of his dearly beloved son. In 1844 he delivered, in Concord, an address on the emancipation of the negroes in the British West Indies.

In 1844 the "Second Series of Essays" appeared. It includes:

"The Poet," "Experience," "Character," "Manners," "Gifts," "Nature," "Politics," "Nominalist and Realist," and "New England Reformers."

In 1847 Emerson's first volume of poems was published. This was chiefly a collection of poems which had appeared before, most of them in "The Dial."

In October, 1847, he sailed for Europe on an English lecture tour. Many of the lectures he delivered on this trip were published in a volume, "Representative Men," which appeared in 1850. It consists of a series of character sketches or mental portraits, each designed to represent a class. The essays are: "Lives of Great Men;" "Plato, or the Philosopher;" "Plato, New Readings;" "Swedenborg, or the Mystic;" "Montaigne, or the Skeptic;" "Shakespeare, or the Poet;" "Napoleon, or the Man of the World;" "Goethe, or the Writer."

In 1849 he returned to the United States. In 1850 he signed the call for the first Woman's Rights Convention. In 1852, conjointly with James Freeman Clarke and William Ellery Channing, he published the "Memoirs of Margaret Fuller Ossoli."

In January, 1855, he gave one of the lectures in a course of Antislavery Addresses, delivered in Boston, and in the same year he delivered an address before the Antislavery Party in New York. The plan he proposed was to buy the slaves from the owners and then liberate them.

"English Traits," the result of his observations in England, was published in 1856. In November, 1857, the "Atlantic Monthly" began its career in Boston with James Russell Lowell as editor. Many of the former contributors of "The Dial" wrote for this paper, among them Emerson, who contributed to it some of his best poems. The " Essay on Persian Poetry " was published in this paper in 1858.

" The Conduct of Life " appeared in 1860. It contains essays on " Fate," " Power," " Wealth," " Culture," " Manners," " Behavior," " Worship," " Beauty," " Illusions," " Considerations by the Way." When we consider that twenty-five hundred copies of this book were sold in a few days we perceive how much Emerson had grown in favor in the twenty years since the publication of his first volume.

About this time a new paper called " The Dial " was started in Cincinnati, for which Emerson wrote several articles. In 1862 he delivered an address at Boston on the Emancipation Proclamation. The " Boston Hymn " was read by him in Music Hall, Jan. 1, 1863.

" Voluntaries " was published in the "Atlantic Monthly " in 1863, and " Saadi " in 1864, " My Garden " in 1866, and " Terminus " in 1867. These poems and others were collected in 1867 in a volume entitled " May Day and Other Pieces."

In 1866 Emerson received the degree of LL.D. from Harvard University, and in 1867 he was elected to their board of overseers. In the same year he delivered an oration on the Progress of Culture before the Phi Beta Kappa Society of Cambridge. This year practically marked the close of his literary career. Most of the works of note which appeared at a later date were published from manuscript written by him at an earlier period.

In 1868–70 he delivered a series of lectures at Harvard University on the " Natural History of the Intellect." " Society and Solitude," a new collection of essays, was published in 1870. The essays include: " Society and Solitude," " Civilization," "Art,"

" Eloquence," " Domestic Life," " Farming," " Weeks and Days," " Books," " Clubs," " Courage," " Success," " Old Age."

In 1871, accompanied by his daughter Edith, he made a trip to California. In July, 1872, his house caught fire. The shock he received on this occasion greatly hastened his mental decline. He was induced to go to Europe for his health, and on his return he found his house perfectly restored to its former condition by friends who had paid for it by voluntary subscriptions.

In December, 1874, he edited " Parnassus," a collection of poems by British and American authors. In the same year " Letters and Social Aims " appeared, containing the following essays: " Poetry and Imagination," " Social Aims," " Eloquence," " Resources," " The Comic," " Quotation and Originality," " Progress of Culture," " Persian Poetry," " Inspiration," " Greatness," " Immortality."

On March 30, 1878, he delivered a lecture in the Old South Church, Boston, on the " Fortune of the Republic." " The Sovereignty of Ethics " was published in the " North American Review " in 1878. In May, 1879, he read his address on " The Preacher " in Divinity College, Harvard. In 1881 he read a paper on Carlyle before the Massachusetts Historical Society. His essay on " Superlatives " appeared in the " Century " for February, 1882.

In April, 1882, Emerson caught a severe cold, which developed into pneumonia, of which he died on April 27. He was buried in Concord near the graves of Hawthorne and Thoreau.

In addition to many short poems hitherto unpublished, two volumes of essays, " Miscellanies " and " Biographical Sketches," have appeared since his death.

To understand Emerson's works, we must inquire into his religious belief, since it permeates and colors all his writings. He belongs to the school of transcendentalism, but this word admits of many interpretations. Emerson himself defines it as "modern idealism." "The materialist," he tells us, "insists on facts, on history, on the force of circumstances and the animal wants of man; the idealist, on the power of Thought and of Will, on inspiration, on miracle, on individual culture. . . . The idealist takes his departure from his consciousness and reckons the world an appearance. . . . His thought,— that is the universe."

His precise attitude as to the conception of the Deity is difficult to define. He declares in one of his essays that "there is a sublime and friendly destiny by which the human race is guided — the race never dying, the individual never spared — to results affecting masses and ages."

Perhaps the following passage from Oliver Wendell Holmes will give us as good a conception as any, of Emerson's religious attitude:

"His creed was a brief one, but he carried it everywhere with him. In all he did, in all he said, and, so far as all outward signs could show, in all his thoughts, the indwelling Spirit was his light and guide; through all nature he looked up to nature's God; and if he did not worship the 'man Christ Jesus' as the churches of Christendom have done, he followed his footsteps so nearly that our good Methodist, Father Taylor, spoke of him as more like Christ than any man he had known."

But, whatever we may think of his theological views, we cannot fail to admire his ethics. He aimed to be a teacher of man, a reformer of reformers. He preached by life as well as by pen a new code of morals. He was an idealist, and he insisted on the application of idealism to the everyday matters of life. His was a courageous and hopeful nature. He had unbounded confidence in the power for good in the human soul, and he preached untiringly the worth of the moral sentiment. He explored every province of human life and thought; he lent his voice in behalf of all great public measures; and he never lost an opportunity to prove himself a good citizen. His mission in life was to inspire others, to make life nobler, purer, loftier.

There is, perhaps, no writer regarding whom there is less consensus of opinion than of Emerson. The judgments formed of him are as various as the habits of thought in the critics. We may regard him in three phases: Emerson the essayist, Emerson the poet, and Emerson the philosopher and moral leader. In all these phases we find the most diverse opinions and criticisms regarding him.

Some say there never before was such a writer, poet, sage; others can find no sense in his writings and pronounce them mere empty words. One critic accords him a high place as a philosopher, but characterizes his poetry as inartistic and harsh; another ranks him among the greatest poets, and says of him, "The great poets addressed him as one of themselves; he was not of their audience, but of their choir;" while a third declares that his poetry is as devoid of life as his philosophy of wisdom. We give a few of these criticisms by men whose opinions are valued.

First let us hear what Oliver Wendell Holmes says:—

"The poet in Emerson never accurately differentiated itself from the philosopher. . . . Emerson is so essentially a poet that whole pages of his are like so many litanies of alternating chants and recitations. His thoughts slip on and off their light rhythmic robes just as the mood takes him. Many of the metrical preludes to his lectures are a versified and condensed abstract of the leading doctrine of the discourse. Emerson was not only a poet, but a very remarkable one. . . . He was a man of intuition, of insight, a seer, a poet with a tendency to mysticism which renders him sometimes obscure and once in a while almost, if not quite, unintelligible. He made desperate work now and then with rhyme and rhythm, showing that though a born poet he was not a born singer. . . . After all our criticisms we have to recognize that there is a charm in his poems which cannot be defined any more than the fragrance of a rose or a hyacinth. . . . No man would accuse Emerson of parsimony of ideas. He crams his pages with the very marrow of his thought. But in weighing out a lecture he was as punctilious as Portia about the pound of flesh. When the lecture had served its purpose it came before the public in the shape of an essay, but the essay never lost the character it borrowed from the conditions under which it was delivered ; it was a lay sermon."

Now let us listen to Matthew Arnold : —

" And, in truth, one of the legitimate poets, Emerson, in my opinion, is not. His poetry is interesting ; it makes one think, but it is not the poetry of one of the born poets. . . . I do not, then, place Emerson among the great poets. But I go farther and say that I do not place him among the great writers, the great men of letters. . . . Emerson has passages of noble and pathetic eloquence ; he has passages of shrewd and felicitous wit ; he has crisp epigram ; he has passages of exquisitely touched observation of nature. Yet he is not a great writer ; his style has not the requisite wholeness of good tissue. . . . Emerson cannot, I think, be called with justice a great philosophical writer. He cannot build; his arrangement of philosophical ideas has no progress in it — no evolution; he does not construct a philosophy."

Lastly, the Rev. C. A. Bartol, criticising the critic, says: —

" Mr. Arnold, who has forgot the dreams and got so bravely over the supposed illusions of his youth, putting for them the depressing doubts and hopeless speculations of his age, while he prizes Emerson's spiritual substance, eschews as not good tissue his literary style. Moses, David, Paul, James, and Jesus, as reported by his amanuenses, under this self-confident critic's cleaver, must lose their heads as writers and authors on the same block. They, too, are no weavers of words whose work is figured by the loom; but brief, sententious, pictorial, ejaculatory, a quiver full of arrows being rather their type. Is there not a good prophetic and oracular as well as a didactic or dialectic style? "

So we see that it is not safe to trust the opinion of any one critic. It is not always easy to understand Emerson; his sentences are full of hidden meaning which cannot be detected at a glance; they must be read and re-read to perceive the full drift of the thought; but the thought in its fullness well repays us for the trouble. With unbiased mind and earnest purpose we must go to the storehouse of Emerson's works, take from thence all the material we can gather, and with this as the basis, each according to his understanding, form his own judgment.

" The American Scholar " has been well called our literary declaration of independence. In it Emerson deplores the tendencies of Americans to devote their energies exclusively in the direction of mechanical skill, and he fearlessly accuses them of subserviency to European taste and style.

In treating of the education of the scholar, he recognizes three great influences, — Nature, the Past with its accumulation of books, and Action.

Nature he regards as the most important influence. "Know thyself" and "Study nature" are to him as one maxim. The classifying instinct is one of the first to be developed; we must learn to see that many things are governed by one law.

In speaking of the influence of the past, he dwells chiefly on books. The danger, he tells us, is in placing too much faith in books. "Instead of Man Thinking we have the bookworm. Books are the best of things, well used; abused, among the worst."

Action, though subordinate to the other influences, still is an essential factor in education. "It is the raw material out of which the intellect molds her splendid product." He emphasizes the dignity and necessity of labor, and spurns the idea that the scholar must withdraw from the practical issues of life. Having spoken of the scholar's education, he eloquently describes his duties, which, he tells us, are all included in self-trust. If we would be true to ourselves, we must never yield to the popular cry, but manfully declare our independence, cost what it may, and hold to our belief though the whole world decry it.

Lastly, he makes special application of these principles to the American Scholar. He rejoices in the fact that people are beginning to be interested in near and common things instead of in the "doings in Italy and Arabia." "What would we really know the meaning of — the meal in the firkin, the milk in the pan, the ballad in the street." And he closes in that hopeful strain, so characteristic of Emerson, by expressing the utmost faith and confidence in the American Scholar.

Perhaps no other work of Emerson's has been less criticised or more universally approved. James Russell Lowell, in speaking of its delivery, says: "It was an event without any former parallel in our literary annals, a scene to be always treasured in the memory for its picturesqueness and its inspiration. What crowded and breathless aisles, what windows clustering with eager heads, what enthusiasm of approval, what grim silence of foregone dissent!"

In this oration are to be found the germs of those thoughts and principles which animate all the author's later works, — self-trust, self-culture, the dignity of labor, harmony and analogy in nature, intellectual and moral independence. Emerson has been accused of burying his thoughts so deep that common seekers cannot find them; but in this essay, at least, few passages can be found which are not perfectly intelligible. Some of them, indeed, are so exquisitely expressed as to constitute veritable prose poems. The address, like all of Emerson's works, is full of quotations and allusions; yet Emerson is essentially original. He is the champion of mental freedom, and continually urges others to free themselves from the fetters of conventionality.

He practiced what he preached in this oration, and set the example of ignoring European methods and manners. The humblebee and the pine tree rather than the nightingale and the asphodel furnished his models.

Let us rejoice that Emerson no longer need complain of our subserviency to European taste. Since this address was delivered, we have had a host of original writers, — Cooper, Irving, Hawthorne, Bryant, Longfellow, Whittier, Lowell, Holmes, Whitman, and many others. The whole tendency of American literature has changed. As with one impulse it has grown more original and more American. Emerson's rich and vigorous fresh-ness has undoubtedly proved a stimulant to his contemporaries, and to him, more than to any other, we are indebted for the development of American scholarship.

It is hardly necessary to explain the theme of "Self-Reliance." The title is self-explanatory. It is the doctrine which Emerson preaches in "The American Scholar," reiterated and elaborated. When we read there, " In self-trust all the virtues are compre-hended," we strike the keynote of this later essay. To the self-reliant man everything is possible ; he may become a genius, a leader of men, but without this one virtue, his case is hopeless.

Some of us, perhaps, cannot agree with Emerson when he tells us it is right to ignore many of the ordinary duties of life for the sake of maintaining our individuality ; but certain it is that con-formity to the conventionalities of society stamps out from many a man his originality and individuality, and makes of him merely one of a mass of men. Let us see how it is in our own case. Suppose some one took enough interest in you or me to write our biography. Would it not read somewhat like this? " Mr. —— was of such a nationality (Order). He belonged to such a religious sect (Class). He followed such a profession or engaged in such a business (Genus). He was a member of such a club, was interested in such a movement, etc. (Species)." These are all class distinctions, but where, we ask, is the attribute that shows his individuality, that makes him himself and distinguishes him from his companions B and C and D? Of this, alas! most men's lives leave no record.

In times of revolution, when conventionalities are forcibly thrust aside, our great men grow up like mushrooms in a night.

So we find in our own history that at no other time did our country produce so many great men as during the Revolutionary period and the period of the Civil War. Must we, then, wish for war and turmoil, or shall we rather believe with Emerson that if we would but be as brave as he would have us, the most peaceful times might fill our records with the achievements of men who now sink into unknown graves?

In "Compensation" we strike one of Emerson's deeper and more philosophic veins, — that great theory of retribution on earth which makes us pause and hold our breath. Is it indeed true that "every excess causes a defect, every defect an excess?" that "for everything you have missed you have gained something else, and for everything you gain you lose something?" that "every secret is told, every crime is punished, every virtue rewarded, every wrong redressed, in silence and certainty?" The universal acceptation of this doctrine would work a revolution in society: for would not the wicked man fear to do wrong if he knew the punishment to be as inevitable as the laws of nature, and not dependent upon a possible detection and conviction by the judges of the world? And where would be the motive for his crime if he felt that he already possessed his full allotment of happiness, and that for everything he gained in one direction he would lose something in another? And would not the virtuous man be encouraged to persist all the more in his virtue if he knew that for every sacrifice he made there would be some reward, — a gain in character, if not a material compensation?

But the doctrine is one that is not easily learned. To be well understood it must be carefully taught by inspired men, by men like Emerson himself: for all men have not his penetrating eye; they cannot see below the surface, and so long as the wrongdoer succeeds in his wrongdoing and the wicked man is rich and surrounded by friends, so long will he be envied. No matter what his mental turmoil may be, no matter though the poorest beggar in the street have greater peace of mind, to the world at large he appears happy and successful, and men continue to look for retribution in a life to come.

THE AMERICAN SCHOLAR.[1]

Mr. President and Gentlemen,—

I greet you on the recommencement of our literary year. Our anniversary is one of hope, and, perhaps, not enough of labor. We do not meet for games of strength or skill, for the recitation of histories, tragedies, and odes, like the ancient Greeks;[2] for parliaments of love and poesy, like the Troubadours;[3] nor for the advancement of science, like our contemporaries in the British and European capitals. Thus far, our holiday has been simply a friendly sign of the survival of the love of letters amongst a people too busy to give to letters any more. As such, it is precious as the sign of an indestructible instinct. Perhaps the time is already come, when it ought to be, and will be, something else; when the sluggard intellect of this continent will look from under its iron lids,[4] and fill the postponed expectation of the world with something better than the exertions of

---

[1] This oration was delivered in August, 1837, before the Cambridge chapter of the Phi Beta Kappa Society, a society composed of honor students graduated from the various colleges.

[2] Public games were a religious institution in ancient Greece. The most important were the Olympic games celebrated in honor of Zeus. At first they comprised simply feats of strength, races, etc. ; but later it became customary to indulge in intellectual exercises. Dramatic pieces and discourses were delivered, and artists exhibited their work while the games were in progress.

[3] Minstrels of Provence, in southern France, in the eleventh, twelfth, and thirteenth centuries. Their poetry was about love and gallantry or about war and chivalry. They sang at public festivals or at the courts of great barons or princes. They were also known as Provençal minstrels.

[4] Heavy lids.

mechanical skill.   Our day of dependence, our long apprentice-
ship to the learning of other lands, draws to a close.   The
millions, that around us are rushing into life, cannot always be fed
on the sere remains of foreign harvests.   Events, actions arise,
that must be sung, that will sing themselves.   Who can doubt,
that poetry will revive and lead in a new age, as the star in the
constellation Harp, which now flames in our zenith, astronomers
announce, shall one day be the polestar[1] for a thousand years?

In this hope, I accept the topic which not only usage, but the
nature of our association, seem to prescribe to this day, — The
AMERICAN SCHOLAR.   Year by year, we come up hither to read
one more chapter of his biography.   Let us inquire what light new
days and events have thrown on his character, and his hopes.

It is one of those fables, which, out of an unknown antiquity,
convey an unlooked-for wisdom, that the gods, in the beginning,
divided Man into men, that he might be more helpful to himself;
just as the hand was divided into fingers, the better to answer its
end.

The old fable covers a doctrine ever new and sublime; that
there is One Man, — present to all particular men only partially,
or through one faculty; and that you must take the whole society to find the whole man.   Man is not a farmer, or a professor,
or an engineer, but he is all.   Man is priest, and scholar, and
statesman, and producer, and soldier.   In the *divided* or social
state, these functions are parceled out to individuals, each of
whom aims to do his stint of the joint work, whilst each other
performs his.   The fable implies, that the individual, to possess
himself, must sometimes return from his own labor to embrace
all the other laborers.   But unfortunately, this original unit, this
fountain of power, has been so distributed to multitudes, has
been so minutely subdivided and peddled out, that it is spilled
into drops, and cannot be gathered.   The state of society is one
in which the members have suffered amputation from the trunk,

---

[1] The north star, or the star in the zenith of the north pole of the earth.

and strut about so many walking monsters,— a good finger, a neck, a stomach, an elbow, but never a man.

Man is thus metamorphosed into a thing, into many things. The planter, who is Man sent out into the field to gather food, is seldom cheered by any idea of the true dignity of his ministry. He sees his bushel and his cart, and nothing beyond, and sinks into the farmer, instead of Man on the farm. The tradesman scarcely ever gives an ideal worth to his work, but is ridden[1] by the routine of his craft, and the soul is subject to dollars. The priest becomes a form ; the attorney, a statute book ; the mechanic, a machine ; the sailor, a rope of a ship.

In this distribution of functions, the scholar is the delegated intellect. In the right state, he is, *Man Thinking*. In the degenerate state, when the victim of society, he tends to become a mere thinker, or, still worse, the parrot[2] of other men's thinking.

In this view of him, as Man Thinking, the theory of his office is contained. Him nature solicits with all her placid, all her monitory pictures ; him the past instructs ; him the future invites. Is not, indeed, every man a student, and do not all things exist for the student's behoof? And, finally, is not the true scholar the only true master? But the old oracle said, "All things have two handles: beware of the wrong one."[3] In life, too often, the scholar errs with mankind and forfeits his privilege. Let us see him in his school, and consider him in reference to the main influences he receives.

I. The first in time and the first in importance of the influences upon the mind is that of nature. Every day, the sun ;[4] and, after

---

[1] Tyrannized over.   [2] Imitator.

[3] The teachings of Epictetus (60–120), a Roman Stoic philosopher, have been handed down by one of his pupils, and preserved in two treatises, Discourses of Epictetus, and Enchiridion. From the latter of these works the quotation is made.

[4] The predicate must be supplied,— a construction which occurs frequently in this oration.

sunset, night and her stars. Ever the winds blow; ever the grass grows. Every day, men and women, conversing, beholding and beholden. The scholar is he of all men whom this spectacle most engages. He must settle its value in his mind. What is nature to him? There is never a beginning, there is never an end, to the inexplicable continuity of this web of God, but always circular[1] power returning into itself. Therein it resembles his own spirit, whose beginning, whose ending, he never can find, — so entire, so boundless. Far, too, as her splendors shine, system on system shooting like rays, upward, downward, without center, without circumference, — in the mass and in the particle, nature hastens to render account of herself to the mind. Classification begins. To the young mind, everything is individual, stands by itself. By and by, it finds how to join two things, and see in them one nature; then three, then three thousand; and so, tyrannized over by its own unifying[2] instinct, it goes on tying things together, diminishing anomalies, discovering roots running under ground, whereby contrary and remote things cohere, and flower out from one stem. It presently learns, that, since the dawn of history, there has been a constant accumulation and classifying of facts. But what is classification but the perceiving that these objects are not chaotic, and are not foreign, but have a law which is also a law of the human mind? The astronomer discovers that geometry, a pure abstraction of the human mind, is the measure of planetary motion. The chemist finds proportions and intelligible method throughout matter; and science is nothing but the finding of analogy, identity, in the most remote parts. The ambitious soul sits down before each refractory fact; one after another, reduces all strange constitutions, all new powers, to their class and their law, and goes on forever to animate the last fiber of organization, the outskirts of nature, by insight.

Thus to him, to this schoolboy under the bending dome of

---

[1] Circular, because without beginning and without end.
[2] Uniting into one.

day,[1] is suggested, that he and it proceed from one root; one is leaf and one is flower; relation, sympathy, stirring in every vein. And what is that Root? Is not that the soul of his soul?—A thought too bold,—a dream too wild. Yet when this spiritual light shall have revealed the law of more earthly natures,—when he has learned to worship the soul, and to see that the natural philosophy that now is, is only the first gropings of its gigantic hand, he shall look forward to an ever-expanding knowledge as to a becoming creator.[2] He shall see, that nature is the opposite of the soul, answering to it part for part. One is seal, and one is print. Its beauty is the beauty of his own mind. Its laws are the laws of his own mind. Nature then becomes to him the measure of his attainments. So much of nature as he is ignorant of, so much of his own mind does he not yet possess. And, in fine, the ancient precept, " Know thyself,"[3] and the modern precept, " Study nature," become at last one maxim.

II. The next great influence into the spirit of the scholar, is, the mind of the Past,—in whatever form, whether of literature, of art, of institutions, that mind is inscribed. Books are the best type of the influence of the past, and perhaps we shall get at the truth,—learn the amount of this influence more conveniently,—by considering their value alone.

The theory of books is noble. The scholar of the first age received into him the world around; brooded thereon; gave it the new arrangement of his own mind, and uttered it again. It came into him, life; it went out from him, truth. It came to him, short-lived actions; it went out from him, immortal thoughts. It came to him, business; it went from him, poetry. It was dead fact; now, it is quick thought. It can stand, and it can go. It now endures, it now flies, it now inspires. Precisely in propor-

---

[1] " Dome of day," i.e., the sky.

[2] " Knowledge as to," etc., i.e., knowledge will become a creator for him.

[3] A maxim of Chilo, one of the seven sages of Greece, who lived in the sixth century B.C.

tion to the depth of mind from which it issued, so high does it soar, so long does it sing.

Or, I might say, it depends on how far the process had gone, of transmuting life into truth. In proportion to the completeness of the distillation, so will the purity and imperishableness of the product be. But none is quite perfect. As no air pump can by any means make a perfect vacuum, so neither can any artist entirely exclude the conventional, the local, the perishable from his book, or write a book of pure thought, that shall be as efficient, in all respects, to a remote posterity, as to contemporaries, or rather to the second age. Each age, it is found, must write its own books; or rather, each generation for the next succeeding. The books of an older period will not fit this.

Yet hence arises a grave mischief. The sacredness which attaches to the act of creation, — the act of thought, — is transferred to the record. The poet chanting, was felt to be a divine man: henceforth the chant is divine also. The writer was a just and wise spirit: henceforward it is settled, the book is perfect; as love of the hero corrupts into worship of his statue. Instantly, the book becomes noxious: the guide is a tyrant. The sluggish and perverted mind of the multitude, slow to open to the incursions of Reason, having once so opened, having once received this book, stands upon it, and makes an outcry, if it is disparaged. Colleges are built on it. Books are written on it by thinkers, not by Man Thinking; by men of talent, that is, who start wrong, who set out from accepted dogmas, not from their own sight of principles. Meek young men grow up in libraries, believing it their duty to accept the views, which Cicero,[1] which Locke,[2]

---

[1] Marcus Tullius Cicero (106–43 B.C.), Roman author, orator, and statesman. He stands preëminent as a specimen of the highest moral and intellectual culture of the ancient world.

[2] John Locke (1632–1704), English philosopher and theologian. His aim was to inquire into the original certainty and extent of human knowledge. His most famous work is his Essay on the Human Understanding.

which Bacon,[1] have given, forgetful that Cicero, Locke, and Bacon were only young men in libraries,[2] when they wrote these books.

Hence, instead of Man Thinking, we have the bookworm. Hence, the book-learned class, who value books, as such; not as related to nature and the human constitution, but as making a sort of Third Estate[3] with the world and the soul. Hence, the restorers of readings, the emendators, the bibliomaniacs of all degrees.

Books are the best of things, well used; abused, among the worst. What is the right use? What is the one end, which all means go to effect? They are for nothing but to inspire. I had better never see a book, than to be warped by its attraction clean out of my own orbit, and made a satellite instead of a system. The one thing in the world, of value, is the active soul. This every man is entitled to; this every man contains within him, although, in almost all men, obstructed, and as yet unborn. The soul active sees absolute truth; and utters truth, or creates. In this action, it is. genius; not the privilege of here and there a favorite, but the sound estate of every man. In its essence, it is progressive. The book, the college, the school of art, the institution of any kind, stop with some past utterance of genius. This is good, say they,— let us hold by this. They pin me down. They look backward and not forward. But genius looks forward: the eyes of man are set in his forehead, not in his hindhead:[4] man hopes: genius creates. Whatever talents may be, if the man create not, the pure efflux of the Deity is not his; —

[1] Francis Bacon (1561–1626), English philosopher and statesman. He tried to recall philosophy from speculation and use it as an interpreter of nature. His most important work is the Novum Organum (New Method).

[2] " Young men in libraries," i.e., young men like themselves.

[3] In some countries the population has been divided into three classes or estates, with respect to political rights and powers, as nobility, clergy, and people; lords temporal, lords spiritual, and commons, etc. The common people represent the " third estate."

[4] The back part of the head.

cinders and smoke there may be, but not yet flame.   There are
creative manners, there are creative actions, and creative words;
manners, actions, words, that is, indicative of no custom or
authority, but springing spontaneous from the mind's own sense
of good and fair.

On the other part, instead of being its own seer, let it receive
from another mind its truth, though it were in torrents of light,
without periods of solitude, inquest, and self-recovery, and a
fatal disservice is done.   Genius is always sufficiently the enemy
of genius by overinfluence.   The literature of every nation bears
me witness.   The English dramatic poets have Shakespearized[1]
now for two hundred years.

Undoubtedly there is a right way of reading, so it be sternly
subordinated.   Man Thinking must not be subdued by his instruments.   Books are for the scholar's idle times.   When he can
read God directly, the hour is too precious to be wasted in other
men's transcripts of their readings.   But when the intervals of
darkness come, as come they must,— when the sun is hid, and
the stars withdraw their shining,— we repair to the lamps which
were kindled by their ray, to guide our steps to the East again,
where the dawn is.   We hear, that we may speak.   The Arabian
proverb says, "A fig tree, looking on a fig tree, becometh fruitful."

It is remarkable, the character of the pleasure we derive from
the best books.   They impress us with the conviction, that one
nature wrote and the same reads.   We read the verses of one of
the great English poets, of Chaucer,[2] of Marvell,[3] of Dryden,[4]

---

[1] Imitated Shakespeare.   This is one of the many words which Emerson
has coined.

[2] Geoffrey Chaucer (1340–1400), the " Father of English Poetry," author
of the famous Canterbury Tales.

[3] Andrew Marvell (1621–78), English poet, called the " British Aristides "
on account of his great probity, the allusion being to the Athenian statesman
Aristides, surnamed " the Just."   The Emigrants in the Bermudas is Marvell's greatest poem.

[4] John Dryden (1631–1700), English poet.   He was appointed poet lau-
reate in 1668.   One of his most popular poems is The Ode for St. Cecilia's Day.

with the most modern joy,—with a pleasure, I mean, which is in great part caused by the abstraction of all *time* from their verses. There is some awe mixed with the joy of our surprise, when this poet, who lived in some past world, two or three hundred years ago, says that which lies close to my own soul, that which I also had well-nigh thought and said. But for the evidence thence afforded to the philosophical doctrine of the identity of all minds, we should suppose some preëstablished harmony, some foresight of souls that were to be, and some preparation of stores for their future wants, like the fact observed in insects, who lay up food before death for the young grub they shall never see.

I would not be hurried by any love of system, by any exaggeration of instincts, to underrate the Book. We all know, that, as the human body can be nourished on any food, though it were boiled grass and the broth of shoes, so the human mind can be fed by any knowledge. And great and heroic men have existed, who had almost no other information than by the printed page. I only would say, that it needs a strong head to bear that diet. One must be an inventor to read well. As the proverb says, " He that would bring home the wealth of the Indies, must carry out the wealth of the Indies."[1] There is then creative reading as well as creative writing. When the mind is braced by labor and invention, the page of whatever book we read becomes luminous with manifold allusion. Every sentence is doubly significant, and the sense of our author is as broad as the world. We then see, what is always true, that, as the seer's hour of vision is short and rare among heavy days and months, so is its record, perchance, the least part of his volume. The discerning will read, in his Plato[2] or Shakespeare,[3] only that least part,—only

---

[1] Spanish proverb.

[2] Plato (429–347 B.C.), Athenian author and philosopher, the father of idealism. He was a disciple of Socrates, whose memory and teachings he preserved in his Dialogues.

[3] William Shakespeare (1564–1616), the greatest of English poets and dramatists. His most popular plays are Merchant of Venice and Hamlet.

the authentic utterances of the oracle; — all the rest he rejects, were it never so many times Plato's and Shakespeare's.

Of course, there is a portion of reading quite indispensable to a wise man. History and exact science he must learn by laborious reading. Colleges, in like manner, have their indispensable office, — to teach elements. But they can only highly serve us, when they aim not to drill, but to create; when they gather from far every ray of various genius to their hospitable halls, and, by the concentrated fires, set the hearts of their youth on flame. Thought and knowledge are natures in which apparatus and pretension avail nothing. Gowns, and pecuniary foundations, though of towns of gold, can never countervail[1] the least sentence or syllable of wit.[2] Forget this, and our American colleges will recede in their public importance, whilst they grow richer every year.

III. There goes in the world a notion, that the scholar should be a recluse, a valetudinarian, — as unfit for any handiwork or public labor, as a penknife for an ax. The so-called "practical men" sneer at speculative men, as if, because they speculate or *see*, they could do nothing. I have heard it said that the clergy, — who are always, more universally than any other class, the scholars of their day, — are addressed as women; that the rough, spontaneous conversation of men they do not hear, but only a mincing and diluted speech. They are often virtually disfranchised; and, indeed, there are advocates for their celibacy. As far as this is true of the studious classes, it is not just and wise. Action is with the scholar subordinate, but it is essential. Without it, he is not yet man. Without it, thought can never ripen into truth. Whilst the world hangs before the eye as a cloud of beauty, we cannot even see its beauty. Inaction is cowardice, but there can be no scholar without the heroic mind. The preamble[3] of thought, the transition through which it passes from

---

[1] Prevail against.   [2] Sound sense.   [3] Prelude, or preliminary.

the unconscious to the conscious, is action. Only so much do I know, as I have lived. Instantly we know whose words are loaded with life, and whose not.

The world,—this shadow of the soul, or *other me*, lies wide around. Its attractions are the keys which unlock my thoughts and make me acquainted with myself. I run eagerly into this resounding tumult. I grasp the hands of those next me, and take my place in the ring to suffer and to work, taught by an instinct, that so shall the dumb abyss be vocal with speech. I pierce its order; I dissipate its fear; I dispose of it within the circuit of my expanding life. So much only of life as I know by experience, so much of the wilderness have I vanquished and planted, or so far have I extended my being, my dominion. I do not see how any man can afford, for the sake of his nerves and his nap, to spare any action in which he can partake. It is pearls and rubies to his discourse. Drudgery, calamity, exasperation, want, are instructors in eloquence and wisdom. The true scholar grudges every opportunity of action passed by, as a loss of power.

It is the raw material out of which the intellect molds her splendid products. A strange process too, this, by which experience is converted into thought, as a mulberry leaf is converted into satin.[1] The manufacture goes forward at all hours.

The actions and events of our childhood and youth, are now matters of calmest observation. They lie like fair pictures in the air. Not so with our recent actions,—with the business which we now have in hand. On this we are quite unable to speculate. Our affections as yet circulate through it. We no more feel or know it, than we feel the feet, or the hand, or the brain of our body. The new deed is yet a part of life,—remains for a time immersed in our unconscious life. In some contemplative hour, it detaches itself from the life like a ripe fruit, to become a thought of the mind. Instantly, it is raised, transfigured; the

---

[1] The silkworm feeds on the mulberry leaf, which furnishes the material from which it spins the silk that is manufactured into satin.

corruptible has put on incorruption.[1] Henceforth it is an object
of beauty, however base its origin and neighborhood. Observe,
too, the impossibility of antedating this act. In its grub state, it
cannot fly, it cannot shine, it is a dull grub. But suddenly, without observation, the selfsame thing unfurls beautiful wings, and is
an angel of wisdom. So is there no fact, no event, in our private
history, which shall not, sooner or later, lose its adhesive, inert
form, and astonish us by soaring from our body into the empy-
rean. Cradle and infancy, school and playground, the fear of
boys, and dogs, and ferules,[2] the love of little maids and berries,
and many another fact that once filled the whole sky, are gone
already; friend and relative, profession and party, town and
country, nation and world, must also soar and sing.

Of course, he who has put forth his total strength in fit actions,
has the richest return of wisdom. I will not shut myself out
of this globe of action, and transplant an oak into a flowerpot,
there to hunger and pine; nor trust the revenue of some single
faculty, and exhaust one vein of thought, much like those Savoy-
ards,[3] who, getting their livelihood by carving shepherds, shep-
herdesses, and smoking Dutchmen, for all Europe, went out one
day to the mountain to find stock, and discovered that they had
whittled up the last of their pine trees. Authors we have, in
numbers, who have written out their vein, and who, moved by
a commendable prudence, sail for Greece or Palestine, follow
the trapper into the prairie, or ramble round Algiers, to replenish
their merchantable stock.

If it were only for a vocabulary, the scholar would be covetous
of action. Life is our dictionary. Years are well spent in country labors; in town,—in the insight into trades and manufactures;

---

[1] 1 Cor. xv. 54.

[2] Corporal punishment at school administered with the ferule.

[3] Inhabitants of Savoy, south of Lake Geneva, the loftiest mountain region of Europe. Wood-carving was one of their chief industries, for which
the forests of beech, birch, and pine, which have suffered deplorable clear-
ances, furnished ample material.

in frank intercourse with many men and women; in science; in art; to the one end of mastering in all their facts a language by which to illustrate and embody our perceptions. I learn immediately from any speaker how much he has already lived, through the poverty or the splendor of his speech. Life lies behind us as the quarry from whence we get tiles and copestones[1] for the masonry of to-day. This is the way to learn grammar. Colleges and books only copy the language which the field and the work-yard made.

But the final value of action, like that of books, and better than books, is, that it is a resource. That great principle of Undulation[2] in nature, that shows itself in the inspiring and expiring of the breath; in desire and satiety; in the ebb and flow of the sea; in day and night; in heat and cold; and as yet more deeply ingrained in every atom and every fluid, is known to us under the name of Polarity,[3] — these "fits of easy transmission and reflection," as Newton[4] called them, are the law of nature because they are the law of spirit.

The mind now thinks; now acts; and each fit reproduces the other. When the artist has exhausted his materials, when the fancy no longer paints, when thoughts are no longer apprehended, and books are a weariness, — he has always the resource *to live*. Character is higher than intellect. Thinking is the function. Living is the functionary. The stream retreats to its source. A great soul will be strong to live, as well as strong to think. Does he lack organ or medium to impart his truths? He can still fall back on this elemental force of living them. This is a total act. Thinking is a partial act. Let the grandeur of justice shine in his affairs. Let the beauty of affection cheer

---

[1] Headstones of a wall.   [2] Wave motion.

[3] That quality or condition of a body by virtue of which it exhibits opposite or contrasted powers or properties in opposite directions.

[4] Sir Isaac Newton (1642–1727), English philosopher and mathematician. He discovered the law of gravitation and is regarded as the greatest of natural philosophers. His most important work was the Principia.

his lowly roof. Those "far from fame," who dwell and act with him, will feel the force of his constitution in the doings and passages of the day better than it can be measured by any public and designed display. Time shall teach him, that the scholar loses no hour which the man lives. Herein he unfolds the sacred germ of his instinct, screened from influence. What is lost in seemliness is gained in strength. Not out of those, on whom systems of education have exhausted their culture, comes the helpful giant to destroy the old or to build the new, but out of unhandseled[1] savage nature, out of terrible Druids[2] and Berserkirs[3] come at last Alfred[4] and Shakespeare.

I hear therefore with joy whatever is beginning to be said of the dignity and necessity of labor to every citizen. There is virtue yet in the hoe and the spade, for learned as well as for unlearned hands. And labor is everywhere welcome; always we are invited to work; only be this limitation observed, that a man shall not for the sake of wider activity sacrifice any opinion to the popular judgments and modes of action.

I have now spoken of the education of the scholar by nature, by books, and by action. It remains to say somewhat of his duties.

[1] A handsel is a gift; hence, ungifted or uncultured.

[2] An order of priests among the ancient Celts of Gaul, Britain, and Ireland. They believed in one Supreme Being and in the transmigration of the soul from one body to another. They were held in great awe, as disobedience to their mandates was followed by excommunication, in those days a terrible fate. They guarded the secret archives of the religion and acted as instructors and judges. Though they were well educated and understood many of the sciences, they also practiced divination and magic, and sacrificed human beings as part of their worship. The Druids reverenced the oak and the mistletoe, and their most profound ceremonies were performed in the depths of oak forests or in caves.

[3] Berserkir, or Berserker, was a hero in Scandinavian mythology who fought without armor, but overcame all opponents by his valor; hence the name Berserkirs was given to a class of warriors who fought naked under the influence of frenzy.

[4] Alfred the Great (849–901), King of the West Saxons, a distinguished

They are such as become Man Thinking. They may all be comprised in self-trust. The office of the scholar is to cheer, to raise, and to guide men by showing them facts amidst appearances. He plies the slow, unhonored, and unpaid task of observation. Flamsteed[1] and Herschel,[2] in their glazed observatories, may catalogue the stars with the praise of all men, and, the results being splendid and useful, honor is sure. But he, in his private observatory, cataloguing obscure and nebulous stars of the human mind, which as yet no man has thought of as such,— watching days and months, sometimes, for a few facts; correcting still his old records; — must relinquish display and immediate fame. In the long period of his preparation, he must betray often an ignorance and shiftlessness in popular arts, incurring the disdain of the able who shoulder him aside. Long he must stammer in his speech; often forego the living for the dead. Worse yet, he must accept,— how often! poverty and solitude. For the ease and pleasure of treading the old road, accepting the fashions, the education, the religion of society, he takes the cross of making his own, and, of course, the self-accusation, the faint heart, the frequent uncertainty and loss of time, which are the nettles and tangling vines in the way of the self-relying and self-directed; and the state of virtual hostility in which he seems

scholar and patron of learning. He is characterized by historians as the wisest, best, and greatest king that ever reigned in England.

[1] John Flamsteed (1646–1719), first English astronomer royal under Charles II. He was the first to explain the true principles of the equation of time. His Historia Cœlistis Britannicæ, in which he determined the position of nearly 3000 stars, was the first trustworthy catalogue of the stars.

[2] Sir William Herschel (1738–1822) was of German birth, but all his astronomical work was done in England. He accomplished more than any other man in the field of astronomy. He discovered the planet Uranus, and made many remarkable observations upon the physical constitution of the sun, and upon comets; but his most valuable service to the cause of astronomy consisted in his accurate observations upon variable and binary stars. He demonstrated the action upon the most distant members of the firmament of the same mechanical laws that bind together our solar system.

to stand to society, and especially to educated society. For all this loss and scorn, what offset? He is to find consolation in exercising the highest functions of human nature. He is one, who raises himself from private considerations, and breathes and lives on public and illustrious thoughts. He is the world's eye. He is the world's heart. He is to resist the vulgar prosperity that retrogrades ever to barbarism, by preserving and communicating heroic sentiments, noble biographies, melodious verse, and the conclusions of history. Whatsoever oracles the human heart, in all emergencies, in all solemn hours, has uttered as its commentary on the world of actions,— these he shall receive and impart. And whatsoever new verdict Reason from her inviolable seat pronounces on the passing men and events of to-day,— this he shall hear and promulgate.

These being his functions, it becomes him to feel all confidence in himself, and to defer never to the popular cry. He and he only knows the world. The world of any moment is the merest appearance. Some great decorum, some fetish[1] of a government, some ephemeral trade, or war, or man, is cried up by half mankind and cried down by the other half, as if all depended on this particular up or down. The odds are that the whole question is not worth the poorest thought which the scholar has lost in listening to the controversy. Let him not quit his belief that a popgun is a popgun, though the ancient and honorable of the earth affirm it to be the crack of doom. In silence, in steadiness, in severe abstraction, let him hold by himself; add observation to observation, patient of neglect, patient of reproach; and bide his own time,— happy enough, if he can satisfy himself alone, that this day he has seen something truly. Success treads[2] on every right step. For the instinct is sure, that prompts him to tell his brother what he thinks. He then learns, that in going down into the secrets of his own mind, he has descended into the secrets of all minds. He learns that he who has mastered any

---

[1] An idol or object of blind devotion.
[2] Follows.

law in his private thoughts, is master to that extent of all men whose language he speaks, and of all into whose language his own can be translated. The poet, in utter solitude remembering his spontaneous thoughts and recording them, is found to have recorded that, which men in crowded cities find true for them also. The orator distrusts at first the fitness of his frank confessions, — his want of knowledge of the persons he addresses, — until he finds that he is the complement of his hearers; — that they drink his words because he fulfills for them their own nature; the deeper he dives into his privatest, secretest presentiment, to his wonder he finds, this is the most acceptable, most public, and universally true. The people delight in it; the better part of every man feels, This is my music; this is myself.

In self-trust, all the virtues are comprehended. Free should the scholar be, — free and brave. Free even to the definition of freedom, "without any hindrance that does not arise out of his own constitution." Brave; for fear is a thing, which a scholar by his very function puts behind him. Fear always springs from ignorance. It is a shame to him if his tranquillity, amid dangerous times, arise from the presumption, that, like children and women, his is a protected class; or if he seek a temporary peace by the diversion of his thoughts from politics or vexed questions, hiding his head like an ostrich in the flowering bushes,[1] peeping into microscopes, and turning rhymes, as a boy whistles to keep his courage up. So is the danger a danger still; so is the fear worse. Manlike let him turn and face it. Let him look into its eye and search its nature, inspect its origin, — see the whelping of this lion, — which lies no great way back; he will then find in himself a perfect comprehension of its nature and extent; he will have made his hands meet on the other side, and can henceforth defy it, and pass on superior. The world is his, who can see through its pretension. What deafness, what stone-blind custom, what overgrown error you behold is there only by sufferance, —

---

[1] The ostrich, when hunted, thrusts its head into a bush and imagines itself invisible because it cannot see the hunter.

by your sufferance.   See it to be a lie, and you have already
dealt it its mortal blow.

Yes, we are the cowed, — we the trustless.   It is a mischievous
notion that we are come late into nature; that the world was
finished a long time ago.   As the world was plastic and fluid in
the hands of God, so it is ever to so much of his attributes as we
bring to it.   To ignorance and sin, it is flint.[1]   They adapt themselves to it as they may; but in proportion as a man has anything in him divine, the firmament flows before him and takes his
signet and form.   Not he is great who can alter matter, but he
who can alter my state of mind.   They are the kings of the
world who give the color of their present thought to all nature
and all art, and persuade men by the cheerful serenity of their
carrying the matter, that this thing which they do, is the apple
which the ages have desired to pluck, now at last ripe, and inviting nations to the harvest.   The great man makes the great
thing.   Wherever Macdonald sits, there is the head of the table.[2]
Linnæus[3] makes botany the most alluring of studies, and wins
it from the farmer and the herb-woman; Davy,[4] chemistry; and

[1] "It is flint," i.e., hard or unimpressionable as flint.

[2] In Cervantes' Don Quixote, Sancho Panza, Don Quixote's squire, relates
a story of a gentleman who, having invited a poor farmer to dine with him,
pressed him to take the head of the table.   The countryman, piquing himself
on his good breeding, refused to take the place of honor, until his host, losing all patience, exclaimed, "Sit thee down, clodpole, for let me sit wherever
I will, that will still be the upper end and the place of worship to thee."
The same thought, modified in expression, is placed by different authors in
the mouths of various men, and it is uncertain to which of several famous
Scotchmen Emerson ascribes it.

[3] Carolus Linnæus, or Carl von Linne (1707–78), Swedish botanist.   He
established natural science upon its modern basis, and was, in botany and
zoölogy, the foremost man of his time.   His artificial system of plant classification, though now discarded, was simple and easily followed, and has
greatly facilitated the study of botany.

[4] Sir Humphry Davy (1778–1829), English chemist.   His greatest
achievement was his account of the decomposition by galvanism of the fixed
alkalies, by which he proved that these alkalies are metallic oxides.

Cuvier,[1] fossils. The day is always his, who works in it with serenity and great aims. The unstable estimates of men crowd to him whose mind is filled with a truth, as the heaped waves of the Atlantic follow the moon.[2]

For this self-trust, the reason is deeper than can be fathomed, — darker than can be enlightened. I might not carry with me the feeling of my audience in stating my own belief. But I have already shown the ground of my hope, in adverting to the doctrine that man is one. I believe man has been wronged; he has wronged himself. He has almost lost the light, that can lead him back to his prerogatives. Men are become of no account. Men in history, men in the world of to-day are bugs, are spawn, and are called "the mass" and "the herd." In a century, in a millennium, one or two men; that is to say,— one or two approximations to the right state of every man. All the rest behold in the hero or the poet their own green and crude being,— ripened; yes, and are content to be less, so *that* may attain to its full stature. What a testimony,—full of grandeur, full of pity, is borne to the demands of his own nature, by the poor clansman, the poor partisan, who rejoices in the glory of his chief. The poor and the low find some amends to their immense moral capacity, for their acquiescence in a political and social inferiority. They are content to be brushed like flies from the path of a great person, so that justice shall be done by him to that common nature which it is the dearest desire of all to see enlarged and glorified. They sun themselves in the great man's light, and feel it to be their own element. They cast the dignity of man from their downtrod selves upon the shoulders of a hero, and will perish to add one drop of blood to make that great heart beat, those

---

[1] George Cuvier (1769–1832), French naturalist. He first applied to zoölogy the natural method, and founded a system of classification of animals based on their anatomical structure. He is regarded as the founder of the science of comparative anatomy.

[2] The attraction of the moon heaps up the waters of the sea into a broad, low wave, the passage of which forms the ebb and flow of the tide.

giant sinews combat and conquer.   He lives for us, and we live
in him.

Men such as they are, very naturally seek money or power;
and power because it is as good as money,—the "spoils," so
called, "of office."   And why not? for they aspire to the highest,
and this, in their sleep-walking, they dream is highest.   Wake
them, and they shall quit the false good, and leap to the true, and
leave governments to clerks and desks.   This revolution is to
be wrought by the gradual domestication of the idea of Culture.
The main enterprise of the world for splendor, for extent, is the
upbuilding of a man.   Here are the materials strown[1] along the
ground.   The private life of one man shall be a more illustrious
monarchy,—more formidable to its enemy, more sweet and serene
in its influence to its friend, than any kingdom in history.   For
a man, rightly viewed, comprehendeth the particular natures of
all men.   Each philosopher, each bard, each actor, has only
done for me, as by a delegate, what one day I can do for myself.   The books which once we valued more than the apple
of the eye, we have quite exhausted.   What is that but saying,
that we have come up with the point of view which the universal mind took through the eyes of one scribe; we have
been that man, and have passed on.   First, one; then another;
we drain all cisterns, and, waxing greater by all these supplies,
we crave a better and more abundant food.   The man has
never lived that can feed us ever.   The human mind cannot be
enshrined in a person, who shall set a barrier on any one side to
this unbounded, unboundable empire.   It is one central fire,
which, flaming now out of the lips of Etna,[2] lightens the capes
of Sicily; and, now out of the throat of Vesuvius,[3] illuminates
the towers and vineyards of Naples.   It is one light which

---

[1] Strewn.

[2] A celebrated volcanic mountain of Sicily, the largest island in the Mediterranean Sea.

[3] A famous volcano, the most active in Europe, situated near Naples, the
largest town in Italy.

beams out of a thousand stars. It is one soul which animates all men.

But I have dwelt perhaps tediously upon this abstraction of the Scholar. I ought not to delay longer to add what I have to say, of nearer reference to the time and to this country.

Historically, there is thought to be a difference in the ideas which predominate over successive epochs, and there are data for marking the genius of the Classic, of the Romantic, and now of the Reflective or Philosophical age. With the views I have intimated of the oneness or the identity of the mind through all individuals, I do not much dwell on these differences. In fact, I believe each individual passes through all three. The boy is a Greek; the youth, romantic; the adult, reflective. I deny not, however, that a revolution in the leading idea may be distinctly enough traced.

Our age is bewailed as the age of Introversion.[1] Must that needs be evil? We, it seems, are critical; we are embarrassed with second thoughts; we cannot enjoy anything for hankering to know whereof the pleasure consists; we are lined with eyes; we see with our feet; the time is infected with Hamlet's unhappiness, —

"Sicklied o'er with the pale cast of thought."[2]

Is it so bad then? Sight is the last thing to be pitied. Would we be blind? Do we fear lest we should outsee nature and God, and drink truth dry? I look upon the discontent of the literary class, as a mere announcement of the fact, that they find themselves not in the state of mind of their fathers, and regret the coming state as untried; as a boy dreads the water before he has learned that he can swim. If there is any period one would desire to be born in, — is it not the age of Revolution; when the old and the new stand side by side, and admit of being compared;

---

[1] Literally, turning inward: hence, reflection.
[2] Shakespeare's Hamlet, act iii., sc. 1.

when the energies of all men are searched by fear and by hope;
when the historic glories of the old, can be compensated by the
rich possibilities of the new era? This time, like all times, is a
very good one, if we but know what to do with it.

I read with joy some of the auspicious signs of the coming
days, as they glimmer already through poetry and art, through
philosophy and science, through church and state.

One of these signs is the fact, that the same movement which
effected the elevation of what was called the lowest class in the
state, assumed in literature a very marked and as benign an
aspect. Instead of the sublime and beautiful; the near, the low,
the common, was explored and poetized. That, which had been
negligently trodden under foot by those who were harnessing
and provisioning themselves for long journeys into far countries,
is suddenly found to be richer than all foreign parts. The literature of the poor, the feelings of the child, the philosophy of the
street, the meaning of household life, are the topics of the time.
It is a great stride. It is a sign,— is it not? of new vigor, when
the extremities are made active, when currents of warm life run
into the hands and the feet. I ask not for the great, the remote,
the romantic; what is doing in Italy or Arabia; what is Greek
art, or Provençal minstrelsy; I embrace the common, I explore
and sit at the feet of the familiar, the low. Give me insight
into to-day, and you may have the antique and future worlds.
What would we really know the meaning of ? The meal in the
firkin; the milk in the pan; the ballad in the street; the news
of the boat; the glance of the eye; the form and the gait of the
body;— show me the ultimate reason of these matters; show
me the sublime presence of the highest spiritual cause lurking, as
always it does lurk, in these suburbs and extremities of nature;
let me see every trifle bristling with the polarity that ranges it
instantly on an eternal law; and the shop, the plow, and the
leger,[1] referred to the like cause by which light undulates and
poets sing;— and the world lies no longer a dull miscellany and

---

[1] Old form of "ledger."

lumber room, but has form and order; there is no trifle; there is no puzzle; but one design unites and animates the farthest pinnacle and the lowest trench.

This idea has inspired the genius of Goldsmith,[1] Burns,[2] Cowper,[3] and, in a newer time, of Goethe,[4] Wordsworth,[5] and Carlyle.[6] This idea they have differently followed and with various success. In contrast with their writing, the style of Pope,[7] of Johnson,[8] of Gibbon,[9] looks cold and pedantic. This writing is blood-warm. Man is surprised to find that things near are not less beautiful and wondrous than things remote. The near explains the far. The drop is a small ocean. A man is related to all nature. This perception of the worth of the vulgar is fruitful

[1] Oliver Goldsmith (1728–74), Irish poet, historian, and novelist. The charm of his poetry lies in the fact that he enlists simple and universal feelings in behalf of the moral principle he seeks to establish. His best known poem is The Deserted Village, and his famous and only novel, The Vicar of Wakefield.

[2] Robert Burns (1759–96), Scottish poet, the poet of the people and of homely human nature. Tam O'Shanter, and The Cotter's Saturday Night are his most noted poems.

[3] William Cowper (1731–1800), English poet of simple human affections. He is best known by The Task, and Table Talk.

[4] Johann Wolfgang von Goethe (1749–1832), Germany's greatest philosophical poet. His masterpieces are Faust, and Wilhelm Meister.

[5] William Wordsworth (1770–1850), English poet of nature and of man. His longest poems are The Prelude, and The Excursion.

[6] Thomas Carlyle (1795–1881), British essayist and historian, noted for his deep insight into the nature of things. His most famous works are History of the French Revolution, and Sartor Resartus.

[7] Alexander Pope (1688–1744), English poet. Pope was a critical poet of no great originality. He cast other men's thoughts into finished verse. His most noted works are the Essay on Man, and the Dunciad.

[8] Samuel Johnson (1709–84), English miscellaneous writer, author of the didactic novel Rasselas and of the Dictionary of the English Language. He was a man of wonderful conversational powers, and his language is condensed and well-balanced like Pope's.

[9] Edward Gibbon (1737–94), English historian. His language is elaborate but he displays little sympathy with humanity. His great work is The Decline and Fall of the Roman Empire.

in discoveries. Goethe, in this very thing the most modern of
the moderns, has shown us, as none ever did, the genius of the
ancients.

There is one man of genius, who has done much for this
philosophy of life, whose literary value has never yet been rightly
estimated; — I mean Emanuel Swedenborg.[1] The most imaginative of men, yet writing with the precision of a mathematician,
he endeavored to ingraft a purely philosophical Ethics on the
popular Christianity of his time. Such an attempt, of course,
must have difficulty, which no genius could surmount. But he
saw and showed the connection between nature and the affections of the soul. He pierced the emblematic or spiritual character of the visible, audible, tangible world. Especially did his
shade-loving muse[2] hover over and interpret the lower parts of
nature; he showed the mysterious bond that allies moral evil to
the foul material forms, and has given in epical parables[3] a theory of insanity, of beasts, of unclean and fearful things.

Another sign of our times, also marked by an analogous political movement, is the new importance given to the single person.
Everything that tends to insulate the individual, — to surround
him with barriers of natural respect, so that each man shall feel
the world is his, and man shall treat with man as a sovereign
state with a sovereign state; — tends to true union as well as
greatness. "I learned," said the melancholy Pestalozzi,[4] "that
no man in God's wide earth is either willing or able to help any

---

[1] Emanuel Swedenborg (1688–1772), founder of the New Jerusalem
Church. He first applied himself to the problem of discovering the nature
of the soul and spirit by anatomical studies, but a change came over him
which made of the scientific inquirer a supernatural prophet.

[2] An inspiring power.

[3] An epic is a poem about heroic or great events; a parable is a moral
fable or an allegory; hence, allegorical relations of great events or things.

[4] Johann Heinrich Pestalozzi (1746–1827), Swiss educational reformer,
and author of Leonard and Gertrude. He was deeply in earnest in his work
and spent his life with his pupils, sharing in their sufferings as well as in
their play.

other man." Help must come from the bosom alone. The scholar is that man who must take up into himself all the ability of the time, all the contributions of the past, all the hopes of the future. He must be an university of knowledges. If there be one lesson more than another, which should pierce his ear, it is, The world is nothing, the man is all; in yourself is the law of all nature, and you know not yet how a globule of sap ascends; in yourself slumbers the whole of Reason; it is for you to know all, it is for you to dare all. Mr. President and Gentlemen, this confidence in the unsearched might of man belongs, by all motives, by all prophecy, by all preparation, to the American Scholar. We have listened too long to the courtly muses of Europe. The spirit of the American freeman is already suspected to be timid, imitative, tame. Public and private avarice make the air we breathe thick and fat. The scholar is decent, indolent, complaisant. See already the tragic consequence. The mind of this country, taught to aim at low objects, eats upon itself. There is no work for any but the decorous and the complaisant. Young men of the fairest promise, who begin life upon our shores, inflated by the mountain winds, shined upon by all the stars of God, find the earth below not in unison with these, — but are hindered from action by the disgust which the principles on which business is managed inspire, and turn drudges, or die of disgust, — some of them suicides. What is the remedy? They did not yet see, and thousands of young men as hopeful now crowding to the barriers for the career, do not yet see, that, if the single man plant himself indomitably on his instincts, and there abide, the huge world will come round to him. Patience, — patience ; — with the shades[1] of all the good and great for company ; and for solace, the perspective of your own infinite life ; and for work, the study and the communication of principles, the making those instincts prevalent, the conversion of the world. Is it not

[1] Spirits or spiritual influence; so called because it was formerly believed that the soul, after its separation from the body, was perceptible to the sight, but not to the touch, in which respect it resembled a shadow or shade.

the chief disgrace in the world, not to be. an unit; — not to be reckoned one character; — not to yield that peculiar fruit which each man was created to bear, but to be reckoned in the gross, in the hundred, or the thousand, of the party, the section, to which we belong; and our opinion predicted geographically, as the north, or the south?   Not so, brothers and friends, — please God, ours shall not be so.   We will walk on our own feet; we will work with our own hands; we will speak our own minds. The study of letters shall be no longer a name for pity, for doubt, and for sensual indulgence.   The dread of man and the love of man shall be a wall of defense and a wreath of joy around all. A nation of men will for the first time exist, because each believes himself inspired by the Divine Soul which also inspires all men.

SELF-RELIANCE.

"Ne te quæsiveris extra." [1]

" MAN is his own star; and the soul that can
Render an honest and a perfect man,
Commands all light, all influence, all fate;
Nothing to him falls early or too late.
Our acts our angels are, or [2] good or ill,
Our fatal shadows that walk by us still."

Ep. to BEAUMONT *and* FLETCHER'S *Honest Man's Fortune.*

[1] " Do not seek for anything outside of thyself."
[2] Whether.

Cast the bantling on the rocks,
Suckle him with the she-wolf's teat;
Wintered with the hawk and fox,
Power and speed be hands and feet.

SELF-RELIANCE.

I READ the other day some verses written by an eminent
painter which were original and not conventional. The soul
always hears an admonition in such lines, let the subject be what
it may. The sentiment they instill is of more value than any
thought they may contain. To believe your own thought, to
believe that what is true for you in your private heart is true for
all men, — that is genius. Speak your latent conviction, and it
shall be the universal sense;[1] for the inmost in due time becomes
the outmost, — and our first thought is rendered back to us by the
trumpets of the Last Judgment. Familiar as the voice of the
mind is to each, the highest merit we ascribe to Moses, Plato,[2]
and Milton[3] is, that they set at naught books and traditions, and
spoke not what men, but what they thought. A man should
learn to detect and watch that gleam of light which flashes
across his mind from within, more than the luster of the firmament[4] of bards and sages. Yet he dismisses without notice his
thought, because it is his. In every work of genius we recognize
our own rejected thoughts: they come back to us with a certain
alienated majesty. Great works of art have no more affecting
lesson for us than this. They teach us to abide by our spontaneous impression with good-humored inflexibility then most[5]
when the whole cry of voices is on the other side. Else, to-mor-

---

[1] Opinion.   [2] See Note 2, p. 29.

[3] John Milton (1608–74), one of the greatest and most original of English
poets, author of Paradise Lost.

[4] The heavens or canopy in which the stars appear to be placed; hence,
to carry out the metaphor, the firmament, rather than the world, of bards
and sages.   [5] " Then most," i.e., most at that time.

row a stranger will say with masterly good sense precisely what
we have thought and felt all the time, and we shall be forced to
take with shame our own opinion from another.

There is a time in every man's education when he arrives at
the conviction that envy is ignorance; that imitation is suicide;
that he must take himself for better, for worse, as his portion;
that though the wide universe is full of good, no kernel of nour-
ishing corn can come to him but through his toil bestowed on
that plot of ground which is given to him to till. The power
which resides in him is new in nature, and none but he knows
what that is which he can do, nor does he know until he has
tried. Not for nothing one face, one character, one fact, makes
much impression on him, and another none. This sculpture [1] in
the memory is not without preëstablished harmony. The eye
was placed where one ray should fall, that it might testify of that
particular ray. We but half express ourselves, and are ashamed
of that divine idea which each of us represents. It may be
safely trusted as proportionate and of good issues, so [2] it be faithfully imparted, but God will not have his work made manifest
by cowards. A man is relieved and gay when he has put his
heart into his work and done his best; but what he has said or
done otherwise, shall give him no peace. It is a deliverance
which does not deliver. In the attempt his genius deserts him;
no muse befriends; no invention, no hope.

Trust thyself: every heart vibrates to that iron string. Accept the place the divine providence has found for you, the society of your contemporaries, the connection of events. Great
men have always done so, and confided themselves childlike to
the genius of their age, betraying their perception that the absolutely trustworthy was seated at their heart, working through
their hands, predominating in all their being. And we are now
men, and must accept in the highest mind the same transcendent

---

[1] Image.

[2] "Proportionate," etc., i.e., of correct proportions and of good results,
so long as.

destiny; and not minors and invalids in a protected corner, not cowards fleeing before a revolution, but guides, redeemers, and benefactors, obeying the Almighty effort, and advancing on Chaos[1] and the Dark.

What pretty oracles nature yields us on this text, in the face and behavior of children, babes, and even brutes! That divided and rebel mind, that distrust of a sentiment because our arithmetic has computed the strength and means opposed to our purpose, these[2] have not. Their mind being whole, their eye is as yet unconquered, and when we look in their faces, we are disconcerted. Infancy conforms to nobody: all conform to it, so that one babe commonly makes four or five[3] out of the adults who prattle and play to it. So God has armed youth and puberty[4] and manhood no less with its own piquancy and charm, and made it enviable and gracious and its claims not to be put by, if it will stand by itself. Do not think the youth has no force, because he cannot speak to you and me. Hark! in the next room his voice is sufficiently clear and emphatic. It seems he knows how to speak to his contemporaries. Bashful or bold, then, he will know how to make us seniors very unnecessary.

The nonchalance[5] of boys who are sure of a dinner, and would disdain as much as a lord to do or say aught to conciliate one, is the healthy attitude of human nature. A boy is in the parlor what the pit is in the playhouse;[6] independent, irresponsible, looking out from his corner on such people and facts as pass by, he tries and sentences them on their merits, in the swift,

---

[1] The confused or formless elementary state in which the universe is supposed to have existed before order was developed; hence, disorder in general.

[2] Children, babes, and brutes.   [3] Supply "babes."

[4] The age of maturity.   [5] Indifference.

[6] In the early theaters the floor of the house, below the level of the stage, was known as the pit. The seats in this part were the cheapest in the house, and the people who assembled there were of a class who did not care much what others thought of them, but shouted and stamped their applause and hissed their disapproval, as the occasion seemed to demand.

summary way of boys, as good, bad, interesting, silly, eloquent, troublesome. He cumbers himself never about consequences, about interests; he gives an independent, genuine verdict. You must court him: he does not court you. But the man is, as it were, clapped into jail by his consciousness. As soon as he has once acted or spoken with *éclat*[1] he is a committed person, watched by the sympathy or the hatred of hundreds, whose affections must now enter into his account. There is no Lethe[2] for this. Ah, that he could pass again into his neutrality! Who[3] can thus avoid all pledges, and having observed, observe again from the same unaffected, unbiased, unbribable, unaffrighted innocence, must always be formidable. He would utter opinions on all passing affairs, which being seen to be not private, but necessary, would sink like darts into the ear of men, and put them in fear.

These are the voices which we hear in solitude, but they grow faint and inaudible as we enter into the world. Society everywhere is in conspiracy against the manhood of every one of its members. Society is a joint-stock company, in which the members agree, for the better securing of his bread to each shareholder, to surrender the liberty and culture of the eater. The virtue in most request is conformity. Self-reliance is its aversion. It loves not realities and creators, but names and customs.

Whoso would be a man must be a nonconformist.[4] He who would gather immortal palms[5] must not be hindered by the name of goodness, but must explore if it be goodness.[6] Nothing is at

[1] A French word (pronounced ā klä′) meaning brilliancy of success which attracts applause.

[2] Oblivion; from the ancient Greek myth of Lethe, the personification of oblivion, or from the river Lethe, in the lower world, of which the souls of the departed drank and forgot all they had done in the upper world.

[3] He who.

[4] One who does not conform to established opinions or creeds.

[5] Undying fame. A branch or leaf of the palm was anciently worn as a symbol of victory or rejoicing.

[6] " Explore," etc., i.e., himself investigate if the thing so called be really goodness.

last sacred but the integrity of your own mind. Absolve you to yourself,[1] and you shall have the suffrage[2] of the world. I remember an answer which when quite young I was prompted to make to a valued adviser, who was wont to importune me with the dear old doctrines of the church. On my saying, What have I to do with the sacredness of traditions, if I live wholly from within? my friend suggested, — "But these impulses may be from below, not from above." I replied, "They do not seem to me to be such; but if I am the Devil's child, I will live then from the Devil." No law can be sacred to me but that of my nature. Good and bad are but names very readily transferable to that or this; the only right is what is after my constitution, the only wrong what is against it. A man is to carry himself in the presence of all opposition, as if everything were titular and ephemeral[3] but he. I am ashamed to think how easily we capitulate to badges and names, to large societies and dead institutions. Every decent and well-spoken individual affects and sways me more than is right. I ought to go upright and vital,[4] and speak the rude truth in all ways. If malice and vanity wear the coat of philanthropy, shall that pass?[5] If an angry bigot assumes this bountiful cause of Abolition, and comes to me with his last news from Barbadoes,[6] why should I not say to him, "Go love thy infant; love thy wood-chopper: be good-natured and modest: have that grace; and never varnish your hard, uncharitable ambition with this incredible tenderness for black folk a thousand miles off. Thy love afar is spite at home." Rough and graceless would be such greeting, but truth is handsomer than the affectation of love. Your goodness must have some

---

[1] "Absolve," etc., i.e., justify yourself.   [2] Approval.

[3] "Titular and ephemeral," i.e., existing in name only and of short duration.   [4] "I ought," etc., i.e., I ought to act as if I were alive.

[5] Be tolerated.

[6] An island in the Atlantic Ocean, belonging to Great Britain, one of the Lesser Antilles. The inhabitants are mainly negroes who, prior to 1834, were slaves.

edge to it, — else it is none. The doctrine of hatred must be preached as the counteraction of the doctrine of love, when that pules and whines. I shun father and mother and wife and brother, when my genius calls me. I would write on the lintels of the doorpost, *Whim.*[1] I hope it is somewhat better than whim at last, but we cannot spend the day in explanation. Expect me not to show cause why I seek or why I exclude company. Then, again, do not tell me, as a good man did to-day, of my obligation to put all poor men in good situations. Are they *my* poor? I tell thee, thou foolish philanthropist, that I grudge the dollar, the dime, the cent, I give to such men as do not belong to me. and to whom I do not belong. There is a class of persons to whom by all spiritual affinity I am bought and sold; for them I will go to prison, if need be; but your miscellaneous popular charities; the education at college of fools; the building of meetinghouses to the vain end to which many now stand; alms to sots; and the thousand-fold Relief Societies; — though I confess with shame I sometimes succumb and give the dollar, it is a wicked dollar which by and by I shall have the manhood to withhold.

Virtues are, in the popular estimate, rather the exception than the rule. There is the man *and* his virtues. Men do what is called a good action, as some piece of courage or charity, much as they would pay a fine in expiation of daily nonappearance on parade. Their works are done as an apology or extenuation of their living in the world, — as invalids and the insane pay a high board. Their virtues are penances. I do not wish to expiate, but to live. My life is for itself and not for a spectacle. I much prefer that it should be of a lower strain, so it be genuine and equal, than that it should be glittering and unsteady. I wish it to be sound and sweet, and not to need diet and bleeding.[2] I

---

[1] Emerson means to convey the idea that he would rather have his actions ascribed to mere caprice than to be compelled to spend his time in explaining them.

[2] A use of the sign for the thing signified. "Not to need diet and bleed-

ask primary evidence that you are a man, and refuse this appeal from the man to his actions. I know that for myself it makes no difference whether I do or forbear those actions which are reckoned excellent. I cannot consent to pay for a privilege where I have intrinsic right. Few and mean as my gifts may be, I actually am, and do not need for my own assurance or the assurance of my fellows any secondary testimony.

What I must do is all that concerns me, not what the people think. This rule, equally arduous in actual and in intellectual life, may serve for the whole distinction between greatness and meanness. It is the harder, because you will always find those who think they know what is your duty better than you know it. It is easy in the world to live after the world's opinion; it is easy in solitude to live after our own; but the great man is he who in the midst of the crowd keeps with perfect sweetness the independence of solitude.

The objection to conforming to usages that have become dead to you is, that it scatters your force. It loses your time and blurs the impression of your character. If you maintain a dead church, contribute to a dead Bible-society, vote with a great party either for the government or against it, spread your table like base housekeepers, — under all these screens I have difficulty to detect the precise man [1] you are. And, of course, so much force is withdrawn from your proper life. But do your work, and I shall know you. Do your work, and you shall reënforce yourself. A man must consider what a blindman's-buff is this game of conformity. If I know your sect, I anticipate your argument. I hear a preacher announce for his text and topic the expediency of one of the institutions of his church. Do I not know beforehand that not possibly can he say a new and spontaneous word? Do I not know that, with all this ostentation of examining the

ing" means not to be unhealthy, a special course of diet being frequently prescribed in cases of illness, and bleeding having been one of the first resources of the old medical practitioners.

[1] " The precise man," i.e., precisely what kind of a man.

grounds of the institution, he will do no such thing? Do I not know that he is pledged to himself not to look but at one side, — the permitted side, not as a man, but as a parish minister? He is a retained attorney, and these airs of the bench[1] are the emptiest affectation. Well, most men have bound their eyes with one or another handkerchief,[2] and attached themselves to some one of these communities of opinion. This conformity makes them not false in a few particulars, authors of a few lies, but false in all particulars. Their every truth is not quite true. Their two is not the real two, their four not the real four; so that every word they say chagrins us, and we know not where to begin to set them right. Meantime nature is not slow to equip us in the prison-uniform of the party to which we adhere. We come to wear one cut of face and figure, and acquire by degrees the gentlest asinine[3] expression. There is a mortifying experience in particular, which does not fail to wreak itself also in the general history; I mean "the foolish face of praise," the forced smile which we put on in company where we do not feel at ease in answer to conversation which does not interest us. The muscles, not spontaneously moved, but moved by a low usurping willfulness, grow tight about the outline of the face with the most disagreeable sensation.

For nonconformity the world whips you with its displeasure. And therefore a man must know how to estimate a sour face. The bystanders look askance on him in the public street or in the friend's parlor. If this aversation[4] had its origin in contempt and resistance like his own, he might well go home with a sad countenance; but the sour faces of the multitude, like their sweet faces, have no deep cause, but are put on and off as the wind blows and a newspaper directs. Yet is the discontent of the multitude more formidable than that of the senate and the

---

[1] Court of justice.
[2] An extension of the metaphor of the blindman's-buff.
[3] Like an ass, or stupid.
[4] A turning away from.

college. It is easy enough for a firm man who knows the world to brook the rage of the cultivated classes. Their rage is decorous and prudent, for they are timid as being very vulnerable themselves. But when to their feminine[1] rage the indignation of the people is added, when the ignorant and the poor are aroused, when the unintelligent brute force that lies at the bottom of society is made to growl and mow,[2] it needs the habit of magnanimity and religion to treat it godlike as a trifle of no concernment.

The other terror that scares us from self-trust is our consistency; a reverence for our past act or word, because the eyes of others have no other data for computing our orbit[3] than our past acts, and we are loth to disappoint them.

But why should you keep your head over your shoulder? Why drag about this corpse of your memory, lest you contradict somewhat[4] you have stated in this or that public place? Suppose you should contradict yourself; what then? It seems to be a rule of wisdom never to rely on your memory alone, scarcely even in acts of pure memory, but to bring the past for judgment into the thousand-eyed[5] present, and live ever in a new day. In your metaphysics you have denied personality to the Deity; yet when the devout motions of the soul come, yield to them heart and life, though they should clothe God with shape and color. Leave your theory, as Joseph[6] his coat in the hand of the harlot, and flee.

A foolish consistency is the hobgoblin of little minds, adored by little statesmen and philosophers and divines. With consistency a great soul has simply nothing to do. He may as well concern himself with his shadow on the wall. Speak what you think now in hard[7] words, and to-morrow speak what to-morrow

---

[1] Feminine, because decorous and timid.   [2] To make grimaces.

[3] Course or path in life.   [4] Something.

[5] Thousand-eyed, because there may be thousands of witnesses to things that happen in the present, while for the past we must rely on memory and history.   [6] Gen. xxxix. 12.   [7] Strong and enduring.

thinks in hard words again, though it contradict everything you said to-day. — "Ah, so you shall be sure to be misunderstood." — Is it so bad, then, to be misunderstood?   Pythagoras was misunderstood, and Socrates, and Jesus, and Luther, and Copernicus, and Galileo, and Newton,[1] and every pure and wise spirit that ever took flesh.   To be great is to be misunderstood.

I suppose no man can violate his nature.   All the sallies[2] of his will are rounded in by the law of his being, as the inequalities of Andes and Himmaleh[3] are insignificant in the curve of the sphere.   Nor does it matter how you gauge and try him.   A character is like an acrostic or Alexandrian stanza; — read it forward, backward, or across, it still spells the same thing.[4]   In this pleasing, contrite wood-life which God allows me, let me record

---

[1] Pythagoras (560–510 B.C.), a famous Greek philosopher, and leader in a movement for ethical and religious reform.   He died in banishment. Socrates (470–399 B.C.), one of the most famous of Athenian philosophers and teachers of truth, virtue, and self-control, was ridiculed, imprisoned, and died a martyr; Jesus was crucified; Martin Luther (1483–1546), a German Augustine monk, protested against certain abuses that had grown up within the Catholic Church, and became the leader of the Reformation or religious revolution.   He was excommunicated by the church and outlawed by the state.   Nicholas Copernicus (1473–1543), a Polish astronomer, was the originator of the theory that the planets revolve around the sun.   This theory was opposed to the prejudices and dogmas of the time and was not generally accepted until many years after his death.   Galileo, or Galilei (1564–1642), was a famous Italian astronomer, mathematician, physicist, and inventor of the refracting telescope by means of which he discovered the mountainous character of the moon, the phases of the planet Venus, the satellites of Jupiter, and the rings of Saturn.   His physical discoveries were heard with incredulity by the physicists of his time, and he was subjected to persecution and imprisonment by the Inquisition because of them.   Sir Isaac Newton (1642–1727), the great English philosopher and mathematician who discovered the law of gravitation.   His teachings were hotly contested and only adopted after many years.   [2] Digressions.

[3] Andes and Himmaleh (Himalaya), the great mountain ranges of South America and Asia respectively.

[4] It is the palindrome, not the acrostic or Alexandrian stanza, which has this peculiarity.

day by day my honest thought without prospect or retrospect,[1] and, I cannot doubt, it will be found symmetrical, though I mean it not, and see it not. My book should smell of pines and resound with the hum of insects. The swallow over my window should interweave that thread or straw he carries in his bill into my web also.[2] We pass for what we are. Character teaches above our wills. Men imagine that they communicate their virtue or vice only by overt actions, and do not see that virtue or vice emit a breath every moment.

There will be an agreement in whatever variety of actions, so they be each honest and natural in their hour. For of one will, the actions will be harmonious, however unlike they seem. These varieties are lost sight of at a little distance, at a little height of thought. One tendency unites them all. The voyage of the best ship is a zigzag line of a hundred tacks.[3] See the line from a sufficient distance, and it straightens itself to the average tendency. Your genuine action will explain itself, and will explain your other genuine actions. Your conformity explains nothing. Act singly, and what you have already done singly will justify you now. Greatness appeals to the future. If I can be firm enough to-day to do right, and scorn eyes, I must have done so much right before as to defend me now. Be it how it will, do right now. Always scorn appearances, and you always may. The force of character is cumulative. All the foregone days of virtue work their health into this. What makes the majesty of the heroes of the senate and the field, which so fills the imagination? The consciousness of a train of great days and victories behind. They shed an united light on the advancing actor. He is attended as by a visible escort of angels. That is it which throws thunder into Chatham's[4] voice, and dignity into Wash-

---

[1] "Without prospect," etc., i.e., without looking backward or forward.

[2] Emerson means to express by this whole passage that our lives should be natural, not artificial or conventional.

[3] The short, oblique courses back and forth by which a sailing vessel advances against a headwind.

[4] William Pitt, Earl of Chatham (1708–78), one of the most distinguished

ington's port, and America into Adams's[1] eye. Honor is venerable to us because it is no ephemeris.[2] It is always ancient virtue. We worship it to-day because it is not of to-day. We love it and pay it homage, because it is not a trap for our love and homage, but is self-dependent, self-derived, and therefore of an old immaculate pedigree, even if shown in a young person.

I hope in these days we have heard the last of conformity and consistency. Let the words be gazetted[3] and ridiculous henceforward. Instead of the gong for dinner, let us hear a whistle from the Spartan fife.[4] Let us never bow and apologize more. A great man is coming to eat at my house. I do not wish to please him; I wish that he should wish to please me. I will stand here for humanity, and though I would make it kind, I would make it true. Let us affront and reprimand the smooth mediocrity and squalid contentment of the times, and hurl in the face of custom, and trade, and office, the fact which is the upshot of all history, that there is a great responsible Thinker and Actor working wherever a man works; that a true man belongs to no other time or place, but is the center of things. Where he is, there is nature. He measures you, and all men, and all events. Ordinarily, everybody in society reminds us of somewhat else, or of some other person. Character, reality, reminds you of nothing else; it takes place of the whole creation. The man must be so much, that he must make all circumstances indifferent. Every

of English statesmen. He was possessed of great eloquence and all his actions were impelled by deep patriotic feeling.

[1] Samuel Adams (1722–1803), American statesman. Adams was a conspicuous agitator of the popular cause in America, a prominent member of the Continental Congress at Philadelphia, and one of the signers of the Declaration of Independence. He is called the " Father of the Revolution."

[2] A journal or account of daily transactions.

[3] Officially announced.

[4] The Spartans of ancient Greece were especially noted for their courage and valor. The signal of attack in battle was given by the music of the fife or flute. Hence, " instead of the gong," etc., instead of a mere summons to dinner let us have something that will inspire us to bravery.

true man is a cause, a country, and an age; requires infinite spaces and numbers and time fully to accomplish his design; — and posterity seem to follow his steps as a train of clients. A man Cæsar[1] is born, and for ages after we have a Roman Empire. Christ is born, and millions of minds so grow and cleave to his genius, that he is confounded with virtue and the possible[2] of man. An institution is the lengthened shadow of one man; as, Monachism, of the Hermit Antony;[3] the Reformation, of Luther; Quakerism, of Fox;[4] Methodism, of Wesley;[5] Abolition, of Clarkson.[6] Scipio, Milton called "the height of Rome;"[7] and all history resolves itself very easily into the biography of a few stout and earnest persons.

Let a man then know his worth, and keep things under his feet. Let him not peep or steal, or skulk up and down with the air of a charity-boy, a bastard, or an interloper, in the world which exists for him. But the man in the street, finding no worth in himself which corresponds to the force which built a

---

[1] Julius Cæsar (100–44 B.C.), the great Roman general, one of the greatest the world has ever seen, also preëminent as a statesman and as an orator. After subduing Gaul he crossed the Rubicon against his enemies in Rome. He became undisputed master of the known world, was made imperator for life, and sought to promote the true interests of his country. He laid a strong foundation to the imperial power of his successors.

[2] "Possible," i.e., that which it is possible for man to accomplish.

[3] Saint Antony or Anthony (250–356), a voluntary hermit of Upper Egypt, founder of Monachism, the doctrine of a life of religious seclusion, asceticism, and devotion.

[4] George Fox (1624–91), an Englishman, founder of the Society of Friends, or Quakers.

[5] John Wesley (1703–91), an Englishman, founder of the religious sect of the Methodists.

[6] Thomas Clarkson (1760–1846), English philanthropist. He devoted his life to the abolition of the slave trade and the relief of the oppressed. Through his influence Parliament declared the slave trade illegal in 1807.

[7] See Milton's Paradise Lost, Book IX., line 510. Publius Cornelius Africanus Scipio Major (237 or 234–184 B.C.), the greatest Roman general before Cæsar. By his defeat of Hannibal he ended the long struggle between Rome and Carthage.

tower or sculptured a marble god, feels poor when he looks on these. To him a palace, a statue, a costly book, have an alien and forbidding air, much like a gay equipage, and seem to say like that, "Who are you, Sir?" Yet they all are his, suitors for his notice, petitioners to his faculties that they will come out and take possession. The picture waits for my verdict: it is not to command me, but I am to settle its claims to praise. That popular fable of the sot who was picked up dead drunk in the street, carried to the duke's house, washed and dressed and laid in the duke's bed, and, on his waking, treated with all obsequious ceremony like the duke, and assured that he had been insane,[1] owes its popularity to the fact, that it symbolizes so well the state of man, who is in the world a sort of sot, but now and then wakes up, exercises his reason, and finds himself a true prince.

Our reading is mendicant and sycophantic. In history, our imagination plays us false. Kingdom and lordship, power and estate, are a gaudier vocabulary than private John and Edward in a small house and common day's work; but the things of life are the same to both; the sum total of both is the same. Why all this deference to Alfred,[2] and Scanderbeg,[3] and Gustavus?[4] Suppose they were virtuous; did they wear out virtue? As great a stake depends on your private act to-day, as followed their public and renowned steps. When private men shall act with original views, the luster will be transferred from the actions of kings to those of gentlemen.

The world has been instructed by its kings, who have so mag-

---

[1] It is difficult to say where this fable originated. See the story of " The Sleeper Awakened " in the Arabian Nights, and the Introduction to Shakespeare's Taming of the Shrew.

[2] See Note 4, p. 34.

[3] Scanderbeg (George Castriota, 1410–67), an Albanian chief who abjured Islamism, and successfully conducted several crusades against the Turks.

[4] Gustavus II. (Gustavus Adolphus, 1594–1632), King of Sweden. Law, order, and national spirit were encouraged during his reign, schools were everywhere established, roads made, and foreign trade extended. He even established model farms.

netized the eyes of nations. It has been taught by this colossal symbol the mutual reverence that is due from man to man. The joyful loyalty with which men have everywhere suffered the king, the noble, or the great proprietor to walk among them by a law of his own, make his own scale of men and things, and reverse theirs, pay for benefits not with money but with honor, and represent the law in his person, was the hieroglyphic[1] by which they obscurely signified their consciousness of their own right and comeliness, the right of every man.

The magnetism which all original action exerts is explained when we inquire the reason of self-trust. Who is the Trustee? What is the aboriginal[2] Self, on which a universal reliance may be grounded? What is the nature and power of that science-baffling star, without parallax,[3] without calculable elements, which shoots a ray of beauty even into trivial and impure actions, if the least mark of independence appear? The inquiry leads us to that source, at once the essence of genius, of virtue, and of life, which we call Spontaneity or Instinct. We denote this primary wisdom as Intuition, whilst all later teachings are tuitions. In that deep force, the last fact behind which analysis cannot go, all things find their common origin. For, the sense of being which in calm hours rises, we know not how, in the soul, is not diverse from things, from space, from light, from time, from man, but one with them, and proceeds obviously from the same source whence their life and being also proceed. We first share the life by which things exist, and afterwards see them as appearances in nature, and forget that we have shared their cause. Here is the fountain of action and of thought. Here are the lungs[4] of that inspiration which giveth man wisdom, and

---

[1] Hidden sign.　　　　　　[2] Primitive, first.

[3] Apparent displacement of an object as observed from different points of view. The parallax of a heavenly body is used in estimating its distance, and decreases as the distance increases; hence, the exact location of a star so far distant as to have no parallax cannot be calculated.

[4] The source from which it draws breath; hence, the origin.

which cannot be denied without impiety and atheism. We lie in the lap of immense intelligence, which makes us receivers of its truth and organs of its activity. When we discern justice, when we discern truth, we do nothing of ourselves, but allow a passage to its beams. If we ask whence this comes, if we seek to pry into the soul that causes, all philosophy is at fault. Its presence or its absence is all we can affirm. Every man discriminates between the voluntary acts of his mind, and his involuntary perceptions, and knows that to his involuntary perceptions a perfect faith is due. He may err in the expression of them, but he knows that these things are so, like day and night, not to be disputed. My willful actions and acquisitions are but roving; — the idlest reverie, the faintest native emotion, command my curiosity and respect. Thoughtless people contradict as readily the statement of perceptions as of opinions, or rather much more readily; for, they do not distinguish between perception and notion. They fancy that I choose to see this or that thing. But perception is not whimsical, but fatal. If I see a trait, my children will see it after me, and in course of time, all mankind, — although it may chance that no one has seen it before me. For my perception of it is as much a fact as the sun.

The relations of the soul to the divine spirit are so pure, that it is profane to seek to interpose helps. It must be that when God speaketh he should communicate, not one thing, but all things; should fill the world with his voice; should scatter forth light, nature, time, souls, from the center of the present thought; and new date and new create the whole. Whenever a mind is simple, and receives a divine wisdom, old things pass away, — means, teachers, texts, temples fall; it lives now, and absorbs past and future into the present hour. All things are made sacred by relation to it, — one as much as another. All things are dissolved to their center by their cause, and, in the universal miracle, petty and particular miracles disappear. If, therefore, a man claims to know and speak of God, and carries you backward to the phraseology of some old moldered nation in another country, in another world, believe him not. Is the acorn better than the oak which is its fullness and completion? Is the parent better than the child into whom he has cast his ripened being? Whence, then, this worship of the past? The centuries are conspirators against the sanity and authority of the soul. Time and space are but physiological colors which the eye makes, but the soul is light; where it is, is day; where it was, is night; and history is an impertinence and an injury, if it be anything more than a cheerful apologue or parable[1] of my being and becoming.

Man is timid and apologetic; he is no longer upright; he dares not say "I think," "I am," but quotes some saint or sage. He is ashamed before the blade of grass or the blowing rose. These roses under my window make no reference to former roses or to better ones; they are for what they are; they exist with God to-day. There is no time to them. There is simply the rose; it is perfect in every moment of its existence. Before a leaf bud has burst, its whole life acts; in the full-blown flower there is no more; in the leafless root there is no less. Its nature is satisfied, and it satisfies nature, in all moments alike. But man postpones or remembers; he does not live in the present, but with reverted[2] eye laments the past, or, heedless of the riches that surround him, stands on tiptoe to foresee the future. He cannot be happy and strong until he too lives with nature in the present, above time.[3]

This should be plain enough. Yet see what strong intellects dare not yet hear God himself, unless he speak the phraseology of I know not what David, or Jeremiah, or Paul. We shall not always set so great a price on a few texts, on a few lives. We are like children who repeat by rote the sentences of grandames[4] and tutors, and, as they grow older, of the men of talents and character they chance to see, — painfully recollecting the exact words they spoke; afterwards, when they come into the point of

---

[1] See Note 3, p. 44.   [2] Turned back.
[3] That is, apart from time past or time to come.
[4] Old women; grandmothers.

5

view which those had who uttered these sayings, they understand them, and are willing to let the words go; for, at any time,
they can use words as good when occasion comes. If we live
truly, we shall see truly. It is as easy for the strong man to be
strong, as it is for the weak to be weak. When we have new perception, we shall gladly disburden the memory of its hoarded treasures as old rubbish. When a man lives with God, his voice shall be
as sweet as the murmur of the brook and the rustle of the corn.

And now at last the highest truth on this subject remains un-
said; probably cannot be said; for all that we say is the far-off
remembering of the intuition. That thought, by what I can now
nearest approach to say it, is this. When good is near you,
when you have life in yourself, it is not by any known or accustomed way; you shall not discern the footprints of any other;
you shall not see the face of man; you shall not hear any
name;—the way, the thought, the good, shall be wholly strange
and new. It shall exclude example and experience. You take
the way from man, not to man. All persons that ever existed
are its forgotten ministers. Fear and hope are alike beneath it.
There is somewhat low even in hope. In the hour of vision,
there is nothing that can be called gratitude, nor properly joy.
The soul raised over passion beholds identity and eternal causa-
tion, perceives the self-existence of Truth and Right, and calms
itself with knowing that all things go well. Vast spaces of
nature, the Atlantic Ocean, the South Sea,—long intervals of
time, years, centuries,—are of no account. This which I think
and feel underlay every former state of life and circumstances,
as it does underlie my present, and what is called life, and what
is called death.

Life only avails, not the having lived. Power ceases in the
instant of repose; it resides in the moment of transition from a
past to a new state, in the shooting of the gulf, in the darting to
an aim. This one fact the world hates, that the soul *becomes;*
for that forever degrades the past, turns all riches to poverty, all
reputation to a shame, confounds the saint with the rogue, shoves

Jesus and Judas equally aside. Why, then, do we prate of self-reliance? Inasmuch as the soul is present, there will be power not confident but agent.[1] To talk of reliance is a poor external way of speaking. Speak rather of that which relies, because it works and is. Who has more obedience than I masters me, though he should not raise his finger. Round him I must revolve by the gravitation of spirits. We fancy it rhetoric, when we speak of eminent virtue. We do not yet see that virtue is Height, and that a man or a company of men, plastic and permeable to principles, by the law of nature must overpower and ride [2] all cities, nations, kings, rich men, poets, who are not.

This is the ultimate fact which we so quickly reach on this, as on every topic, the resolution of all into the ever-blessed ONE. Self-existence is the attribute of the Supreme Cause, and it constitutes the measure of good by the degree in which it enters into all lower forms. All things real are so by so much virtue as they contain. Commerce, husbandry, hunting, whaling, war, eloquence, personal weight, are somewhat, and engage my respect as examples of its presence and impure action. I see the same law working in nature for conservation and growth. Power is in nature the essential measure of right. Nature suffers nothing to remain in her kingdoms which cannot help itself. The genesis and maturation of a planet, its poise and orbit, the bended tree recovering itself from the strong wind, the vital resources of every animal and vegetable, are demonstrations of the self-sufficing, and therefore self-relying soul.

Thus all concentrates: let us not rove; let us sit at home with the cause. Let us stun and astonish the intruding rabble of men and books and institutions, by a simple declaration of the divine fact. Bid the invaders take the shoes from off their feet, for God is here within.[3] Let our simplicity judge them, and our

---

[1] Power not reliant but active.

[2] " Overpower," etc., i.e., have power over and rule.

[3] The Mohammedans are obliged to take off their shoes before they are permitted to enter a mosque.

docility to our own law demonstrate the poverty of nature and fortune beside our native riches.

But now we are a mob. Man does not stand in awe of man, nor is his genius admonished to stay at home, to put itself in communication with the internal ocean, but it goes abroad to beg a cup of water of the urns of other men. We must go alone. I like the silent church before the service begins, better than any preaching. How far off, how cool, how chaste the persons look, begirt each one with a precinct or sanctuary! So let us always sit. Why should we assume the faults of our friend, or wife, or father, or child, because they sit around our hearth, or are said to have the same blood? All men have my blood, and I have all men's.[1] Not for that will I adopt their petulance or folly, even to the extent of being ashamed of it. But your isolation must not be mechanical, but spiritual, that is, must be elevation. At times the whole world seems to be in conspiracy to importune you with emphatic trifles. Friend, client, child, sickness, fear, want, charity, all knock at once at thy closet door, and say,— "Come out unto us." But keep thy state; come not into their confusion. The power men possess to annoy me, I give them by a weak curiosity. No man can come near me but through my act. "What we love that we have, but by desire we bereave ourselves of the love."

If we cannot at once rise to the sanctities of obedience and faith, let us at least resist our temptations; let us enter into the state of war, and wake Thor and Woden,[2] courage and constancy, in our Saxon breasts. This is to be done in our smooth times by speaking the truth. Check this lying hospitality and lying affection. Live no longer to the expectation of these deceived and deceiving people with whom we converse. Say to them, O father, O mother, O wife, O brother, O friend, I have lived

---

[1] An allusion to the fact that all men are brothers.

[2] In Norse mythology the god Woden was held to be all-powerful and noted for his constancy, while his eldest son Thor, the god of thunder, was the personification of strength and courage.

with you after appearances hitherto. Henceforward I am the truth's. Be it known unto you that henceforward I obey no law less than the eternal law. I will have no covenants but proximities.[1] I shall endeavor to nourish my parents, to support my family, to be the chaste husband of one wife,—but these relations I must fill after a new and unprecedented way. I appeal from your customs. I must be myself. I cannot break myself any longer for you, or you.[2] If you can love me for what I am, we shall be the happier. If you cannot, I will still seek to deserve that you should. I will not hide my tastes or aversions. I will so trust that what is deep is holy, that I will do strongly before the sun and moon whatever inly[3] rejoices me, and the heart appoints. If you are noble, I will love you; if you are not, I will not hurt you and myself by hypocritical attentions. If you are true, but not in the same truth with me, cleave to your companions; I will seek my own. I do this not selfishly, but humbly and truly. It is alike your interest, and mine, and all men's, however long we have dwelt in lies, to live in truth. Does this sound harsh to-day? You will soon love what is dictated by your nature as well as mine, and, if we follow the truth, it will bring us out safe at last.—But so may you give these friends pain. Yes, but I cannot sell my liberty and my power, to save their sensibility. Besides, all persons have their moments of reason, when they look out into the region of absolute truth; then will they justify me, and do the same thing.

The populace think that your rejection of popular standards is a rejection of all standard, and mere antinomianism;[4] and the bold sensualist will use the name of philosophy to gild[5] his

---

[1] " I will," etc., i.e., I will agree to govern my conduct only according to the dictates of my inner consciousness, of my soul's intuitive sense of right.

[2] You in the singular, i.e., the particular person whom Emerson imagines himself as addressing.   [3] Within the soul.

[4] The doctrine that Christians are freed from the moral law as set forth in the Old Testament by the new dispensation of grace in the Gospel. ·

[5] Cover or conceal.

crimes. But the law of consciousness abides. There are two confessionals, in one or the other of which we must be shriven.[1] You may fulfill your round of duties by clearing yourself in the *direct*, or in the *reflex* way. Consider whether you have satisfied your relations to father, mother, cousin, neighbor, town, cat, and dog; whether any of these can upbraid you. But I may also neglect this reflex standard, and absolve me to myself. I have my own stern claims and perfect circle. It denies the name of duty to many offices that are called duties. But if I can discharge its debts, it enables me to dispense with the popular code. If any one imagines that this law is lax, let him keep its commandment one day.

And truly it demands something godlike in him who has cast off the common motives of humanity, and has ventured to trust himself for a taskmaster. High be his heart, faithful his will, clear his sight, that he may in good earnest be doctrine, society, law, to himself, that a simple purpose may be to him as strong as iron necessity is to others!

If any man consider the present aspects of what is called by distinction *society*, he will see the need of these ethics. The sinew and heart of man seem to be drawn out, and we are become timorous, desponding whimperers. We are afraid of truth, afraid of fortune, afraid of death, and afraid of each other. Our age yields no great and perfect persons. We want men and women who shall renovate life and our social state, but we see that most natures are insolvent, cannot satisfy their own wants, have an ambition out of all proportion to their practical force, and do lean and beg day and night continually. Our housekeeping is mendicant, our arts, our occupations, our marriages, our religion, we have not chosen, but society has chosen for us. We are parlor soldiers. We shun the rugged battle of fate, where strength is born.

If our young men miscarry in their first enterprises, they lose all heart. If the young merchant fails, men say he is *ruined*. If

---

[1] Confessed.

the finest genius studies at one of our colleges, and is not installed in an office within one year afterwards in the cities or suburbs of Boston or New York, it seems to his friends and to himself that he is right in being disheartened, and in complaining the rest of his life. A sturdy lad from New Hampshire or Vermont, who in turn tries all the professions, who *teams it, farms it,*[1] *peddles,* keeps a school, preaches, edits a newspaper, goes to Congress, buys a township, and so forth, in successive years, and always, like a cat, falls on his feet, is worth a hundred of these city dolls. He walks abreast with his days, and feels no shame in not " studying a profession," for he does not postpone his life, but lives already. He has not one chance, but a hundred chances. Let a Stoic[2] open the resources of man, and tell men they are not leaning willows, but can and must detach themselves; that with the exercise of self-trust, new powers shall appear; that a man is the word made flesh,[3] born to shed healing to the nations, that he should be ashamed of our compassion, and that the moment he acts from himself, tossing the laws, the books, idolatries, and customs out of the window, we pity him no more, but thank and revere him,— and that teacher shall restore the life of man to splendor, and make his name dear to all history.

It is easy to see that a greater self-reliance must work a revolution in all the offices and relations of men; in their religion; in their education; in their pursuits; their modes of living; their association; in their property; in their speculative views.

1. In what prayers do men allow themselves![4] That which they call a holy office is not so much as brave and manly. Prayer

---

[1] " Teams it," etc., i.e., drives a team or engages in farming as a profession.

[2] A disciple of the philosopher Zeno, who founded a sect and taught that men should be free from passion, unmoved by joy or grief, and should submit uncomplainingly to the inevitable; hence, the name is applied to any one who professes to be indifferent to pleasure or pain.

[3] See John i. 14.

[4] " In what prayers," etc., i.e., in what prayers do men allow themselves to indulge.

looks abroad and asks for some foreign addition to come through some foreign virtue, and loses itself in endless mazes of natural and supernatural, and mediatorial and miraculous. Prayer that craves a particular commodity,— anything less than all good,— is vicious. Prayer is the contemplation of the facts of life from the highest point of view. It is the soliloquy of a beholding and jubilant soul. It is the spirit of God pronouncing his works good. But prayer as a means to effect a private end is meanness and theft. It supposes dualism[1] and not unity in nature and consciousness. As soon as the man is at one with God, he will not beg. He will then see prayer in all action. The prayer of the farmer kneeling in his field to weed it, the prayer of the rower kneeling with the stroke of his oar, are true prayers heard throughout nature, though for cheap ends. Caratach, in Fletcher's "Bonduca,"[2] when admonished to inquire the mind of the god Audate, replies,—

> "His hidden meaning lies in our endeavors;
> Our valors are our best gods."

Another sort of false prayers are our regrets. Discontent is the want of self-reliance: it is infirmity of will. Regret calamities, if you can thereby help the sufferer; if not, attend your own work, and already the evil begins to be repaired. Our sympathy is just as base. We come to them who weep foolishly, and sit down and cry for company, instead of imparting to them truth and health in rough electric shocks, putting them once more in communication with their own reason. The secret of fortune is joy in our hands. Welcome evermore to gods and men is the self-helping man. For him all doors are flung wide: him all tongues greet, all honors crown, all eyes follow with desire. Our

[1] A twofold division.

[2] Caratach, or Caractacus, was a character in the play of Bonduca (another name for Boadicea), written by the English dramatist and poet John Fletcher (1576–1625). The scene of the play is laid in ancient Britain, where the characters were historical. Audate is another name for the Celtic goddess (not god) Audrasta.

love goes out to him and embraces him, because he did not
need it.   We solicitously and apologetically caress and celebrate
him, because he held on his way and scorned our disapproba-
tion.   The gods love him because men hated him.   "To the
persevering mortal," said Zoroaster,[1] "the blessed Immortals are
swift."

As men's prayers are a disease of the will, so are their creeds
a disease of the intellect.   They say with those foolish Israelites,
"Let not God speak to us, lest we die.   Speak thou, speak any
man with us, and we will obey."   Everywhere I am hindered of
meeting God in my brother, because he has shut his own temple
doors, and recites fables merely of his brother's, or his brother's
brother's God.   Every new mind is a new classification.   If it
prove a mind of uncommon activity and power, a Locke,[2] a
Lavoisier,[3] a Hutton,[4] a Bentham,[5] a Fourier,[6] it imposes its
classification on other men, and lo! a new system.   In proportion to the depth of the thought, and so to the number of the
objects it touches and brings within reach of the pupil, is his
complacency.   But chiefly is this apparent in creeds and churches,
which are also classifications of some powerful mind acting on
the elemental thought of duty, and man's relation to the Highest.
Such is Calvinism,[7] Quakerism, Swedenborgism.[8]   The pupil
takes the same delight in subordinating everything to the new
terminology, as a girl who has just learned botany in seeing a

---

[1] The founder of the ancient Persian religion.   The time in which he lived
is uncertain.   [2] See Note 2, p. 26.

[3] Antoine Laurent Lavoisier (1743–94), illustrious French chemist.   He
discovered the composition of water.

[4] James Hutton (1726–97), great Scotch geologist.   He wrote the Theory
of Rain, and Theory of the Earth.

[5] Jeremy Bentham (1748–1832), English philosopher and reformer.   He
devoted himself to reforms in legislature and government.

[6] François Marie Charles Fourier (1772–1837), French socialist.

[7] The doctrine of the followers of John Calvin (1509–64), French theologian.

[8] The doctrine taught by Emanuel Swedenborg.   See Note 1, p. 44.

new earth and new seasons thereby. It will happen for a time, that the pupil will find his intellectual power has grown by the study of his master's mind. But in all unbalanced minds, the classification is idolized, passes for the end, and not for a speedily exhaustible means, so that the walls of the system blend to their eye in the remote horizon with the walls of the universe; the luminaries of heaven seem to them hung on the arch their master built. They cannot imagine how you aliens have any right to see, — how you can see; "It must be somehow that you stole the light from us." They do not yet perceive, that light, unsystematic, indomitable, will break into any cabin, even into theirs. Let them chirp awhile and call it their own. If they are honest and do well, presently their neat new pinfold [1] will be too strait [2] and low, will crack, will lean, will rot and vanish, and the immortal light, all young and joyful, million-orbed, million-colored, will beam over the universe as on the first morning.

2. It is for want of self-culture that the superstition of Traveling, whose idols are Italy, England, Egypt, retains its fascination for all educated Americans. They who made England, Italy, or Greece venerable in the imagination did so by sticking fast where they were, like an axis of the earth. In manly hours, we feel that duty is our place. The soul is no traveler; the wise man stays at home, and when his necessities, his duties, on any occasion call him from his house, or into foreign lands, he is at home still, and shall make men sensible by the expression of his countenance, that he goes the missionary of wisdom and virtue, and visits cities and men like a sovereign, and not like an interloper or a valet.

I have no churlish objection to the circumnavigation of the globe, for the purposes of art, of study, and benevolence, so that the man is first domesticated, or does not go abroad with the hope of finding somewhat greater than he knows. He who travels to be amused, or to get somewhat which he does not carry, travels away from himself, and grows old even in youth

---

[1] An inclosure for beasts.   [2] Narrow.

among old things. In Thebes,[1] in Palmyra,[2] his will and mind have become old and dilapidated as they. He carries ruins to ruins.

Traveling is a fool's paradise. Our first journeys discover to us the indifference of places. At home I dream that at Naples, at Rome, I can be intoxicated with beauty, and lose my sadness. I pack my trunk, embrace my friends, embark on the sea, and at last wake up in Naples, and there beside me is the stern fact, the sad self, unrelenting, identical, that I fled from. I seek the Vatican,[3] and the palaces. I affect to be intoxicated with sights and suggestions, but I am not intoxicated. My giant goes with me wherever I go.

3. But the rage of traveling is a symptom of a deeper unsoundness affecting the whole intellectual action. The intellect is vagabond, and our system of education fosters restlessness. Our minds travel when our bodies are forced to stay at home. We imitate; and what is imitation but the traveling of the mind? Our houses are built with foreign taste; our shelves are garnished with foreign ornaments; our opinions, our tastes, our faculties, lean, and follow the Past and the Distant. The soul created the arts wherever they have flourished. It was in his own mind that the artist sought his model. It was an application of his own thought to the thing to be done and the conditions to be observed. And why need we copy the Doric[4] or the Gothic[5] model? Beauty, convenience, grandeur of thought, and quaint expression are as near to us as to any, and if the American

1 The ruined prehistoric city, capital of Upper Egypt.

2 A ruined city, founded by Solomon, in an oasis of the Syrian desert, a hundred and twenty miles northeast of Damascus.

3 The residence of the Pope in Rome, the largest palace in the world, consisting of over four thousand rooms. It contains the finest existing collection of marbles, bronzes, frescoes, paintings, gems, and statues.

4 A style of architecture distinguished for simplicity and strength, which originated in Doris in ancient Greece.

5 A style of architecture derived from the Goths, with high and sharply pointed arches and clustered columns.

artist will study with hope and love the precise thing to be done
by him, considering the climate, the soil, the length of the day,
the wants of the people, the habit and form of the government,
he will create a house in which all these will find themselves
fitted, and taste and sentiment will be satisfied also.

Insist on yourself; never imitate. Your own gift you can
present every moment with the cumulative force of a whole life's
cultivation; but of the adopted talent of another, you have only
an extemporaneous, half possession. That which each can do
best, none but his Maker can teach him. No man yet knows
what it is, nor can, till that person has exhibited it. Where is
the master who could have taught Shakespeare?[1]   Where is the
master who could have instructed Franklin,[2] or Washington, or
Bacon,[3] or Newton? Every great man is a unique. The Scip-
ionism of Scipio is precisely that part he could not borrow.
Shakespeare will never be made by the study of Shakespeare.
Do that which is assigned you, and you cannot hope too much
or dare too much. There is at this moment for you an utterance
brave and grand as that of the colossal chisel of Phidias,[4] or
trowel[5] of the Egyptians, or the pen of Moses, or Dante,[6] but
different from all these. Not possibly will the soul all rich, all
eloquent, with thousand-cloven[7] tongue, deign to repeat itself;
but if you can hear what these patriarchs say, surely you can
reply to them in the same pitch of voice; for the ear and the
tongue are two organs of one nature. Abide in the simple and

[1] See Note 3, p. 29.

[2] Benjamin Franklin (1706–90), American philosopher, statesman, and
writer. He discovered the nature of lightning, invented the lightning rod,
performed important diplomatic services during the Revolution, and compiled
the famous Poor Richard's Almanac.

[3] See Note 1, p. 27.

[4] Phidias (400–432 B.C.), the greatest sculptor of Greece if not of all
lands.   [5] The tool with which they reared the pyramids.

[6] Dante Alighieri (1265–1321), the greatest Italian poet, author of the
Inferno.

[7] Divided into many parts; that is, capable of speaking in many ways.

noble regions of thy life, obey thy heart, and thou shalt reproduce the Foreworld[1] again.

4. As our Religion, our Education, our Art look abroad, so does our spirit of society. All men plume themselves on the improvement of society, and no man improves.

Society never advances. It recedes as fast on one side as it gains on the other. It undergoes continual changes; it is barbarous, it is civilized, it is christianized, it is rich, it is scientific; but this change is not amelioration. For everything that is given, something is taken. Society acquires new arts, and loses old instincts. What a contrast between the well-clad, reading, writing, thinking American, with a watch, a pencil, and a bill of exchange in his pocket, and the naked New Zealander, whose property is a club, a spear, a mat, and an undivided twentieth of a shed to sleep under! But compare the health of the two men, and you shall see that the white man has lost his aboriginal strength. If the traveler tell us truly, strike the savage with a broad ax, and in a day or two the flesh shall unite and heal as if you struck the blow into soft pitch, and the same blow shall send the white to his grave.

The civilized man has built a coach, but has lost the use of his feet. He is supported on crutches, but lacks so much support of muscle. He has a fine Geneva[2] watch, but he fails of the skill to tell the hour by the sun. A Greenwich nautical almanac[3] he has, and so being sure of the information when he wants it, the man in the street does not know a star in the sky. The solstice he does not observe; the equinox he knows as little; and the whole bright calendar of the year is without a dial in his mind. His notebooks impair his memory; his libraries overload his wit; the insurance office increases the number of accidents; and

---

[1] A previous state of the world.

[2] Geneva, Switzerland, at one time produced the best watches in the world.

[3] An almanac for the use of navigators and astronomers, calculated at the Royal Observatory at Greenwich, England.

it may be a question whether machinery does not encumber;
whether we have not lost by refinement some energy, by a Christianity intrenched in establishments and forms, some vigor of
wild virtue. For every Stoic was a Stoic; but in Christendom
where is the Christian?

There is no more deviation in the moral standard than in the
standard of height or bulk. No greater men are now than ever
were. A singular equality may be observed between the great
men of the first and of the last ages; nor can all the science,
art, religion, and philosophy of the nineteenth century avail to
educate greater men than Plutarch's[1] heroes, three or four and
twenty centuries ago. Not in time is the race progressive. Phocion,[2] Socrates, Anaxagoras,[3] Diogenes,[4] are great men, but they
leave no class. He who is really of their class will not be called
by their name, but will be his own man, and, in his turn, the
founder of a sect. The arts and inventions of each period are
only its costume, and do not invigorate men. The harm of the
improved machinery may compensate its good. Hudson[5] and
Bering[6] accomplished so much in their fishing boats, as to astonish
Parry[7] and Franklin,[8] whose equipment exhausted the resources

[1] A Grecian philosopher living in the first century A.D. He was also a
prolific writer. His most noted work is Parallel Lives, a series of forty-six
biographies divided into pairs, one taken from Greek and one from Roman
history, and each accompanied by a psychological and moral comparison between the characters described.   [2] An Athenian general (402–317 B.C.).

[3] Eminent Greek philosopher (500–426 B.C.). He maintained the eternity of matter.

[4] A famous Greek cynic philosopher (400–323 B.C.). He affected a
contempt for the comforts of life and the customs of the world. According
to tradition he lodged in a tub.

[5] Henry Hudson, distinguished English discoverer, discovered Hudson
River and Hudson Bay.

[6] A Danish navigator (1680–1741). He discovered Bering Strait in 1728,
and ascertained that Asia was not joined to America, as was formerly supposed.

[7] Sir William Edward Parry, English navigator (1790–1855). In 1819–23
he penetrated the Arctic regions farther than any previous explorer.

[8] Sir John Franklin (1786–1845), English Arctic explorer.

of science and art. Galileo, with an opera glass, discovered a more splendid series of celestial phenomena than any one since. Columbus[1] found the New World in an undecked boat. It is curious to see the periodical disuse and perishing of means and machinery, which were introduced with loud laudation a few years or centuries before. The great genius returns to essential man. We reckoned the improvements of the art of war among the triumphs of science, and yet Napoleon[2] conquered Europe by the bivouac,[3] which consisted of falling back on naked valor, and disencumbering it of all aids. The Emperor held it impossible to make a perfect army, says Las Casas,[4] "without abolishing our arms, magazines, commissaries, and carriages, until, in imitation of the Roman custom, the soldier should receive his supply of corn, grind it in his handmill, and bake his bread himself."

Society is a wave. The wave moves onward, but the water of which it is composed does not. The same particle does not rise from the valley to the ridge. Its unity is only phenomenal. The persons who make up a nation to-day, next year die, and their experience with them.

And so the reliance on Property, including the reliance on governments which protect it, is the want of self-reliance. Men have looked away from themselves and at things so long, that they have come to esteem the religious, learned, and civil institutions as guards of property, and they deprecate assaults on these, because they feel them to be assaults on property. They measure their esteem of each other by what each has, and not by

---

1 Christopher Columbus (about 1436-1506), the discoverer of America.

2 See note 2, page 101.

3 An encampment of soldiers in the open air, without tents, each soldier remaining dressed, with his weapons at hand.

4 Emmanuel Augustin Dieudonné, Comte de las Cases (1766-1842); author of "Mémorial de St. Hélène," and a friend of Napoleon Bonaparte's. Note that Emerson's spelling of the name is wrong. He confused it with that of the great Bartolomé de las Casas, the Spanish missionary.

what each is. But a cultivated man becomes ashamed of his
property, out of new respect for his nature. Especially he hates
what he has, if he see that it is accidental, — came to him by inheritance, or gift, or crime; then he feels that it is not having;
it does not belong to him, has no root in him, and merely lies
there, because no revolution or no robber takes it away. But
that which a man is does always by necessity acquire,[1] and
what the man acquires is living property, which does not wait
the beck of rulers, or mobs, or revolutions, or fire, or storm, or
bankruptcies, but perpetually renews itself wherever the man
breathes. "Thy lot or portion of life," said the Caliph Ali,[2] "is
seeking after thee; therefore be at rest from seeking after it."
Our dependence on these foreign goods leads us to our slavish
respect for numbers. The political parties meet in numerous
conventions; the greater the concourse, and with each new uproar of announcement, The delegation from Essex! The Dem-
ocrats from New Hampshire! The Whigs of Maine! The
young patriot feels himself stronger than before by a new thousand of eyes and arms. In like manner the reformers summon
conventions, and vote and resolve in multitude. Not so, O
friends! will the God deign to enter and inhabit you, but by a
method precisely the reverse. It is only as a man puts off all
foreign support, and stands alone, that I see him to be strong and
to prevail. He is weaker by every recruit to his banner. Is
not a man better than a town? Ask nothing of men, and in
the endless mutation, thou only firm column must presently appear the upholder of all that surrounds thee. He who knows
that power is inborn, that he is weak because he has looked for
good out of him and elsewhere, and so perceiving, throws himself unhesitatingly on his thought, instantly rights himself, stands
in the erect position, commands his limbs, works miracles; just

[1] Become his own.

[2] An Arabian caliph, surnamed the " Lion of God," a cousin and follower
of Mohammed. He is distinguished as an author of many maxims and
proverbs which have been handed down and published.

as a man who stands on his feet is stronger than a man who stands on his head.

So use all that is called Fortune. Most men gamble with her, and gain all, and lose all, as her wheel rolls. But do thou leave as unlawful these winnings, and deal with Cause and Effect, the chancellors of God. In the Will work and acquire, and thou hast chained the wheel of Chance,[1] and shalt sit hereafter out of fear from her rotations. A political victory, a rise of rents, the recovery of your sick, or the return of your absent friend, or some other favorable event, raises your spirits, and you think good days are preparing for you. Do not believe it. Nothing can bring you peace but yourself. Nothing can bring you peace but the triumph of principles.

[1] Fortuna, the goddess of fortune or chance in Roman mythology, was represented with her eyes bound, standing on a ball or wheel to indicate that luck rolls, like a ball, without choice.

COMPENSATION.

THE wings of Time are black and white,
Pied [1] with morning and with night.
Mountain tall and ocean deep
Trembling balance duly keep.
In changing moon, in tidal wave,
Glows the feud of Want and Have.
Gauge of more and less through space
Electric star and pencil plays.
The lonely Earth amid the balls [2]
That hurry through the eternal halls,[3]
A makeweight [4] flying to the void,
Supplemental asteroid,
Or compensatory spark,
Shoots across the neutral Dark.

[1] Spotted.   [2] Planets.   [3] Space.
[4] Something added to fill a deficiency.

Man's the elm, and Wealth the vine,
Stanch and strong the tendrils twine:
Though the frail ringlets thee deceive,
None from its stock that vine can reave.[1]
Fear not, then, thou child infirm,
There's no god dare wrong a worm.
Laurel crowns[2] cleave to deserts,
And power to him who power exerts;
Hast not thy share?   On winged feet,
Lo! it rushes thee to meet;
And all that Nature made thy own,
Floating in air or pent[3] in stone,
Will rive[4] the hills and swim the sea,
And, like thy shadow, follow thee.

[1] Take away.
[2] Honors, from the custom of the ancient Greeks to use laurel crowns as a mark of honor.
[3] Confined.   [4] Rend asunder.

COMPENSATION.

EVER since I was a boy, I have wished to write a discourse on Compensation: for it seemed to me when very young, that on this subject life was ahead of theology, and the people knew more than the preachers taught. The documents,[1] too, from which the doctrine is to be drawn, charmed my fancy by their endless variety, and lay always before me, even in sleep; for they are the tools in our hands, the bread in our basket, the transactions of the street, the farm, and the dwelling house, greetings, relations, debts and credits, the influence of character, the nature and endowment of all men. It seemed to me, also, that in it might be shown men a ray of divinity, the present action of the soul of this world, clean from all vestige of tradition, and so the heart of man might be bathed by an inundation of eternal love, conversing with that which he knows was always and always must be, because it really is now. It appeared, moreover, that if this doctrine could be stated in terms with any resemblance to those bright intuitions in which this truth is sometimes revealed to us, it would be a star[2] in many dark hours and crooked passages in our journey that would not suffer us to lose our way.

I was lately confirmed in these desires by hearing a sermon at church. The preacher, a man esteemed for his orthodoxy, unfolded in the ordinary manner the doctrine of the Last Judgment. He assumed, that judgment is not executed in this world; that the wicked are successful; that the good are miserable; and then urged from reason and from Scripture a compensation to

---

[1] Data.   [2] A guiding star; hence, guide.

be made to both parties in the next life. No offense appeared to be taken by the congregation at this doctrine. As far as I could observe, when the meeting broke up, they separated without remark on the sermon.

Yet what was the import[1] of this teaching? What did the preacher mean by saying that the good are miserable in the present life? Was it that houses and lands, offices, wine, horses, dress, luxury, are had[2] by unprincipled men, whilst the saints are poor and despised; and that a compensation is to be made to these last hereafter, by giving them the like gratifications another day,—bank stock and doubloons,[3] venison and champagne? This must be the compensation intended; for what else? Is it that they are to have leave to pray and praise? to love and serve men? Why, that they can do now. The legitimate inference the disciple would draw was,—"We are to have *such* a good time as the sinners have now;"—or, to push it to its extreme import,—"You sin now; we shall sin by and by; we would sin now, if we could; not being successful, we expect our revenge to-morrow."

The fallacy lay in the immense concession, that the bad are successful; that justice is not done now. The blindness of the preacher consisted in deferring[4] to the base estimate of the market[5] of what constitutes a manly success, instead of confronting and convicting the world from the truth; announcing the presence of the soul; the omnipotence of the will: and so establishing the standard of good and ill, of success and falsehood.

I find a similar base tone in the popular religious works of the day, and the same doctrines assumed by the literary men when occasionally they treat the related topics. I think that our popular theology has gained in decorum, and not in principle, over the superstitions it has displaced. But men are better than this

---

[1] Meaning.   [2] Possessed.

[3] Spanish and Portuguese coins worth about $15.60 each.

[4] Bowing to; accepting.   [5] Those engaged in commercial life.

theology. Their daily life gives it the lie.[1] Every ingenuous and aspiring soul leaves the doctrine behind him in his own experience; and all men feel sometimes the falsehood which they cannot demonstrate. For men are wiser than they know. That which they hear in schools and pulpits without afterthought, if said in conversation, would probably be questioned in silence. If a man dogmatize in a mixed company on Providence and the divine laws, he is answered by a silence which conveys well enough to an observer the dissatisfaction of the hearer, but his incapacity to make his own statement.

I shall attempt to record some facts that indicate the path of the law of Compensation; happy beyond my expectation, if I shall truly draw the smallest arc of this circle.

POLARITY,[2] or action and reaction, we meet in every part of nature; in darkness and light; in heat and cold; in the ebb and flow of waters; in male and female; in the inspiration and expiration of plants and animals; in the equation of quantity and quality in the fluids of the animal body; in the systole[3] and diastole[4] of the heart; in the undulations of fluids, and of sound; in the centrifugal[5] and centripetal[6] gravity; in electricity, galvanism, and chemical affinity. Superinduce[7] magnetism at one end of a needle; the opposite magnetism takes place at the other end. If the south attracts, the north repels. To empty here, you must condense there. An inevitable dualism bisects nature, so that each thing is a half, and suggests another thing to make it whole; as, spirit, matter; man, woman; odd, even; subjective, objective; in, out; upper, under; motion, rest; yea, nay.

Whilst the world is thus dual, so is every one of its parts. The

---

[1] Proves it false.   [2] See Note 3, p. 33.

[3] Contraction of the heart and arteries.

[4] Dilatation of the heart and arteries.

[5] Tending to recede from the center.

[6] Tending to move towards the center.

[7] Develop.

entire system of things gets represented in every particle. There is somewhat that resembles the ebb and flow of the sea, day and night, man and woman, in a single needle of the pine, in a kernel of corn, in each individual of every animal tribe. The reaction, so grand in the elements, is repeated within these small boundaries. For example, in the animal kingdom the physiologist has observed that no creatures are favorites, but a certain compensation balances every gift and every defect. A surplusage[1] given to one part is paid out of a reduction from another part of the same creature. If the head and neck are enlarged, the trunk and extremities are cut short.

The theory of the mechanic forces is another example. What we gain in power is lost in time; and the converse. The periodic or compensating errors of the planets is another instance. The influences of climate and soil in political history is another. The cold climate invigorates. The barren soil does not breed fevers, crocodiles, tigers, or scorpions.

The same dualism underlies the nature and condition of man. Every excess causes a defect; every defect an excess. Every sweet hath its sour; every evil its good. Every faculty which is a receiver of pleasure has an equal penalty put on its abuse. It is to answer for its moderation with its life. For every grain of wit there is a grain of folly. For everything you have missed, you have gained something else; and for everything you gain, you lose something. If riches increase, they are increased[2] that use them. If the gatherer gathers too much, nature takes out of the man what she puts into his chest, swells the estate, but kills the owner. Nature hates monopolies and exceptions. The waves of the sea do not more speedily seek a level from their loftiest tossing, than the varieties of condition tend to equalize themselves. There is always some leveling circumstance that puts down the overbearing, the strong, the rich, the fortunate, substantially on the same ground with all others. Is a man too

---

[1] Excess.   [2] That is, their needs or wants are increased.

strong and fierce for society, and by temper and position a bad
citizen,—a morose ruffian, with a dash of the pirate in him?—
nature sends him a troop of pretty sons and daughters, who are
getting along in the dame's[1] classes at the village school, and
love and fear for them smooths his grim scowl to courtesy. Thus
she contrives to intenerate[2] the granite and felspar, takes the
boar out and puts the lamb in, and keeps her balance true.

The farmer imagines power and place are fine things. But
the President has paid dear for his White House.[3] It has commonly cost him all his peace, and the best of his manly attributes. To preserve for a short time so conspicuous an appearance before the world, he is content to eat dust[4] before the real
masters who stand erect behind the throne. Or do men desire
the more substantial and permanent grandeur of genius? Neither
has this an immunity. He who by force of will or of thought is
great, and overlooks[5] thousands, has the charges of that eminence. With every influx of light comes new danger. Has he
light? he must bear witness to the light, and always outrun that
sympathy which gives him such keen satisfaction, by his fidelity
to new revelations of the incessant soul. He must hate father
and mother, wife and child. Has he all that the world loves and
admires and covets?—he must cast behind him their admiration,
and afflict them by faithfulness to his truth, and become a byword
and a hissing.

This law writes the laws of cities and nations. It is in vain
to build or plot or combine against it. Things refuse to be mis-
managed long. *Res nolunt diu male administrari.*[6] Though no
checks to a new evil appear, the checks exist, and will appear.
If the government is cruel, the governor's life is not safe. If
you tax too high, the revenue will yield nothing. If you make
the criminal code sanguinary, juries will not convict. If the law

---

[1] Schoolmistress.   [2] Soften.
[3] The official residence of the President in Washington.
[4] " Eat dust," i.e., humble himself.   [5] Superintends.
[6] The Latin rendering of the sentence preceding.

is too mild, private vengeance comes in. If the government is a terrific democracy, the pressure is resisted by an overcharge of energy in the citizen, and life glows with a fiercer flame. The true life and satisfactions of man seem to elude the utmost rigors or felicities of condition, and to establish themselves with great indifferency[1] under all varieties of circumstances. Under all governments the influence of character remains the same,— in Turkey and in New England about alike. Under the primeval despots of Egypt, history honestly confesses that man must have been as free as culture could make him.

These appearances indicate the fact that the universe is represented in every one of its particles. Everything in nature contains all the powers of nature. Everything is made of one hidden stuff; as the naturalist sees one type under every metamorphosis, and regards a horse as a running man, a fish as a swimming man, a bird as a flying man, a tree as a rooted man. Each new form repeats not only the main character of the type, but part for part all the details, all the aims, furtherances,[2] hindrances, energies, and whole system of every other. Every occupation, trade, art, transaction, is a compend of the world, and a correlative of every other. Each one is an entire emblem of human life; of its good and ill, its trials, its enemies, its course and its end. And each one must somehow accommodate the whole man, and recite all his destiny.

The world globes itself in a drop of dew.[3] The microscope cannot find the animalcule[4] which is less perfect for being little. Eyes, ears, taste, smell, motion, resistance, appetite, and organs of reproduction that take hold on eternity,— all find room to consist in the small creature. So do we put our life into every act. The true doctrine of omnipresence is, that God reappears with all his parts in every moss and cobweb. The value of the

---

[1] Impartiality.   [2] Things which help its progress.

[3] "The world," etc., i.e., the laws which make the world a globe give the same shape to a drop of dew.

[4] An animal so small as to be nearly or quite invisible to the naked eye.

universe contrives to throw itself into every point. If the good is there, so is the evil; if the affinity, so the repulsion; if the force, so the limitation.

Thus is the universe alive. All things are moral. That soul, which within us is a sentiment, outside of us is a law. We feel its inspiration; out there in history we can see its fatal strength. "It is in the world, and the world was made by it." Justice is not postponed. A perfect equity adjusts its balance in all parts of life. Οἱ κύβοι Διὸς ἀεὶ εὐπίπτουσι,[1]— The dice of God are always loaded.[2] The world looks like a multiplication table, or a mathematical equation, which, turn it how you will, balances itself. Take what figure you will, its exact value, nor[3] more nor less, still returns to you. Every secret is told, every crime is punished, every virtue rewarded, every wrong redressed, in silence and certainty. What we call retribution is the universal necessity by which the whole appears wherever a part appears. If you see smoke, there must be fire. If you see a hand or a limb, you know that the trunk to which it belongs is there behind.

Every act rewards itself, or, in other words, integrates itself, in a twofold manner; first, in the thing, or in real nature; and secondly, in the circumstance, or in apparent nature. Men call the circumstance the retribution. The causal retribution is in the thing, and is seen by the soul. The retribution in the circumstance is seen by the understanding; it is inseparable from the thing, but is often spread over a long time, and so does not become distinct until after many years. The specific stripes[4] may follow late after the offense, but they follow because they accompany it. Crime and punishment grow out of one stem. Punishment is a fruit that unsuspected ripens within the flower of the pleasure which concealed it. Cause and effect, means and ends,

---

[1] *Hoi kōō'boi Deéŏs äi ŭpiptoósee* — the Greek of the sentence which follows.

[2] "The dice," etc., i.e., God does not play a game of chance.

[3] Neither.

[4] Blows made with a lash; hence, punishment.

seed and fruit, cannot be severed; for the effect already blooms in the cause, the end preëxists in the means, the fruit in the seed.

Whilst thus the world will be whole, and refuses to be disparted,[1] we seek to act partially, to sunder, to appropriate; for example, — to gratify the senses, we sever the pleasure of the senses from the needs of the character. The ingenuity of man has always been dedicated to the solution of one problem, — how to detach the sensual sweet, the sensual strong, the sensual bright, etc., from the moral sweet, the moral deep, the moral fair; that is, again, to contrive to cut clean off this upper surface so thin as to leave it bottomless; to get a *one end*, without an *other end*. The soul says, Eat; the body would feast. The soul says, The man and woman shall be one flesh and one soul; the body would join the flesh only. The soul says, Have dominion over all things to the ends of virtue; the body would have the power over things to its own ends.

The soul strives amain[2] to live and work through all things. It would be the only fact. All things shall be added unto it, — power, pleasure, knowledge, beauty. The particular man aims to be somebody; to set up for himself; to truck and higgle for a private good; and, in particulars, to ride, that he may ride; to dress, that he may be dressed; to eat, that he may eat; and to govern, that he may be seen. Men seek to be great; they would have offices, wealth, power, and fame. They think that to be great is to possess one side of nature, — the sweet, without the other side, — the bitter.

This dividing and detaching is steadily counteracted. Up to this day, it must be owned, no projector has had the smallest success. The parted water reunites behind our hand. Pleasure is taken out of pleasant things, profit out of profitable things, power out of strong things, as soon as we seek to separate them from the whole. We can no more halve things and get the sensual

---

[1] Divided.   [2] Vigorously.

good, by itself, than we can get an inside that shall have no outside, or a light without a shadow. " Drive out nature with a fork, she comes running back."[1]

Life invests itself with inevitable conditions, which the unwise seek to dodge, which one and another brags that he does not know; that they do not touch him; — but the brag is on his lips, the conditions are in his soul. If he escapes them in one part, they attack him in another more vital part. If he has escaped them in form, and in the appearance, it is because he has resisted his life, and fled from himself, and the retribution is so much death. So signal is the failure of all attempts to make this separation of the good from the tax, that the experiment would not be tried, — since to try it is to be mad, — but for the circumstance, that when the disease began in the will, of rebellion and separation, the intellect is at once infected, so that the man ceases to see God whole in each object, but is able to see the sensual allurement of an object, and not see the sensual hurt; he sees the mermaid's[2] head, but not the dragon's tail; and thinks he can cut off that which he would have, from that which he would not have. " How secret art thou who dwellest in the highest heavens in silence, O thou only great God, sprinkling with an unwearied providence certain penal blindnesses upon such as have unbridled desires!"[3]

The human soul is true to these facts in the painting of fable, of history, of law, of proverbs, of conversation. It finds a tongue in literature unawares. Thus the Greeks called Jupiter,[4] Supreme Mind; but having traditionally ascribed to him many base actions, they involuntarily made amends to reason, by tying up the hands[5] of so bad a god. He is made as helpless as a king of

---

[1] A proverb, quoted by Horace, the origin of which is lost in antiquity.

[2] A fabled marine being, represented as having the upper part of the body like a woman and the lower part like a fish, serpent, or dragon.

[3] St. Augustine, Confessions, Book I.

[4] Jupiter, Jove, or Zeus, the supreme god of the Greeks and Romans.

[5] Limiting the power.

England.[1] Prometheus[2] knows one secret which Jove must bargain for; Minerva,[3] another. He cannot get his own thunders;
Minerva keeps the key of them.

> " Of all the gods, I only know the keys
> That ope the solid doors within whose vaults
> His thunders sleep."

A plain confession of the in-working of the All, and of its
moral aim. The Indian mythology ends in the same ethics;
and it would seem impossible for any fable to be invented and
get any currency which was not moral. Aurora[4] forgot to ask
youth for her lover, and though Tithonus is immortal, he is old.
Achilles[5] is not quite invulnerable; the sacred waters did not
wash the heel by which Thetis held him. Siegfried,[6] in the

[1] Parliament has supreme power in England.

[2] Prometheus, in Greek mythology the regenerator of mankind, used
knowledge as a weapon to defeat evil. He stole Jupiter's fire and taught
mortals how to use it. Jupiter punished him by chaining him to a rock
where he was tortured by an eagle. There was a prophecy afloat in heaven
portending the fall of Jupiter, and only Prometheus knew the secret of avert-
ing it. Jupiter offered him his freedom if he would reveal it. For a long
time he steadfastly refused, and endured untold tortures; but at length,
according to some traditions, he revealed the secret that if Jupiter became
the father of a son by Thetis, that son would deprive him of his sovereignty.
Prometheus was thereupon set free. According to another story he never
divulged the secret, but was at length released by Hercules, who killed the
eagle.

[3] Minerva, Athena, or Pallas, a goddess in Greek and Roman mythology,
who sprang full-armed from the head of her father Jupiter. She was the goddess of wisdom and of war, and sometimes wielded Jupiter's thunderbolts.

[4] Aurora, Roman goddess of the dawn, became enamored of Tithonus,
son of Laomedon, King of Troy. She stole him away and persuaded Jupiter
to grant him immortality, but she forgot to have youth added to the gift, and
soon began to discern that he was growing old. She grew angry at this and
finally turned him into a grasshopper.

[5] Achilles is the hero of the Iliad, Homer's great epic. His mother,
Thetis, dipped him in the river Styx to render him immortal.

[6] The Nibelungenlied is the great epic poem of the old Germans, as the

Nibelungen, is not quite immortal, for a leaf fell on his back whilst he was bathing in the dragon's blood, and that spot which it covered is mortal. And so it must be. There is a crack in everything God has made. It would seem, there is always this vindictive circumstance stealing in at unawares, even into the wild poesy in which the human fancy attempted to make bold holiday, and to shake itself free of the old laws,— this back-stroke, this kick of the gun, certifying that the law is fatal; that in nature nothing can be given, all things are sold.

This is that ancient doctrine of Nemesis,[1] who keeps watch in the universe, and lets no offense go unchastised. The Furies,[2] they said, are attendants on justice, and if the sun in heaven should transgress his path, they would punish him. The poets related that stone walls, and iron swords, and leathern thongs had an occult sympathy with the wrongs of their owners; that the belt which Ajax gave Hector dragged the Trojan hero over the field at the wheels of the car of Achilles, and the sword which Hector gave Ajax was that on whose point Ajax[3] fell. They recorded, that when the Thasians erected a statue to Theagenes,[4] a victor in the games, one of his rivals went to it by night, and endeavored to throw it down by repeated blows, until at last he moved it from its pedestal, and was crushed to death beneath its fall.

Iliad is of the ancient Greeks. Siegfried is the mythical hero of the former as Achilles is of the latter story.

[1] In Greek mythology, a goddess personifying moral reverence for law. She visited the righteous anger of the gods upon the proud and insolent.

[2] The Furies were three mythological deities, Alecto, Tisiphone, and Megæra, who punished crimes by their secret stings.

[3] Ajax and Hector are mythological heroes in the Trojan War as related in the Iliad, the former a Greek and the latter a Trojan. After a personal combat, they exchanged arms, and when subsequently Ajax committed suicide, he used the sword which had been Hector's, and when Achilles killed Hector, he used the belt which had belonged to Ajax to fasten the corpse to his chariot or car.

[4] See Pausanias's Description of Greece, Book VI., line 11. Theagenes, an inhabitant of Thasos, an island in the Ægean Sea, was renowned for his strength and swiftness and his numerous victories in athletic contests.

This voice of fable has in it somewhat divine. It came from thought above the will of the writer. That is the best part of each writer, which has nothing private in it; that which he does not know, that which flowed out of his constitution, and not from his too active invention; that which in the study of a single artist you might not easily find, but in the study of many, you would abstract as the spirit of them all. Phidias[1] it is not, but the work of man in that early Hellenic[2] world, that I would know. The name and circumstance of Phidias, however convenient for history, embarrass when we come to the highest criticism. We are to see that which man was tending to do in a given period, and was hindered, or, if you will, modified in doing, by the interfering volitions of Phidias, of Dante,[3] of Shakespeare,[4] the organ whereby man at the moment wrought.

Still more striking is the expression of this fact in the proverbs of all nations, which are always the literature of reason, or the statements of an absolute truth, without qualification. Proverbs, like the sacred books of each nation, are the sanctuary of the intuitions. That which the droning world, chained to appearances, will not allow the realist to say in his own words, it will suffer him to say in proverbs without contradiction. And this law of laws which the pulpit, the senate, and the college deny, is hourly preached in all markets and workshops by flights of proverbs, whose teaching is as true and as omnipresent as that of birds and flies.

All things are double, one against another. — Tit for tat; an eye for an eye; a tooth for a tooth; blood for blood; measure for measure; love for love. — Give and it shall be given you. — He that watereth shall be watered himself. — What will you have? quoth God; pay for it and take it. — Nothing venture, nothing have. — Thou shalt be paid exactly for what thou hast done, no more, no less. — Who doth not work shall not eat. — Harm watch, harm catch. — Curses always recoil on the head of him

---

[1] See Note 4, p. 76.   [2] Greek.   [3] See Note 6, p. 76.
[4] See Note 3, p. 29.

who imprecates them. — If you put a chain around the neck of
a slave, the other end fastens itself around your own. — Bad
counsel confounds the adviser. — The Devil is an ass.

It is thus written, because it is thus in life. Our action is
overmastered and characterized above our will by the law of
nature. We aim at a petty end quite aside from the public good,
but our act arranges itself by irresistible magnetism in a line with
the poles of the world.

A man cannot speak, but he judges himself. With his will, or
against his will, he draws his portrait to the eye of his companions by every word. Every opinion reacts on him who utters it.
It is a thread-ball[1] thrown at a mark, but the other end remains
in the thrower's bag. Or, rather, it is a harpoon hurled at the
whale, unwinding, as it flies, a coil of cord in the boat, and if
the harpoon is not good, or not well thrown, it will go nigh to
cut the steersman in twain, or to sink the boat.

You cannot do wrong without suffering wrong. " No man
had ever a point of pride that was not injurious to him," said
Burke.[2] The exclusive in fashionable life does not see that he
excludes himself from enjoyment, in the attempt to appropriate
it. The exclusionist in religion does not see that he shuts the
door of heaven on himself, in striving to shut out others. Treat
men as pawns[3] and ninepins, and you shall suffer as well as they.
If you leave out their heart, you shall lose your own. The senses
would make things of all persons; of women, of children, of
the poor. The vulgar proverb, " I will get it from his purse or
get it from his skin," is sound philosophy.

All infractions of love and equity in our social relations are
speedily punished. They are punished by fear. Whilst I stand

---

[1] A ball of thread.

[2] Edmund Burke (1729–97), Irish statesman, orator, and political writer.
His best known works are his Speech on American Conciliation and Reflections on the French Revolution.

[3] A piece of lowest rank in the game of chess; hence, a mere figure to be
moved about at the will of another.

7

in simple relations to my fellow-man, I have no displeasure in meeting him. We meet as water meets water, or as two currents of air mix, with perfect diffusion and interpenetration[1] of nature. But as soon as there is any departure from simplicity, and attempt at halfness, or good for me that is not good for him, my neighbor feels the wrong; he shrinks from me as far as I have shrunk from him; his eyes no longer seek mine; there is war between us; there is hate in him and fear in me.

All the old abuses in society, universal and particular, all unjust accumulations of property and power, are avenged in the same manner. Fear is an instructor of great sagacity, and the herald of all revolutions. One thing he teaches, that there is rottenness where he appears. He is a carrion crow, and though you see not well what he hovers for, there is death somewhere. Our property is timid, our laws are timid, our cultivated classes are timid. Fear for ages has boded and mowed and gibbered[2] over government and property. That obscene[3] bird is not there for nothing. He indicates great wrongs which must be revised.

Of the like nature is that expectation of change which instantly follows the suspension of our voluntary activity. The terror of cloudless noon, the emerald of Polycrates,[4] the awe of prosperity, the instinct which leads every generous soul to impose on itself tasks of a noble asceticism and vicarious virtue, are the tremblings of the balance of justice through the heart and mind of man.

[1] A penetrating between other substances.

[2] " Fear," etc., i.e., fear has presaged evil, made faces, and spoken incoherently.   [3] Ill-omened.

[4] Polycrates, a celebrated Greek tyrant of Samos, had such unvarying good fortune that he was counseled to cast from him that which he valued most in order to allay the jealousy of the gods. Accordingly he threw into the sea an emerald ring of extraordinary beauty; but in a few days he regained it from inside a fish presented to him by a fisherman. Soon after this Polycrates' prosperity deserted him and he suffered an ignominious death on the cross.

Experienced men of the world know very well that it is best to pay scot and lot[1] as they go along, and that a man often pays dear for a small frugality. The borrower runs in his own debt. Has a man gained anything who has received a hundred favors and rendered none? Has he gained by borrowing, through indolence or cunning, his neighbor's wares, or horses, or money? There arises on the deed the instant acknowledgment of benefit on the one part, and of debt on the other; that is, of superiority and inferiority. The transaction remains in the memory of himself and his neighbor; and every new transaction alters, according to its nature, their relation to each other. He may soon come to see that he had better have broken his own bones than to have ridden in his neighbor's coach, and that " the highest price he can pay for a thing is to ask for it."

A wise man will extend this lesson to all parts of life, and know that it is the part of prudence to face every claimant, and pay every just demand on your time, your talents, or your heart. Always pay; for, first or last, you must pay your entire debt. Persons and events may stand for a time between you and justice, but it is only a postponement. You must pay at last your own debt. If you are wise, you will dread a prosperity which only loads you with more. Benefit is the end of nature. But for every benefit which you receive, a tax is levied. He is great who confers the most benefits. He is base — and that is the one base thing in the universe — to receive favors and render none. In the order of nature we cannot render benefits to those from whom we receive them, or only seldom. But the benefit we receive must be rendered again, line for line, deed for deed, cent for cent, to somebody. Beware of too much good staying in your hand. It will fast corrupt and worm[2] worms. Pay it away quickly in some sort.[3]

Labor is watched over by the same pitiless laws. Cheapest,

---

[1] Scot and lot, formerly a parish assessment laid on subjects according to their ability.

[2] Beget.   [3] Manner.

say the prudent, is the dearest labor. What we buy in a broom, a mat, a wagon, a knife, is some application of good sense to a common want. It is best to pay in your land a skillful gardener, or to buy good sense applied to gardening; in your sailor, good sense applied to navigation; in the house, good sense applied to cooking, sewing, serving; in your agent, good sense applied to accounts and affairs. So do you multiply your presence, or spread yourself throughout your estate. But because of the dual constitution of things, in labor as in life there can be no cheating. The thief steals from himself. The swindler swindles himself. For the real price of labor is knowledge and virtue, whereof wealth and credit are signs. These signs, like paper money, may be counterfeited or stolen, but that which they represent, namely, knowledge and virtue, cannot be counterfeited or stolen. These ends of labor cannot be answered but by real exertions of the mind, and in obedience to pure motives. The cheat, the defaulter, the gambler, cannot extort the knowledge of material and moral nature which his honest care and pains yield to the operative. The law of nature is, Do the thing, and you shall have the power: but they who do not the thing have not the power.

Human labor, through all its forms, from the sharpening of a stake to the construction of a city or an epic, is one immense illustration of the perfect compensation of the universe. The absolute balance of Give and Take, the doctrine that everything has its price,—and if that price is not paid, not that thing but something else is obtained, and that it is impossible to get anything without its price,—is not less sublime in the columns of a leger than in the budgets of states, in the laws of light and darkness, in all the action and reaction of nature. I cannot doubt that the high laws which each man sees implicated in those processes with which he is conversant, the stern ethics which sparkle on his chisel edge, which are measured out by his plumb and foot rule, which stand as manifest in the footing of the shop bill as in the history of a state,—do recommend to him his trade, and though seldom named, exalt his business to his imagination.

The league between virtue and nature engages all things to assume a hostile front to vice. The beautiful laws and substances of the world persecute and whip the traitor. He finds that things are arranged for truth and benefit, but there is no den in the wide world to hide a rogue. Commit a crime, and the earth is made of glass.[1] Commit a crime, and it seems as if a coat of snow fell on the ground, such as reveals in the woods the track of every partridge and fox and squirrel and mole. You cannot recall the spoken word, you cannot wipe out the foot-track, you cannot draw up the ladder, so as to leave no inlet or clew. Some damning circumstance always transpires. The laws and substances of nature — water, snow, wind, gravitation — become penalties to the thief.

On the other hand, the law holds with equal sureness for all right action. Love, and you shall be loved. All love is mathematically just, as much as the two sides of an algebraic equation. The good man has absolute good, which like fire turns everything to its own nature, so that you cannot do him any harm; but as the royal armies sent against Napoleon,[2] when he approached, cast down their colors and from enemies became friends, so disasters of all kinds, as sickness, offense, poverty, prove benefactors : —

> "Winds blow and waters roll
> Strength to the brave, and power and deity,
> Yet in themselves are nothing."

The good are befriended even by weakness and defect. As no man had ever a point of pride that was not injurious to him, so no man had ever a defect that was not somewhere made useful

---

[1] There is no place where you can hide; every spot will be transparent.

[2] Napoleon Bonaparte (1769–1821), Emperor of France. For many years he was one of the most successful generals the world has ever seen, and he seemed destined to conquer the whole of Europe, but was finally defeated at Waterloo by the English and Prussians, and exiled to St. Helena, where he died.

to him.　The stag in the fable[1] admired his horns and blamed
his feet, but when the hunter came, his feet saved him, and afterwards, caught in the thicket, his horns destroyed him.　Every
man in his lifetime needs to thank his faults.　As no man thoroughly understands a truth until he has contended against it, so
no man has a thorough acquaintance with the hindrances or
talents of men, until he has suffered from the one, and seen the
triumph of the other over his own want of the same.　Has he a
defect of temper that unfits him to live in society?　Thereby he
is driven to entertain himself alone, and acquire habits of self-
help; and thus, like the wounded oyster, he mends his shell with
pearl.

Our strength grows out of our weakness.　The indignation
which arms itself with secret forces does not awaken until we
are pricked and stung and sorely assailed.　A great man is
always willing to be little.　Whilst he sits on the cushion of
advantages, he goes to sleep.　When he is pushed, tormented,
defeated, he has a chance to learn something; he has been put
on his wits, on his manhood; he has gained facts; learns his
ignorance; is cured of the insanity of conceit; has got moderation and real skill.　The wise man throws himself on the side of
his assailants.　It is more his interest than it is theirs to find his
weak point.　The wound cicatrizes[2] and falls off from him like
a dead skin, and when they would triumph, lo! he has passed
on invulnerable.　Blame is safer than praise.　I hate to be defended in a newspaper.　As long as all that is said is said against
me, I feel a certain assurance of success.　But as soon as
honeyed words of praise are spoken for me, I feel as one that
lies unprotected before his enemies.　In general, every evil to
which we do not succumb is a benefactor.　As the Sandwich
Islander believes that the strength and valor of the enemy he
kills passes into himself, so we gain the strength of the temptation we resist.

[1] One of Æsop's fables.
[2] Heals by forming a skin over dead flesh.

The same guards which protect us from disaster, defect, and enmity, defend us, if we will, from selfishness and fraud. Bolts and bars are not the best of our institutions, nor is shrewdness in trade a mark of wisdom. Men suffer all their life long, under the foolish superstition that they can be cheated. But it is as impossible for a man to be cheated by any one but himself, as for a thing to be and not to be at the same time. There is a third silent party to all our bargains. The nature and soul of things takes on itself the guaranty of the fulfillment of every contract, so that honest service cannot come to loss. If you serve an ungrateful master, serve him the more. Put God in your debt. Every stroke shall be repaid. The longer the payment is withholden,[1] the better for you; for compound interest on compound interest is the rate and usage of this exchequer.[2]

The history of persecution is a history of endeavors to cheat nature, to make water run up hill, to twist a rope of sand. It makes no difference whether the actors be many or one, a tyrant or a mob. A mob is a society of bodies voluntarily bereaving themselves of reason, and traversing its work. The mob is man voluntarily descending to the nature of the beast. Its fit hour of activity is night. Its actions are insane like its whole constitution. It persecutes a principle; it would whip a right; it would tar and feather justice, by inflicting fire and outrage upon the houses and persons of those who have these. It resembles the prank of boys, who run with fire engines to put out the ruddy aurora streaming to the stars. The inviolate spirit turns their spite against the wrongdoers. The martyr cannot be dishonored. Every lash inflicted is a tongue of fame; every prison, a more illustrious abode; every burned book or house enlightens the world; every suppressed or expunged word reverberates through the earth from side to side. Hours of sanity and consideration are always arriving to communities, as to individuals, when the truth is seen, and the martyrs are justified.

. [1] Old form of " withheld."   [2] Treasury.

Thus do all things preach the indifferency of circumstances. The man is all. Everything has two sides, a good and an evil. Every advantage has its tax. I learn to be content. But the doctrine of compensation is not the doctrine of indifferency. The thoughtless say, on hearing these representations, — What boots[1] it to do well? there is one event to good and evil; if I gain any good, I must pay for it; if I lose any good, I gain some other; all actions are indifferent.

There is a deeper fact in the soul than compensation, to wit, its own nature. The soul is not a compensation, but a life. The soul *is*. Under all this running sea of circumstance, whose waters ebb and flow with perfect balance, lies the aboriginal[2] abyss of real Being. Essence, or God, is not a relation, or a part, but the whole. Being is the vast affirmative, excluding negation, self-balanced, and swallowing up all relations, parts, and times within itself. Nature, truth, virtue, are the influx from thence. Vice is the absence or departure of the same. Nothing, Falsehood, may indeed stand as the great Night or shade, on which, as a background, the living universe paints itself forth, but no fact is begotten by it; it cannot work; for it is not. It cannot work any good; it cannot work any harm. It is harm inasmuch as it is worse not to be than to be.

We feel defrauded of the retribution due to evil acts, because the criminal adheres to his vice and contumacy, and does not come to a crisis or judgment anywhere in visible nature. There is no stunning confutation of his nonsense before men and angels. Has he therefore outwitted the law? Inasmuch as he carries the malignity and the lie with him, he so far deceases from nature. In some manner there will be a demonstration of the wrong to the understanding also; but should we not see it, this deadly deduction makes square the eternal account.

Neither can it be said, on the other hand, that the gain of rectitude must be bought by any loss. There is no penalty to virtue; no penalty to wisdom; they are proper additions of

---

[1] Profits.   [2] See Note 2, p. 63.

being. In a virtuous action, I properly *am;* in a virtuous act, I add
to the world; I plant into deserts conquered from Chaos and
Nothing, and see the darkness receding on the limits of the horizon. There can be no excess to love; none to knowledge; none
to beauty, when these attributes are considered in the purest
sense. The soul refuses limits, and always affirms an Optimism,[1]
never a Pessimism.

His life is a progress, and not a station. His instinct is trust.
Our instinct uses "more" and "less" in application to man, of
the *presence of the soul*, and not of its absence; the brave man
is greater than the coward; the true, the benevolent, the wise, is
more a man, and not less, than the fool and knave. There is no
tax on the good of virtue; for that is the incoming of God himself, or absolute existence without any comparative. Material
good has its tax, and if it came without desert or sweat, has no
root in me, and the next wind will blow it away. But all the
good of nature is the soul's, and may be had, if paid for in nature's
lawful coin, that is, by labor which the heart and the head allow.
I no longer wish to meet[2] a good I do not earn, for example, to
find a pot of buried gold, knowing that it brings with it new
burdens. I do not wish more external goods, — neither possessions, nor honors, nor powers, nor persons. The gain is apparent; the tax is certain. But there is no tax on the knowledge
that the compensation exists, and that it is not desirable to dig
up treasure. Herein I rejoice with a serene eternal peace. I
contract the boundaries of possible mischief. I learn the wisdom
of St. Bernard,[3] — "Nothing can work me damage except myself; the harm that I sustain I carry about with me, and never
am a real sufferer but by my own fault."

In the nature of the soul is the compensation for the inequali-

[1] The doctrine that everything in nature is ordered for the best. Pessimism is the reverse.

[2] To receive, or have bestowed on me.

[3] St. Bernard of Clairvaux, France (1091–1153), one of the most influen-
tial theologians of the middle ages.

ties of condition. The radical tragedy of nature seems to be the distinction of More and Less. How can Less not feel the pain; how not feel indignation or malevolence towards More? Look at those who have less faculty, and one feels sad, and knows not well what to make of it. He almost shuns their eye; he fears they will upbraid God. What should they do? It seems a great injustice. But see the facts nearly, and these mountainous inequalities vanish. Love reduces them, as the sun melts the iceberg in the sea. The heart and soul of all men being one, this bitterness of *His* and *Mine* ceases. His is mine. I am my brother, and my brother is me. If I feel overshadowed and out-done by great neighbors, I can yet love; I can still receive; and he that loveth maketh his own the grandeur he loves. Thereby I make the discovery that my brother is my guardian, acting for me with the friendliest designs, and the estate I so admired and envied is my own. It is the nature of the soul to appropriate all things. Jesus and Shakespeare are fragments of the soul, and by love I conquer and incorporate them in my own conscious do-main. His virtue, — is not that mine? His wit, — if it cannot be made mine, it is not wit.

Such, also, is the natural history of calamity. The changes which break up at short intervals the prosperity of men are ad-vertisements of a nature whose law is growth. Every soul is by this intrinsic necessity quitting its whole system of things, its friends, and home, and laws, and faith, as the shellfish crawls out of its beautiful but stony case, because it no longer admits of its growth, and slowly forms a new house. In proportion to the vigor of the individual, these revolutions are frequent, until in some happier mind they are incessant, and all worldly relations hang very loosely about him, becoming, as it were, a transparent fluid membrane through which the living form is seen, and not, as in most men, an indurated[1] heterogeneous[2] fabric of many dates, and of no settled character, in which the man is imprisoned. Then there can be enlargement, and the man of to-day scarcely

---

[1] Hardened.   [2] Composed of differing things.

recognizes the man of yesterday. And such should be the out-ward biography of man in time, a putting off of dead circum-stances day by day, as he renews his raiment day by day. But to us, in our lapsed estate, resting, not advancing, resisting, not coöperating with the divine expansion, this growth comes by shocks.

We cannot part with our friends. We cannot let our angels go. We do not see that they only go out, that archangels may come in. We are idolaters of the old. We do not believe in the riches of the soul, in its proper eternity and omnipresence. We do not believe there is any force in to-day to rival or recre-ate[1] that beautiful yesterday. We linger in the ruins of the old tent, where once we had bread and shelter and organs, nor believe that the spirit can feed, cover, and nerve us again. We cannot again find aught so dear, so sweet, so graceful. But we sit and weep in vain. The voice of the Almighty saith, " Up and on-ward forevermore!" We cannot stay amid the ruins. Neither will we rely on the new; and so we walk ever with reverted eyes, like those monsters who look backwards.

And yet the compensations of calamity are made apparent to the understanding also, after long intervals of time. A fever, a mutilation, a cruel disappointment, a loss of wealth, a loss of friends, seems at the moment unpaid loss, and unpayable. But the sure years reveal the deep remedial force that underlies all facts. The death of a dear friend, wife, brother, lover, which seemed nothing but privation, somewhat later assumes the aspect of a guide or genius; for it commonly operates revolutions in our way of life, terminates an epoch of infancy or of youth which was waiting to be closed, breaks up a wonted[2] occupation, or a household, or style of living, and allows the formation of new ones more friendly to the growth of character. It permits or constrains the formation of new acquaintances, and the reception of new influences that prove of the first importance to the next years; and the man or woman who would have remained a

---

[1] Create again.   [2] Customary.

sunny garden flower, with no room for its roots and too much sunshine for its head, by the falling of the walls and the neglect of the gardener, is made the banian[1] of the forest, yielding shade and fruit to wide neighborhoods of men.

[1] Banyan, an East Indian tree of the mulberry family. Aërial roots descending from the branches become fixed in the ground, and thicken into supports or pillars. Thus the branches spread over an immense area, and a single tree has the appearance of a whole grove.